PRAISE FOR TAHOE NIGHT

"BORG HAS WRITTEN ANOTHER WHITE-KNUCKLE THRILLER... A sure bet for mystery buffs waiting for the next Robert B. Parker and Lee Child novels."
- Jo Ann Vicarel, Library Journal

"AN ACTION-PACKED THRILLER WITH A NICE-GUY HERO, AN EVEN NICER DOG..."
- Kirkus Reviews

"A KILLER PLOT... EVERY ONE OF ITS 350 PAGES WANTS TO GET TURNED... *FAST*"
- Taylor Flynn, Tahoe Mountain News

"PLENTY OF ACTION TO KEEP YOU ON THE EDGE OF YOUR SEAT... An excellent addition to this series."
- Gayle Wedgwood, Mystery News

"ANOTHER PAGE-TURNER OF A MYSTERY, with more twists and turns than a roller coaster ride."
- Midwest Book Review

"A FASCINATING STORY OF FORGERY, MURDER..."
- Nancy Hayden, Tahoe Daily Tribune

PRAISE FOR TAHOE AVALANCHE

ONE OF THE TOP 5 MYSTERIES OF THE YEAR!
- Gayle Wedgwood, Mystery News

"BORG IS A SUPERB STORYTELLER...A MASTER OF THE GENRE"
- Midwest Book Review

"TAHOE AVALANCHE WAS SOOOO GOOD... A FASCINATING MYSTERY with some really devious characters"
- Merry Cutler, Annie's Book Stop, Sharon, Massachusetts

"EXPLODES INTO A COMPLEX PLOT THAT LEADS TO MURDER AND INTRIGUE"
- Nancy Hayden, Tahoe Daily Tribune

"READERS WILL BE KEPT ON THE EDGE OF THEIR SEATS"
- Sheryl McLaughlin, Douglas Times

"WORTHY OF RECOGNITION"
- Jo Ann Vicarel, Library Journal

"INCLUDE BORG IN THE GROUP OF MYSTERY WRITERS that write with a strong sense of place such as TONY HILLERMAN"
- William Clark, The Union

PRAISE FOR TAHOE SILENCE

WINNER, BEN FRANKLIN AWARD, BEST MYSTERY OF THE YEAR!

"A HEART-WRENCHING MYSTERY THAT IS ALSO ONE OF THE BEST NOVELS WRITTEN ABOUT AUTISM"
STARRED REVIEW - Jo Ann Vicarel, Library Journal

CHOSEN BY LIBRARY JOURNAL AS ONE OF THE FIVE BEST MYSTERIES OF THE YEAR

"THIS IS ONE ENGROSSING NOVEL...IT IS SUPERB"
5-QUILL REVIEW - Gayle Wedgwood, Mystery News

"ANOTHER GREAT READ!!"
5-STAR REVIEW - Shelly Glodowski, Midwest Book Review

"ANOTHER EXCITING ENTRY INTO THIS TOO-LITTLE-KNOWN SERIES"
- Mary Frances Wilkens, Booklist

"A REAL PAGE-TURNER"
- Sam Bauman, Nevada Appeal

"LOFTY STUFF INDEED... But Borg manages to make it all go down like a glass of white wine on a summer afternoon"
- Heather Gould, Tahoe Mountain News

PRAISE FOR TAHOE KILLSHOT

"BORG BELONGS ON THE BESTSELLER LISTS with Parker, Paretsky and Coben"
- Merry Cutler, Annie's Book Stop, Sharon, Massachusetts

TAHOE HEAT

by

Todd Borg

THRILLER PRESS

AUTHOR'S NOTE

One of the Tahoe landmarks featured in this story is Cave Rock on the east shore of Lake Tahoe. For thousands of years, Cave Rock has been a sacred place for the Washoe, the Native Americans who lived at Tahoe in the summer and wintered to the east in Carson Valley. It has been relatively few years since people of European ancestry came to Tahoe, occupied it, and claimed it as their own. During that time, the beliefs and traditions of the Washoe Tribe have been almost universally disrespected.

Early in the development of Tahoe, twin tunnels were blasted through Cave Rock for Highway 50, and in later years, Cave Rock became a rock climber's paradise for its challenging routes.

Gradually, the Forest Service has begun to recognize the special history of Cave Rock, and they recently banned climbing and ordered the removal of countless climbing aids that had been pounded into its many climbing routes.

While the blasting of the tunnels can't be undone, it is this author's wish that all people who come to Tahoe be aware of the sacredness of Cave Rock. Let's all appreciate and care for this special place as we would have others appreciate and care for our places of worship.

ACKNOWLEDGMENTS

I am indebted to Mike and Denise Geissinger for introducing me to their Mustangs and answering many questions about them. Their beautiful horses were the inspiration for part of this story.

Liz Johnston is a great editor. Can't thank her enough.

Eric Berglund is a great editor. Can't thank him enough.

Keith Carlson produced another spectacular cover. Can't thank him enough.

Kit kept her eye on the subjects, the composition, and the colors of the big picture, while I was lost in the brush strokes. Can't thank her enough, either.

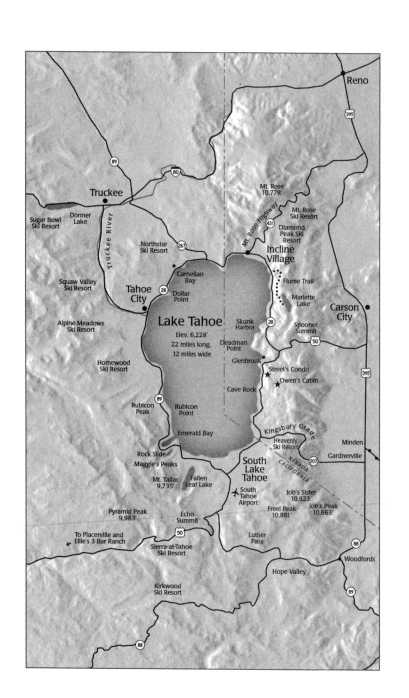

PROLOGUE

"Don't do it, Eli!" Sydney shouted from below the cliff. "This is a sacred Washoe Indian site. Climbers are no longer allowed here. You'll bury yourself in bad Karma."

She stared up at her wild, skinny, genius boyfriend on the vertical wall of Cave Rock, the 100-foot prominence that rose from the East Shore of Lake Tahoe. They had parked at the State Park lot to meet a friend, got there early, and Eli suddenly decided to try a route. He put on his climbing shoes, chalked his fingers, and started up the rock.

"It's not worth the rush," she yelled.

Elijah Nathan didn't respond to Sydney, didn't even fully hear her warning, so focused was he on the crack that zig-zagged up the craggy face over the highway where the southbound lanes of Highway 50 emerged from the Cave Rock tunnel. If he could follow the fracture line to the top, it would absolutely be worth the risk.

Elijah was free climbing without a belay rope. No climbing nuts or cams or chocks, no carabiners to hold a rope, nothing to anchor him if his sweaty, chalked fingertips should slip.

The whole point of free climbing was the rush.

He reached out his right hand, feeling, searching, found a grip, shifted his right foot to a tiny edge, moved his body up and to the side.

"Eli, you're freaking crazy, you know that?!" Sydney shouted from below. "You're moving out of my sight line. I couldn't advise you even if you wanted another set of eyes."

Elijah didn't hear her. Listening to others was not one of his skills. CalBioTechnica, Inc., the company that he and his two partners founded, wouldn't even exist if he had listened to the dozen experts who said you couldn't compete with pharmaceutical giants. The recombinant DNA concepts that his buddy invented were new, and the formulas for a new class of biological drugs were unusual. Only Eli's mentor, Old Man Martin, at Stanford's Business School understood.

"You got a vision, kid," the 44-year-old geezer had said to the student working on his post-doctoral project. "Go for it. Don't let their expertise get in your way. Only way to prove they're wrong is to prove they're wrong."

So Elijah Nathan took his friend's concepts and designed a company around them. He wrote the business plan, structured a new kind of manufacturing model, and enticed several bio-tech equipment makers into donating CalBioTechnica's first lab in return for future marketing possibilities. Then Eli recruited math wizard Jeanie Samples to come onboard as VP of Finance, and she pulled together their initial financing as if spinning gold out of burlap.

Now, five years later, CBT had lucrative development contracts with big pharma, and a steady revenue stream from manufacturing for the name-brand companies. The first drugs to be marketed under the CalBioTechnica name were in the home stretch for FDA approval. Annual sales were approaching $100 million, and when the FDA approvals came through, CBT's sales would explode.

Elijah knew the numbers better than his accountants. A little less than a hundred million at a 70% gross margin, less fixed expenses, variable expenses, salaries for 197 employees, and other miscellaneous costs still added up to real money. And this was just the beginning. After their scorching five-year sales arc into the big leagues, Elijah had decided that the way to build a monster money-maker was to listen very carefully to expert advice and then run as fast as possible in the opposite direction.

The result was a thrill. But still nothing like the rush of free climbing.

Elijah made another, smaller, crab shift up and to the left, his chalk bag swinging from his belt. Forty feet below him, a pickup came out of the tunnel at high speed, followed by two cars, bumper-to-bumper, like in a NASCAR race. Elijah didn't even notice. He wasn't aware of the sun broiling his head. He didn't notice the vast blue of Lake Tahoe shimmering under a strong August breeze. The world had shrunk down to a wall of rock and a network of fracture lines. Following them up and across the rock without placing any safety was beyond a thrill. It was better than skiing off of a cornice, better than riding the curl of a wave. Better than sex.

The air flowing into his lungs felt mentholated, the product, he knew from past experience, of endorphins flooding his brain.

He shifted farther to the right, out of Sydney's range of vision. Two more feet and he'd be able to reach a vertical crack that rose up toward the heavens.

Four more cars raced by underfoot, one after another.

Compared to the surrounding mountains, the little hump of cave-riddled rock didn't look like much, but it had been a stubborn obstacle to all of the early Tahoe travelers who wanted to trek north or south along the East Shore. With typical disdain for sacred Native American places of worship, the white men decided that the only solution to Cave Rock's implacable obstruction to easy travel was to dynamite two tunnels through it. They blasted two lanes each for both the northbound and southbound sides of Highway 50.

To the Washoe, it was an unforgivable desecration of sacred land. And long after the endless violation of cars and trucks and RVs roaring through Cave Rock, many members of the small remaining Washoe tribe still refused to use the tunnel, even if that refusal necessitated a 75-mile detour around the giant lake.

Eventually, the U.S. Forest Service, under mounting legal pressure, declared Cave Rock off-limits to climbers. They even ordered that all of the dozens of world-famous climbing routes be stripped of the countless pitons and bolts and other climbing aids that had been pounded into the rock.

But Eli didn't care.

It wasn't that he rejected the Washoe's long history at Cave Rock and their claim to the land. Eli was simply a narrow-minded prodigy who only saw the world through his own perspective. What mattered to him was what he wanted. And what he wanted was to be in charge, to be in control, and to never again let the bullies of his childhood have their way. Eli had discovered that the power of his intelligence led to the power of money. And now that he, along with his partners, had become very wealthy while still in their twenties, he wasn't going to play by anyone else's rules ever again.

Eli lost track of the passage of time as he climbed. He followed the cracks in the rocks like an ant sniffing out the path to sweet nectar. He went up 10 feet, moved laterally 6 feet, then up another 10. After 50 feet of ascent, his body began to tire, first in the hand muscles, then the forearms, then across his back. Because he was climbing without the protection of aids or belay, he had no opportunity to rest. That was what made it exciting. And that was what drew the crowd gathering below and made drivers pull their cars over to the side of the highway to park and watch. A free climber lives or dies based on his or her skill and strategy. And steel fingertips.

A few minutes later, Eli had conquered yet another class 5 route, and he pulled himself up and over the edge near the top. The burst of neurotransmitters flooding his brain was as great a feeling as he'd ever had. It was as if his body were filled with a blinding light.

After a hands-and-knees scramble up the last portion of steep slope, he stood up at the top of Cave Rock. Slowly, he inched back down toward the edge, his lungs still puffing hard, and looked down the vertical cliff, savoring his accomplishment.

Directly below him, 80 feet down, cars and trucks raced out of the southbound tunnel, their drivers and passengers oblivious to the drama that had played out above their heads.

"Eli!"

A loud voice. Close behind him.

"Payback!"

Elijah turned toward the sound, twisting on his right foot. Something sharp cut into his ankle. His foot slipped. The motion jerked diagonally through his body, knocked him off balance.

Elijah fell to the left. His palms hit the rock, ground into the rough surface. His left knee bent and slammed down onto a protruding shard of rock. Pain shot up his leg. Eli grabbed at the rock with both hands, but he fumbled at loose grit.

His motion carried him the last few inches toward the edge as he scrambled for a hold on the granular surface. He ignored the pain in his knee and his ankle, and clawed at the surface.

Eli was a serious climber. He'd climbed some real walls in Yosemite and was planning to eventually tackle El Cap. His ultimate goal was the Trango Towers in Pakistan. Serious climbers didn't succumb to a slippery slope above a little bump of rock that was barely 100 feet high.

But his hands and feet couldn't find a grip.

Just as he slipped off the edge of the steep rock and began his plunge down the vertical face, his right hand found a good, solid hold, his fingers wedging into a crack, knuckles jamming against rock.

For a moment, he felt the huge relief that came with arresting his fall. But his body swung hard, a 160-pound pendulum suspended from a two-knuckle pivot point. At the bottom of his swing, his finger bones broke skin. His feet flailed against the smooth rock below. Left fingers clawed at the rough surface, but found no hold.

His right knuckles ground so hard into the rock, they left bloody, pulverized chips of bone behind. Electric pain pulsed up his arm. His hand lost its grip.

Elijah Nathan fell 80 feet and hit a protruding rock above the tunnel opening. He flipped over in the air before his life ended against the hood of an eighteen-wheel Peterbilt logging truck loaded down with 40,000 pounds of Ponderosa pine.

A minute later, several bits of what looked like red confetti were still coming down from the sky, swirling on the breeze.

ONE

The light was blinking on the machine when I walked into my office. I hit the Play button while Spot searched for a good place to lie down.

It sounded like a young man. His voice was stressed.

"Mr. McKenna, my name is Ryan Lear. I think I'm in serious trouble. Please call me. Any time, night or day. I can be reached at one of four numbers. In the Bay Area, in Tahoe, cell, and at work. Cell is best." He recited the four numbers.

I dialed them in order, got three voicemail services, and finally, a secretary at the work number.

"CalBioTechnica," she said.

"Owen McKenna returning Ryan Lear's call."

"Let me check. I'm sorry, he's in a meeting."

"He said it was important."

"I'll have him call you as soon as he's available."

Ryan already had my office number, so I gave her my cell. I thanked her and hung up.

I'd heard the company name, CalBioTechnica, but I didn't know anything about it.

I Googled the company and found that it was a bio-tech company, specializing in recombinant DNA research and, according to the media, responsible for some promising emerging drugs in the new class of biologicals. Despite the excitement, it struggled in the shadows of companies like Genentech. CalBioTechnica was scraping by on development and production contracts that were estimated at $93 million in the current year, its fifth year of operation.

I was in my third year of self-employment after quitting the SFPD and scraping by on even less.

The coffee maker finished gurgling. I drank some, paid some bills, grabbed some bagels and water out of the mini-fridge, collected the Matisse monograph that I'd left at the office the last time I was there, and left.

Like nearly all summer days in Lake Tahoe, this one was more of the same weather, almost boring in its predictability. Clear skies that were a light cobalt blue at the edges and pushed toward ultramarine at the zenith, high-altitude sunshine turned up to the barbecue setting, air temperature that was dialed down to the mid-seventies.

I took Spot to Nevada Beach for a little exercise. It was still early enough in the morning that few tourists were out on the miles-long stretch of perfect sand. Despite the August heat, the white snow cross on Mt. Tallac across the lake was still substantial.

I found a stick and threw it down the beach. Great Danes don't fetch with the dedication of retrievers, but Spot ran with gusto. He likes to retrieve, but he isn't wild about giving the stick back to me. I was patient, having learned long ago that you can't simply decide to take a stick from the mouth of a 170-pound Great Dane unless he wants to let it go. He ran around, taunting me with the stick. I acted bored. Eventually, he dropped it.

This time I threw the stick into the water. Spot ran into the water until it reached his chest, then stopped. Danes have a thin coat and no body fat, and Tahoe's icy water never warms up much even near the shore.

He looked at the floating stick, trotted left, then right, whining, wondering whether there was a shallower, warmer way to get the stick. He got up his nerve and leaped in. Just like a person jumping into freezing water, he made a lot of splashy, inefficient movement, his front paws breaking the water's surface as he thrashed out to the stick and brought it back. He came out of the water in a rush and raced up and down the beach to celebrate life in warm sunshine.

Eventually, he dropped the stick.

I threw it back into the water.

From the water's edge, Spot watched it arc toward its splash-landing. Then he turned and looked at me.

"You're not working to ability," I said.

He sighed, walked back from the water until he reached dry, hot sand, and lay down.

"A Black lab would keep chasing the stick no matter how cold the water is," I said.

Spot ignored me and flopped down onto his side, soaking up the sunshine.

Two para-sailors were out on the lake. Their parachutes, big billowy bursts of color, looked like giant flowers being towed behind boats. Over by the Tahoe Keys was a regatta, fifteen or twenty sailboats all racing north toward the windward mark. Close to the beach, three jet skis raced by, bouncing on the light chop. The MS Dixie sternwheeler headed west on its morning cruise to Emerald Bay.

My cell phone rang. I expected the young man who thought he was in danger. It was Diamond Martinez.

"Busy?" he said.

"Working hard as always, Sergeant," I said.

"Office office, or one of your outdoor offices?"

"Nevada Beach."

"Gonna be there for a few more minutes?"

"Judging by how long it'll take me to get the sand off my dog, another hour."

"Okay if I stop by?"

"If you bring treats. We're a couple of stick throws north of the parking lot."

Diamond showed up fifteen minutes later with two coffees. He looked and smelled freshly washed, his thick black hair shiny and combed back. He twisted the coffees down into the sand, then pulled a doggie biscuit out of his pocket.

"I meant treats for me," I said.

Diamond pointed at the coffee.

Spot had been sleeping, but when Diamond bent down in front of him, he opened his eyes. He made a big yawn without lifting his head. His giant tongue flopped out.

"He just got sand in his mouth," Diamond said.

"Helps abrade the plaque off his teeth," I said.

Diamond held out the biscuit and gave it a little toss.

Spot caught the biscuit and chewed it up fast.

Diamond lifted up on the creases of his trousers, then sat down on the sand.

I sipped my coffee. "You been siesta-ing? It looks like you just got out of the shower."

"Been on a long, sweaty hike." Diamond pulled out a map, unfolded it. "Yesterday afternoon, two hikers found human remains up by Genoa Peak. This morning I went up with two of our deputies and had a look. Felt like I should get cleaned up after that."

"Any thoughts on how recent the death was?"

"No idea. The body was quite desiccated, and the skull and neck bones were dragged some distance away, probably by a bear or coyote."

"You get up there on one of those Jeep trails?"

"Yeah, part of the way. We had to park and hike the Tahoe Rim Trail for a bit, then make a long, steep descent down into a canyon below. The return trip was way worse. My hiking motto is always go up first, then the return trip is easy."

"You pack out the bones?"

"Not yet. Wanted to see if your sweetheart had time to go up and collect samples. There wasn't much insect activity, but I did see some flies buzzing around. The remains have been there some time, so I figured one more day wouldn't hurt, especially if Street could make an estimate of time of death. We took photos, and hiked back. I called Street when we got back, and she said she'd be willing to go up tomorrow morning."

"Any indication of the cause of death?"

"Nah," Diamond said." There wasn't anything but stinky leather and bones. Some of the skin remaining on the skull had long hair. And the body seemed small. So maybe it was a woman. We'll bag the bones after Street's done. But I've only got one free deputy. We've been running a lot of overtime the last few days. Lots of stuff keeping us busy."

"Like the climber who fell off Cave Rock last week," I said.

"Yeah. Don't they know it's illegal to climb there now? Talk about stupid. He dies, and we get stuck cleaning up the mess. We had to close the highway for three hours." Diamond picked up a pine cone and threw it down the beach. Spot watched it go, but didn't move. "Anyway, I wondered if you might come along with Street and me. Help me out."

I looked at the lake. A big motor yacht was rumbling by, a group of people already drinking beer up on the flying bridge.

"I'm pretty busy," I said.

Diamond looked at me, held his hands out gesturing at the beach, decided not to respond. He bent over the map and pointed at the topographical lines that showed the contour of the land. "The body was found here, down a canyon on the Carson Valley side of Genoa Peak. Street says her tool box is a bit heavy to carry a long way, and this site is pretty remote."

"I'll carry it."

"That's what she suggested. But I had a better idea. I called Maria. She's got a friend, Lana Madrone, who lives near Hidden Woods. Pretty much straight down from Genoa Peak on the Tahoe side. Lana's got a stable and some horses. You can haul Street's gear in on horseback." Diamond grinned at me.

"And you're grinning because you're pleased with the idea of seeing me on horseback?"

"Possibly. Anyway, I want to preserve the bones in their current position. Like on an archaeology dig. I thought I could get them onto a foam-covered board, then put more foam and another board on top. Strap them all together and carry the package out on a horse. I figure I'll go up with a deputy. We'll do like we did today, take a Jeep to the saddle, then hike down to the body. You and Street can ride the entire way. After we pack up the remains, you and me and the deputy can walk, and your horse can carry the remains. Once we get back up to the saddle, we can transfer everything to the Jeep. Then you and Street can ride back down."

I thought about it. "I don't remember any stable near Hidden Woods."

"It's private. Lana took early retirement from Intel. She runs a program for battered women. She has a friend in Chicago who runs a shelter there. Three or four times a summer Lana brings small groups of women from Chicago out to Tahoe to learn to ride. It's about building self-esteem through acquiring new skills. She takes them in for a week at a time. Pays all of their expenses."

"So she's a nice lady. Doesn't mean that I can't hike and carry

Street's stuff."

Diamond looked at me. "You're not excited about the idea of riding a horse. I understand. Big, macho guys don't want to do anything where they look like a neophyte."

"Just because I've never been on a horse, you think I'm a neophyte," I said.

"Right," Diamond said. He pointed on the map. "You probably know this Jeep trail. The closest it goes to the place with the body is this saddle at eighty-six hundred feet. From there you have to traverse this slope on the Tahoe Rim Trail, then descend down toward Carson Valley. This circle here is my best estimate of where the body was. I wrote down the GPS coordinates. The elevation is about seven thousand. So that's about sixteen hundred vertical down and then back up."

"The town of Genoa is over here," I said. "Not too far. Could we come up from there?"

"Probably, but Genoa's at, what, forty-eight hundred feet. That would be even more vertical, coming up from below. It was one of my guys who said that we should have gone in on horses. As soon as he said it, I realized he was right."

We went over times and what else to bring. Diamond was standing up to go when my phone rang.

"Owen McKenna," I said.

"This is Ryan Lear. Thanks for calling me back. I really need to talk to you. But I can't get to Tahoe for another day. Can you meet me tomorrow night?"

"On my machine, you said that you're in trouble."

There was a pause. "I think someone is planning to kill me."

"Why do you think this?"

"I got a threatening note. Then my friend Eli Nathan fell and died at Cave Rock."

"Climbers fall and die all the time."

"Sure. But I can't believe Eli would fall off of Cave Rock. He was very skillful, very sure of himself. Someone must have done something to make him fall. I know that as much as I know anything."

"Is his death why you think you're in danger?"

"Partly, yes."

"I don't mean to sound impertinent, but if someone wanted to kill you, why kill your friend?"

Diamond turned to stare at me, frowning.

"I don't know," Ryan said.

"You said your friend's death was partly the reason you think you're in danger. What is the other reason?"

"My other friend has gone missing. Jeanie Samples. I haven't heard from her in two weeks. I'm worried to death. I went to her house in Palo Alto. I called all of her friends and her parents. Nobody's heard from her. Last I talked to her, she was packing for her summer vacation. But I don't know if she ever even left the Bay Area."

"Where was she going on vacation?"

"Her plan was to go up to Tahoe and hike the Tahoe Rim Trail."

TWO

I saw no reason to speculate on the phone about Ryan's missing friend. Despite the coincidence, the body up on the mountain could be anyone.

"Where do you want to meet?" I asked.

"Can you come to my house? I'm on the East Shore, about a mile south of Cave Rock."

"What time?"

"I'll call when I get there tomorrow night. Eight or nine o'clock."

"Okay," I said.

"Since I've never been up on the Tahoe Rim Trail, is there cell phone coverage up there? Would it be possible that Jeanie could still be hiking and camping her way around the basin and not be able to call out?"

"There are dead spots, but there are many more live spots. Especially on the prominent high places with good views. When you can see a long way, your cell phone can see a tower and get reception. She wouldn't be able to hike any serious distance without getting reception. Unless her phone broke, or she lost it. She could have been checking it and dropped it off one of those viewpoints or something."

"Now I'm even more worried. I was hoping her silence was just because she was camping."

"Have you or her family filed a missing persons report?"

"Yes. Her parents and I both made reports at our local police stations. That was ten days ago."

"So she went missing before Eli fell climbing."

"Yes." Ryan sounded like he was talking through clenched teeth.

"Maybe she was up here at the lake and she found out that Eli died," I said. "Would the shock and distress cause her to go silent? Hole up in a hotel or something?"

"No. If she'd heard about Eli, the first thing she would have done would be to call me and her other friends. Jeanie would have wanted to be with us at Eli's funeral."

"There are some things I'd like you to bring when you come."

"What?"

"A picture or two of Jeanie and Eli. Also, do you have access to Jeanie's house or apartment?"

"Sure," he said. "We're like siblings. Water each other's plants."

"Look around and find a hairbrush or comb or something similar, but don't take the hair out of it."

"I don't understand," Ryan said.

I didn't want to say that I wanted her DNA for comparing to the body. "Scent," I said. "I probably won't need it. But in case we need to send out a search party. We would scent search dogs on the hair brush."

"Got it."

"Okay, Ryan. I'll see you tomorrow night."

I hung up.

"You make out the gist of it?" I said to Diamond.

"I think so. Guy you were talking to knows the guy who fell from Cave Rock. He also knows a missing woman who may or may not be our body."

"Right."

"And he thinks these deaths aren't natural."

"Right."

"Hard to imagine that Eli Nathan's fall wasn't natural. We'll know more about the body up on the mountain after we get the remains to the coroner."

THREE

Street, Spot, and I left early the next morning, went south through the Cave Rock tunnel, and found Lana Madrone's driveway down around the next big curve, just south of Hidden Woods on the southeast side of the lake. We turned off onto a curving ribbon of asphalt that crawled up away from the highway on the mountain side of the road.

The drive crested a rise, wound past a large, silver horse trailer, then widened in front of a large house, done in a modern mountain lodge design. We all got out, and Street pressed the doorbell. I held Spot's collar as we waited a couple of minutes, but no one came. In the distance, we heard the sound of someone laughing. We walked around the house.

"Look," Street said, pointing.

Up in the trees was a small barn painted like a Mondrian, with vertical and horizontal black stripes dividing the barn walls up into rectangles of varying size. The rectangles were filled in with brilliant yellows and reds and oranges and blues.

"What a delight," I said. "I hope the Tahoe Color Police never see it."

Just outside of the open barn door stood three women, two black and one who was white a few days ago but now sported one of the most painful-looking sunburns I'd ever seen. One of them had her hand on a canted hip, thumb forward, elbow waving. Her other hand was up in the air, a long index finger tracing circles as she talked. She saw us approach and spoke to her friends in a strong South-Side-Chicago accent.

"Y'all think horses only come black or brown like me and Belle, check out the polka-dot pony approaching."

The others turned to look at us, gasped at Spot, and laughed hearty bellows.

"Afternoon," I said. "The pony is Spot, who will be pleased to make your acquaintance."

The first woman said, "That's the biggest hound dog I've ever seen. He isn't going to bite us, right? Where we come from, any white folks who walk the neighborhood always have a dog. And we know to keep our distance. But no one ever had a dog that big."

The white woman said, "I'm white and I walk the neighborhood, and I ain't got a dog."

"Yeah, but you're one of us."

I said, "The only danger with Spot is that he might slobber on you as he licks you. Or if you sit down, he'll try to climb on your lap, and he's not light."

They made cooing sounds, and each bravely reached out to pet him.

"We're here to meet Lana. Is she around?"

One of them shouted into the barn. "Lana, hon, you've got company!"

A muffled voice came back, "Soon as I get this hay out of the loft!"

While we waited, I said, "I'm Owen McKenna, and this is Street Casey." We shook hands all around.

"I'm Janelle, she's Belle and she," she pointed at the white woman, "is Chanelle. You can call any of us Elle, and we'll all answer."

"Have you been riding?" Street asked.

"Yeah!" they said in exaggerated unison.

"Tell them about Paint," Chanelle said, giggling.

"No way," Belle said. "You tell 'em. I'll tell 'em about Prancer. She's my kind of girl."

"Yeah, but Paint, he's got this huge..."

"Shut up. I rode Peppy, and she's so sweet."

"Good," I said. "If Peppy's sweet, that'll be perfect for a greenhorn like me. Street's done the horse thing, but the last time I sat on an animal, it was the donkey ride at the amusement park when I was ten years old."

All three of them looked at each other.

"Should we tell him about Peppy?" Chanelle said. "Hate to bring him down."

"What?" I said.

Belle spoke up. "We should let Lana tell him."

"What?" I said again.

"Tory will tell him. It'll be better, one man to another."

Street said, "I'm guessing that there's some kind of a counterpoint to Peppy's sweet side."

"You listen to her," Chanelle said.

"Counterpoint is good in music," I said. "Gotta be good for a horse."

"Not this counterpoint," Janelle said.

"She doesn't like men," Belle said.

"Who?"

"Peppy. She bucks them off." Belle didn't seem all that disappointed about it.

"All men, or just the guys who are jerks?" I said.

"There's a difference?" Belle said. They all exploded in laughter.

Lana came through the barn door. She was a big, strong white woman in her fifties. She had huge hands and a red face. She smiled so sweetly, I could see how she could convince a city-dweller that climbing up on a thousand-pound animal and galloping through the forest was a reasonable activity.

"You must be Owen and Street."

We introduced ourselves.

Lana said, "I've heard about you from Maria and Diamond, and they both extol your virtues."

"Extol your virtues," Chanelle repeated. She turned to her friends. "You're right. Some white folk do talk funny."

Lana grinned as Belle and Janelle laughed. It was obvious that they had a great relationship.

"We're not taking your horses away at the wrong time, are we?" Street asked.

"Not at all," Lana said. "Chanelle has a blister on her hand and a sunburn that might as well have come from a frying pan, and Janelle and Belle said they need a day off to unstiffen their legs."

"I don't know why you say that," Belle said. She walked a slow, pained circle, keeping her feet at least three feet apart from each other.

Janelle and Chanelle shrieked.

"You Elles are a riot," I said. I turned to Street. "Maybe you should do the ride, and I'll hang with them. That way I don't have to worry about Peppy throwing me off the mountain."

"Oh, oh," Lana said. "They told you about that?"

"No problem. What was the other horse's name? Prancer. I'll ride her."

"She doesn't like men either," Janelle said.

"Lot of that going around," I said.

More laughter.

"Let me call my nephew," Lana said. "He can help us saddle up." She pulled a walkie talkie off her belt. "Tory, the couple I told you about are here. Can you come chip in?"

"Be right there," came a voice.

Lana clipped her walkie talkie back on her belt. "We're in a cell phone shadow," she said.

An electric golf cart came humming up the drive. The driver, a rugged looking guy with a shaved head, was about twenty years younger than Lana. He jumped out of the golf cart.

"Hi. I'm Tory."

We shook hands. He smiled at Street, but his look to me was more of a grimace. Spot appeared from the woods.

"That your dog?" Tory looked alarmed.

"Yeah. He's friendly." A phrase I'd said a thousand times.

"While I show Street the map," Lana said to Tory, "you could go over the saddles and such with Owen."

Tory looked at me, up and down. It was the look a coach gives a player who's destined to sit on the bench. "You ever ridden before?"

"Nope. Street's a competent rider, but I'm a greenhorn."

"Okay, come with me."

I followed Tory into the barn. We went past the horse stalls and into a tack room. Tory looked at me, looked at the various items of tack, and held his finger up.

"Give me a sec." He walked out.

I heard Lana say, "Missing something?"

"Guy's awful tall. I need the big saddle. I think I left it in the horse trailer after that desert ride."

"I already set it on the paddock fence," Lana said. "And the trailer was parked over the edge of my flowers again."

"I didn't do that," Tory said, sounding defensive. "I've been very careful about that."

"Okay, it moved itself."

Tory came back into the tack room, shaking his head, carrying a large saddle. He began explaining about sizes of saddles and cinch straps, and which bridles were for which horses, and how to check saddle blankets for any sharp bits of pine needles or grit before putting them on the horses, and why they rode Western-style, and how little a horse should be allowed to eat on a ride, and many other details that I was already forgetting as he heaped information on top of more information. Combined with Tory's gruff, brusque manner, I gathered that his intent was to overwhelm me.

Tory handed a saddle blanket to me and draped another blanket over a saddle.

"Your saddle is outside." He grabbed his saddle and blanket, and we walked outside and set the tack over the fence.

We went back into the barn and Tory opened one of the stalls, clipped a short line to the halter of the horse inside and handed me the line.

"This guy will be your horse," Tory said. The huge gelding looked like its front half had been dipped in chocolate and its back half dipped in cream and then sprayed with chocolate drops. "His name is Paint. He's twelve hundred pounds of muscle, so he'll have no trouble hauling someone your size up the mountain."

Tory took another, smaller horse out of its stall.

"This one's Prancer," he said.

We brought both horses outside into the bright light and looped their short halter ropes over fence posts.

Tory showed me how to bridle and saddle both Paint and Prancer. I noticed that of the two saddles, Tory's was the one with the padded seat and mine was made of leather so hard it may as well have been made of wood.

"Lana told me that you're going all the way up to the Tahoe

Rim Trail, then down the east side fifteen hundred feet, and back again."

"Yeah," I said. "You think we're crazy?"

"No. You'll be fine. Your lady friend knows what she's doing?"

"It was quite a few years ago," I said. "When she was in college she worked a couple of summers at a dude ranch in Jackson, Wyoming."

"Then she'll be your guide. It just takes one person who knows horses to lead a group, so to speak. First, you and I will go on a check-ride, make sure you're comfortable and your saddle fits and all that."

"Sounds good," I said.

Tory went over more things to keep in mind, tips about climbing into the saddle, and how not to get my feet caught in the stirrups, and leaning forward when going up a steep trail. I got up on Paint, and he adjusted the height of the stirrups.

"There, easy as one, two, three," Tory said in a condescending manner as if I were a three-year-old. "Now try letting go of the saddle horn, and sit up a little straighter. You know, when they teach flying lessons, they always stress holding the yoke gently."

I knew where he was going with that. "Yeah, I'm actually a sometime pilot. The key is a light touch on the yoke, fingertips of one hand. The plane flies better when you stay relaxed."

"Exactly the same with horses."

"Difference is, planes do exactly what you tell them," I said. "Not so sure about horses."

"You can be sure. Horses are naturally obedient."

Right, I thought.

"I'll jump on Prancer," Tory said. "Then we can take a turn through the forest together and get you up to speed." He turned toward Prancer and swung himself up and into the saddle in one smooth motion.

"I thought Prancer bucks men off," I said.

"Who told you that?"

"The Elles."

"Then I'll ride her like a girl, all soft and gentle." He gave me a look that was half sneer. "We'll start on a wide trail where we can ride two abreast." He made a little motion with his hand on the reins, and Prancer trotted up a trail heading north into the woods.

I didn't do anything, and Paint walked along after Prancer. I shook Paint's reins like I'd seen in the movies, and he sped up to a trot, naturally drawing alongside of Tory and Prancer. I didn't even have to steer.

The trot was excruciating in its jarring bounce.

Tory must have read my mind. Or maybe he saw one of my fillings come out. "A little faster is easier," he said. He must have made a secret signal, for Prancer sped up into a kind of loping gait. Paint followed, just a touch behind and to the left.

"This is called a canter," Tory said, his voice louder to carry over the beating hooves. "Feels just like sitting in a rocking chair, doesn't it?"

I thought nothing of the kind, but it was smoother than a trot. We went for some distance. Spot ran large circles around us.

"There's a trail coming up that turns off to the right," Tory shouted. "It's single track, so I'll pull ahead. Then you follow me."

Without any telltale movement, he got Prancer to speed up ahead of me, then he veered off on a narrower trail. I pretended I knew how to indicate the same intentions to Paint, and, like magic, Paint followed him.

We were now galloping fast through the forest. Trees rushed by at a dangerous speed.

Tory and Prancer leaned into two or three S-turns. In time, we came to another fork in the trail. Tory shouted back toward me.

"If we go straight, this trail would take us up to Cave Rock. Instead, we'll make a sharp right just up ahead."

"Got it," I shouted back.

Tory didn't slow Prancer at all as he shot off onto the new trail, leaning hard to the right.

I understood that he was trying to push me far past my abilities. Yet Paint followed Prancer. We made a loop through the woods. In a minute, we came back around toward the Mondrian box. Prancer slowed, as did Paint. Tory brought Prancer to a stop, and jumped off. He took Paint's bridle and pet Paint's forehead.

"That was great, Owen. You're a natural," he said with obvious sarcasm.

"You say that to everyone." I swung my leg over and got off. My legs and groin were already sore. It was going to be a long day.

"No, I'm serious. You're practically a trail hound."

I had no idea why Tory had such an attitude about me. Maybe he had expected me to be more obsequious as he played the role of equestrian expert. Or maybe it was something about my appearance. Although Tory was muscular, he was about eight inches short of my six-six. I'd seen it before, men who want to make tall guys pay for the unearned advantages that the world gives us.

"Well," I said, "I felt a little out of balance when we hit top speed back there," I said. "But I didn't fall off, so I guess that's a good sign."

"That was barely a slow gallop. Maybe you and I should ride together sometime. All the riders around here are women. It would be good to do a guy's ride for a change. We could get out and let these horses really open up. Burn off some of their energy."

"They go much faster than what we were just doing?"

He scoffed. "Twice that fast."

"Thanks for the offer. I'll keep it in mind."

FOUR

Fifteen minutes later, Street, Spot, and I were well down the single-track trail, with Street's toolbox of forensic gear strapped onto the back of her saddle.

"Watch out when Paint's ears go flat against his head like that," Street said. "It means he might take a nip out of your leg."

"Good to know," I said. Now that Paint was preparing to swing that huge jaw around for a taste of my shinbone, the merits of riding instead of hiking up under the hot August sun seemed less clear.

I gave Paint my best Clint Eastwood glare. But according to Tory, he had 1200 pounds to my 215. I don't think he was fooled into thinking that I was the alpha male on this journey. Reaching forward, I patted his big neck just behind his right ear.

"Easy, boy. We're pals. I'm just along for the ride."

Paint turned his head just enough that I could see the evil look in his right eye. Then he resumed walking, slower than before. Paint labored his way up the dusty trail with all the enthusiasm of the kiddie-carnival donkey of my youth, groaning with each step.

Street and Prancer were ahead of me, giving me a good view. Street had grown out her auburn hair. She'd folded it like ribbon candy into loops and gathered it into a clip. She wore tight jeans that were tucked into boots with tall heels that hooked on her stirrups so that her feet couldn't accidentally slip through. Golden, stitched patterns danced up the sides of the boots. On Street's long, thin legs, they looked like a special feature in the Victoria's Secret Cowgirl catalog.

Paint and I were falling behind again. I gave him a squeeze with my legs and shook the reins.

"C'mon, big guy. Maybe pick up the pace?" He came to a

stop, swung his head around and leered at me, ears back.

"It wasn't a critique, bud. Just a soft sell. I'm on your side."

Paint turned away and jerked his head out, loosening the reins, then stepped off the trail to munch fresh grass with vigor. At least he had enthusiasm for something.

Spot appeared, running through the trees on one side of the trail. He crossed in front of Street and Prancer and ran through the trees on the other side.

Street stopped and turned back toward me. "Spot likes this exploration stuff. Look how he gambols through the forest."

"Street, my sweet, Great Danes don't gambol. Deer and their fawns and the occasional pair of young girls gambol. Spot's cheery Harlequin exterior belies the reality that he is a predator with fang and claw. He hunts and stalks and pursues his prey with relentless cunning and focus."

Spot ran out of the trees and did a quick stop in the trail. A dust cloud wafted off on the gentle breeze. He had a bent stick in his mouth and dirt on his nose. A purple wildflower was stuck in the toes of his left rear foot. He looked up at us, wagged, then chewed the stick into pieces.

"I see what you mean," Street said. "Ferocious predator." She appeared to do nothing, yet Prancer trotted ahead.

Paint walked behind. I shook the reins to attempt to get him to speed up, but he did not take the hint.

Unlike Paint, Prancer was a deep mahogany color. Unlike Paint, Prancer had a surfeit of enthusiasm. As Prancer trotted, Street went up and down with every other beat. The horse bounced, but she looked smooth.

"What is that you're doing?" I called out.

"It's called posting," she shouted back at me. "Keeps your brain from getting loose when a horse trots." She pulled Prancer to a stop and gazed out across the lake.

"How does a childhood runaway who studies bugs know about posting?" I asked. "They teach that at dude ranches?"

"Yeah. But I learned about horses the same way I know about bugs. Books. You should try posting when you trot."

"You should try making Paint trot," I said.

Street headed up the trail, walking Prancer now as the trail grew steeper and started to wind. We came to the second Y in the trail and took the high road once again as instructed by Lana.

A youngish man with a camera around his neck and a pack on his back came hiking down toward us. The camera had a long telephoto lens. Despite the warmth of summer, he wore long sleeves and a red knit cap. He had no hair below the cap. When men shave their heads - guys like Tory - they usually don't put on caps to cover up. Maybe this guy was in chemo.

"Morning," he said, giving us a pleasant smile. He stepped off the trail to let us by. Spot walked up to him, sniffing, wagging. The man was hesitant, but he didn't voice any fear. He slowly reached out and pet Spot.

"Get any good shots?" I asked, pausing Paint as Street rode on ahead.

"Not really. But I'm not after scenic shots. I'm looking for our newly famous forest resident." He pet Paint on his forehead.

"Who's that?" I said.

"You haven't heard of our wild Mustang?"

"I didn't know there were any Mustangs in Tahoe."

"There aren't supposed to be. A few people own Mustangs that they adopted from the Carson City Prison program, but those are kept in stables like all the other horses in Tahoe. They don't live here naturally. Too much snow for them to survive in winter. Even so, we've got a wild one now."

"You've seen it?"

He nodded. "I read about it in the Herald before I saw it. The reporter hadn't seen it, either, but other people had phoned in sightings. The reporter even gave it a name, called it Heat. Now I've seen Heat twice. Not today, though. He's become a kind of obsession for me. I've even put up a website about him. People can post sightings and trade info on what might be the best way to bring him safely back home, wherever that is. If we can't catch him, his chances are pretty bleak. He'll get mired in the snow. If you see him, will you let me know?"

"Sure."

He pulled a home-printed business card out of his shirt pocket and handed it up to me. "Otherwise, you could go to my website and post the time and location you saw him."

I took the card.

The man continued to hold his hand out. "I'm Travis Rundell, by the way."

"Owen McKenna." We shook. "Heat is a funny name for a horse," I said.

"It's because the people who've seen him say he likes to stand in the sun. He seeks out the little open meadow areas in the forest. It makes sense when you think of it. Mustangs live on the open range. They spend their whole lives in the sun. It would be hard to go from that to life under the forest canopy. You should check out the reporter's blog. Her name is Glenda Gorman, and she's been writing daily reports."

"We know Glennie," I said. "A friend of ours. Where's Heat been seen?"

"Right here in these forests of the East Shore. That's why I'm so excited about it."

"What's Heat look like?"

"Prettiest horse you've ever seen. Deep cherry color, with a triangular blaze on his forehead. The triangle points down. Heat is large for a Mustang. But not big like this horse, of course."

"I'm curious about how a wild Mustang would end up in Tahoe."

"Me too," Travis said. "The most likely explanation is that someone adopted him, but he wasn't really domesticated. So he escaped into the forest. Both times I saw him, he ran away and disappeared. Same thing as when other people have seen him. The only other possibility is that he somehow came by himself up and over the mountains into the Tahoe Basin.

"Anyway, I hope you enjoy your ride. The views up on the mountain are great. Oh, one more thing before you go."

"Yeah?"

"There are two guys who've been out riding these local trails over the last couple of weeks or so. We think they're just summer visitors who are staying near one of the stables. They're a bit intimidating. They drink and carry on, and they harass other riders. I just saw them up this trail, about a half-hour hike above us. They were pretty drunk, so I just thought I'd warn you."

"Appreciate that," I said.

I rejoined Street and Spot. I told her about the Mustang as we followed the trail up the mountain. Paint went slowly, always looking for a tuft of grass to eat. Street and Spot gradually got far ahead of us. They were waiting as Paint and I finally labored our way up to the four-wheel-drive trail below Genoa peak. We both dismounted to drink water, stretch, and enjoy the view.

A few minutes later, we got back on our horses and, with Street leading, worked our way over to the saddle.

There was no Jeep waiting for us. We'd gotten there before Diamond and his deputy.

"There's a cairn on top of that boulder." Street pointed to a small stack of rocks that someone, Diamond perhaps, had assembled. "That probably marks the trail that descends down the canyon toward Genoa."

It was indeed a trail, and it showed recent footprints.

"Do you think we should wait for Diamond?" Street said.

"No. We agreed that if we didn't see each other, both parties would head down to the site. Getting there before them will give you more time to collect your goodies."

"Never thought of forensic specimens as goodies," she said.

The view now showed Carson Valley in one direction, and Lake Tahoe in the other. Carson Valley was 1600 feet lower than the surface of the lake. Because the lake just happened to be a bit over 1600 feet deep, the bottom of the lake was the same elevation as Carson Valley, making it easy to visualize the depth of the lake.

Street started down, and I followed. After twenty minutes, Paint saw an opportunity. He stepped to the side and gobbled fresh green where a late-season water seepage oozed out of the rocky slope and fed a serpentine tail of wildflowers and grass.

"How much farther? This giant food processor won't be happy until we get back to the barn and give him dinner."

Street paused Prancer at a switchback where there was a small level area. She held up her map, compared it to the landscape, then pointed down the mountain. "If you look south to that descending ridge, then follow it down to where it intersects with our canyon, that point is near our destination."

I nodded. Street started up again, and I followed. A half mile down the trail, Street stopped and studied the map again.

Paint had fallen behind, and he wheezed his way down toward them. He reached out and bit down on a Manzanita bush as we went by. And I thought horses knew their food. The Manzanita bush, tough as steel, would not give way. Paint, maybe dumb as steel, kept walking, his teeth clamped onto the bush. We rotated around it until we were facing the opposite direction, back up the mountain, at which point Paint, in danger of losing his molars, let go.

"Owen, where are you going?" Street called up to me.

"Not to worry," I yelled.

I gave Paint a jerk on the reins and a kick with my heels. To my astonishment, he reared up until we were pointing directly at the sky, pivoted on his hind legs, and did a skidding gallop down the trail toward Street and Spot. I hung onto the saddle horn with one hand, the reins with the other.

With a dangerous collision imminent, Street yelled, "Whoa, boy! Whoa!"

I took up the chorus, yelling, "Whoa!" and "Stop!" while I pulled back on the reins. At the last possible moment, Street gave Prancer a kick, and she jumped out of my way. Spot leaped sideways as Paint and I blasted through where they'd been standing. Finally, I brought Paint to a standstill, at which point he stretched out his neck and commenced mowing another tuft of grass. I sat there, my breathing pronounced.

"Honey," Street said, drawing alongside, "if you take your hands off the saddle horn, you'll be better at hanging onto the reins. It would help your balance, too."

I looked down at where my hand had a death grip on the saddle. I pulled it away, and tried to straighten my aching knuckles. "Just wanted to find out if this old boy could move."

"Right," Street said.

Spot was watching with a certain wariness from the other side of an outcropping of rock.

Street stared across the canyon to a short cliff and frowned. "Something over there," she said. "Just visible below that cliff."

She and Prancer turned off and headed toward the cliff.

FIVE

Street approached the cliff and dismounted like a pro. She hooked Prancer's reins onto a Manzanita bush and walked over to the base of the cliff. As Paint and I crested the rise, I saw the yellow crime scene tape that encircled the remains. It made a rough circle 40 feet in diameter. Diamond had put it low to the ground so that it didn't advertise from a distance.

Street squatted down to look at the bones. I climbed off Paint, looped his reins around the same bush, and walked over to see what she'd found.

It was an ugly sight, human bones in a human shape, with just enough dried skin and other tissue to destroy the disconnect that we have when we see clean bones and perceive them as an artifact of a human. In contrast, this looked very much like the recent leftovers of an actual person, and it was disturbing.

Spot approached the body, stopped a short distance away. He sniffed the air, made a little cry, and backed away.

I knew that he was reacting to the lingering smell of a dead human, a smell that professional search dogs often find depressing and occasional helpers like Spot struggle with as well.

His eyes were droopy and sad. He walked away from the body, over toward the cliff, sniffing the ground aimlessly, then lay down in the shade. He put his head down on the dirt, facing at an angle away from us as if to focus on something else.

Street managed to telegraph a scientific remove, but I knew that inside she was experiencing the same free-fall as I was.

The bones were dressed in hiking shorts and shirt and boots. The body lay chest down in a bed of sandy dirt. The back of the olive-green, short-sleeved shirt had been torn open. The skull and top couple of cervical vertebrae were missing. One set of arm bones was flung out as if pointing toward the north. A small silver ring holding a sapphire sparkled on the index finger. The other arm was bent underneath the chest. The spine was twisted a quarter turn so that the pelvis, contained within dark gray shorts, lay on its side. The legs were both bent at the knees. The lower tibias and fibulas disappeared into tall wool socks and hiking boots that looked improbably large on the bones.

The skin that remained was dried and darkened. It draped the bones like a dirty fabric. In a few places, the skin was completely gone, the exposed bone cleaned and white.

Street astonished me with her control.

She opened her toolbox, pulled out the tools and vials she uses for collecting insects. She poked and prodded about the body as she looked for insects. She moved around to the other side and continued her search, lifting bits of sun-dried skin, scraping at the dirt under the edges of the corpse.

"No luck?" I said, looking for a way to break the silence and lighten the mood.

"Just some dermestids." She pointed to a few small beetles.

"No maggots or flies?"

She pointed to a group of small brown objects on a nearby bush.

"These are their pupal cases," she said.

I bent down to look. They were like miniature, long, skinny footballs with an opening in one end.

Street said, "The blow flies lay eggs on a corpse very soon after the person or animal dies. The eggs hatch to maggots. When the maggots are fully grown, they leave the corpse and crawl like worms to a place like this to pupate. They form a little oblong container where they undergo metamorphosis into adult flies. Now the pupal cases are empty."

"Hate it when those little buggers fly the coop," I said, attempting levity.

"Yeah. Can't tell how long ago they did their thing."

"Their thing being lunch on the corpse."

"Right," she said. "If we saw adult flies emerging from the pupal cases, or if we saw pupa inside the cases..."

"Or if you saw the maggots in their various instar stages, you could tell how long since the person had died."

Street turned. "I had no idea you paid so much attention during those other cases."

I moved around the corpse, saw another cairn about seventy or eighty feet away, walked over and took a look.

"Skull's over here," I called out to Street. I saw Spot's ears move as I spoke, but he didn't lift his head, didn't move.

The skull and cervical vertebrae were exposed and white in some places, covered with skin in others. Unlike a live person, the flesh under the skin was gone, making it look like the skull had been shrink-wrapped with skin. The head, void of flesh under the skin, darkened, and without eyes, wouldn't have bothered me, except that this one still had most of its hair. Some tufts of hair had come out and gotten caught on some brush nearby. But what remained was still thick and red and long. The hair, unlike the rest of the corpse, still looked alive, as if the person had just brushed it that morning.

I wanted some of the hair so that I could have a lab compare its DNA with that of any hair that Ryan Lear would hopefully bring me. So I broke off a few strands, carefully folded them into one of the baggies I carried, and slid it into the slot of my wallet.

Street came over.

I said, "With the adult flies gone and the head dragged over here, it could be a very long time since the person died, right?"

"That's what I would have thought."

"Except for," I said.

"Except for the dermestids."

"Remind me again what they do," I said.

"Dermestids are hide beetles," Street said.

"Meaning they eat skin," I said.

"Yes. The moisture content has to be relatively low before they are attracted to a corpse. But the corpse can't be completely desiccated or even the dermestids will pass it by."

"If hide beetles like a dry corpse," I said, "the maggots must've reduced it to mostly skin and bones some time ago. How long ago do you think the victim died?"

"Impossible to say with any accuracy if we don't have maggots present." Street thought about it. "The weather has been hot for

Tahoe, up into the upper eighties in town. Even at this elevation, the temps would have been up into the seventies in the afternoon. But it still would drop to freezing at night. That kind of cold really slows the work of maggots. It would probably take at least two weeks for the blow flies to go through all the stages from eggs to maggots to pupas to adults and then fly away. Maybe more. At that point, the corpse would be desiccated enough for hide beetles."

"So we're looking at a rough time-of-death of two-to-three weeks ago."

"Yeah," she said. "Very rough."

I looked up at the small cliff from which the person probably fell. It stood about twenty feet high.

"Not a very tall cliff," Street said. "And the rock here is somewhat crumbly, not always the firmest footing."

"I'll hike up there and have a look while you get your samples," I said.

"Be careful." Street bent down towards the skull.

Spot came with me as I climbed up and around to get to the place from which the victim may have fallen. It was steep, and I had to use my hands in a couple of places. Spot is too big to be an especially agile dog, but he made it up without any problem, and the two of us stood on a rocky projection and looked down at Street and the horses as well as at Carson Valley spread out 2000-plus feet below.

The place would make a spectacular lunch overlook, but it was a bit of a distance from the trail, so only explorers like the people who discovered the body would find it. It was easy to imagine that someone who'd fallen from the cliff to the rocks below could go undiscovered for a long time.

I looked around for any indications of what might have happened, but nothing stood out. There was rock, and there was air, and the transition from one to the other would take nothing more than a small distraction.

I was turning to leave when a tiny glimmer of red caught my eye. I stopped and turned back, but saw nothing. I went through the motions again, trying to remember where I'd seen the color.

Still nothing.

So I did a spiral grid search, starting at my best guess at where the red came from. Visualize a 2-inch square and look closely at it. Now move one square to the left. Then one square up. Now right. Right again. Down. And so on in an expanding clockwise pattern. It is slow and tedious and frustrating. I'd had some experience with the process back on the SFPD. A 3-foot square has 324 2-inch squares contained within. A 6-foot square has 1296 squares. It can take all day. But if you're careful and thorough, you will almost always find the missing item.

I was lucky. On square 32, just a hand-span away from where I'd started, was a tiny piece of red paper next to a rock. I picked it up. Not paper. Leather. Very thin, very light, very red. It was torn most of the way through.

The red was too bright to be any natural thing from a plant or animal. I bagged it and put it in my wallet with the victim's hair.

Spot and I climbed back down to Street. She was putting vials into a rack inside her toolbox.

"See anything?" she asked.

"Just a tiny piece of red leather."

"A piece of clothing?"

"I doubt it." I took it out and showed it to her.

"Looks like a piece of fringe from a purse or something. You think the victim died falling off the cliff?"

"It's likely. A fall from that height could easily kill someone if they landed on their head. But any other landing would probably leave a person wounded, perhaps still able to call out to hikers on the trail across the arroyo. I'll be interested in the Medical Examiner's report. If the skull and cervical bones show no damage, then it's likely the victim didn't land on their head and lived for some time. Which makes me wonder why someone didn't hear them calling."

"Maybe no one was on the trail to hear," Street said.

I saw movement and looked up to see Diamond and another man. They carried foam boards and a shovel.

"Any luck with bugs?" he said to Street.

"Dermestids," she said.

"Ah," he said. "I'd be premature to ask about time of death, right?"

"Yeah. But I'm guessing two to three weeks."

He nodded, then introduced us to his deputy, a man named Smithy. Street went over to comfort Spot, while Diamond and Smithy and I dug under the main portion of the corpse and got it sandwiched between Diamond's foam-covered boards.

The skull went faster, although at one point we had to wait while Smithy took a breather. He walked over to a boulder that was in the shade of a scrubby juniper. Like Spot, he sat down facing the valley below, and took his hat off. After five minutes he came back, and we finished our packing and wrapping. Throughout the entire process, Smithy said no more than a dozen words. He was young, and I guessed that this was his first body. We strapped the foam boards onto Paint and walked with him back up the mountain as Street led the way on Prancer.

"I can walk, and one of you can ride Prancer," she said.

"Thanks," I said. "But remember, she bucks men off."

"Oh, right."

Spot brought up the rear, his mood depressed, no doubt failing to comprehend why some people, just like those who feed him and play with him, end up dead.

When we got to the Jeep trail, Diamond and Smithy transferred the cargo into their Douglas County SUV, and, with Spot still trailing behind, Street and I rode the horses back down the lake side of the mountain toward Lana and Tory's ponderosa.

About half way down the mountain we came to a trail intersection. Near it stood two horses with saddles, their reins tied to a tree. In the shade nearby sat two guys wearing jeans and muscle shirts. Their cowboy hats didn't go with their Nikes. They lounged back on one elbow each, and drank beer from cans.

"Afternoon," I said.

"Sho'nuff," one of them said.

The other laughed and said, "You come up from the place with the multi-cultural tourists. We was riding down there earlier and saw your hound dog when you were saddling up."

"You are tourists, too," I said, not specifically knowing it, but certain nonetheless. "Just not as multi-cultural."

"Way we like it," he said.

Street spoke up, "Let's go, Owen," she said with tension in her voice. She rode on past, through the intersection. Spot stayed.

After she had gone a short way but was still within hearing distance, the other guy said, "Skinny broad, but she looks good in them jeans." He finished his beer, crunched his can, and threw it onto the trail in front of me.

"We don't leave litter in Tahoe," I said.

"You gonna make me pick it up?"

"I could. My dog could. Instead, I'll just pick it up the next time I come through. C'mon, Spot," I said.

I gave Paint a shake of the reins and we went on down the mountain. The two guys laughed behind me.

Lana, Tory, and the Elles were not in sight when we got down, maybe napping in the afternoon.

Street helped me take the saddles and the toolbox off the horses. We put the horses back in their stalls. Street found a large brush and brushed down both horses while I watched.

"How many years since you rode?" I asked.

"Sixteen or seventeen, I guess."

"You still seem to remember it well."

"Like a bicycle," she said. She looked into Prancer's big brown eye, brushed her neck. "But horses are special. These guys have a soul unlike anything else."

We were walking past Tory and Lana's pickup on the way out to my Jeep when Street glanced into the pickup bed and stopped. She frowned, moved around to the other side of the truck, leaned over and looked into the corner of the bed. She pulled a toothpick from out of her shirt pocket, reached down into the pickup, and used the toothpick to pick up a dark object that contrasted with the white paint of the truck.

She walked over and showed me. It was dark brown, tubular, about a quarter inch in diameter, and an inch or more long.

"Like a little tube of bark that slipped off a twig," I said.

"No, look. See the segments? All the little rings?"

"Yeah?"

"This is what happens to a millipede after a glowworm encounter."

"What does that mean?" I asked.

"Have you ever seen fireflies?"

"Sure. Bright, blinking lights low down over fields at night. But I don't recall them since I was a kid. Back east."

"Yeah. That's because the California versions of fireflies don't have the fire. At least, not the flying versions. For example," she gestured with the toothpick, "this involved a California Phengodid. The male of the species matures into a flying beetle similar to other firefly species. Except our guy doesn't have any light action."

"He's light impotent?" I asked.

"Yeah. But the female more than makes up for his lack of performance."

"She's into bright lights, or hot sex?"

"Both. She's got pheromones that drive the males crazy. But she's also a strange creature. She doesn't mature into a typical adult beetle. She stays larviform."

"Not sure I like the sound of that."

"No. You wouldn't like watching what she does, either."

I took a deep breath. "Okay, I'm ready."

"She looks like a moist, yellow caterpillar with big brown spots. She's naked, no hair, and she glows in the dark."

"And her perfume drives the guys wild," I said.

"Yeah. But I'm not sure how they would react if they took the time to watch her eat."

"Not a pretty sight?"

"No. She likes nice, big millipedes. She grabs them by wrapping her body around them, and gives them a death-bite right behind their head. Then she commences her dinner."

"Perhaps I should fortify myself with a beer before you give me the details."

"You can take it," Street said, grinning. "Her particular Thanksgiving feast behavior is to dive right into the millipede's body, and tunnel through the entire creature, starting just behind the head, eating her way through, and exiting out the tail, leaving only the hollow shell."

I pointed at the brown thing on Street's toothpick. "The tube you're holding."

"Yeah. But you want to know the best part?"

"Maybe not."

"Sure you do. Her lights are so bright, that you can watch her glowing through the millipede's shell as she eats her way through him at night."

"Lovely world you study," I said.

"Have you ever seen a glowing snail?" Street said, her grin moving from mischievous to maniacal.

"No, and I don't want to."

"They look quite pretty in the woods at night, the shell colors illuminated from inside." She held up the toothpick and its millipede remains. "The cousins of the girl who ate this guy from the inside out are the pink glowworms. They eat snails."

"And I thought a snail's shell was for protection," I said. "Instead they're just lamp shades so we don't get blinded by the glowworms as they eat their dinner."

Street beamed. "You could be an entomologist."

"And if I were, what useful information would I deduce from such arcane knowledge?"

"I don't know." Street looked around. "Maybe just that this pickup truck has recently been down to lower elevations, because the California Phengodids don't live up this high.

"Ah. Be a bummer if I didn't know that."

Street nodded with earnestness.

SIX

Street, Spot, and I went to Street's condo. She got out of the Jeep and walked up to her door like a normal person. I struggled just to stand up straight. Street had her boots off and was already opening a bottle of wine by the time I got inside.

She poured a glass and handed it to me.

"Will a Seghesio Rockpile Zin work for loosening stiff muscles?" she said.

"We can always try," I said, and sipped a delicious jammy wine with such an intense garnet color that it would shame any gemstone. "Tastes great. Full report in the morning."

The sun was getting low in the sky, and the air coming through the screen was cold. While Street did food stuff in the kitchen, I sat on her big chair, feet up on the hassock, and drank my wine. Spot was already asleep in front of the cold fireplace. Some time later, Street came out to say something and woke me up.

"Dinner's ready."

She brought me a bowl of chili with crackers on the side, and set it on the arm of my chair. She set a tall glass of milk on the other arm. It was delicious. The only problem was that I yawned continuously as I ate.

"Maybe you'd better go home to bed," she said.

"Good idea." When I was done eating, I got up to go. I was kissing Street goodbye when my cell rang. I answered.

"Hello, Mr. McKenna? This is Ryan Lear. I'm up at the lake, now. You were going to come by this evening?"

After my big horse-riding debut, I'd forgotten. "Yeah. Of course. Tell me again where I'm going?"

He recited his address for me. South of Cave Rock about a mile, on the lake side of Highway 50. Spot and I were there ten minutes later.

I left Spot in the Jeep, sound asleep in back. I got out, feeling as stiff-legged as Belle had demonstrated early that morning. After my all-day ride on Paint, I tried to walk normally, but I couldn't manage it.

Judging by the sizable lakeshore house, Ryan looked to be a typical bankbook baby living at mom and dad's spread. The place was a large, semi-modern house on the water. It would have seemed quite out-sized but for comparison with a real mansion on the next lot to the north.

To the south of Ryan's house, close enough to easily see in Ryan's windows, was a log cabin. On the front porch of the cabin was a seat made from an old chairlift. On the seat sat an old man wearing a winter jacket to ward off the chill of the high altitude evening.

I waved and said, "How are you?"

He waved, but he didn't say anything.

To the lake side of the cabin was a construction site. Long trenches for foundation, bundles of rebar, piles of crushed rock. All around the perimeter of the construction was the mandated, temporary, Day-Glo orange fencing and rolled straw mats to absorb and prevent construction runoff.

I walked past a kid-sized red bicycle leaning against a Lexus SUV, and headed for the front door. A little Douglas squirrel with a silver dollar-sized shock of white hair on its back sat on the mat by the door casually making a big mess out of a Jeffrey pine cone. He screamed at me, waited until I got close, then finally ran away carrying the large cone in his teeth, as I went up the broad front steps and pressed the doorbell. I heard the deadbolt being turned a few seconds later. The big oak door opened until it was restrained by a chain at eye level and another at knee level.

"Hello?" The young man was striking, with heavy arched eyebrows on a strong brow, projecting cheekbones, broad white teeth. But he came across like a skinny high-school kid who was afraid to look you in the eye. Even his baritone voice cracked with nerves.

"I'm Owen McKenna."

"Hold on a sec."

He shut the door, unhooked the chains and reopened the door. In full view, he looked more like he was in his mid-twenties, but with the ashen quality of someone who plays video games 18 hours a day and never sees the sun. He didn't look at me, but instead stared past me to the left and then to the right, peering out to the road and the forest. His eyes seemed to flit back and forth in a head that nearly vibrated with nervousness. He reminded me of a twitchy chipmunk, constantly quivering, ready to bolt in an instant should a raptor swoop down out of the sky.

"Come in," he said.

As soon as I was through the door he shut it, turned the lock and latched both of the chains.

He turned and reached out to shake my hand. His hand was soft and moist and clammy.

"You can sit if you like." He pointed to the big great room ahead of me. "But first I should give you this." He handed me a couple of photos of what I remembered would be his friends Eli Nathan and Jeanie Samples. He also handed me a hairbrush with lots of hair still in it.

"I hope that will work for scenting search dogs."

"Perfect," I said. I held it up to catch the light, and knew that a search would not be necessary. The hair was bright red.

SEVEN

Ryan waved his hand as if to push me toward the great room to sit down.

The great room projected out of the lake-side of the house, and it had windows on three sides. It was bigger than my log cabin and had an excess of furniture. I sat down on a leather chair and set the photos and hairbrush on an end table.

"Unless you don't want to sit," Ryan said, too late. "That's okay. Whatever you want. Sorry, I don't know much about real world stuff like being a host."

"What world do you know?"

"Besides the world of computer games, I'm a biologist by training. A medical futurist by vocation. Some would call me a bio-geek. But before I tell you about what I think is happening to me, I need to explain something. Full disclosure and all that."

His eyes darted around the room, stopped for an intense moment on me, took flight again. He rubbed his hands over each other repeatedly, as if washing them.

"You can sit, too, Ryan. Relax, and we'll talk."

"Oh. Right." He sat in a facing chair, put one foot up over the other knee, held onto his lower leg with both hands, then put the foot back down on the floor. He radiated discomfort.

"Anyway," he said, "I've been under a lot of personal stress. And for a long time I've had a little problem with obsessive compulsive behavior and paranoia."

I didn't expect that comment.

"We all have moments of thinking things are stacked against us," I said.

He nodded with vigor. "In my case, it would be, um, more than what most people experience."

"Maybe explain that?"

"The doctors usually refer to it as suffering from paranoid delusions. Like I'm crazy."

"Are you crazy?" I asked.

"I don't think so. I'm out at the end of the bell curve, I admit. My thoughts have been paranoid in the past. But it's probably been three years since it was a problem."

I nodded, unsure of how to respond to that. I decided to be straight. "Isn't that what a paranoid person would say? 'Not this time? This time my thoughts are real'?"

"Yeah. Unfortunately, that's exactly what a paranoid person would say."

"So what makes you think this time is different?"

"The things that have happened." By this time, he'd crossed and uncrossed his ankles three or four times.

"Which are," I said.

"A note I got. Eli Nathan's death at Cave Rock. Jeanie Sample's disappearance, and when I was up for Eli's funeral, a vision I had of a wild Mustang in the forest."

"What do you mean, a vision of a wild Mustang?"

"Just that. A vision. I'd just come up to the lake, and I went for a walk down my street to get some fresh air. The sun was hot and I felt a little dizzy. I hadn't eaten since I left the Bay Area. I stopped in the shade of the woods. I sensed movement in the forest. In the far distance, between the tree trunks came the shape of a horse's head. It had a blaze in the shape of an inverted triangle. It was in a spot of sunlight. Then it vanished."

"What made you think this horse was a wild Mustang and not just an ordinary horse?"

"I know horses a bit. This guy seemed wild."

"Other people have seen the Mustang," I said.

Ryan stared at me. "So I'm not the only one. At any rate, the horse was a bad sign for me. Wild Mustangs don't live in Tahoe. He probably came from two mountain ranges east of here. So it is an upset of nature. It suggests something deeper and more important is amiss."

Ryan was agitated, doing the hand-washing movement, blinking his eyes.

"What exactly do you think these various events mean?"

"I think they are all connected to this." He walked over to a built-in bookcase and reached some papers off of the highest shelf. He handed them to me.

It was several layers of newspaper. I unfolded it to see the San Francisco Chronicle Obituary page. Stapled to it was a half-sheet of copy paper with computer printing on it. All caps. Times Roman.

"YOU'LL BE ON THIS PAGE SOON"

"Where did this come from?" I asked.

"My Sunday paper in the paper box at my house in Palo Alto."

"Have you had any other specific threats?"

"No," Ryan said.

"Why tell me about your delusions?"

"Because I did some research on you. I made some calls and got directed to a Sergeant O'Hara in Palo Alto. I guess he used to work with you in San Francisco. He told me that you are very thorough. So I realized that when you looked into my situation, you would discover my history of psychiatric problems. Then you would naturally think that this was just another case of delusions. But in telling you up front, I thought that would make me seem more forthright and believable."

"Or," I said, "it could be a sophisticated way of getting me to believe your delusions. But regardless of whether I thought they were legitimate, wouldn't you assume I'd look into your concerns anyway, just to collect my fee?"

Ryan shook his head. "No. Because O'Hara told me that you are principled."

"He said that? Principled?"

"Yes. But he did put a kind of unpleasant inflection on the word. So I got the message that you wouldn't pursue something if you thought it was frivolous even if it meant a lot of money. That was what made me think I should call you."

"If I knew about your past delusions, I might be better at believing your current thoughts."

Ryan thought about it, his eyes flinching as if bats were flying around his head, and he was trying not to move.

"It started around puberty, in middle school. I was a skinny weakling then, just like I am now. There were one or two kids that were out to get me. They hit me, threw things at me. Later, there were more kids that picked on me. I stopped going to school because of my fears that I would be beaten up. My father made me see the school psychologist. She told me that my persecution was simple bullying. She explained that bullying was bad, but that it wasn't anything more than that.

"Later, in college, it got worse. Not only were the other kids out to get me, but first one professor and then another went after me. I went to a shrink who explained that I was having paranoid delusions. He put me on medication. I was inconsistent in taking my pills, and it got worse. I began to think that the shrink was out to get me, too, so I went to another shrink. She concurred with the first. It was then that I believed that they were conspiring together. After a few months it got so bad that I couldn't function. I never left my dorm room, and I pretty much stopped eating.

"My roommate was Eli Nathan. He saved me by tricking me into going out for a cup of coffee. He took me to a café where he'd assembled a group of people who knew me, along with two doctors I'd never met. They did a kind of intervention, eventually getting me to agree to sign myself into a hospital. After a lot of drugs and therapy, they got me stabilized. I've been in therapy and on medication ever since. I'm also on an exercise program. I started walking on a treadmill. I have one here and in the Bay Area. I believe that walking has helped more than the drugs."

"Are these current thoughts you're having similar to what you used to have?"

"That someone is out to get me? Yes. Very similar. The difference is that this time there is physical evidence. The first and main incident was the death of Eli. I believe it was a murder staged to look like an accident. Eli was my best, and longest friend."

I wasn't sure what to say. Ryan had lost not just one friend, but probably two friends in a short period of time. He would be dealing with a great deal of stress and pain and misery. But for him to think his friends' deaths were the result of someone tormenting him was extreme.

"Look, Ryan," I said, talking slowly, carefully. "When

someone dies by accident, and another person believes it was a murder connected to them, that's getting way off the charts into the land of delusions. I think you need to talk to a doctor, not an investigator."

"But what if it's true?" Ryan's voice had risen to a near-shout.

I wanted to to change the subject for a few moments. I stood and looked out at the lake in the approaching twilight. A shiny wooden boat in a hoist at the large dock reflected the sunset afterglow over the mountains to the west of the lake.

"Good looking watercraft," I said. "What is it? A Gar Wood? Chris-Craft?"

"It's a Riva. It came with the house. But I've never used it."

I couldn't believe he'd never taken it out.

"What is the circular stone arrangement near the shore?"

"A custom fire pit."

"Looks like a great spot to have a campfire and watch the setting sun across the lake."

"I haven't tried it. Actually, I've never had a campfire."

"What do you mean?" I asked.

"Just that. I've never done it."

"You've never sat around a campfire? Roasted hotdogs? S'mores?"

He shook his head. "Anyway, fires are dangerous. Unless you live in a rainforest or something, you could burn something down."

"From here it looks like the fire pit is surrounded by a large stone sitting area, and there is nothing combustible to speak of within forty or fifty feet. Even that closest Jeffrey pine is a good distance away, and its lowest branches are probably sixty feet off the ground. We've even had rain this summer. Just last week. They've never announced a burning ban."

"There's a lot of things I haven't done," Ryan said, his voice small and sad.

A sound came from another room. A young girl in the age range of someone just starting school came running in carrying an open notebook computer.

"Ryan! Ryan, look!" She saw me and stopped. She had eyes like in a Disney animated feature, large and round and so dark that you couldn't see her pupils. Her hair was black as obsidian, long and coarse and shiny like a horse's tail.

"Lily, this is Mr. McKenna."

"Hi, Lily," I said. "You can call me Owen. I'm glad to meet you."

"Hello, Owen. And the pleasure is all mine." Her eyes sparkled. She shifted the computer under her left arm, and we shook, her tiny hand lost in mine.

"Where did you hear that phrase?" Ryan said to her, "'The pleasure is all mine'?" He was visibly more relaxed now that Lily was in the room.

"That old movie you watched last night. Remember when Cary Grant met the woman pilot? She said that."

"You have a good memory," I said.

Lily nodded. "Yes, I do. And I have lots of good ideas, too."

"I bet you do," I said, already hoping she'd run for president some day. "What's on your computer?"

"A game. I won. I got awarded the Silver Venus insignia and bonus points for my next game!" She showed the computer to me, then turned it toward Ryan.

"That's great, Lily. Maybe you should play another game while Owen and I talk."

"This time I'll win the Gold!" As she turned, her eyes flashed up toward the windows, looked for a second, then looked away.

I turned to look at what she'd seen. The orange glow was now a sliver beneath the midnight blue of the sky above. Maybe she looked because of the pretty colors.

She left.

"Your daughter is a smart kid. How old is she?"

"Thank you. Lily is actually my sister. She's six." Ryan made a small smile, the first since I'd arrived.

Ryan's personality had undergone a transformation. He'd stopped flinching for the moment, and he was much calmer. If I ended up working for him, I would want to have Lily around as much as possible.

"Ryan!" came Lily's shout from around the corner.

"What?"

"Look out the window. There's a big animal."

"Sammy the squirrel?"

"No," Lily said. "Sammy's by the door. This is in a car. By the post light."

"That's my dog," I said.

Lily came running into the room. "Can I go see him?"

"No," Ryan said. "You shouldn't approach strange dogs."

"In this case, she should," I said. "If I'm going to work for you, then you both need to meet Spot."

Without waiting for Ryan's approval, I walked out the front door and got Spot out of the Jeep.

They were both standing just inside the front door as we approached, Ryan in front of Lily, air-washing his hands as if to rub the skin off. As we came close, Ryan looked alarmed. He picked up Lily and stepped back.

"This is Spot." Spot looked at them and wagged.

Ryan's eyes twitched with fear. Lily strained to get out of his arms.

"Come in, Spot." I took his collar and walked him through the doorway. I didn't want him approaching Ryan or Lily. The fear in the air was too intense. They could approach him when ready.

"Spot, sit."

He sat. His tale swept the floor. I shut the door, locked the deadbolt, and hooked the chains to make Ryan feel comfortable.

"Spot, please meet Ryan and Lily." She waved at him.

I said to her, "Do you know what he's thinking?"

She shook her head.

"He's thinking that the pleasure is all his."

Lily grinned. "He has an earring."

"Yeah. Spot, come here." I kept hold of his collar so he wouldn't greet them with too much enthusiasm. I walked him over to the great room. He turned to look behind at Ryan and Lily as we went past. I had him lie down on the rug in front of the fireplace.

"Lily, come over and meet Spot. He wants you to pet him."

Ryan put her down. She ran to us and put her hand out to pet Spot.

If children haven't been repeatedly cautioned about dogs, they have no natural fear. Just as dogs have evolved to direct their primary attachments to humans, humans have evolved similar hard-wiring and feel a natural desire to approach and pet and hold and talk to dogs. Lily couldn't have weighed more than thirty or forty pounds, a fifth of Spot's 170, yet she walked up to him with no hesitation.

Lying down, his head was almost shoulder height on Lily as she stood before him. She put her tiny hand between his big ears and stroked him as gently as if he were a new-born kitten. Over and over she stroked. Spot shut his eyes under the delicious touch of the little girl.

She fingered his rhinestone ear stud. "How come he has an earring?"

"An accident made a little hole in his ear. So my girlfriend got him the stud to fill the hole."

Lily kneeled in front of him. She reached her arms up and hugged his neck, his giant head over her diminutive shoulder.

Ryan came over, sat on a nearby chair. He watched Lily and Spot and seemed to relax.

"Are you from the Bay Area?" I asked.

"No. Just down the hill on the Nevada side. In Gardnerville."

"How did you come here? Move in with your parents?"

"No. My mother ran away when I was three. I don't remember her. My dad died two years ago. Lily was the result of a second marriage. Shortly after Lily was born, her mother divorced my dad and moved to Mexico with a truck driver. Dad didn't have much luck with women. He began his career as a teacher, then became a principal. He lived in Reno the last part of his life until he died. This is my house."

"You're what, mid-twenties?"

"I'm twenty-six."

"Twenty-six is young. Forgive my prying, but how does someone your age come to have this place? A house of this size, on the lake, would be several millions. What do you do for CalBioTechnica? Or did you inherit?"

"It's my company. I'm founder and Chairman."

EIGHT

"So you bought this house," I said.

"This is the age of technology," Ryan said. "Like many young people who are educated techies, I have money. More than I could ever spend."

"How did you start the company?" I asked, thinking that he couldn't be too delusional and still put together something as demanding and complex as a large bio-tech company like CalBioTechnica.

"I invented a new approach for doing recombinant DNA projects. Easier, cheaper, faster. My friends Jeanie Samples and Elijah Nathan believed I could start a company based on my concepts. But I had no idea of how to begin. Their enthusiasm was so strong, they convinced me to pursue it. They believed that the three of us had most of what we needed to make it work."

"They're friends in addition to being business partners."

"Right. We met in college, and we've been best friends and business confidants ever since."

"Where did you go to college?"

"Stanford. We all stayed on at Stanford to pursue graduate school as well. Both Jeanie and Eli got their Ph.D.s, hers in math, his in physics. I stopped at a masters in biology.

"Early on, there was actually a fourth in our group, William Hughes, who was a wizard video game programmer from the time he was very young. When we started CBT, he did some critical computer modeling that helped me with my original DNA research. We asked him to be part of our company, but he declined. He's probably smarter than the rest of us, but he wasn't good at follow-through on anything except video games. He dropped out of Stanford in his third year. He actually ended up starting his own company, and he's been very successful. He's a classic basement gamer, maybe a little autistic, a loner who relates more to binary code than to people. So he declined our invitation.

"We ended up a troika of geeks, socially maladroit kids who had difficult childhoods. None of us fit in. Even as we found success, we still felt like we were unfit for society. The kids who did well in our high schools went on to become doctors and lawyers, and some ran for political office, and some went into entertainment. Meanwhile, we pursued our geek focus and got quite rich. It's a weird position to be in. So incompetent at mixing with people and yet owning a portion of the future of American industry and the wealth that comes with it."

Ryan was much more relaxed as he talked about subjects that were distant from his current stress and worries. "Our coping mechanism was to celebrate our weirdness. We had an ongoing joke about not having time to be second rate, that the real losers are the bullies who kicked sand in our faces when we were young. That came from a line in the Queen song, We Are The Champions. Eli had these micro portable speakers he plugged into his iPod. At the end of our weekly café meetings, we three would walk down the sidewalk, arm-in-arm, singing along with Freddie Mercury. We Are The Champions.

"We discovered in college that there are lots of kids like us. Stanford is full of people who can invent the new world but don't know how to play sports or ask a girl or a boy out on a date. And the school nurtures our community."

"The San Francisco Chronicle ran an article on that," I said. "About the crucible of the top schools, a technology culture, and venture capital that gives birth to technology companies."

"Yeah. I remember what one of my professors said. That the Bay Area economy kicks out more dollars per capita than anywhere in the world. And a huge portion of Bay Area business is high-tech. You've heard all the names. What people sometimes forget is that those name-brand companies and the thousands of others coming up are mostly started by, owned by, and run by young techies like me. It's like there's a new geek dynasty."

A loud phone rang, and Ryan leaped as if he'd stepped on a tarantula. He put his hand to his chest as if to calm himself, then walked over and looked at the readout.

"Private!" He made a stifled cry that was half fear and half anger.

"What does that mean?" I asked. The phone was still ringing.

Ryan shook with tension. "Nearly every time it says private number, it's like a creep show. I don't answer it any more."

I reached for the phone. Ryan handed it to me.

"Lear residence," I said.

First there was silence. Then came the slow, creepy creaking of a rusty hinge. It reverberated like the sound of the basement door opening in a horror movie. Then came a woman's scream. Even from a distance, Ryan heard it, and he recoiled.

I hung up the phone.

"You've had those calls before," I said.

"Many times."

"You have no idea who is making them?"

He shook his head. He looked sad and scared, like he was about to cry.

"Is the call different each time?" I asked.

"Yes. Sometimes it's like a ghost laughing. Sometimes it's a woman crying out, 'Help me, help me.' Sometimes it's a man screaming, 'No, not the knife! Don't use the knife!' Then he screams as if he's being killed. You hear the gurgling of blood in his lungs. It's horrible."

"Someone is using a sound-effects recording to scare you."

"More than scare me. They're trying to take me apart, make me come unglued. And I'm afraid they are succeeding."

"Do they call you at your Bay Area house?"

"Yes. Only my cell phone is safe. But now, when I get a private call on my cell, I start shaking and sweating. When I answer, I'm so upset that I can barely talk."

"Who could benefit from you coming unglued?"

"I don't know. I've tried to think, but it makes no sense! It's like the person simply wants to torture me."

"Why don't you get yourself something to drink, calm you down."

He nodded, a dazed look on his face. Like someone in shock. He went toward the kitchen, then turned back.

"Do you want something?"

"Whatever you're having."

He left, then came back with two glasses of water.

"Tell me about your partners," I said.

He took a deep breath, shut his eyes, eventually spoke.

"Of the geek troika, Elijah Nathan was the business genius. He was the one who came up with the concept of how we could build a company around my DNA manipulation techniques. He learned how to start a corporation and helped orchestrate the process. It was his idea that we would each own twenty percent of the company. Together, we'd always have a controlling interest of sixty percent, and we could sell forty percent to outside investors in order to get funding for growth. Our pact was that, as a group, we'd never give up control of the company. Eli thought that because the company was based on my ideas, I should be chairman. He and Jeanie would each be vice presidents, she of finance, he of sales and marketing. I'd also be temporary President, but our plan was to bring in an experienced grayhair to be President and CEO. And we'd each sit on the Board of Directors. We'd all have equal compensation packages regardless of how successful we became." As Ryan talked, he relaxed a little.

"All for one, and one for all," I said.

Ryan nodded. "Right. The Three Musketeers. As long as our Geek Troika stayed unified, no one could take away our company. We'd always have a majority."

"Not to segue too far," I said. "But don't venture capitalists often demand fifty-one percent in return for investing?"

"Often, yes. But we figured that once it was obvious that our company had huge potential, we wouldn't have any problem getting someone to come in for forty percent. In fact, we even discussed the psychology of how an outside investor would be the single largest shareholder, and they would be reassured by the concept that if they had a really good idea, they would only have to sway one of us over to their side to have a majority voting block. Of course, in our minds that could never happen. So we felt that we could entice investors with no worry for us."

"And did someone come in for forty percent?"

"Eventually, yeah. In our second year, Eli sold a ten million dollar production contract to one of the biggest pharmaceutical companies. A few months later, he got two big development contracts with other giants. Once we had that revenue flowing, we got Bob Mendoza to come onboard as President and CEO and steer the ship.

"Then Business Week did a story on us. And Forbes ran a big feature. The Chronicle did a human interest piece on our new biologicals and how they were already saving lives. With all that attention, we ended up having a little auction of sorts among three investors. We knew the guy who won. You've probably heard of him. Preston Laurence. He put up forty-five million for forty percent of CBT.

"Anyway, Eli was our master of the universe. He pretty much excelled at everything."

"What does Jeanie Samples do?"

"Jeanie is our financial guru and our visionary. When I first got the idea for using my new DNA technique to make a different kind of biological cancer drug, she was the one who saw how unique and potent it was. She also created a new kind of mathematical model that we could use to predict our future business and pharmacology environment. She says it's like the complex equations they use for meteorology, only it's for forecasting conditions in our business arena instead of forecasting the weather."

"Your expertise is biology," I said. "What else do you bring to this Geek Troika?"

Ryan looked uncomfortable. "I'm not sure how to say this. Aside from the core of our business, our DNA work, what I brought to the group was a kind of sensitivity. In the world of technology - like any world, I suppose - people can be bulls. Especially Stanford, Harvard, MIT, and Caltech alums. These highly educated techies often have an unshakable confidence in their intelligence. They believe that they're better than anyone else in the world when it comes to their particular specialty. As a result, they sort of charge ahead without any sense of consequence. Even though they might be meek in social situations, they can be almost tyrants in their geek world. Both Eli and Jeanie needed someone to be a human interface.

"Of course, you're thinking that no way could I be a stand-in for how regular humans function. That's true, and I know it better than anyone. But I have always been good for Eli and Jeanie by visualizing how other people would see our products. I'm like an editor, cleaning up Eli and Jeanie's concepts before they submit them to their target audience."

"Is CalBioTechnica growing?"

"Yeah. Pretty fast. We've had a few offers to buy the company outright, which would have put a much bigger sum into our bank accounts, but we've never wanted to sell. It's too exciting to be at the leading edge of medical research. And anyway, it's not like I would know what to do with more money. I have an accountant who spends a lot of time figuring out how I should be structuring my compensation. Much of it is deferred of course, and much of the rest gets invested. But I still have a lot of regular income to dispose of. That's part of why I bought this place along with the next property to the south. A house and an old lakeshore cabin. I'm incorporating the cabin into the new building, a Washoe Spirit Lodge for my people."

"You are Washoe?"

"Half, yes. My father was Washoe. My mother was a white woman named Mary Thomas. Lily's mom, my dad's second wife, was Brenda. Now there's an interesting mix, because Brenda is mostly Maidu Indian. You probably know that for all the thousands of years that the Washoe were in Tahoe, the Maidu lived in the foothills, and they didn't get along well with the Washoe. Well guess what? Brenda and my dad didn't get along, either."

Ryan looked over at Lily. She was sitting next to Spot, slumped against him, one arm draped over his back, her head leaning against his shoulder, apparently asleep.

Ryan lowered his voice. "Brenda was much younger and had a taste for men closer to my age than my dad's age. I don't even know what she saw in him other than a decent income. So not long after Lily was born, Brenda and dad got a divorce."

"What's your spirit lodge going to be about?"

"Whites invented land ownership, and they decided that they owned Tahoe even though it was Washoe country for ten thousand years. The only property the Washoe have left in Tahoe is the Meeks Bay Resort. Maybe I'm wrong - I hope I'm wrong -

but to my knowledge, I'm the only person of Washoe descent who owns a house on the lake. Our lake."

Ryan paused. "I know a spirit lodge sounds like it's about the Washoe shamans, like what I'm building is directed by the tribal elders and such. But the reality is that I'm not very tight with the elders. My dad moved me away to Reno when I was young. In fact, the elders might not like what I'm doing. But my goal is to build a lodge where other Washoe can come and be at the lake. No obligations. No questions. Just a chance to come back and experience a tiny bit of what their ancestors had. My ultimate goal would be to get some kind of tax exempt status in place, like for a church, and then deed the property to the Washoe Tribe."

"Did Eli know that you are half Washoe?"

"Yes."

"Did he know that it is now illegal to climb at Cave Rock?"

"Yes, I'm sure he did. All climbers know it. The ban has been well publicized. What he did was terrible, separate from getting himself killed. He knew that it's a sacred site. He knew that I would disapprove. Climbing there is a desecration. Like going into a church and climbing the altar."

"Then why did he do it?"

"I can only guess that it's because he didn't respect others. He was bullheaded and self-centered. He didn't care what other people thought. If he went into a great cathedral, he'd probably climb the flying buttresses if he could get away with it."

I nodded. "Your dad raised you alone?"

"I was raised by my dad and neighbor ladies and people from the Unitarian church and teachers and anyone else who thought that I needed and deserved help."

"And now you're raising Lily," I said.

"Yes." Ryan glanced at Lily. "When her mother Brenda moved to Mexico, I became Lily's legal guardian. A year ago, after word of CBT's success started making the papers, Brenda wanted back into our life. She started sending me postcards. Not to Lily, but to me. That's when you know that Lily is really loved. When the mother who abandoned her doesn't contact her, but reconnects with me in an attempt to get money.

"Of course, I'm in the Bay Area a fair amount, so Lily has

Hannah Serrano, a nanny who stays here at the house when she's working. Hannah takes care of Lily and does the domestic stuff whenever I'm gone. But I'm here quite a bit. Being chairman has some advantages. I do what works for me and Lily."

It was now dark outside. There were no drapes on the big windows that faced the lake. I wondered about privacy in a house where a little girl lived.

"Do you have a nice home in the Bay Area?"

"Sure. Why do you ask?"

"Why not just live in the Bay Area, and come up here on vacation?"

Ryan hesitated. "I like Tahoe."

"C'mon, Ryan, tell me the truth."

He looked away, flicked his eyes around the room, then looked back to me. "We have some business in Tahoe."

"What kind?"

"It doesn't matter."

"Ryan, whatever you're trying to hide from me could be the crux of what is going on."

"I don't think that could be true."

I stood up. "I can't work for you without your cooperation."

"Wait. Don't leave. I'll tell you. But I need your word that you won't mention what I say to anyone."

"I won't unless I have to."

"No, that's not good enough."

"Ryan, you can trust me to respect your privacy, but I won't keep a secret if it puts someone in danger, or if I have to break the law, unless it is appropriate to the situation. In general, you can know that I won't tell anyone. But I won't agree to a blanket condition that eliminates my discretion."

"Okay. We do some bio-tech research here."

"In Tahoe," I said. It took me a second to place the idea of bio-tech research in an area that is focused on outdoor recreation.

"Yes," Ryan nodded. "It may actually become the centerpiece of our future plans for CalBioTechnica. We envision a new class of biologicals that we expect to develop in the future. We think they will transform part of medicine. So we acquired a building and built a research facility just out of Incline Village. Four scientists work up there, and I do some work at that lab as well."

"What could Tahoe possibly have that the Bay Area doesn't?"

"Altitude."

"What does altitude have to do with bio-research?" I asked.

"It's a bit hard to explain. We're studying hypoxic stress and related genetic adaptations."

"Which, in lay-speak, means?"

Another pause. "You've heard of recombinant DNA?"

"Sure. That's when you take our genetic code and rearrange things to punch it up, right?" I said.

If I'd told Mozart that he took simple songs and made them sound fancy by using different instruments, I would have gotten the same withering look that Ryan gave me.

"I wrote a White Paper on our process. It was part of our information packet for potential investors. I'll get it for you."

He walked out of the room and was gone for a minute. He came back and said, "I must have left my briefcase in my car. I'll be right back."

Ryan went out, leaving the front door ajar. Several seconds later I heard a grunt like when someone is punched in the solar plexus, followed by a couple of thuds like car doors shutting. An engine revved, tires screeched.

I ran outside into the dark. His Lexus was still there.

"Ryan!" I shouted. "Ryan!"

No response.

In the distance through the trees was the flicker of red taillights. Then nothing.

NINE

I shouted Ryan's name again. No answer. I ran back into the house. Dialed Diamond as I sprinted inside. The phone rang on the other end of the line.

"Lily," I said. "Come with me. We need to go find Ryan."

She was still sleeping against Spot. She looked up, alarmed.

"Where is Ryan?" she asked, her eyes pinched with fright and worry. She'd met me, but she didn't know me. I was a stranger in her house.

"He went outside," I said to Lily, my heart thumping, struggling for a way to present a kidnapping. "Somebody took him for a ride. We should go look. Let's hurry. Spot will come with us."

Diamond answered.

I turned away from Lily, took fast steps out the front door. "Ryan Lear was just kidnapped out of his driveway," I said in a low voice. "I didn't see the vehicle. I saw taillights through the trees. The spacing seemed like a large vehicle. I couldn't see anything else."

"Nothing to go on," Diamond said.

"No. I'm going to take Lily and head out to the highway. I'll be in touch."

I hung up, went back inside.

"Ready, Lily?"

She was standing near Spot, her hand reaching up to his collar as if it were a life ring. I reached for her hand. Picked her up and held her at my side.

"Where did Ryan go?" she said, her voice high and tiny and scared.

"I don't know."

She didn't fight me, but she was rigid with fear.

"Spot, come."

I headed out the door. I didn't have a key, so I left it unlocked.

I put Spot in the back seat of the Jeep, and pushed him over to the side. He would give Lily more comfort than I could, so I put Lily in next to him, and buckled her belt. I got in the driver's side and drove off.

Up at the highway, there was no traffic. I saw a tiny, distant flash of red taillight far to the south. I turned right, accelerated hard. I caught up to the taillights a mile south. It was a Ford Expedition, all three seats stuffed with people. Summer tourists. Probably heading to the late show at the casino showroom. I went past them, drove into town, turned around and headed back north.

"Where did Ryan go?" Lily asked, tremolo in her voice.

"I don't know. But you watch out your window. I'll watch out mine. Maybe we'll see him."

I drove back north, past the turnoff to Ryan's, pulled over by Cave Rock. I called Street.

"Hello?"

I tried to sound calm for Lily's benefit. "It's me. I'm with Lily and Spot in my Jeep. Someone took Ryan."

"I don't understand."

"Lily and I were inside. He went outside. Someone took him for a ride."

"He was kidnapped?!"

"Yeah. I could use some help."

"Does Lily understand?"

"Somewhat. How about we pick you up, and you come over."

"Yes. Of course."

I drove north through the Cave Rock tunnel, and pulled into Street's condo a few minutes later. She came running out, got in the front seat.

She turned around, reached over to touch Lily behind her.

"Hi Lily. My name is Street. I'm so sorry that Ryan went away suddenly."

"Where did he go?" Lily's voice quaked.

"We don't know, yet. We're going to find him."

I pulled out onto the highway.

"You think we should go back to Ryan and Lily's house?" Street asked.

"Yeah. Familiar territory for Lily."

Street nodded. She turned back to Lily, while I called Diamond and explained where we were.

"Smithy and I are at Ryan's," he said. "The house is empty. No sign of trouble."

"Do you have your light bar off?"

"Yeah. Smithy knows that there is a child involved, and we want to minimize the trauma. Another patrol unit is on the way. I'll radio them, too."

"Thanks."

We were back in Ryan's drive in five minutes.

Diamond stood at Ryan's door. Smithy was in their patrol unit. I told Street and Lily that I'd be right back. I let Spot out of the Jeep, and we went up to the house.

"What do you think?" Diamond said.

"No idea. If it's a ransom demand, we'll know soon. If it's a murder, it could be weeks before we find something."

"Like the body up on the Rim Trail," Diamond said.

"You check the house?" I asked.

"Found the door unlocked. Looked inside, briefly."

"I'll have Spot check." I turned to him. "Spot, I want you to find the suspect!" I grabbed his chest, pointed him inside the house, and vibrated him to get him primed. "Do you understand, Spot? Find the suspect!" I smacked him on his rear, and he ran into the house."

"Lot's of human scents in there," Diamond said. "You think he can sort out which are remnants and which, if any, are current occupants."

I nodded. I went inside. I heard Spot moving upstairs. He came down. There was no excitement in him. I pointed him toward the stairs that led to the lower level.

"Find the suspect!" I said.

All he did was sniff the air, then turn back to me, a clear sign that no one else was in the house.

I went back out and escorted Lily and Street inside. Street took

Lily into her bedroom. Spot went with them.

I went back outside.

A second patrol unit had arrived.

"Leave a deputy here overnight?" I said.

"That's what I thought," Diamond said. "You have a plan?"

I shook my head.

It was a long night. Street finally got Lily to sleep by lying next to her on her bed and reading stories to her.

I wandered the house, napped on one of the couches, paced in the dark, made a pot of coffee and brought a cup out to Smithy in his Douglas County SUV. We spoke a bit, then I went back inside.

In the morning, Street tried to be upbeat for Lily, whose curiosity and cheerful demeanor had been replaced by a somber depression.

She asked, "Where's Ryan?" and, "Is he okay?" and "When will he be back?"

Street and I both struggled with answers.

Street made breakfast for Lily. I found Ryan's home answering machine. No blinking light. His other phone numbers would have voicemail boxes, but I couldn't access them.

I left Street and Lily with Spot, told Street I was going to my office. I stopped and talked to Smithy in the SUV out front. He said it was a quiet night, said he would stay there while I was gone.

It was a beautiful summer day, calm and aromatic of pine trees, an idyll that was a complete disconnect from the trauma of kidnapping.

There were no messages on my office machine.

I got Diamond on the phone.

"Anything?" he said.

"No. You?"

"Just talked to Smithy," he said. "We're juggling. Praeger will replace him in an hour and stay at the Lear house for today, at least. Not that it will matter. Best keep the girl inside with Spot and Street when you're not there."

"Yeah."

I hung up, and called Street. Nothing had changed.

I walked out of my office, self-critique making it hard to breathe. There was a nearby path that led to the woods, a path where I knew there was cell coverage. Maybe I could think in the trees.

Ryan Lear knew that his situation was bad enough to call me. When you want to accurately assess any situation, you get a professional who works the territory, a person whose job it is to read the indicators and gauge the threat.

And I let Ryan walk out into the dark alone.

I began to run, going hard up the trail, pushing my heart and lungs, pushing my psyche. You run hard enough, it goes from exercise to punishment.

When I was drenched in sweat, I turned around and headed back to the Jeep. I was getting into the driver's seat when I thought I should check the office machine once again.

There was a note on the floor just inside my office door. I picked it up with a piece of tissue even though I assumed it would contain no prints.

It was printed on a piece of copy paper. The font looked like Times Roman. Same as the note stapled to the obits page.

> "You're falling down on the job, McKenna. Ryan Lear
> got a taste of his future last night. But we don't want
> him to die just yet. If you hurry, he may still be alive.
> Look for him at the top of Ski Run."

I ran to my Jeep. Ski Run is on the California side, out of Diamond's jurisdiction, so I called Mallory of the South Lake Tahoe PD as I drove.

"Yeah," he answered.

"Commander," I said. "McKenna calling."

"Heard from Diamond that you've got a kidnapping."

"Why I'm calling. Just found a note at my office. Ryan Lear, the kidnap victim, is at the top of Ski Run. I'm heading there now."

"See you there." Mallory hung up.

The town was full of tourists. Stop and go traffic. Long waits at stoplights.

Just after Heavenly Village, I cut off on Pioneer Trail. The traffic was still heavy. I turned left at Ski Run, went up the long hill as far as the road goes, parked and got out.

I saw trees, rocks, the lake view. No person.

"Ryan?" I yelled. No response. "Ryan!"

If I went higher, I could see more. I ran up the steep slope, my legs still burning from my earlier run.

"Ryan!"

I went around an outcropping, looked off to the side.

"Ryan!"

If I climbed up on the outcropping, I'd be able to see farther.

I scrambled up, turned a complete circle, studying the trees, the rocks, the downed logs.

"Ryan!"

Far down on Ski Run came two South Lake Tahoe PD cars, racing up the big hill, lights flashing, sirens off. In the distance behind them was the Fire Department Rescue vehicle.

I kept turning, looking. I had no idea what to expect. Would Ryan be stumbling and hypothermic from all-night exposure? Or would I find a body?

I turned again.

Something moved.

Far up the slope, in the trees. One of the trees had a dark bulge on the trunk, well up from the ground. Green.

I dropped off of the outcropping and sprinted up the mountain.

There was a huge boulder. In front of it, two feet away, was a small pine.

Ryan stood in the tree with his feet perched on two branches that were ten feet off the ground. His back was to the pine. His arms were behind him, wrapped behind the tree trunk. A dark green pillow case had been pulled over his head and tied around his neck.

Someone had made him climb up on the boulder, made him step out to the tree branches, then cuffed his arms so that he leaned forward, out from the tree. If his feet didn't slip, he'd be okay. If they did slip, he'd fall and his arms would be jerked up behind him, tearing out his shoulder joints.

"It's Owen, Ryan. Hang in there. I'll have you down in a few minutes. Don't move. I'm coming up the boulder from behind."

I got myself into position, leaning from the boulder to the tree.

"Almost there," I said.

He'd been up on the tree long enough that his muscle strength had given away, leaving his arms stretched tight behind him. But his feet were still on the branches.

"First, I'm cutting the pillowcase off your head. Concentrate on not moving your feet."

I got my jackknife under what looked like hay-bale twine, cut it away, gently pulled the pillowcase off.

Ryan's head lolled.

With my other arm, I got the knife into position near his wrists, knowing that he would fall forward off the perch as soon as I freed his arms. I could wait for the SLT cops to get up the long slope and catch him. But I didn't know if Ryan could wait that long.

"Okay, Ryan, hold still. I'm going to cut the zip tie on your wrists."

I shifted my shoulder against the tree, reached out around the tree, and grabbed Ryan across his chest.

He shivered violently despite the warming sun.

With one motion, I cut the tie, tossed the knife to the boulder, and grabbed another handful of Ryan's shirt.

Ryan made an agonizing cry of pain as his arms dropped forward.

"We're going to move you to the right. Lift up your right foot. Reach it back."

He made a weak motion with his foot.

"Farther. A little more."

I had all my weight leaning against the tree. I shifted him in my arms, lifting him up and to the right, back toward the boulder.

"You're only three inches away from the rock. Two inches. There, contact. Keep your foot planted while I swing you around the tree and up onto the rock."

I took a breath and swung him, lifting with all of my strength.

Ryan landed on the boulder, made a guttural yell as he

collapsed.

I stepped back onto the boulder, rolled him onto his back.

"My arms," he mumbled, his eyes shut in pain.

I straightened his body and gently pulled his arms into a more natural position, elbows at his sides, hands on his stomach.

"You got your shoulders seriously stressed. Lie still, and the pain will gradually diminish."

Mallory and one of the SLT cops came around the uphill side of the boulder and climbed up onto the rock. The other cop walked to the base of the tree, used a baggie to pick up the zip tie I'd cut from Ryan's wrists. Two paramedics ran up the slope, carrying a gurney. By the time they got close, they'd slowed to a walk, their lungs huffing.

They handed the gurney up to me, and I lay it down next to Ryan.

We got Ryan strapped on, arms immobilized, and lowered him off the big rock. He was in the hospital 15 minutes later.

Doc Lee was on duty. He asked Ryan some questions about the pain, about the position he'd been in. While I explained to Mallory what had happened, a nurse cut Ryan's shirt off so that Doc Lee could examine his shoulders.

Lee decided that Ryan probably had numerous small tears in his ligaments and tendons, but that with time his shoulders would heal without any surgical intervention. He also said that the cuts on Ryan's wrists from the zip tie were bad enough to leave scars, but said that they would eventually heal well. Lee bandaged Ryan's wrists, and put his arms in slings. He gave him some pain medication, and told him to take the slings off and use his arms as the pain diminished.

I took Ryan home.

When we went inside, Lily ran and clung to Ryan, asked him what happened. He said that he'd hurt his arms and had to go to the hospital.

Eventually, Ryan convinced her to let go of him, and he took a three-hour nap. He got up to take a pain pill, and was finally able to talk. Because the kidnapping happened on the Nevada side, I called Diamond to let him know that Ryan was awake. Diamond came to take a statement.

Street thought that it wasn't a good idea for Lily to hear all of the details, so she took Lily and Spot into Lily's bedroom to play a game while Ryan, Diamond, and I sat in the dining room.

"Tell me what happened from the moment you walked out the door," Diamond said.

Ryan shook from the memory. His voice wavered.

"I went to my car, and hit the key fob to open the rear hatch. I never heard anyone approach. Someone pulled the pillowcase over my head. Someone else punched me in the stomach. The blow doubled me over. I couldn't breathe. They pulled my arms behind me and tied my wrists."

"There were two people?"

"Yeah. Well, it seemed like it. But I didn't see anyone. There could have been more, for that matter."

"What did they say?"

"Nothing. That was one of the things that made it so terrifying. No one spoke a word until they put me in the tree."

"What happened after they grabbed you?"

"They shoved me into a vehicle and drove away fast."

"Did you get a sense of what kind of vehicle?"

"No. The seat was high up, like a van. I was lying down in the back seat."

"When they put you in the vehicle, how many doors did you hear open and shut?"

Ryan thought.

"Three, I think. The door on my side after they pushed me in. The door in front of me on the passenger side. Then the driver's door."

"Did they make any stops on their way to Ski Run?"

"No. They just drove, then stopped, then marched me up the mountain."

"When they took you out of the vehicle, did you hear three doors open and shut?"

Ryan pondered. He looked down at his bandaged wrists, then shut his eyes.

"I really don't remember. I could tell we were going up a hill. And when they took me out, it was obvious that we were on a steep slope. I thought they were taking me into the woods to kill me. I kept thinking about Eli and Jeanie." Ryan was shivering.

"You want me to get you a sweater or something?" I asked.

"No. It's just nerves." Even though his arms were in slings, he could still air-wash his hands.

"They say anything when they put you in the tree?" Diamond said.

"Just a few words. They marched me up the mountain, cut the tie off my wrists and said stuff like, 'There's a boulder in front of you. Use your hands to climb up.' Then, 'Move your foot. Put it here. You slip off the branch, you'll die.' When they got me in position, they tied my wrists behind the tree."

"What did their voices sound like?"

"I think only one guy talked, and he had a high voice. But kind of gruff. If he hadn't handled me with such strength, I might have thought it was a woman's voice. Maybe he was trying to talk high. Like a disguise."

"Was there anything that happened that indicated how many guys there were?"

Ryan thought about it, shook his head.

"So it was probably two guys," I said, "but it could have been three. Or even one."

"But multiple car doors..."

"A single person could have done that as disguise. Reached over and pushed you from behind or from the side as a misdirection, too."

"Yeah, I guess so."

Diamond finished making his notes, put his little pad in his pocket.

"What's your guess about this?" I said to Ryan.

Ryan shook his head. "I don't know. If these guys wanted to kill me, they would have done it, right? So they must be trying to terrorize me."

"Can you think of a reason why?"

"No. Maybe it's a kind of blackmail. First, they show me what they're capable of. Then they demand money."

Diamond spoke. "You get a money demand, it'll say don't call the cops. It'll mention some threat against you or Lily. But if you do what they say, you'll just make it worse. You must keep us informed about this. It's our only chance to get these guys. Do you understand?"

Ryan looked at him, then me. "Yeah," he said. "I'll be sure to let you know." He turned back to me. "Thanks for taking care of Lily last night."

"Certainly."

"I don't know what to do now."

"If you're okay with the expense, I can arrange to hire off-duty deputies on rotation here. You and Lily will be safer with a twenty-four-hour guard outside your house."

"Of course," Ryan said.

"Diamond?" I said. "Do you have some guys who can do some moonlighting?"

He nodded. "Yeah, but I don't know about twenty-four seven."

"See what you can pull together. I'll call Mallory for additional help."

I followed Diamond outside, and gave him the hairbrush that Ryan had brought.

"The hair belongs to Jeanie Samples, the missing woman," I said. "Do you want to send it to the lab Douglas County uses?"

"Sure."

"Do you have an envelope?"

Diamond found one in his patrol unit.

I pulled out my wallet, removed the hair I'd pulled off the corpse, put it into the envelope, and handed it to Diamond.

"From the body up on the mountain?"

"Yeah. I didn't know if you'd taken any off the remains."

Diamond shook his head.

"Then this will save you the trouble of getting some from the coroner."

Diamond left, and I went back inside.

"Thanks for getting the police to come here, but I still feel lost," Ryan said. "Can I go? Are Lily and I going to be trapped here in the house?"

"Somewhat," I said. "Another choice for you is your Bay Area house if you feel safer there."

Ryan shook his head. "That's where the message on the obituary page was left. They know everywhere I go. At least up here, I have you helping."

"You could take Lily and go out of town, but that would likely just postpone the process of trying to find out who kidnapped you. My best guess is that we won't figure this out until the person makes another move. If you leave, that might only delay the person's actions. So I think the best thing is for you to stay here and send Lily out of town."

"Where?"

"Do you have a relative far away?"

"No."

"A friend?"

He shook his head. "My only friends are here and in the Bay Area. And with Eli dead and Jeanie missing, the only other possibilities would be too obvious to the kidnapper."

"Then I would keep Lily near to you at all times." I paused, considering what I was getting myself into. "If you like, Spot and I could move in with you for the time being."

Ryan's immediate relief was obvious. "You would? That would be great. I have lots of bedrooms. I would of course pay you whatever you need."

"I'll have to leave from time to time. But I can stay at night. And when I leave during the day, Spot can stay with you. He will be a good guard for Lily."

"Is he a trained guard dog? I mean, obviously, he's huge. But he seems very docile."

"He's always gentle, especially with children. He's not a professional police dog. But he's good protection. Are you familiar with dogs?"

"Not really. I have an acquaintance who has a poodle. It likes me. But I've never had a dog. I couldn't claim to really know dogs."

"Then I can tell you that all dogs understand threatening behavior. They don't have to be trained for that. They have an instinctive desire to protect the people they've come to know. So we'll show Spot your house. We'll let him explore your bedrooms, get familiar with the scents and sounds. He already understands that the two of you are a unit. Because you are my friends, you are his friends. We can feed him in your garage, take him into your kitchen and give him some of your food treats. After that, he'll know that this is another home for him. If he hears something out of place, he'll bark. If the worst should happen, and a stranger tries to come in against your will, Spot will prevent that."

"What does that mean? What if someone comes in a window even if Spot's barking?"

"He'll subdue the person and hold him until I tell him to let go."

"You mean he'll bite?"

"Just enough to put the person on the ground and keep him immobile. If the suspect struggles, Spot will bite harder. If the suspect is passive, Spot will let go, but stay next to him, ready to growl if the suspect moves. If the suspect tries to run, Spot will prevent him from getting away."

Ryan lowered his voice. "What if the person has a gun?"

"What people do is hold out their weapon. Dogs instinctively go for the hand that comes out first. Of course, a determined person with a gun can shoot whatever they want. But if a person breaks in with a gun, I wouldn't give him real good odds. Dogs don't care about guns. So the gun doesn't slow them down or affect their judgment."

Ryan nodded.

"Do you carry a gun?"

"No, I don't."

"You used to be a cop," he said.

"Twenty years. Most of us carry after we quit. But I don't. I don't like having that choice available to me."

Ryan looked somber even as his eyes twitched.

I understood that he needed time to process what had happened.

TEN

That afternoon, while I was on the phone, Lily's nanny Hannah reported for work. I saw her from down the hall as she said a few words to Ryan about his arm slings, appearing to show no concern. She then went downstairs to do laundry while Ryan took another nap. Street stayed near Lily, and Lily stayed virtually attached to Spot, her hand around his neck or in his collar. He appeared intoxicated by the attention.

Come evening, I heard Ryan up and talking to Hannah in the kitchen, sending her out to get groceries.

After she left, I asked everyone else to stay out of the great room with its undraped windows.

"You should have motion lights outside," Street said.

"Of course," Ryan said. "That's obvious now that you say it. I'll call someone in the morning."

Lily dragged Street and Spot down to the walkout basement so that she could show Street a new video game on Ryan's console. I went down briefly to check the door and windows. Everything looked strong and secure.

Back upstairs in the dining room, I asked Ryan for more background on his company.

"Do you think my kidnapping has something to do with my business?"

"Possibly. There's a lot of money involved. It's always smart to see who might benefit financially if you're severely stressed."

"You mean, if I go crazy."

"That, or if you merely lose your edge. If your competitors can get your business."

"So where do we start?"

"Tell me more about what CBT does. Before you were

kidnapped, you talked about something called hypoxic stress. Start there."

Ryan air-washed his hands despite the slings, then laced his fingers together as if to hold them still.

"It goes back to DNA," he said. "As you know, DNA is the helical structure of molecules that encode everything about the form and function of an organism. All plants and animals, from bacteria to humans, have DNA."

"The difference being the complexity of the sequence," I said. I could have been a scientist.

"True," Ryan said. "But the difference is not as much as you might think. About half of your DNA is shared by a fruit fly."

How to win friends and influence people, I thought. "So, you slice and dice a fruit fly's DNA, and what, make it more like me?"

Ryan's look of strained tolerance returned, a healthy sign, I thought, after the ordeal of kidnapping.

"Or make me more like the fruit fly," I added.

He made a little smile, caught himself, took it back. "Let's just say that by altering a sequence of DNA, we can alter the form and function of the organism."

I nodded. "I've heard about recombinant DNA a lot, but is this just pure scientific inquiry, or has it actually helped in some area?"

"Oh, it has been amazing. Uncountable lives have been saved by recombinant technology. For example, insulin for diabetics used to be extracted from animals, and we never had enough. Then scientists figured out how to rearrange the DNA of a certain type of bacteria and basically turned it into an insulin factory. The result is that we feed the bacteria, and it produces all the insulin we need."

Ryan spread his arm slings wide. "This is happening all across the spectrum. Recombinant DNA has produced plants that produce dramatically higher yields, plants that are resistant to disease, plants that are resistant to freezing weather, fish that grow faster and larger, specialized bacteria that eat and break down toxic garbage, vaccines that provide immunity against influenza and hepatitis and herpes. One day we will use the technology to actually cure genetic diseases like muscular dystrophy. The list is huge, and the future possibilities are endless."

"How does it work? I mean, the actual cut and paste of these molecules? They're too small for you to get in there with little scalpels and scissors."

"Actually, we're learning to use laser beams for some of those purposes. But in general, the molecules are much too small. We're talking about objects on a nano-scale. You could put four hundred thousand DNA molecules side by side on the head of a pin. So we use what we call vectors to manipulate DNA in a cell. There are many kinds of vectors. Bacteria and restriction enzymes and viruses."

"A virus can cut apart DNA?"

"Viruses are little micro snippets of wanna-be life that are helpless if they're just sitting there on the surface of that table. But they are very good at invading a cell, taking over its command structure, and turning it into a virus reproduction machine."

"Like pirates taking over a ship and turning it in a new direction."

"Exactly. It's taken many decades and the entire careers of thousands of scientists to develop the techniques. But now it's quite routine. These vectors are our tools.

"At CBT our main focus is producing a category of drugs called biologicals. These drugs alter the genetic growth mechanisms of cancer. Ordinary drugs basically try to poison cancer to death, whereas biologicals get into the cancer cells and put on the parking brakes, shift the cancer transmissions into neutral and turn off the cancer engines."

"Earlier, you used the word hypoxic. So the reason to do DNA research in Tahoe must have something to do with oxygen levels?"

"Very good," Ryan said. "You could have been a scientist."

I was right.

Ryan raised the back of his left hand to his mouth, chewed on the knuckle of his index finger. "As you go up in elevation, the barometric pressure gets less, and what we call the partial pressures of the component gases get proportionally less, too. You know how flatlanders sometimes suffer from high altitude when they go hiking or skiing up in the mountains."

My turn for the smile of tolerance.

"Where I'm going with this is that our bodies are fine with the loss of nitrogen pressure. Same for other gasses. But when oxygen pressure is reduced, less of it crosses the cellular threshold from the air in our lungs to our red blood cells. Our bodies try to accommodate that by producing more red blood cells. Some studies suggest that after you've lived in Tahoe for a month, you develop an extra pint of blood volume. The other obvious accommodation is that we move a little slower and we breathe faster.

"That accommodation works well at altitudes in the Sierra. But at the much higher altitudes of the Andes and the Himalayas, it doesn't work well. The percentage of oxygen in the atmosphere is still about twenty-one percent, but the partial pressure of the oxygen is too low to help drive it from the air into our red blood cells. What we've discovered is that native populations in those high mountains are genetically different from the rest of us."

"Sherpas have different genes?" I asked.

"Yes. Their DNA has evolved for optimal oxygenation of their cells."

"How?"

"I think you'd find the science a bit inscrutable," he said.

"Try me."

"Well, relative to the hypoxia-inducible factor on one of their genes, we've found a dinucleotide repeat polymorphism."

"Of course," I said. "I figured that would be it. So how does this research help your company make biologicals?"

"It doesn't. Not yet, anyway. This is pure science. Any resulting future benefit that I might guess at is nothing but speculation and wouldn't stand up to any rigorous examination. I'd be like a science fiction writer dreaming up possibilities."

"But..." I said, sensing the direction of his thought.

"But science fiction writers have a long history of conjuring up the wildest things, like, say, geo-synchronous satellites, which then are actually developed and revolutionize the world."

Ryan continued, "So our notion is that if we can unlock what is happening with this high-altitude adaptation, it may help us develop treatments for people with diseases that make it difficult to breathe and starve their bodies of oxygen. Cystic fibrosis, pneumonia, asthma, emphysema."

"Seems like a great idea, doing this research at high altitude."

"We're also trying to learn how natural adaptations occur. So we take primitive organisms and bring them from sea level to high altitude. We've already made some interesting discoveries. If we can understand the adaptation mechanisms..." he trailed off, looking at me, but seeing some other world.

"The nuclear repeating morphological Pollyanna," I said.

Ryan grinned. "Yeah, that." He'd stopped with the hand-wringing, the nervous tics, the glances at the doors and windows. He was a natural scientist, much more comfortable talking about biology and physics than matters of emotion and feeling. The irony was that when he immersed himself in scientific subjects, he became warmer, more human.

"Anyway," he said, "this may all come to nothing. Or it may..." Ryan stopped in mid-sentence as a clinking sound permeated the house. My sense was that it came from the direction of the front door. I turned and listened.

It was like metal hitting metal. Or metal clinking on glass.

I stood and walked over to the front door. I could send Spot out to do a search. But that might be just what someone wanted.

"Lock the door behind me," I said as I opened the door.

ELEVEN

The breeze was cold. In the driveway sat the Douglas County Sheriff's SUV, engine running, lights off. It was still an official presence. The off-duty moonlighting wouldn't start until the morning. I stood motionless until my eyes adjusted. Then I walked to the patrol unit.

The driver's window rolled down. It was Deputy Praeger.

"Heard a clinking sound from inside," I whispered.

"Didn't hear anything out here," he said. "But I had to turn on the engine for some warmth. The night breeze off the lake feels like winter." He got out of the vehicle and shut the door.

"I'll walk around the house," I said. "Best if you stay here."

I walked around to the lake side of the house, stepping carefully, feeling my way, watching the shadows. In the distance I heard the soft lap of waves against the shore. Nothing moved. I went back around the other direction.

A clinking sound came from the trees near the road.

I ran along the side of Ryan's house, took a shortcut through dense, dark bushes, letting my footfalls be loud, hoping to startle and flush out anyone who was near.

A small animal, a raccoon maybe, scurried into brush.

I stopped and listened. The clinking had stopped.

I went back, made contact with Deputy Praeger, and knocked on the front door, calling out, "It's me."

Ryan opened up.

"Find anything?"

"No. All looks calm."

We sat down. Ryan's chest was still rising and falling with worry. I knew he would calm if I brought the subject back to his high-altitude research.

"Why come all the way to Tahoe?" I asked. "Couldn't you make a room in your Bay Area lab where the atmospheric pressure is lower? Compression pumps or something?"

"Yeah. That's what our forty-percent investor advocated. He said that our workers were there and our other facilities were there. But there are two reasons why I chose Tahoe. First, it was cheaper. Building a hypobaric chamber is very expensive. It has to be perfectly sealed against air leakage, and you need airlock rooms for people to come and go. Just reinforcing the walls and ceiling of a two thousand square-foot lab is an engineering nightmare. The increased load to handle an atmospheric reduction of thirty percent works out to over seven hundred pounds per square foot, or one and a half million pounds for two thousand square feet. It would be building a room that can withstand the weight of twenty fully-loaded semi-trucks on each wall. Even the floor would have to be hugely reinforced. Not to handle weight on the floor, but air pressure from below trying to push the floor up."

"Got it," I said. "Would you have to worry about the bends when people go inside such a chamber?"

"No. The bends happen when you reduce surrounding pressures by fifty percent or more, as when a scuba diver spends a long time at depths greater than thirty-three feet and then comes up to the surface. The reduced pressure allows dissolved nitrogen to bubble out of the blood. Like when you open a Coke and the carbon dioxide bubbles out of the liquid. We're talking about reducing pressure by only thirty percent. But going in and out of a hypobaric chamber is still uncomfortable on the ears. Standing in the airlock while the pumps equalize the pressure would be like riding an elevator in a building seven or eight times as high as the Empire State Building."

"How high is your facility?"

"Ten thousand, one hundred feet."

"Where is it located?"

Ryan hesitated.

"If you can't trust me, then why am I here? The kidnapper no doubt already knows the location of your lab."

Ryan stood silent for a time. He chewed on his lower lip. "I'm sorry. It's an adjustment for me. We went to great lengths to keep this place secret. The financial stakes are very high. The lab is up near the Mount Rose Meadows. Near the pass, there's a dirt road. A good distance up from the highway is a locked gate that the Forest Service put in to close the road. One of our lawyers found some language in the land lease and used that to get us a key.

"The road climbs up toward a utility building that a power company built years ago. About twenty years ago, the building was sold to a cell phone company, which was in turn bought out by one of the major carriers. They still use the nearby tower, but the building sat vacant for several years. We were able to buy it relatively cheap because it's on Forest Service land with only thirty-one years left on a ninety-nine year lease. The Forest Service is unlikely to renew the lease, and when the term is done, the building will have to be torn down. It's just a plain concrete block box in the woods, painted forest green, out of sight. They originally built it for big electrical equipment. No interior walls. It was easy for us to retrofit it for our use. And it's very secure. We added steel doors and barred windows.

"The end result is a high-altitude lab only forty minutes from Reno's airport. Reno is a thirty-minute flight from San Jose. We can even get in there in winter on snowmobiles. It's as perfect a location as we could hope for."

"You said there were two reasons to do your research up here instead of down in the Bay Area. One was the ease of obtaining a low pressure facility. What was the other one?"

"Privacy," Ryan said with emphasis. "We hired a Reno contractor to make modifications to the building, but he had no idea what the purpose of the building was. We personally hauled in our own equipment. If we'd built a hypobaric lab in the Bay Area, the unusual construction would have advertised our intentions to the entire world. As you know, corporate espionage is a big problem. Because of the enormous value of certain drugs, some disreputable companies will pay huge dollars to a spy who can bring them insider info.

"Putting this research lab up on the mountain kept us out of sight. Also, it reinforces the privacy issue to our own researchers. If they were in Palo Alto lunching every day with their colleagues, eating dinner with friends who work at other bio-tech companies, casual slip-ups would be much more likely. Being physically removed from the corporate centers creates more of an awareness of how precious our intellectual property is."

"Who works there?"

"We moved four of our scientists up from Palo Alto. We bought a house in Incline Village, and three of them live there. The fourth, Selena, lives with her parents who retired to Incline."

"What exactly do they do? Work with viruses and such?

"Some. Everything is designed to fall under what the National Institutes of Health calls their Section Three-F experiments. Those are exempt research projects that don't require registration with the Institutional Biosafety Committee."

"Meaning you aren't using hazardous materials," I said. "None of the yellow Hazmat suits we see in the movies."

"Right. Nevertheless, we use bio-safety cabinets, and we have accident protocols in place. We have our Biological Safety Officer review all of our experiments and procedures just to be sure. He's very thorough. Plus, he likes to get out of the Bay Area and come up to the lake."

Street and Lily and Spot came up the stairs from the basement level and turned into the kitchen.

"Snack break," Street said. "Need anything?"

Ryan and I both shook our heads.

"Is your Tahoe lab making any money for you?" I asked.

Ryan shook his head. "Like most of bio-tech research, it costs millions. Until we get a really successful biological drug, our main revenue stream is the development and production contracts with big pharma. But we have some promising projects for ourselves to market in the future.

"Our investor wants to take us public because he believes that other investors across the spectrum will see our potential. He thinks a giant cash infusion will allow us to do our research much faster. I'm his biggest irritation because I disagree. I think that our future breakthroughs will come from original insight and not pharmacological number crunching."

"You think your company will eventually make big money?"

Ryan's grin turned to a look of terror when a scream came from the kitchen.

TWELVE

"Sammy!" Lily screamed.

I bolted from my chair and ran into the kitchen. Lily stood by the center island, hiding behind it, her fingers gripping its top edge as she stared over it toward the big window above the sink. Street stood next to her, holding her head, trying to comfort her.

Ryan rushed in behind me and grabbed Lily up into his arms.

The squirrel with the shock of white hair hung from its neck by a tiny white thread, just outside of the kitchen window, lit from the inside by the canned lights above the sink and adjacent countertops. It swung slightly in the breeze.

"Spot, come!"

I ran out the front door. Spot loped after me.

The yard on the right side of Ryan's house was open to the back. On the left side, it was planted in with bushes. Good cover. I went left.

The plantings were thick. I charged through them, hoping to startle anyone hiding in the dark. I spun around the far corner of the house. Spot had caught up to me. I went over to the kitchen window. The squirrel and the cord that suspended it was too high to reach unless the person was very tall or had something to stand on.

Nearby was a wheelbarrow, on its side, pushed away in haste. I brought Spot over, had him sniff the handles.

"Do you have the scent? Do you, Spot?" I shook his chest to indicate that he was to get excited about the scent.

"Okay, Spot, find the suspect! Find the suspect!"

I patted him on his rear.

He spun around the other direction and ran off.

I sprinted after him. He went through the bushes at the side of the house, past the construction site, down the street.

Fifty yards down, he stopped, put his nose to the dirt at the side of the road. Then he lifted his head high, turned a circle. Air-scenting. He went down the street several paces, came back, put his nose back to the ground.

Spot's motions suggested that whomever had last moved the wheelbarrow had gotten into a car at that point in the road. We went back to the driveway.

Praeger was out, flashlight in hand.

"I saw you and your dog," he said.

"We followed a scent down the street to a point out of sight from you. I think a person got into a vehicle there, and left. Come around to the back side of the house." I brought him around, pointed up at the squirrel.

"I'll boost you up," I said.

I found a stick, handed it to Praeger, locked my fingers for his shoe and boosted him up.

He got the stick inside the loop of thread, lifted the thread up. It appeared to have been hooked over a piece of window moulding. I lowered Praeger down. He shined his light on the squirrel.

"It's got something around its neck with writing on it, but I can't see what," he said.

"Let's bring it around, put it in your headlight beams," I said.

Praeger carried the stick with the suspended squirrel around the house.

I reached inside his patrol unit and turned on the headlights.

Praeger angled the squirrel.

"It's a twisty label like the ones you write the food number on in the healthfood aisle at the grocery store. This says DRTX-thirty-three."

"No word?" I said.

"Here, look," Praeger said.

I leaned in close. The DRTX-33 was written in careful block letters.

"Got a plastic garbage bag in the back," he said. "Not much else to check for, right? Looks like the thread is dental floss. Maybe that can tell us something?" He was looking to me for guidance.

"Maybe," I said. "But not likely. Hold onto the squirrel just in case." I opened the rear hatch of his SUV, found a bag in a box, pulled it out. We bagged the squirrel.

I went back to the front door. I assumed Ryan had locked it behind me.

I knocked again, worried that I was wrong and that the person outside had stepped indoors right after I came out, locking the door behind them. My heart pounded.

THIRTEEN

"Who is it?" came Ryan's voice.

"Owen."

He opened the door.

I went inside, thinking that one cop on guard duty outside wasn't enough. But Street's thought to have motion lights installed would make a difference.

"Where are Lily and Street?" I asked Ryan.

"Street took her into her bedroom," Ryan said. "Did you see anybody?"

"No. Somebody turned your wheelbarrow over and stood on it to get up and tie the squirrel. Spot smelled the wheelbarrow handles, and followed the scent down the street to a scent dead-end. The suspect probably got into a car and drove off. There was a twisty around the squirrel's neck. It had writing on it."

"What? A message like the obituary?" His voice was tense.

"No. It makes no sense to me. Maybe it will to you. It said DRTX-thirty-three."

Ryan started shaking.

"You know what it means?"

Ryan backed up, reached out, collapsed into a chair. He bent over, head between his knees. He started bobbing, crying.

"Tell me, Ryan."

He lifted up his head, looked at me with terrified eyes.

"It's about Lily."

"What do you mean?" I asked.

"DRTX-thirty-three is a gene on chromosome eleven. It's a type of gene that prevents runaway cell growth. We call genes like this tumor suppressors. If it is damaged, it can lead to a nephroblastoma, a tumor in the kidney. A guy named Babbett first discovered it. It's now called Babbett's Syndrome." Ryan lowered his head to his knees again, made a deep sob, raised up again. "It's a rare genetic defect, but children who have it usually develop cancerous tumors before the age of five."

"Lily has the genetic defect," I said.

He nodded, his eyes and cheeks wet. "She lost her left kidney and part of her right kidney three years ago, a month after her third birthday. A year later, they went in to take out more. Maybe they got it all. Probably not. She's got enough of her kidney left to function, but just barely."

"Does she understand?"

"She knows she's sick. She remembers her hospital stays for the surgeries in great detail. She remembers the chemo. But I don't think she understands how serious it is."

"What's the prognosis?"

"For most children who have a tumor in just one kidney, it's quite good. But she got it in both kidneys, a stage five cancer when they found it. She's been in remission since the chemo. But one of the bad indicators was up in her blood tests this last month. There is a substantial risk that the cancer will metastasize to her lungs or her brain. They want to start another round of chemo, but the last time it nearly killed her."

Ryan paused. He was panting.

"I've got a large team that's spent the last three years working on a biological treatment. That's part of the reason why I can never lose majority control of CBT. I can't risk that someone else would pull that team off of their research."

"When do you expect results?"

"We've had a new trial going the last six months. We expect to get a preliminary report in a week or so." Ryan looked at me, his eyes pinched with fear. "If the results are good, I believe I can get her doctor to administer it under the terms of the FDA clinical trial protocols. If he won't, I'm going to give it to her myself."

"The penalties are substantial either way," I said.

Ryan nodded, his eyes twitching. "If the FDA finds me breaching the law, they could destroy my company's future. But if Lily's cancer spreads, she dies."

Ryan looked away.

"Who besides a scientist would know about the DRTX-thirty-three gene?" I asked.

"Anyone who knew that Lily was sick."

"How many people know that Lily is sick?"

"Lots. All of the medical people who've worked on her. The people on the team at CBT. No doubt others at CBT as well. When the boss's kid sister gets cancer, word gets around."

"Who named the squirrel Sammy?"

"Lily did. She liked him hanging around our front step."

"Who knows that she named him?"

"No one but me," Ryan said. "Wait. Hannah, our nanny would know. And Herman, the piano tuner neighbor might know. Anybody they talked to."

"Either way, it's a message designed to terrorize you."

He nodded, tears flowing. He stood up.

I followed Ryan into Lily's bedroom, where Street was reading to her. He sat down next to Lily and hugged her hard.

"I'm sorry about Sammy," he said as he cried.

She nodded. "I'll try not to be sad if you try, Ryan."

Ryan wiped the heels of his hands over his eyes.

"What are you reading?"

"Street got one of your books. What's it called again?"

"de Botton's 'How Proust Can Change Your Life'," Street said.

"A bit much for a six-year-old," I said.

Lily looked at me.

"She's smart," Street said.

Lily looked at Street.

"No wonder people think you ivory-tower scholars are out of touch," I said.

"It's not like Ryan has The Cat In The Hat lying around," Street said.

"That's true," Ryan said.

"I already read that at the library," Lily said.

I said, "If Proust doesn't keep her satisfied, I have my Matisse book in the Jeep. We can always fall back on the tried-and-true of picture books."

We heard a car pull up the drive.

"That will be Hannah," Ryan said. "It's about time. Her friend Tammy picked her up, but who knows who will be dropping her off. I better go out and see where's she's been."

Ryan and I walked down to the kitchen. He wiped his eyes on his sleeve.

We heard the distant sound of the side door opening, and Hannah came down the hall.

"Sorry, I'm late," she announced. She was a plump young woman with stringy brown hair. She carried two grocery bags.

"I thought you'd be back a long time ago," Ryan said.

"We saw our friends Sue and John at the market, and they asked us to stop by for a quick visit, and I knew that you'd be here with Lily, so I took that liberty. I hope you don't mind."

She set down the groceries and turned to look at Ryan. Her look was bold and Ryan averted his eyes.

"What if I'd gotten a call and had to leave?" he said.

"Then Lily would have been fine by herself for a few minutes. You worry too much."

Up close I saw that her lipstick was smeared, and her snug black top had been tucked in so hastily that it pulled to the side, and one of her lacy black bra straps showed in the neck opening.

She looked at me. "Hi, I'm Hannah."

I nodded. "Owen."

Ryan held his head bent forward. He shook it back and forth. Without looking up, he said, "Leave the groceries. I'll put them away. And I'll take care of Lily tonight."

"Okay, good," Hannah said. "There's a show I wanted to watch." She left and went down the stairs.

"Good nannies are hard to find," I said.

"It's been a nightmare," Ryan said. "I can't count how many nannies we've had. I pay her well. She has her own apartment in the basement. I give her rides when she needs them. Why can't she visit her friends on her off-hours?"

"When she started, did you explain what you expected?"

"Sure. I told her she was to look after Lily. Get her off to school when it starts in a couple of weeks, be here when she comes home from school. Help with the household. Like that."

"What about boundaries, specific job description, hours you

expect her to be here each week."

"You mean spell out every detail? Why should I do that? Everybody knows what a nanny needs to do. Help raise a child."

I figured I'd already made my point, so I didn't respond.

Ryan continued, "If someone told me every detail of how I was supposed to do my job, it would be like a straightjacket. I can't be creative, innovative, and thoughtful about my work if someone is standing around with a clipboard checking off each item as I do it. But of course, you're thinking that a nanny's job isn't supposed to be about creativity or innovation."

"I think a nanny could benefit from creativity as much as any other job. The difference is that when it comes to work, there are two types of people. You are the type who throws yourself into your work, because that is what makes it worth doing, that is how you have self-respect.

"Hannah is the type who doesn't care. Clock in, put in your time - or in her case, don't even put in your time - clock out, get your pay, and laugh at your employer's gullibility behind his or her back."

"Do you think I should fire her? It's so hard to find nannies."

"Tell me this. If a stranger approached Hannah in the produce aisle or at a bar and chatted her up, asking questions about her employer, would she deflect the questions in respect for your privacy?"

Ryan lifted his head and stared at me.

I continued. "What if that stranger bought her a few drinks, and then made her a lucrative offer. Here's a hundred dollars to start. I'm interested in information about Ryan Lear's work. Just photocopy whatever you can find. You show the papers to me, I'll pay one hundred dollars for each piece of paper I keep."

"And you think this because she was late with the groceries?"

"No. Anyone can be late for anything and have a legitimate reason for it. I think it because she doesn't respect you. Why, I don't know. But her actions tonight showed contempt. I think she would enjoy selling you out."

"God, you are scaring me," he said.

"The person who killed the squirrel scares me."

"This will be her last night here," he said.

FOURTEEN

"Let's say a person did approach Hannah," Ryan said. "How would we find out who it is?"

"We start with a basic question. Of all the people you know as friends or business colleagues or people you bump into in the course of your day, which of them might want to harm you?"

"I've already asked myself that many times. I don't know. I've had no fights with anyone. No one hates me that I know of. No arguments or disagreements, petty or serious."

"Employees who dislike you?" I said.

"I think they mostly like me."

"Not Hannah," I said. "Before tonight, would you have said that about her?"

"I see your point," Ryan said.

"Your company has competitors. Which of them are hurt most by CBT's success?"

"None of them. The need for effective drugs is never-ending. No matter how successful we get, it's unlikely to substantially reduce the demand for the drugs that our competitors produce."

"Who benefits from Eli's death?"

"You mean, financially? His father inherited. I called him. He said that our forty-percent investor asked about purchasing the stock. Eli's dad told him no way, that if he ever sold, it would be to me."

"You said you were your investor's biggest irritation. He wants controlling interest in CBT?"

"All major investors want controlling interest. That's just good business."

"Tell me about him."

"Preston Laurence was Stanford B-School, eight or ten years

older than me. He's super wealthy. Started out writing software, sold his company, then switched to investing. He told me once, why should he ride his own successive waves of entrepreneurship, when he can ride the waves of dozens of successful entrepreneurs at the same time."

"You ever have any disagreements with him?"

Ryan looked into space, then shook his head. "No, we've always gotten along really well."

"I thought you said that he wanted you to build a hypobaric chamber in the Bay Area instead of up on the mountain."

"Sure, but that's not a disagreement."

"It's the kind of thing I'm talking about," I said.

"That was minor. That was just business strategy talk. It's like the times he's offered to buy more stock. Ten percent from each of us. His goal to have a majority stake in CBT wouldn't drive him to destroy me."

"Consider this scenario. What if Preston Laurence did have control over your company? Would he do things differently?"

"Yeah, I suppose so." Ryan frowned.

"Why? Does he think he could make more money if things were run his way?"

"Preston always thinks he can make more money his way. And he's probably right. But I'm doing well for him. His investment has probably doubled in value in the two years since he bought in."

"Anyone else like Preston who you get along with, but who may differ with you about how to do things?"

"Preston, nanny Hannah... Maybe everybody."

"Okay. I'd like to meet the people you are closest to."

Ryan's face was immobile. "Since Eli died and Jeanie disappeared, I'm not close to anybody other than Lily."

"Your colleagues at work, your important employees, any people you see socially. Preston Laurence. Eli's girlfriend. I want to get a feel for how people feel about you, respond to you."

"Mostly, they don't respond to me. I'm a cipher. A basement video gamer. If I weren't running a company that is grossing close to a hundred million, nobody would even know my name."

"Let's not worry about how popular you are. What is the best way for me to meet these people? Can you set up appointments for me in the Bay Area?"

Ryan shook his head. "I don't think so. Some of them, like my closest, most trusted employees, are up here, anyway. Eli's girlfriend is so grief stricken, she hasn't left his house in the Tahoe Keys since he died. She wouldn't even go to his funeral. Preston is usually at his ranch in the foothills."

"Then you could call them, and I'll go to wherever they are."

"I don't know what I would say. I'd get it wrong. They wouldn't see you. Or they'd be so stiff you wouldn't learn anything anyway."

"Then here's another idea. You'll have a party. Invite them all."

"No. No way would that work. I've never had a party. No one would come." Ryan was adamant.

"Sure it will work. We'll hire a band, and have it catered, and put that info on the invitation. We'll invite your neighbors up and down this street. When you send out the email invite, publicly copy everyone else. When they all see who might possibly come, they will show up just to be seen, just to network. Even if they don't care about a party at Ryan Lear's house, the fact of everyone else possibly coming will make it a big deal."

Ryan was shaking his head continuously. "It won't work."

"Yes, it will."

FIFTEEN

Street and Lily were still sitting side-by-side on the bed, leaning back against the headboard. Street held the book about Proust. To Lily's side was the laptop I'd seen her carrying around earlier. Spot was on the carpet at the side of the bed. After the scare and the turmoil and the tears, it was good to see Lily next to Street, happy and content. They looked up.

"Proust is pretty exciting, huh?" I said, looking at the book.

"Well, we talked about 'Remembrance' for a bit, but Lily is more interested in horses."

"I had a good idea," Lily said. "I showed her the website about Heat."

"The one put together by the guy we met on the trail," I said.

Street nodded, then turned to Lily. "How many questions do you think you asked me about Heat?"

"A hundred?" Lily said.

"Sounds about right." Street grinned. "Will he ever be caught, and where will Heat go, and can he find enough food, and do I think that anyone could ever ride Heat."

"I've got a book in the car with a really cool painting that shows a horse," I said. "Do you want to see it, Lily?"

She nodded.

I went outside, waved at Deputy Praeger, went to the Jeep and got the Matisse monograph out from under the seat.

Back inside, I sat next to them and opened the book.

"These are all paintings by a Frenchman named Henri Matisse. One of the best things he did came near the end of his life when he was ill and had to stay in bed. He had his assistants paint color on paper, then Matisse cut them up with a scissors and arranged the pieces into pictures."

I flipped through the color plates near the end of the book. Lily stared, instantly focused on the bold, colorful images.

"Like painting, only with colored paper," she said.

"Yeah." I turned to an image that showed a strong graphic of a horse rendered in hot magenta.

"This one is my favorite. It's called, 'The Horse, the Rider, and the Clown.'"

"There's the horse!" Lily said, pointing.

"Yeah. And this fun decorative stuff above the horse symbolizes the rider."

"It looks like the rider is a girl and this is her skirt." Lily said.

"It is. You have a good eye. And the bright yellow and green area down in the opposite corner symbolizes a clown."

"It doesn't look like a clown," Lily said, shaking her head. "It looks like another skirt."

"There is more than one way to show a clown," I said.

"A round red nose?"

"That's a good way. But here's another. Think about what a clown does."

Lily thought for a moment. "I don't know."

"Sure, you do. A clown makes you laugh and have fun."

Lily pointed to the bright colors in the corner of the picture. "And these colors are fun. Like a clown."

Street looked at me, raised her eyebrows.

"I know," I said to her. "Smart kid."

Lily pretended that she didn't hear us.

Lily looked at more pictures in the book, then came back to The Horse, the Rider, and the Clown. "This is my favorite, too," she said. "The shapes for the two people are almost the same. But a little difference in the color makes one a rider and one a clown."

Ryan came into the room.

"Time for bed, Lily."

"Can I make a copy of this painting for my wall?"

"We can do that in the morning," Ryan said. "Better yet, you can draw a picture like it."

"Can Spot stay with me?"

"Yes," I said. "We'll leave the doors open. He can sleep here for awhile and then someplace else if he likes."

Street and I said goodnight to her as Ryan gave her a kiss.

Ryan caught up with us in the hall. "Thank you. All her life, she's only had me or a nanny to read to her. I have no friends like that, people who would show a book to a kid, no one else to connect with her at bedtime." Ryan stood there, awkward.

"You're welcome, Ryan," Street said, touching him on his shoulder. "I enjoyed it."

Street and I went to bed, chatted about Lily, gradually went to sleep.

In the middle of the night, I awoke to a loud noise followed by a yell and then a groan.

I heard Spot bark. I ran out the open door of our bedroom.

In the glow of the bathroom nightlight, I saw Ryan standing in the bathroom doorway, his hand coming out of the sling and gripping the doorjamb, looking at me approaching as if I were a nighttime stalker. His eyes were wild with nightmare visions. Spot stood nearby, looking for something wrong, not seeing it. Ryan didn't react to Spot, staring instead at the frightening world of his nightmare.

"It's okay, Ryan," I said, approaching slowly. I put my hand on his skinny arm, steered him back to his room, and sat him on his bed.

"I had a bad dream," he said in a whisper.

"It's over now. Everything's okay. Spot will be here watching the house all night. Go back to sleep."

He lay down and pulled the covers over himself. I went back to my room and explained to Street what happened.

In the morning, Street used Ryan's computer to print an outline of the Matisse painting. Lily began to color it.

Ryan fired Hannah and handed her her last paycheck. She yelled and fussed and cried and pleaded. When he didn't give in, she stomped away and gathered her things from the basement apartment, called one of her friends, and left, waiting out on the road for her friend to pick her up.

Ryan made up a list of all the people that I might want to meet, and Street and I made arrangements for a party the coming Friday night. I didn't want music to overwhelm conversation, so

I went online and booked a local acoustic band. Street arranged the catering.

Deputy Praeger left and was replaced by Officer Vistamon from the South Lake Tahoe PD. I explained the routine, showed him the doors to the house, and introduced him to Ryan and Lily and Street. Then Street went to her lab to work on her current bug projects.

I left Spot to tend to his new duties as Ryan and Lily's companion and drove up to my cabin to grab more clothes. I also wrote a letter to a lab I know that does materials testing. I enclosed the little scrap of red leather I'd found on the cliff above the body.

Back at Ryan's house, I brought Ryan and Lily along as I took Spot for a long walk. Ryan took his slings off, and put his hands in his pockets.

"I called a company to put in motion lights," Ryan said. "They're coming day after tomorrow."

"Good," I said, as loud piano sounds came from the log cabin adjacent to Ryan's house and construction site. The notes sounded over and over, some of them quite discordant.

I gestured toward the cabin. "Someone practicing the piano?"

"Tuning," Ryan said. "That's Herman Oleson. He's the piano tuner. He tunes his piano every week."

"When I first came here, I saw a guy with white hair out on the front deck. He nodded at me. But when I said hi, he didn't respond."

"That's him," Ryan said. "He had a stroke a few weeks ago. He lost his speech. But everything else about him seems fine. He still understands what you say, still does his own cooking, washes his clothes. And he's still tuning his piano."

"I call him grandpa Herman," Lily said.

"Yeah," Ryan said. "After our dad died, we got to know Herman a lot better. He's been good for Lily."

"Does he rent the cabin from you?"

"No. He has what we call a life-lease. He was actually born there. Eighty-some years ago. He's lived there all his life. As property values rose, the state of Nevada kept raising his taxes. Even though he is quite a famous piano tuner and made good money, he kept having to sell his possessions to pay his taxes. Art, antique cars, a coin collection started by his grandfather. During the real estate boom when property values went through the roof, his taxes hit eighty thousand dollars a year. So he subdivided his acreage and sold off the parcels that now have my house and my neighbor's mansion.

"Unfortunately, Tahoe lakeshore still kept going up. So his last piece was the parcel with the cabin and the area where I'm now building. Douglas County wouldn't let Herman subdivide any smaller. Yet the assessor was required by law to put a fair value on Herman's cabin. The last adjustment brought his property taxes back up to fifty thousand. Herman was crushed. He put the last piece on the market. I made a deal with him that I would buy the property, and he could keep living in his cabin."

"Nice," I said.

"Yeah, but Herman still lost ownership of the property that had been in his family for over one hundred years. It was very stressful for him."

"He's still tuning pianos?"

"Not his customers'. But he still tunes his own,"

When we had walked a little farther away, Lily said, "I have a good idea!"

"I bet you do," I said.

"I could ride Spot, and then he would have more fun on his walk!"

"Why didn't I think of that." I put her on his back and held her hand while Spot walked along. Lily was thrilled, and she grinned continuously. A quarter-mile later, I thought maybe Spot would want a break, so I lifted her off.

After that, Lily directed the conversation with a constant stream of questions. Which meant that we talked about dogs. Dog games and dog exercise and dog breeds and dog toys and how much dogs shed and how often you brush a dog's teeth and what dogs eat and what dogs think about. Lily appeared to be as brilliant for her age as Ryan was for his, but after an hour of dog talk, I was ready to take a vow of silence and join a monastery.

We were nearly back to the house when something startled Ryan. He was walking at the edge of the road, next to the tall pines when a sudden rustling sound and a movement made him react as if a bomb had gone off. He leaped away from the noise, hitting Lily and almost knocking her over. He landed in the street on the far side of me and grabbed my shoulder as if to get me between him and the devil.

"Ryan, easy, everything's okay."

Ryan stared toward the forest with the same wild, frantic eyes I'd seen in the middle of the night.

"I thought it was..." He stopped and bent over, hands on knees, panting as if he'd just finished running a footrace. "I thought it was the wild Mustang."

"You only saw Heat once, correct?"

"Yes."

"You said it was a bad sign. Is that a Washoe thing? A vision of a Mustang?"

"No. But Mustangs live all over the valleys east of Tahoe. I learned their ways by watching them as I grew up. So I know that Heat is not where he belongs. But I wasn't ever taught specifically about Mustangs. In fact, I was never really taught Washoe customs in a proper sense. I've been around the elders, and I know that they have a long, great, oral history to share. But when my dad got the job as a principal in Reno, we moved away from Dresslerville, the Washoe community near Gardnerville."

"It's unfortunate to have a negative feeling attached to a beautiful wild horse."

Ryan nodded as we walked. "I've had nightmares about Heat. I think his dislocation is symbolic of everything that's wrong with my life."

"If they ever catch Heat, can I ride him?" Lily asked.

"Maybe you can, Lily," I said.

When we got back from our walk, I asked Ryan if he knew how to reach Eli's girlfriend Sydney. He gave me Eli's number and said that he thought they were living together before Eli died.

The phone rang five times, ten times, no machine to pick up. No harm in waiting. Could be someone was there, but was taking out the garbage.

Someone picked up on the fourteenth ring.

"Hello." It was a statement, not a question. A soft, weak voice, young and female.

"My name is Owen McKenna. May I speak to Sydney, please?"

"This is she." She sounded fragile and grief-stricken.

"I'm a private investigator working for Ryan Lear. He believes that Eli's death was not an accident. Some things have happened since Eli's death that make me think there may be something to his idea."

She didn't speak.

"I'm sorry if this upsets you," I said. "But I'm sure you would want to know the truth about Eli's death, especially if there is anything to Ryan's belief."

There was another silence. I waited.

Finally she spoke. "I don't think it was an accident, either."

"May I come over and talk to you?"

The young woman was on delayed response. Perhaps the grief had slowed her brain.

"Yes," she said.

"Where do I go?"

"I'm at Eli's house. Do you know the Tahoe Keys?"

"Yes."

"It's on Beach Drive. On the beach side." She gave me the number. "What time will you come?"

"Would an hour from now work?"

"Yes." Her voice was still so soft, it was hard to hear.

I thanked her and hung up.

I left Spot with Lily and Ryan and drove into South Lake Tahoe. In the middle of town I turned northwest on Tahoe Keys Blvd. A mile up the street I went by the Tahoe Keys sign.

The Keys were one of those great development ideas back in the 1960s. Take hundreds of acres of "useless" wetlands, dredge out a bunch of canals, put up hundreds of upscale houses and a dock out back of each, and market them as homes on lakeshore.

Now the Keys are considered an environmental nightmare, having eliminated the precious wetlands that used to filter runoff before it got to Tahoe's pristine waters.

Yet, even though the Keys get a chunk of blame for declining lake clarity, those homes have gone from merely pricey to some of the hottest real estate in Tahoe.

Everybody wants a dock.

I followed the road as it turned left and became Beach Drive. Eli Nathan's house was on the right, one of the few Keys houses directly on the lake.

As Tahoe beach houses go, Eli's wasn't ostentatious. But it was still 5000 or 6000 square feet. Standard nice-house architecture without any of the excessive timber frame features that make more recent lakeshore houses all look like they're trying to imitate huge 19th century mountain lodges in the Swiss Alps or the Canadian Rockies.

I walked up the flagstone walk and rang the bell.

After a long wait, a petite young woman opened the door. Her sad brown eyes were rimmed with dark circles. She telegraphed a kind of permanent shock. She wore a baggy men's sweater and baggy men's jeans with the cuffs rolled up. She had on a baseball cap that was too big. It sat down low enough on her head that it pushed the tops of her ears out.

"Hi, I'm Owen. You must be Sydney."

"Come in."

She turned and walked into a large, airy entry that had views through to the living room and the beach and lake and mountains beyond the wall of windows.

As I followed her, I saw that she'd pulled her long brown hair into a thick ponytail and threaded it through the opening in the back of the oversized baseball cap. She may have lost the guy, but she was hanging onto the memory of him in every way that she could.

She sat down on one of those over-sized leather couches that are made up of multiple sections that, assembled, created a big 90-degree curve. She pulled her legs up under her. Her hands clenched white-knuckled at the loose fabric of the bottom of the sweater.

I sat on a big chair across from her.

"I'm sorry for your loss, Sydney."

She nodded.

"Ryan told me that Eli was an expert climber. Is that true?"

She nodded again.

"He also told me that while Eli took risks, he didn't do it in a haphazard way, that he approached everything with care."

Another nod. "Eli was into the rush," she said. "But it wasn't like other people going for the thrill. I don't know how to explain it. Like when he wanted to learn skydiving. He didn't just call up the skydiving company and say, 'Sign me up.' He researched it the way he researched science and business. He read books, interviewed other skydivers, learned about the planes they use for jumping. Everything. He sort of became an expert before he even tried something. Only then did he do it."

"So he wasn't an impulsive thrill-seeker."

"He was impulsive, but he only acted when he knew what he was doing. Climbing Cave Rock that day was an impulse. But he wouldn't have done it if he weren't already an expert climber."

Sydney stopped. I waited.

"The problem I had with Eli wasn't that he took risks," she said. "I was okay with that in general because of how thoroughly he learned about the things he tried. My problem was that it was never enough. Instead of just climbing cliffs, he had to escalate it to taller and more vertical cliffs. Even cliffs that were overhangs. Then that wasn't enough, and he had to give up any kind of belay, the rope protection that climbers use. He said that free climbing was the only pure climbing. I had a problem with that, climbing with no safety."

"That push to always want more is probably what made him so successful in business," I said.

"Yeah," she said. "But he took it to extremes. Like when skydiving wasn't enough, and he wanted to try base-jumping."

"Is that where they jump off bridges and buildings?"

"That, and worse. The really extreme version is where they jump off super tall cliffs and wear wing suits."

"Flying suits?"

"Yeah. They have webs of fabric between the legs and between the arms and the body. You point your arms down so that your hands are a foot or so out from your hips."

"So you can fly like Batman?"

She nodded, then shook her head at the craziness of it. "Eli did it. He went to Norway where they have a cliff thousands of feet high. Then he jumped off the cliffs at Lauterbrunnen, Switzerland. Eli showed me videos on the internet. It's beyond nuts. They jump off cliffs, then spread their arms and legs and rocket through the air at something like a hundred fifty miles an hour. Then before they hit the ground, they open their parachutes."

"Do you think his risk-taking contributed to his fall at Cave Rock?"

She shook her head. "No, in fact it was the way he took risks that makes me think something else was involved."

"I don't understand."

She thought for a moment. "He was very careful in how he prepared for it. Before he climbed Cave Rock, Eli said that the route wasn't extreme. Coming from Eli, that tells me that relative to his ability, it was not a big deal. Of course, whenever I'd talk about some climb being dangerous, he would point out that you can kill yourself falling off a ten-foot wall. So it wasn't like he didn't know that he could die climbing Cave Rock. But when he said it wasn't extreme, I don't believe that it would have really taxed him. That's what makes me think that something else was involved."

"Like what?"

"I have no idea."

"Did anyone else know that Eli was climbing that day?"

"Other than the people who saw him and stopped their cars to watch? None that I know of."

"He didn't tell anyone that he was going to climb?"

She shook her head. "No. It was an impromptu thing."

"How did you end up stopping there?"

"He was meeting someone."

"Who?"

"I don't know. Someone called while we were driving. Eli talked a bit, then said that we were on the road, and maybe we should stop someplace where they could talk. They chose Cave Rock."

"Why Cave Rock?"

"I'm not sure. I got the idea that the other person was new to Tahoe and maybe didn't know places very well. Cave Rock is an easy landmark to see, and there's a parking area. We were coming from South Lake Tahoe, so if a person were driving up from Carson City or someplace in that direction, it would make sense that Eli would say that. Hey, let's meet at Cave Rock."

Sydney stopped. She frowned, no doubt thinking about what happened.

"After he hung up, he didn't say anything about the person who called?"

"Nothing significant. I think it was a guy who was coming to Tahoe for vacation. In Eli's business there was always another person he had to meet, always more details he had to discuss with someone. It got so I never really paid much attention to his dealings.

"Anyway, when we got there, Eli looked at his watch and realized that we had twenty or thirty minutes to kill. So he started studying the rock. He saw a route over the southbound tunnel - he called it a line - and he got all excited. He always keeps his climbing shoes in the trunk. So he pulled them out, chalked up, and started climbing. I knew it was against the law to climb on Cave Rock. He knew it, too. I tried everything I could think of to stop him. But he wouldn't listen to me. He kept going up, and I realized it was futile. I stopped shouting. I didn't want to distract him. Then I walked down the highway a bit so I could see him, and there he was, just getting over the crest at the top. He turned and bent down, looking back at the route he just climbed. Then something happened. It was like he slipped or something. He went down on his side and slid. But as he went over the edge, he caught himself, and I thought he was okay. But then he lost his grip, and fell to the highway below."

Sydney shut her eyes, took a deep breath and held it.

"Where did you meet Eli?" I asked, changing the subject to something less dark.

"I'd been going to UC Berkeley. I sort of had an epiphany. I realized that I was majoring in physics because I was good at it, when in fact, I almost hate physics. I don't like the idea that physics may eventually explain everything. I'm more of a romantic. I'm drawn to the concept that there are unexplainable aspects to this life. You can't explain love with physics.

"So I decided to take a year off. I moved in with a friend in Palo Alto, and got a job working in a café. That's where I met Eli and Ryan and Jeanie. The Geek Troika, they called themselves. I waited on them once and I stuck my nose into their conversation. They were talking about some glitch in a scientific experiment, and I overheard them. So I said that it sounded like it was merely entropy inserting itself into the proceedings. And they got all excited and carried on about how there was another scientist in their midst, and joked that I was going to steal their trade secrets and such. After that, they requested that I be their waiter for their weekly meetings.

"After a few weeks, Eli asked me out and we got along well as long as he didn't talk about physics too much."

"Ryan told me that Eli was a physicist, too."

Sydney cracked a tiny smile.

"Eli was everything. His main focus was computer science and applied electronics. But as he liked to say, everything in the universe, at its essence, still gets down to physics. So he got his Ph.D. in physics."

"Were you close?"

"As close as I believe anyone could ever get with Eli. A couple of times I brought up the subject of marriage. He'd challenge me. 'What does marriage give you?' And no matter what I'd answer, he'd say, 'You can have that anyway.' Or, 'You already have that.' It didn't make any difference what my answer was. Permanence? Commitment? Spiritual connection? Legal rights? Societal respect for our relationship?

"He was right, of course. Even so, I guess it's the romantic in me. In that way, I'm more like Ryan, carried away by unrealistic ideals. Ryan's heart is as pure as a heart can get. But Ryan is too broken to have a serious relationship with most people. In spite of all of his success, he's afraid of the world. I think that fear is manifested in his delusions. If he could find courage, I think his delusions would disappear."

"You may be right."

"Eli was a driven businessman scientist, and his rush through life was unrelenting and at times unbearable. But I found that ambition and drive very compelling. When Eli was on, the rest of the world was on a dimmer switch turned down low. With Eli, I felt that I was living a life ten times larger than any I would live without him."

"What are you going to do now?"

"I have no idea. My friend Sheila is a psychologist. She says that the main thing I need to do now is nothing. No plans, no decisions, no changes. She says I should cut myself slack for about six months. It's been ten days. I'm still in shock. Empty inside. Hollow. I still spend most of every day crying. I miss him so much." Sydney looked out at the lake, wiped her eyes with her sleeves.

I told her again that I was sorry for her loss, thanked her for her time, and let myself out.

SIXTEEN

In the morning, I left Spot at the Lear house, headed to my office, paid some bills, and called Diamond.

"Sergeant," I said when he answered. "You know what coroner handled the death of Eli Nathan?"

"Lemme check and call you back," he said, and hung up.

My phone rang two minutes later.

"Captain Robyn Bridbury," Diamond said. "She's one of our Deputy Coroners. Robyn with a Y, not that it matters." He gave me her office number.

I dialed.

"Douglas County Sheriff's Office," a woman said.

"Robyn Bridbury, please."

"I'm sorry, Captain Bridbury is out," the woman said, then added, "Wait, she just walked in. Please hold."

"Captain Bridbury," a woman said in a cheerful feminine voice, like someone planning summer picnics, not investigating suspicious deaths.

"My name is Owen McKenna, buddy of your illustrious Sergeant Martinez. Thanks for taking my call."

"I know about you. And I've heard distinguished and really smart and PITB used to describe Diamond. But wait 'til I lay illustrious on him."

"Pain In The Butt?"

"You got it. What can I do for you?"

"Wondering about the coroner's report on Elijah Nathan," I said.

"Oh, that." It sounded like something she wanted to forget. "Well, I'm just back from one meeting, and off to another in thirty seconds. And my afternoon is full. Let me look at my planner...

Maybe we could talk day after tomorrow, early in the morning."

"You got a lunch date today?" I said.

"Hey, I'm married, and he's a big guy who carries a gun for work."

"Not that kinda date. Pick your spot and I'll buy if you don't mind talking shop over food. Maybe your info will help me catch a murderer."

"That's a bit over-the-top for a guy who took a cliff dive. But you got a deal. You know the Carson Valley Inn?"

"Katie's giant hamsteak?" I guessed.

"You got it. Noon-thirty or so?"

"I'll be there."

I called Diamond back.

"One more thing," I said when he answered. I explained that I'd been thinking about Heat, the mystery horse that roamed through the Tahoe forest. And I remembered that Maria, Diamond's new girlfriend, ran a horse-boarding ranch.

"You nearby?" I asked.

"Up at the top of the grade."

"Meet me for a question?"

"Sure. I'll turn into the pull-over at middle-Kingsbury near the Chart House."

I drove up Kingsbury Grade and spotted Diamond's Explorer half way up. I pulled in next to him, facing the other way, cop-style, so our windows lined up.

"A question about Maria," I said.

"Yeah."

"She boards horses, which means she knows a lot about them."

"Pretty much of an expert," Diamond said.

"I keep wondering how the wild Mustang named Heat got on the wrong side of the mountains. You think Maria would know about Mustangs?"

"She has a Mustang. Probably knows more about Mustangs than the people who thin the Mustang herds. Lotta brains behind her curves."

"You still tight with her?"

"I am but a moth to Maria's flame." His voice was a touch breathy.

"Love the way you roll the R in her name," I said. I attempted the roll. "Maria." A clear failure. "Maria," I tried again, opening my mouth wide and keeping it wide. It sounded like an infection had swollen my tongue and pushed it back into my throat. "We only just met her that one brief time," I said. "And it's been, what, two months since you disappeared into her charms?"

"You noticed," he said.

"Street did, too."

"Imagine you just met Street," he said.

"So?" I said.

"She was like a flower, like an exotic orchid. You must have felt that. Am I right?"

"Right. I still feel it."

"And when she touched you, it was like electricity on your skin. Like hot salsa on your palette."

"An orchid with electricity and salsa?"

Diamond flicked his hand in the air, dismissing my comment.

"I appreciate the romantic impulse," I said, "but it sounds a little rough, not like something from a guy who reads Shakespeare."

"Actually, I've been reading Byron's Don Juan. Not like I'm any Don Juan. But it makes you think."

"Maria is something, no doubt about it."

He ignored me. "So I imagine spending more time with this woman who seemed to walk out of a dream, and I think that if I could spend just one more day with her, my world would be complete. So then I get the chance. Do I show up alone, with flowers and wine and tall candles and the special hot chili sauce I cooked up especially for this occasion and a CD with her favorite mariachi band?"

"I might be getting the picture..."

"Or," Diamond interrupted, "do I bring along my two best friends and settle for a touch of the toes under the table during dinner, a wink and a blown kiss when other faces happen to look away, a..."

"Please tell me this description will terminate before you get to the color of her bras," I said.

"Peach like the sunset on the Pyramid of the Sun at Teotihuacán, magenta like the bougainvillea on my favorite church wall in Guadalajara, turquoise like the waters of Isla Mujeres off the Yucatán Peninsula."

"Got it. So how 'bout you and Maria come to my cabin, and I'll wait on you. Barbecued ribs, spuds, Caesar salad, and I've got a DK Cellars Petite Sirah that will make you consider bagging your job and going into the winery business."

"Part of your fixation on the new Fair Play appellation?"

"Yeah. Took a few decades for the foothills to become the sudden vino hotspot, but it was worth the wait."

"Let me call Maria and see."

Diamond pulled out his cell, dialed, talked in low tones and murmurs, rolling his Rs, making me feel like I was bereft of romance and feeling and poetry. Maybe I should read Byron.

Diamond hung up, shook his head. "Maria has to be at her place to meet a woman who is coming to pick up her horse. A Tennessee Walker called Captain. Maria says she will probably come tomorrow. But she might come tonight. So we will eat there. And she will serve her most famous dinner."

I waited, did the pantomime give-me-a-little-clue hand motion.

"Maria's Numero Uno Hot Chili Swedish Meatball Tortilla Explosion."

"It sounded like you said Swedish."

"Maria jokes about going to Stockholm and waking up those pasty-faced northerners with her gourmet meals."

"Swedish culinary standards done Mexican-style. Probably be a killer business model," I said.

"Bring Street and his largeness," Diamond said. "Eight o'clock."

I drove the rest of the way up Kingsbury Grade and was up and over Daggett Pass and down into the little farm town of Minden a little before 12:30.

My lunch date walked in a few minutes after me, a smallish woman with short sandy hair but looking imposing in her Douglas

County Sheriff's uniform.

"Tallest guy in the room probably means Owen McKenna," she said.

"Captain," I said, nodding.

"Call me Robyn."

We shook hands, found a table, got our food, chatted about Diamond, then got to business.

"We do our basic investigation," she said, "and find nothing particularly unusual except for a young, healthy guy who, according to people who were familiar with his climbing skills, shouldn't have fallen off Cave Rock. We add up all of our information, and it still spells accident. Then you call and ask after him and seriously upset the status quo. What gives?"

"Eli was a partner of Ryan Lear, a guy who is being harassed by unknown persons."

"You're wondering if someone killed your client's partner as a way to harass him? That's some pretty serious harassment, even for a big metropolis like Douglas County, Nevada." She drank coffee. "What kind of place do you think we run?" She cut off a big corner of ham and ate it.

"Just asking," I said. "You got a technical cause of death?"

"The final decision was cardiac arrest caused by brain damage caused by blunt-force trauma. Typical for a fall like that."

"Any interesting details?"

"I knew you'd ask that. So I took another look at the file before I came here. A whole lot of broken bones, lots of road rash from both the rock he hit just above the tunnel and also from the grill of the truck. The guy was pretty banged up."

"You find anything?"

"Nothing to a casual observer. But for you, I might point out that there was an unusual cut on his right ankle."

"Easy to do falling from the cliff," I said.

"Maybe. Maybe not. This cut went halfway around his ankle. Like he hit a sharp rock as he quickly rotated."

"So maybe it's not easy to do," I said.

"We interviewed several people who saw the fall, including his girlfriend. They all said it was a clean fall until he hit the rock above the tunnel. No spinning."

"What did the cut look like?"

"A relatively clean laceration. Something sharp sliced through the skin to the bone."

"The wound was fresh?"

She nodded.

"Any foreign material in the wound?"

"I'll say. Grit and dirt and grime and some tiny pebble-type rocks. We even found motor oil in the cut. Turns out the truck had a little leak and its fan belt was spraying a fine oil mist as the truck drove. Don't they know that's against the keep-the-lake-blue rules?"

"Got a hypothesis?" I asked.

She shook her head. "I'd guess that he got all the way to the top of the cliff, out of sight from the onlookers. Then he stepped against something sharp. Maybe he was turning as he bumped it. Or maybe it was a scruffy little plant with barbed branches, and he jerked away, and it kind of wrapped around his ankle, and the cut startled him enough that he fell back and off the cliff."

"You looked around at the top of Cave Rock?"

"The next morning, yes. Sergeant Martinez led the crusade. But even his illustriousness couldn't find anything that would make that cut."

We talked about it for another five minutes, and then Captain Bridbury had to go.

"One more quick question," I said. "Anything yet on the remains that Diamond brought back from Genoa Peak?"

"Not much. A fresh fracture of the left humerus."

"Upper arm bone," I said.

"Correct."

"No sign of heeling."

"At the micro level, yes. But nothing to speak of. So the person died within hours of sustaining the injury."

I thanked her and drove back up to Tahoe.

SEVENTEEN

After talking to Captain Bridbury, I drove back up and over Kingsbury Grade. My cell rang as I got to the lake and turned north on 50.

"Owen McKenna," I said.

"Owen! Herman is dead!" Ryan said, panicked.

"Your neighbor, the piano tuner?"

"Yes! I went to his cabin, and he didn't answer, so I looked in the window, and he was lying on the floor under his piano! I went inside - the door was unlocked - and he was dead!"

"Are you sure he's dead? Maybe it's another stroke."

"He's dead. I could tell. But I called nine-one-one, anyway. Then I called you. What should I do now?"

"Nothing. I'll be there in a few minutes."

I pulled into Ryan's road a few minutes later. Two sheriff's vehicles, a fire truck, and an ambulance were already there.

I got out of the Jeep and walked over to where Diamond was pacing near Herman's cabin.

He saw me and started talking as if under steam pressure. "I got here first. I told the young EMS guys that Herman was already cold and flexible, past his rigor. But they pulled out their bags of gear and a defibrillator, anyway. I tried to stop them, but they said they're only following orders, that they have a duty to act."

He continued. "Worst insult in this new world is you die - not from electrical shock or something that temporarily stops your heart - but from something final like disease or old age, and someone makes the mistake of calling nine-one-one, and the boys with the uniforms come and start pumping your dead body full of stimulant drugs, and they put the paddles on your chest and the oxygen mask on your face, and they make like they're going to bring you back to life. Of course they can't do that, but what they can do is cost the county or the family of the deceased a huge amount of money for failing at an unachievable goal.

"The public thinks it's not possible or even right to die anymore without being accompanied by red and blue lights flashing, and sirens ripping out the neighbors' ears, and a dozen so-called authorities making decisions about the most private experience you'll ever have. Is this how ordinary people finally get their fifteen minutes of fame? Gimme back the nineteenth century when a guy could die in peace." Diamond was breathing hard.

"Sorry," I said. "Any idea about the cause of death?"

Diamond shook his head. "No physical trauma that I could see. Could be another stroke. Could be a fall."

"Could be someone came in and pushed him down," I said. "Or scared him and his heart gave out."

Diamond nodded. "Either way, every other hour we get another situation at the Lear household. That kid's the black hole of trouble. No problem can escape his gravity."

"You're right," I said. "But it's not his fault. I'll go see how he's doing. Let me know if I can help. Otherwise, see you tonight at Maria's."

Diamond nodded and turned as the two paramedics came back out of the cabin wearing somber faces. They walked past him and out to the ambulance.

I walked over to Ryan's house, waved at Praeger who was back on duty. The door was unlocked, no chains, security overlooked in the commotion. Ryan was pacing the great room. Lily was sitting next to Spot, petting him, sobbing. I picked her up.

"It's a very sad day for Herman," I said.

She nodded, her face swollen and red, her tears voluminous. She touched my face.

"Why did grandpa Herman die? I asked Ryan, but he doesn't know."

"I don't know either, Lily, but we all eventually die. Maybe it was his turn."

"Life was too short for Herman," she said, sounding three times her age.

"Yes, it was."

She looked at me, her large, black eyes young and innocent. "I don't like it," she said.

"Me neither," I said.

"I don't have any ideas about this," she said, crying harder.

"Me neither."

It was two hours before the officials were through officiating and Herman's body had been taken away. Ryan and Lily had calmed a bit. At one point, both of them sat next to Spot on the rug in the great room.

After a time, Ryan took me aside.

"I don't know what to do," he said. "Lily has never had this experience. When dad died, she was very young. But now she understands, and she's devastated."

"Lily will be okay if you keep her active. Talk to her about Herman. Let her grieve. But take her out and show her that the world is alive. Death is part of life. But you can be alive for her."

"You think it's okay for me to leave with her?"

"Yes. You're in a car, moving, probably unknown to the kidnapper. If you stay in public places where there are lots of people, I think you'll be okay. But if you want, you can take your hired off-duty police guard with you."

"Like a chaperone," Ryan said, his eyes squinting.

"Yeah, I guess," I said.

Ryan looked at me, his jaw muscles bulging. He made a single nod and turned away.

EIGHTEEN

An hour later, at my insistence, Ryan, Lily, Spot and I walked down their drive and up their road to the highway. We crossed Highway 50 toward the mountains, what Hawaiians call the mauka side of the highway. After walking back through the forest, we came to one of the many trails and wandered along toward the south. I showed Lily and Ryan some of the wildflowers that grew in late summer. I made them stop and stick their noses into the furrowed bark of the Jeffrey pine to smell the butterscotch. I pointed out the ubiquitous birds of Tahoe, Mountain chickadees and Steller's jays and crows.

We'd gone maybe half a mile when we saw the man with the red knit cap and the camera, the guy who Street and I had met on horseback, the man who was focused on Heat, the man who, based on being hairless, I'd thought had been undergoing chemo. I felt a greater empathy, now that I knew about Lily.

"Travis Rundell," I said, remembering at the last moment.

He looked at me, frowning, trying to remember.

"Owen McKenna," I said. "My girlfriend and I were on horseback. You were after pictures of the wild Mustang."

"Yes. Of course. Good to see you again. I remember now, because I'd just run into those tourist fellows who were drinking. As luck would have it, I saw the same two guys about a half-hour ago. Drinking as before. Really quite unpleasant."

"Yeah, we saw them that other day, too. Making wisecracks and throwing their empties into the woods."

"Oh, I hate that," Rundell said.

"Get any pictures of the horse since we saw you?"

"Yes!" He was effervescent with excitement. "Yesterday, a person posted on my site about seeing Heat quite a ways south of here, not far from the Round Hill Shopping Center. She said that Heat was running north on one of the trails. So today I went out to hike the area where he might've ended up. And about two hours ago, I saw him about a mile south of here!"

Lily looked up at me, a questioning look on her face.

"This is the man who runs the website about Heat," I told her. I looked at Rundell. "Lily, here, is quite taken with Heat."

He held up his camera. "I got some more pictures. He was quite a distance away, so I won't know if any of them turned out until I download them. But if they're good, I'll put them on the website. They should be up by tomorrow if you want to check."

"You'll do that, won't you?" I said to Lily.

She nodded.

"There's one image I'm excited about," he said. "Just as Heat turned to run, he swiveled and kind of reared up. I have this camera set on triple-shot when I push the shutter button, so I'm hoping one of them will show it. That would be cool."

"Good luck," I said, as we moved on.

He nodded. "Not to be a pain," he said, "but if you go south of here very far, don't take that fork to the east. That's where I saw those guys again. They're quite drunk and aggressive. Looking for a fight, I think. I don't understand why they keep hanging around here. It's like they've taken over the forest and made it very unpleasant for the rest of us."

"Good to know," I said.

We said goodbye, and Rundell continued north.

After a moment, Ryan said, "That guy reminds me of someone. Like I've seen his brother. Maybe we shouldn't go toward those guys he was referring to." His voice had a waver in it, and I realized that he had a visceral reaction that traced back to the bullies of his youth.

"We won't," I said. "There's a place where we can take another trail back."

It was a long route, but no doubt good for both Ryan and Lily. As we came over a rise near the highway, there was a small clearing down below. Two small cars and a large pickup were parked off the highway. A group of five people were clustered around the back of the pickup, drinking beers from a case in the pickup's bed. The pickup was white and looked familiar. I paused.

"Ryan, isn't that Hannah sitting on the tailgate of the pickup? The nanny you fired?"

He looked, squinted his eyes.

"Yeah, that's her."

"That's Hannah?" Lily said in a loud voice.

"Shh," Ryan said.

The group below didn't hear us.

I watched a bit longer. One of the guys, a man with a shaved head, turned to reach for another beer. I realized it was Tory, the nephew of Lana, the young man who showed animosity toward me as he instructed me in how to ride the big horse named Paint.

Tory leaned next to Hannah, whispered something in her ear. The sound of her giggle rose up to us.

There was a split in our trail. We took the fork that led north, away from the little party down below.

NINETEEN

I decided to take a chance, and invited Ryan and Lily to join Street and me for dinner with Diamond and Maria.

"Lily can meet Maria's horses," I said. "One of them is a Mustang."

Ryan looked shocked that I would invite them someplace.

"But they don't know we're coming," he said.

"She'll be glad to have you and Lily," I said, hoping it was true. "But Spot takes up most of the back seat of the Jeep, so you'll have to drive, too."

I put Spot in the Jeep, Ryan put Lily in his SUV, and we drove up to the highway. Just after we'd gotten up to speed, I saw a movement in the forest well back from the east side of the highway, not far from the drive up to Lana and Tory's house and stable.

I pulled over and stopped, got out of the Jeep.

Ryan pulled up behind me. He got out.

"What are you doing?"

I walked over to his SUV, opened the passenger door and reached for Lily's hand.

"I saw something move in the forest. I couldn't see what it was. But we know there's a wild Mustang out there."

Lily's sad eyes got wide.

I waited for the traffic to pass, then trotted with Lily across the road. The bank was steep, so I picked her up and scrambled up to the edge of the forest. Ryan followed.

I stopped, set Lily down and put my fingers to my lips. We stood near a large pine and peered around the tree trunk.

The forest of summer evening was mostly in shadows. Nothing moved. Maybe whatever I'd seen decided to leave after it watched us run toward it from the cars.

Or maybe, it was standing motionless, making itself invisible to humans. Our eyesight is stellar compared to many animals, but only if the light is bright. I saw nothing but dark trees and bushes and boulders.

We waited. Lily got restless. I decided to give up. But first it made sense to walk farther into the forest just to be sure.

I took Lily's hand again. We'd moved only eight or ten yards when we saw through to a distant open area where the lowering sun streamed in through the trees. There, in the blaze of golden sunlight, stood a horse, its head high, its mane ruffling in the breeze.

I picked Lily up and pointed to be sure she saw it.

"Heat!" she said in a loud, excited whisper.

The horse nodded its head twice, then turned and vanished into the forest.

We all stopped at Street's lab at the bottom of Kingsbury Grade. Street seemed delighted to see Lily and Ryan, and she gave them the quickie tour, skipping over some of her grosser bug stuff. Then we piled back into the cars, went up and over the summit, and dropped down 3000 feet to Carson Valley. Spot had his head out the right rear window, eager to catalog every smell as the cool, pine-scented air of evening in the mountains was replaced by the warm, verdant, ranch smells of the valley. The cattle of late summer were numerous and heavy, all of them with their mouths to the ground, living up to their rep as world-class eating machines. They were predominantly black with a few of the Oreo-cookie, white-band-around-the-middle type thrown in for variety.

We followed the back roads through hay country, past the towns of Minden and Gardnerville and Dresslerville, where Ryan grew up with many of the Washoe Tribe, then headed into desert lands as we made the gentle climb up the east side of the valley. At one point, I saw a white pickup following well back behind us. It looked similar to a truck that had followed us down Kingsbury Grade. When we turned from the gravel road off onto a dirt road and then into Maria's two-rut drive, the white pickup was not in sight.

Maria's old, single-wide trailer home sat at the crest of a patch of dry, sloping ranchland surrounded by desert dotted with sagebrush. I saw no evidence of an irrigation system, yet her land had grass - albeit dried to a mat of brown - and the nearby land didn't, so the lay of the land must funnel the rare rains her way.

We pulled up and parked between the Green Flame - Diamond's hot-lime Karmann Ghia that he'd been given after I managed to get his Orange Flame blown to pieces - and Maria's camo-rusted, ancient Dodge pickup, the one I'd borrowed in June to help hide the TV talk show lady from the men who were trying to kill her.

Stretching down below Maria's trailer was her ranch, five acres divided by a grid of fencing that was arranged around a small modern barn. The design allowed her to use the various fenced areas as paddocks for the horses. In one fenced area near us was a big black horse, his head over the fence, ears forward, curious about visitors. Behind him in the next paddock over, was a pair, one light tan with a dark brown mane, and the other a mix of brown and white. An unseen horse neighed from the barn. It was obvious that Maria's heart, like her investment dollars, were in the horse accommodations, not the accommodations for people.

Below Maria's fencing, the open desert stretched off toward the ranches and housing developments of Carson Valley and ended with the backdrop of the Carson Range, the 10,000-foot mountains that comprise the south and east sides of Lake Tahoe and are geologically distinct from the shorter but more-jagged mountains of the Sierra Crest that line Tahoe's West Shore.

I let Spot out of the Jeep, and he loped off toward the large black horse. The horse apparently had no fear of the largest of dogs, and he stretched his head out toward Spot.

Street took Lily's hand. Lily's sadness appeared to evaporate in the thick excitement of horses up close.

"Is this a ranch?" Lily asked.

"Yes," Street said. "I bet Maria will show you the horses."

"Do you want to pet the horse?" I asked Lily.

She nodded with vigor.

I picked her up and held her so she could reach his forehead. Her response was the same as when she met Spot. No fear. Natural trust. She reached out her tiny hand and gave the horse the softest, gentlest caress he'd ever had.

Spot reached up his nose to sniff the horse's nose, but stayed interested only for a moment. Then he turned and began to explore as if he'd lived with horses all his life.

I set Lily down and went to fetch a bottle of wine out of the back of the Jeep. Street brought Lily. Ryan kept his distance behind. As we knocked at the thin door, the flimsy trailer wall rattled with the knock.

Maria opened the door. Although Diamond lent me her pickup two months before, we'd only recently met. I remembered her huge, bright smile beneath dark eyes and black eyebrows and blacker hair that curved around her head in a voluptuous swirl.

"Owen and Street! I'm so glad to see you again!" She gave Street a big hug, engulfing Street's thin body with her own, meatier form. "And Owen!" she said turning to me and reaching up. "Praise Mother Mary, you are still as tall as when I met you two weeks ago!"

I bent down and she locked her arms around my neck as if she were saying hello to a long-lost friend.

"And who are these two delightful people?" she said as if nothing could be better than uninvited guests.

"Maria, this is Lily," I said. "Lily, Maria."

Maria bent down as if to pick Lily up or give her a big hug. But Lily put out her hand.

"Well, hello, Lily," Maria said. She shook the little hand. "I'm so glad to meet you."

"The pleasure is all mine," Lily said.

Maria turned to Ryan, who was air-washing his hands at high speed.

I introduced them.

Ryan made a little wave and a nod, but stayed back.

Maria was smooth. If she realized who Ryan and Lily were from things Diamond had said, she didn't show it. "You must come in. Welcome to the castle of the Ponderosa Pomposo!"

We went through the narrow doorway one at a time, Street leading, holding Lily by the hand, me ducking to remain attached to my head, and Ryan following.

The air inside was filled with a luscious mix of cooking smells.

"Of course you know this handsome gentleman," Maria gestured toward Diamond who was folding a newspaper as he stood up from a tattered built-in couch at the end of the eight-foot-wide room that comprised the kitchen, dining, and living area of the trailer, a room that was about the size of the bathroom in Ryan's master suite. "I found him hanging around my back porch, so I gave him a saucer of warm milk. Now he won't leave me alone."

Diamond nodded at us. He didn't look pleased to see extra guests.

"Señor Martinez," Maria said. "Perhaps you could serve libations."

"You want a starter beer?" he said. "Or do we go straight to margaritas?"

I chose the beer. Street said she'd hold for a bit.

"Ryan?" Diamond said.

"Um, sure. A beer would be okay."

Diamond opened Tecates for Maria and me and Ryan and himself and a soda for Lily. We all toasted. Ryan lurked by the door.

Maria set out bowls of chips and salsa and bean dip.

We chatted about cooking and her ranch and, at Street's and my insistence, Maria told us of her long journey, from life as a young, uneducated Mayan girl working on a coffee farm in the Mexican state of Chiapas near the border of Guatemala, to working as a waitress in Carson City. She scraped pennies for two decades, and eventually bought the five-acre scrap that no one believed was good for anything. But she anticipated the growth of Carson Valley and knew it would make a good horse-boarding ranch.

And, at Maria's insistence, Street told of her journey as a 14-year-old runaway from a disastrous childhood in Missouri, and how she worked her way through school, culminating in a Ph.D. in Entomology from UC Berkeley.

Then both Maria and Street proclaimed great embarrassment as Diamond and I counted up the parallels of two young women on their own, without support, making a place in the world starting out with no tools or skills, only astonishing determination, common sense, and intelligence.

"We can change the subject now, sí?" Maria's eyes flashed like black flames.

"Sure," Diamond said.

Marie turned to me. "Diamond said you have seen a horse in the woods."

At that came a woof at the door. Maria opened it and invited Spot in, hugging and kissing him. It took several minutes before we got Maria and Spot separated, with Spot settled in a big curve on the living room rug. Lily sat on the floor and leaned on Spot. Ryan stayed standing, obviously uncomfortable with the close surroundings. With Spot taking up most of the floor space, we completely filled the tiny trailer. I restarted the conversation.

"There is a horse that's been sighted in Tahoe's forests. He's running free. Ryan has seen him before. Lily and I just got our first glimpse of him an hour ago, but others have seen him more often. People claim he's a wild Mustang."

"Up in Tahoe?" Maria started to shake her head, then stopped. "What does he look like?"

"We only saw him from a distance, and it was getting dark, but my first impression was that he seemed strong and agile. And a little smaller than some horses."

"How small? Like a pony?"

I stood up, bending my neck a little to avoid hitting my head on the trailer ceiling, trying to visualize. I put my hands out in front of my face. "Your big black horse out by the barn," I said. "He's about this high."

"Sí. His name is Captain. He belongs to Laura Danner. She's an airline pilot based in San Francisco, but she has a home in Carson Valley. She's gone a lot, so she boards him here." She paused. "Do you know the gaited breeds?"

"All I know about horses is that they are beautiful and they run fast."

"Ah. You have perfectly described the most wonderful animals on the planet. Captain is a Tennessee Walking Horse, what we call one of the gaited breeds. It is a name we give to horses with a particularly comfortable gait. He can do a running walk, one foot always on the ground, so smooth it's a dream. You can ride a gaited horse all day long."

"What is a breed called if it isn't gaited?"

"They are the trotting horses. Good for all of the wonderful things that horses can do. But smooth? No. It's amazing how Captain..." Maria caught herself and stopped. "Sorry. Captain and me, I'm... Enamorado. Anyway, you were saying?"

"I think Captain's eyes would be about even with mine."

"Yes, when he holds his head up high and proud. He's a tall boy, sixteen hands."

"But Heat's eyes would be down here."

"Heat?" Maria said.

"Glennie Gorman, the local reporter," Diamond said. "She named him Heat because he likes to stand in the sun. A guy on the East Shore put up a website about Heat. Glennie has been posting updates about Heat sightings on the site."

Maria nodded. "A horse named Heat. I like it. So Heat is about fourteen hands," Maria said. "What else does he look like?"

"I don't have a horse vocabulary, but I would say his conformation is a little stocky. Not real thin."

"Not like a Thoroughbred," Maria said.

"The race horses," I said.

"Sí. Race horses were bred for speed. That's why they have those long, thin legs and big strong hindquarters."

"Heat looks strong," I said, "but he seems all about function. Like if he fell, he'd just get back up. He wouldn't break a leg just by running too hard."

"Sounds like a Mustang. They are very stout. Strong hooves, teeth, good coat. The opposite of delicate. They can survive and thrive where fancier horses would never make it. They can also go places that would make other horses crazy. Climb trails up steep rocks that I could never scramble up on all fours. I have a Mustang. You want to meet her?"

We all nodded and followed Maria outside.

"You think Heat is a stallion, a gelding, or a mare?" Maria asked as we walked down toward the barn.

"I wouldn't know without seeing him up close. Is there a way to tell from a distance?"

"Attitude. Horses are like people. The boys think they're important. The girls tend to be kinder. The geldings are boys who have been castrated. Take away the sex, you get much less attitude. That's why people like geldings so much."

Diamond was walking on the other side of Maria. His frown was significant.

"Then I'd guess that this guy's a gelding," I said. "But Mustangs are wild, so gelding isn't a choice, correct?"

"If he's really wild, it wouldn't be."

"And if he's a stallion, he'd be, what? Acting out more?" I said.

"Male horses get real focused on hierarchy. The stallion in charge gets all the girls in the area, his own harem, and the other stallions have to keep their distance."

"I don't like it when the toughest guy gets the girl," Diamond said. "Girls should have more sense."

"They don't have a choice. And it's not always the toughest physically who are in charge. It's the one with the most attitude. Sometimes the stallions don't even fight over the girls. They just have shouting matches."

"You mean the males whinny at each other?" Street said.

"Sí. They squeal. The one who squeals the loudest and longest often wins the contest."

Street, giggling, looked first at me, then at Diamond. "That's rich," she said, laughing some more.

I looked at Diamond. "Laughing at our expense," I said. "I don't squeal. Do you?"

"Never squeal," Diamond said, shaking his head.

Lily swung her head back and forth from me to Diamond to me. Ryan stayed behind us.

"It's pretty silly to watch," Maria said. "But the shouting contests save horses from getting injured or even killed, so it kind of makes sense. The horse who wins the shouting match gets the girls."

Diamond was shaking his head. "Why do you say the girls don't have a choice?"

"Because it's forced servitude. The stallion is, how do I put this politely, uncomfortably demanding. The girls have to submit. But this social hierarchy of horses may explain why horses have developed such a close relationship with people." She turned to Street. "I'm sorry, my English is still not all the way there. You are a scientist. What is it when two different kinds of animals benefit from each other?"

"Symbiosis," Street said. "A symbiotic relationship."

"Yes. That is people and horses. Like people and dogs. When people are in control, horses have to serve their needs and can no longer run free. But then the horses eat better, get water easily, live more comfortable lives, and they don't have to fight off predators or even each other."

"Most herd animals just run from predators, right?" I said.

"True. But with horses, the stallion's job is to protect the mares and the foals. If a predator comes near, look out. You've heard the ancient legends about putting a tiger in the ring to fight a stallion and getting stomped to death by the stallion? They can kick from behind and stomp from the front. A horse is an amazing fighter."

Maria walked up to Captain, who was still reaching over the fence. She put her cheek against his forehead and hugged his head, her arms reaching up, hands clasping over his neck just behind his ears.

She let go of Captain's head and turned toward the barn.

"Back to Heat," I said. "You said that Heat wouldn't be a gelding if he were in the wild. You think he's domesticated?"

"Heat could be a runaway from some horse owner in Tahoe. Then Heat would likely be a gelding or a mare. For years there have been problems with too many wild horses. So both the people who don't like Mustangs and the people who love Mustangs have a desire to thin the wild population. The main way is adoption programs. We have one here at the Carson City Prison. They catch the excess Mustangs and bring them to the prison. The prisoners take care of them, give them a good diet, gentle them, and, when they're ready, the Mustangs are put up for adoption."

"Gentle means break them?" Diamond said.

"In the training sense, yes, but gentling a horse is a different mindset than breaking a horse. Better for the horse. Kinder. After one hundred twenty days, they are put up for auction."

I saw where she was going. "And adopted Mustangs, like all horses, sometimes get out of their pastures."

"Sí. When that happens with most horses, you find them and bring them back home."

"But the Mustangs are still mostly wild and they know how to care for themselves," I said.

Maria nodded vigorously. "Exactly. They want to go back to the wild herd, back to their home."

"Do they ever succeed?" Street asked.

"Sometimes. Especially if their new owners live close to the wilds of Nevada. But not if their new owner took them to Tahoe, and they escaped their paddock and are stuck on the wrong side of those mountains." She turned and pointed across the valley to the wall of the Carson Range. "They would be in an unfamiliar forest, without grazing lands other than the rare meadow. Their only hope would be if their new owners found them." Maria went over to the barn and walked in through the open breezeway. We five followed into the dark interior.

A horse neighed from inside one of the stalls.

"Come meet Mandy," Maria said, flipping on the light. "She's my little Mustang sweetheart."

A small horse had its head out, sniffing Maria's jacket, pushing at Maria with her nose.

Maria produced a carrot. Mandy nibbled it out of her hand, chewed it fast, nuzzled Maria for more. As the rest of us walked up, Mandy reached out and nuzzled each of us in turn.

"Lily?" Maria said. "Would you like to feed Mandy a carrot?"

Lily nodded and got so excited that she started bouncing. Maria handed her a carrot. Unlike adults, it didn't even occur to her to ask how to feed the horse. She just walked up, held the carrot up high and Mandy nibbled it out of her hand.

Spot got into the act, and he and Mandy bumped noses. Then, as with Captain, Spot turned and explored the barn.

"Look," Maria said, noticing Spot's behavior as well. "I've seen this many times. Dogs interact with most animals in terms of play, or a chase, or as rivals. They tree bears and mountain lions and chase house cats and herd sheep and kill rodents and play with other dogs and will run deer for miles. Huge animals like cattle and elk and even moose will run from dogs. But not horses. Even wolves will usually stay away from horses. It's just too much trouble to fight the stallion. But dogs are curiously indifferent to horses. I think it's because they sense that horses are not impressed with them. Horses know they are largely untouchable, except by people and other horses, so they don't care very much about what other animals do." Maria grinned at us. "The one exception is amusing. When Mandy sees a coyote, she lowers her head and chases it away."

I reached out to touch Mandy. She was dark brown and, though small, looked very strong. She had an unusual marking on the left side of her neck. Maria saw me touch it.

"It's a BLM freeze brand. The various marks are lines and right-angles turned in different directions indicating numbers. Mandy's number indicates the year of her birth and that she came from Nevada."

"How many other states have wild horses?" Street asked.

"A surprising number. If you draw a north/south line from Montana down to New Mexico, Mustangs are found nearly everywhere to the west. Even in Southern California and up into Oregon. And back east there are also pockets of wild horses, such as the famous herds on the barrier islands from Georgia up to Maryland. The eastern mustangs trace back to early settlers, and, some say, from shipwrecks hundreds of years ago."

"Any wild horses near here?" I asked.

"Just out here, on the ridge behind my trailer, I saw a herd of eight Mustangs. There are herds near Virginia City, herds just north in Washoe Valley. When you drive to Reno, always look to the east. You may see the Mustangs drinking out of Washoe Lake. These western Mustangs go back to horses that escaped from the settlers who migrated west. And the first of those was Cortez."

Maria broke another carrot into thirds so that Lily could feed Mandy more pieces, which the horse nibbled out of Lily's hands with her big soft lips. Then Maria took us back to her trailer for dinner.

While Diamond worked a blender, mixing up margaritas and pouring them into champagne glasses rimmed with salt, Maria served dinner on huge square plates, each a different, brilliant color. Our food lay on over-sized tortillas, cherry tomatoes cut in half, spinach, refried beans, shredded cheddar cheese and, in the center, a pyramid of Swedish meatballs on top of salsa, and a dollop of sour cream on top of that. We all ate with our plates in our laps, except for Ryan who stood and held his plate.

The Swedish meatballs were fire-hot, a taste explosion so powerful that Sweden's favorite pyromaniac homeboy, Alfred Nobel, might have altered his formula for dynamite had he first sampled Maria's recipe.

"You mentioned Cortez," Street said. "Tell us about him." Street was nibbling at her meal, while Maria ate with a hearty appetite and Diamond and I did our best imitation of steam shovels. Both Lily and Ryan appeared to be put off by the fire in the meatballs.

"Cortez's history is kind of a horse history, so I actually know a bit about it. As you probably know, after Columbus, Cortez was the big cheese of Spanish outreach to the New World. Of course, Columbus thought he'd come to the East Indies of the Old World, near Asia. So he called the native people Indians. My people are still called Indians, all because Columbus made a twelve-thousand-mile mistake."

At Maria's mention of her Indian heritage, Ryan looked up.

"Anyway," Maria continued, "Columbus had brought horses to the Caribbean islands. But first I should back up." Maria popped another Swedish ball of fire into her mouth, followed it with spinach and sour cream to dampen the flames and Margarita to put it dead out.

"What is ironic," she said, "is that horses actually evolved here in North America millions of years ago. From here, they traveled over the Alaska land bridge to Asia and spread throughout the world. But then climate changes in the Americas put a great deal of stress on horses, and they began to die off on our continents. Then this pesky new guy on the block called Man started hunting horses for food. This was around the same time that people killed off the last of America's wooly mammoths. And it wasn't just here. Mankind decimated horse populations all over the world. And just as they'd done with the mammoths, people eventually managed to kill off the last of the horses in the Americas."

Maria glanced out the small living room window. In the paddock light stood Captain, his black mane flowing in the breeze as if he were starring in a Disney movie.

Maria continued. "The problems for horses were so severe that the only horses left in the world were just a few small herds in central Asia near the Black Sea. This was about six thousand years ago, around the time that the Sumerians were building the first major civilization in Babylon, which is now Iraq."

Diamond caught my eye and smiled.

I nodded.

In my peripheral vision, I could tell that Ryan watched all of us carefully.

"So anyway," Maria continued, "no one knows exactly what happened, but for some reason the people with the last horses decided not to eat them all. And in the process, they discovered that horses were good for other things. Riding, pulling plows, fighting wars, all that good stuff. So they took care of the last horses, fed them, and helped them breed. Men went from being horses' worst nightmare to their best buds. With the help of the people who nearly killed them all off, horses began to thrive."

"But there still weren't any horses in North or South America," Street said.

"Right," Maria said. "Which brings us to a guy named Hernando."

"Hernando Cortez," Diamond said.

Maria grinned. "Columbus had done his thing for Spain and they knew about all of these islands in the Caribbean, and they'd also visited what is now Central America. But they didn't discover what we call Mexico until fifteen-seventeen. So Cortez decided in fifteen-nineteen that he would take on Mexico with a little over 500 men and about eighteen horses."

"Not much of an army," Street said.

"No. And much of Mexico was run by Montezuma, ruler of the Aztecs, who were fierce warriors. Not only that, the Aztec numbered over two hundred thousand people."

"You'd think that Cortez wouldn't have a chance," I said.

"Sí. A tiny help for him was that when he landed, he found a small tribe of people who were enemies of the Aztecs. He managed to get them to join his men, giving him something like a thousand or twelve hundred men."

"To take on hundreds of thousands of Aztecs," I said.

Maria nodded. "It was crazy. But what happened was that Cortez ran them over, captured Montezuma, and brought down the greatest empire that had ever existed in the Americas."

"With a tiny group," Diamond said. "How could it happen?"

"It was the horses," Maria said.

I felt a collective chill go through our group.

"But even though horses can do a lot for warring men, you said there were only eighteen of them," Diamond said. "What can eighteen horses do against a huge population?"

"It wasn't what they did," Maria said. "It was what they represented." She took a sip of margarita. "Before I go any further, I should point out that we don't really know exactly what happened, and scholars disagree over the fine points. But here's the basics.

"The Aztecs worshiped a light-skinned god named Quetzalcoatl. When Cortez showed up, he was quite light-skinned. There is some scholarly opinion that the Aztecs thought he was their god, and they were unwilling to fight him."

Diamond spoke up. "But even though he was light-skinned, if he came with ill will and not in peace, why would they think he was their god?"

"Well, he was a bit nuts, and acting crazy probably helped his case. But the main reason that scholars put forth for Cortez's success is that he had horses. The Aztecs had never seen horses. So when Cortez and his men - all wearing funny clothes - came charging up on top of these huge, racing animals, it was beyond astonishing. It was as if the deity had arrived. And it was that awe that allowed Cortez to literally ride all all over the Aztecs, and eventually bring the Aztec Empire to an end. The great Aztec city of Tenochtitlán was destroyed. Never again would Native Americans rule any part of their homelands."

We were all silent for a minute.

Eventually, Maria spoke. "The Spanish built Mexico City on the ruins of Tenochtitlán."

"And this was all possible because of the magic and power of eighteen horses," I said.

"Probably," Maria said. She looked out the window. Captain appeared to be looking in at all of us.

"So horses periodically escaped Cortez," Street said. "And some escaped now and then from all of the people who subsequently raised horses. And the descendents of those escapees are the Mustangs."

"Sí. Other Europeans also brought many horses over during the next few centuries. And their various stocks also contributed to our Mustang populations." She looked back out toward the barn. "But it is indeed possible that some of Mandy's DNA came from a horse that rode with Cortez's men."

After dinner, Maria took Lily and Spot outside, and showed Lily how to toss leftover meatballs high into the air. They shrieked at Spot's ability to catch them with only the paddock light for illumination. Other than a little extra tongue and jaw movement, he showed no reaction to the fire in his mouth. After Lily fed him the last meatball, he pressed her for more, staring at her, and wagging hard.

An hour later we thanked Maria. As Street and Lily had a few last words with Maria, Diamond, Ryan and I walked out to Captain's fence and pet him while we stood under the spectacular, star-filled desert sky.

"You're right," I said. "An orchid with hot salsa. Seems like a keeper to me."

Diamond raised two crossed fingers.

TWENTY

The next morning, Street had to leave early. A white pickup arrived at 9:30 a.m. There was a magnetic sign stuck to its door. It said, Image And Sound Security. I looked at Ryan.

"Motion lights?"

"And webcams. Anyone comes near the house again, the lights go on, and their picture is recorded and transmitted to the company."

"Good idea."

Three workmen filled the house and grounds with equipment and wiring and tools.

I asked Ryan if he minded me looking around Herman's cabin.

"No, of course not. There's nothing really to see except how messy he was. Ryan looked away. "It's very upsetting to have Herman die so suddenly. I can't help thinking that someone caused his death."

"Diamond said it looked natural."

"Right," Ryan said. He walked over and opened a kitchen drawer. He pulled out a key and brought it to me. The key fob was shaped like a tiny wrench with a big round handle, presumably a miniature of something a piano tuner would use.

"I don't think Herman ever locked his door, whether at night when he was sleeping or during the day when he was often gone. He grew up back when Tahoe was just a few people who came during the summer. He once told me he never heard of a burglary in Tahoe until he was in his thirties." Ryan looked at me with a furrowed brow. "Maybe you think it's part of my paranoia, always locking the door and putting on the chains." He was talking in a loud voice. "But I always think that if there's no downside to an action, and there's a large potential upside, then..."

I held up my hand to interrupt. "It's okay, Ryan. I'm with you. In fact, you would be hard-pressed to find a cop who leaves his doors unlocked. Many people like the carefree feeling that their neighborhood is perfectly safe, but cops see what actually happens. They have no illusions."

I held up the key, nodded at him and said, "I'll go take a look."

I checked the family room. Spot was sprawled on the floor, his head on Lily's lap. She had a book resting on his head while she read it.

I let myself out. Officer Vistamon was back on duty. He was in his dress blues, standing next to his Toyota, leaning against the hood. I waved and walked across to the old cabin. Herman's homestead was probably built back in the early 1900s. Compared to my little log cabin, it was a grand lodge. I stepped up onto the broad deck that had a large, sloppy pile of split wood on one side and on the other side a row of rustic Adirondack-style furniture near the chairlift seat.

I put the key into an old lock and let myself in through a heavy plank door in the center of the wide front wall.

There was no entry area inside. The front door opened onto a large room that stretched the 40-foot width of the cabin. Directly opposite the door was a huge cobblestone fireplace with a large beam mantle five feet above the stone hearth. There was a braided rug in front of the fireplace. An old stuffed couch sat in front of the rug with a big leather chair on each side. Between the chairs and couch were end tables covered in books, everything from old dusty hardbounds to new, brightly-colored paperbacks.

To the right of the room was the dining area with a heavy wooden table no doubt built in the same era as the cabin and large enough to seat ten people. On the far end of the table sat a TV. The rest of the table was covered with stacks of paper, old bills, a ceramic pot with the withered remains of a plant that must have died months before but never got thrown out. Not even a solo diner could find room to set a plate of food without sweeping papers to the side.

Behind the dining area, to the right rear of the cabin, was the kitchen, largely out of my line of vision from the front door.

It was the left portion of the living room that upstaged the rest. Framed by large windows made up of dozens of small panes, and well-lit by the sunlight that cascaded in, was a huge, black grand piano. It had the Steinway logo above the keys.

I walked over and sat down on the black, upholstered seat.

I didn't know anything about pianos, but it looked like a model from recent decades, with clean modern lines, a perfect matte black finish, and none of the filigree I'd seen on pianos from a hundred years ago.

The Steinway lid was up at a steep angle, exposing the brassy metal framework that supported the strings and the golden wood beneath them. On the music support stand were spiral notebooks. To one side was some sheet music with three bent sheets and dog-eared corners.

I opened the notebooks. They were logbooks of pianos tuned, with dates and names and addresses. Next to each entry were brief notes. 'Replaced broken string on A6. Adjusted action, especially key dip, hammer height, and the let-off.' The handwriting was barely legible.

I leafed through the sheet music. Jazz standards from the 1930s and '40s. Ellington, Porter, Carmichael. Under the sheet music was an assortment of pocket detritus. Paper clips, a bent toothpick, a quarter and seven pennies.

On the floor beneath the piano were piles of books and magazines and other household stuff. A framed certificate of appreciation that wasn't appreciated enough to get hung on a wall, but was too nice an accolade to toss into the garbage. Two pairs of shoes. Cross-country ski boots. A stack of Sunday papers.

A large, red, metal toolbox that showed the dents and scrapes of many decades sat on the floor next to the piano bench. Its top was open.

Herman's tuning tools were out. A wrench very much like the miniature key fob sat on the top of the piano. A long strip of red felt lay draped over the toolbox. Nearby were several black rubber wedges with wire handles coming out of their blunt ends.

The keyboard cover was up, showing the beautiful keys, white and black in that fantastic, iconic repeating pattern.

I knew little about music except the names of the main notes. I struck middle C and immediately noticed that it didn't seem right. It throbbed in a pulsing way that was uncomfortable to listen to. I went up the scale, hitting the white keys, stopping at the next C. All of the notes seemed out of tune to my ears. They all made the pulsing sensation, some even worse than the others. The piano tuner's piano sounded out of tune.

Ryan said that Herman had a stroke in the previous weeks. Had he tuned the piano post-stroke only to discover that he no longer was able to tune? I'd never known a piano tuner, but I imagined that they took the same pride in their work as any artisan. I couldn't picture a tuner purposely mistreating a piano. The only explanation that made sense was that the stroke had caused Herman to lose his faculties.

Still, the idea bothered me. Ryan's comments about Herman being able to understand speech, to cook for himself, wash his clothes and do other common household activities didn't fit with a person losing the activity most intrinsic to their sense of identity, their life-long work.

Before I left, I wandered the rest of the cabin. There were two bedrooms behind and to the left of the fireplace. It was clear that Herman slept in one and stored more stuff in the other. Nothing about them seemed notable.

I walked out into the living room, around through the dining room and back into the kitchen, the only room I hadn't seen.

It was unremarkable, with old appliances, old fixtures, a single bare bulb hanging from the center of the ceiling. I opened a few cupboards and drawers, looking for nothing in particular, and finding the same.

I opened the back door and looked out onto a patio of sorts, created by an indented corner in the log cabin's design. The patio was private. Herman could sit here and not be seen from the neighbors or the road or even the construction site.

Something bothered me, and I tried to figure out what it was. Then I remembered that Ryan had talked about how Herman never locked his door.

It would be easy for someone to walk up to this private patio and let himself into Herman's cabin. No one would see him.

If the person came unannounced and uninvited, Herman would be helpless. The intruder could sit inside Herman's living room and look into Ryan's windows, watch as people came and went, observe their habits.

If Herman had been tuning his piano when the intruder entered, the intruder could tell Herman to continue, which would provide cover. When the intruder was done with his spying or whatever he was doing, he would no longer need Herman's tuning as cover. He could stand him up and push him down. Hit his head on the floor. Or maybe just scare him enough to trigger a heart attack.

I found Ryan outside among the piles of construction materials, walking along and looking down into trenches where the rebar network for the footings awaited another concrete pour. Even though he was in full view of the off-duty cop, he kept stopping to look around as if to see if any stranger was near. It was sad to see such a successful young man so consumed with worry and fear. He saw me and brightened.

"Learn anything?"

"Yeah. If Herman retained most of his abilities after he had his stroke, then why would he mis-tune his piano?"

"What do you mean?"

"I played a few notes. They seem out of tune."

"I doubt that," Ryan said. "Herman was fixated on keeping his piano in tune. He tuned it every week. He played hymns every Sunday. A well-tuned piano was important to him. Anyway, how can you tell if it is out of tune? Are you a musician?"

"No. Even so, I believe Herman's piano is not what it should be. We heard him tuning it when we went for our walk with Spot and Lily. Yet even I can tell that it's out of tune."

Ryan shook his head. "That makes no sense at all."

"I only saw sheet music for jazz standards. But you say that Herman played hymns?"

"He didn't need sheet music for hymns. He was raised on hymns. Knew them all. And he played them in a black Southern Baptist gospel style. This end of the lake really rocked on Sundays. Lily called it God rock."

"He must have died during that last tuning," I said.

"After," Ryan said. "I've watched him several times. There was a regular process he followed. I could tell by the look of his tools that he had finished the last tune."

"How?"

"The felt was out."

"What does that mean?"

"As he would begin tuning, he'd sit at the bench and unroll the strip of felt. He shaped it into loops and pushed the loops down between the strings. If he'd died during the tune, the felt would have still been rolled, or partially inserted in the strings. Once the felt was in place, he would tune the entire piano before he would remove it, bit by bit as he tuned the last of the strings. When I found him, the felt was out, draped over his toolbox. Once the felt was pulled out, the tuning was done. So I'd like to hear what you mean when you say that the piano is out of tune."

We walked up to Herman's cabin. Ryan walked straight to the piano and played a 3-note chord and winced.

"That's not in tune!" He played the chord again, then played a different chord. "I can't believe it. I've never heard his piano ever sound anything but perfect. Herman was really smart. And except for losing his speech after his stroke, he didn't seem much different. So it doesn't make sense."

Ryan frowned. "The thing is, I'm sure he tuned it the week before, and that was post-stroke. If it had been really out of tune like this, we would have noticed when he played his God rock."

"I'd like to bring another piano tuner in to have a look," I said.

"For what purpose?"

"I don't know. Perhaps another tuner can learn something about Herman's last tune. If there's no downside to an action, and there's a large potential upside..."

Ryan made a little grin that quickly faded. "Be my guest."

TWENTY-ONE

I called tuners out of the Yellow Pages and found one in Reno who could come up the next day at ten a.m.

That morning, Ryan had work to do, and Street had a meeting, so I volunteered to be in charge of Lily. After breakfast, Spot and Lily and I went for a walk. We ambled out the drive and down the neighborhood road that paralleled the highway above us. Lily talked about Herman and asked most of the big and small questions about life and death. Her tone wasn't maudlin. She didn't seem to be referencing her own sickness. She just abounded with the curiosity of a child.

Why don't people live forever? Is there a god? What is cremation? Why do we have funerals? Are angels boys or girls? Can dogs smell ghosts? Can Herman hear us talking about him? What does it feel like to be buried in the ground? Can you tell when you're going to die? When we die, is it forever?

I fumbled answers for a couple of her questions and I'm-not-sures for most of them. After a good distance we turned around.

It was getting close to ten o'clock. The tuner was due, so we headed back.

I used the key Ryan had given me and unlocked Herman's door as a 20-year-old Buick, shiny clean despite its sun-damaged blue paint, turned off the street and came down the drive. The driver parked, and turned off the engine.

"Is that the piano tuner?" Lily asked.

"I think so."

The driver's door opened. The man leaned his head out and looked at the ground for a moment. Then he stepped a highly-polished brown wingtip out onto the ground, moving slowly so as not to kick up any dust. He got out of the car and glanced down to be certain that his brown trousers were hanging just so, the creases straight and true. His movements were so precise that they seemed choreographed. He moved like a mime, as if his car didn't exist except in the viewer's imagination.

The man had dark-brown hair the same color as his wingtips. It was medium length, parted down the middle, and was so shiny with hair cream that it sparkled in the sunlight. A small handle-bar moustache featured the same treatment. His long-sleeved shirt was white and stiff as if it had been starched. Over the shirt was a tailored vest, wingtip brown. A gold chain arced from a gold clip into a vest pocket that probably boasted a gold pocket watch.

I stepped off the porch to greet him. Spot jumped off with me and trotted up to the man.

The man froze.

"It's okay," I said. "He's friendly."

"The last time someone told me that, I needed six stitches to close the wound to my arm." He spoke through clenched teeth, like a robot, careful not to even twitch as Spot sniffed him. Spot's tail wagged slowly, like a windshield wiper on one notch of delay.

"But I'm telling the truth. Spot, sit."

Spot turned and looked at me, then turned back to the man and resumed sniffing. His nose was at the base of the man's throat. The man's eyes were white.

"I'm sorry," I said. "Spot, sit," I said again, this time touching Spot on his back. He sat. "My apologies."

The man still stared at Spot as if Spot were waiting for me to avert my eyes so that he could have breakfast.

I held out my hand. "Really," I said. "He's friendly."

He shook my hand, his hand and arm rigid as if he were made of wood and had stiff joints.

"Martin Wellsley," he said.

"Owen McKenna. This is Spot. Up on the deck is Lily."

Wellsley glanced at Lily, then turned back to Spot.

Spot turned to look at me. He was panting in the sun. Little drops of saliva flipped off the tip of his tongue.

One of them hit Wellsley's pants near the waistband. He flinched as if he'd been slapped. The glistening tips of his moustache shook.

"Tell you what," I said. "Spot will stay outside with Lily, while you and I go inside."

"That would be good," Wellsley said. "Let me get my tools." He turned and opened his car trunk. Inside was a large tool box, which he lifted out using both hands.

I brought him up to the front deck of the cabin. Spot ran over to where Lily sat on the chairlift seat, her feet swinging in the air eight inches above the decking.

"Officer Lily," I said in an important voice, "I'm taking Wellsley below decks for an equipment inspection. You and your trusty hound are to stay on the bridge and keep an eye out for pirates. Do I make myself clear?"

Her response was a mischievous grin and devious eyes.

"Lily, the proper response is, 'Yes, sir.'"

"Yes, sir!" she shouted.

I saluted her, then led Wellsley into the cabin.

"I was a bit confused on the phone," Wellsley said. "You'd like me to tune a piano, correct?"

"No. Your confusion is understandable. I want more of an analysis of a tuning. This Steinway was recently worked on by a tuner who is now deceased."

Wellsley frowned and made a slow nod. "I see. You'd like an appraisal of his tuning ability."

"Not exactly. I believe the last tuning he did was bad, although I want you to verify that. If I'm correct, I'm looking for some kind of explanation for why."

Wellsley's frown deepened. He held the look for a long five seconds. He set his tool box on the floor, then sat down on the piano bench. He lifted both arms, held his hands above the keys with fingers arched, paused for effect, then plunged into a chord that rolled from his left little finger, through his hand, then into his right hand, finally ending at his right little finger. It was a fast movement. He jerked his hands away as if the keys were hot.

"Not even the most incompetent tuner would do that to a piano. You said he died?"

"Yes." I said. "He'd had a stroke some weeks before. Then he tuned the piano just before he died."

"Well obviously the stroke burned out his brain so that

he couldn't hear, but he could still go through the motions of tuning."

"That was one of my thoughts. I want you to figure out if that is what happened."

"I just said as much. The piano is worse than if it hadn't been tuned in five years. It's clear that he completely lost command of his faculties."

"Maybe," I said. "But maybe not."

Wellsley stared at me. "You think he tuned it bad on purpose? Like he was trying to be mean to the owner of the piano? I don't think so. Even when we tuners dislike an owner, we still have enormous respect for their pianos. Pianos are our most trusted friends. Speaking for myself, I care more about pianos than people. More than I care about animals." Wellsley glanced around to make certain that Spot was still safely outside. "I would never hurt a piano."

"This was his own piano. He lived here."

"Then his stroke caused major brain damage. There's no other explanation for why he would so mistreat a piano."

"I understand. But I met him. He didn't seem that compromised by his stroke. So I'd still like you to investigate. I'll pay your normal fee."

"What's to investigate? The piano isn't tuned. It's worse than simply not being tuned. It's like the guy wanted to make it bad. He wanted to abuse his own piano."

"As I just said," I reiterated. "I'd like you to take a look. You've driven up from Reno. Spend some time with this piano. See if you can figure out what the tuner was doing."

Wellsley shook his head in disgust as he stood up and walked around the right side of the piano. "It's practically a crime to mistreat a piano. Especially a beauty like this." He ran his hand along the smooth curves of the piano's case, caressing it.

"Of course, I can fix it," he said. "I can make her sing again. But it will take two tunings at least. One to bring it into proper range, then another in a couple of weeks after it has had time to adjust."

"Don't do that. I'd like you not to change a thing. Just analyze."

"Analyze what?" He came back to the keyboard, played the notes of the scale, and winced with a big show of distaste, his eyes shut, cheeks scrunched up into a sneer, head turned as if the piano would ruin his ears. He pulled his hands away.

"Just do what piano tuners do, but without adjusting it. See if something strikes you. See if you can get any sense of what he was doing."

"I'm sorry, but that doesn't make sense. What piano tuners do is tune pianos."

"Then go through the motions as if you're going to tune it. Check the mechanism or whatever the different components are called. Try different note combinations. I don't know what you'd look for."

"A clue?" Wellsley said with a sneer.

"Herman may have done this on purpose. So look for something that would indicate why he did this."

"Herman? You're not referring to Herman Oleson."

"Yeah."

Wellsley's eyes widened. "But he was famous for his tuning ability. We always heard about him down in Reno. I never met him, but I felt that I knew him anyway. He was a real musician's piano tuner."

"What does that mean?"

"Just that you can tune a piano by the book, set each string to the proper mathematical frequency. But it can still sound somewhat dead. Tunings need stretch, especially in the highest octaves, to counteract the relative stiffness of the shorter strings. In fact, that's why serious pianists use grand pianos, because their strings are much longer than those in uprights. That minimizes stiffness and minimizes the need for stretch in the tuning. This is a Parlor Grand, with longer strings than in a Baby Grand or an upright, although nowhere near as long as a Concert Grand.

"The best piano tuners have a musician's ear. Combined with masterful technique, we can hear exactly how much we need to stretch the tuning. We can make a piano sing, give it life, make the harmonics soar. I count myself as one of the best tuners in Nevada, but I never had the presumption to think that I was as good as the famous Herman Oleson."

Wellsley shook his head. "It is doubly sad, that a great tuner would lose his tuning ability. I hope he wasn't aware of what he was doing. Maybe at the end he was completely demented, and he just cranked on his tuning hammer like a child would."

"That's what I want you to determine. Was Herman rendered incompetent by his stroke? Or was something else involved?"

Wellsley nodded. His demeanor was somber now that he realized the tuner was the great Oleson. "All right," he said. "I'll look. I have no idea what for, but I'll see if I can tell anything about what he was doing."

He opened his tool box and pulled out some long, narrow, black rubber wedges with thin wire handles, similar to the ones that Herman had left on the top of the piano. Wellsley also removed a roll of red felt stripping, almost identical to what Herman had draped over his toolbox. Wellsley unrolled the strip of felt and lay it across the strings, then inserted it here and there between the strings so that it looped up and down as it traveled left to right across the center group of strings.

Wellsley played middle C, then played each note, white and black, up the scale until he reached C an octave above. With the felt stuck into the strings, the notes, to my ear, sounded good. Wellsley frowned. He moved down to what I thought was the A note below middle C and played all the notes, both black and white, up to the next A. His frown increased.

Wellsley reached into his toolbox, and pulled out two tuning forks and an electronic device. It had a dial and a digital readout. He held one fork by its base, bounced it on his knee to make it vibrate, then held the end of it against the wood case of the piano. The tuning fork seemed to project its sound into the wood, and became much louder.

Out the window, I saw Spot immediately lift his head up off the deck. He perked his ears and tipped his head. Lily reached down from the chairlift to pet him.

Wellsley played the A note. It sounded the same pitch as the tuning fork. He did the same with the other fork and the C note.

Spot tipped his head the other way, then moaned.

Wellsley turned and looked to see where the moan was coming from. Wellsley's brow was as wrinkled with confusion as Spot's.

Spot moaned louder.

"Sorry," I said. "Apparently my dog wants to sing along." I walked over and opened the door.

"Spot," I said, snapping my fingers. "Quiet." Then I looked at Lily. "Officer Lily, if your hound insists on singing along, please remove him from the bridge."

"Yes, sir!"

I went inside and shut the door behind me.

Wellsley slowly played each note of the scale, looking at the readout on the machine. At the top of the scale, he paused and shook his head.

Next, he reached into the piano and pulled part of the felt strip out. He picked up a rubber wedge and held it against a string and struck a key on the keyboard. Again, he moved the wedge, touched it to another string and played another key.

"My God," he said.

TWENTY-TWO

"Herman Oleson wasn't demented," I said.

"No. Not at all. I almost can't believe it, but the center unisons are in tune. A perfect tempered scale."

Wellsley leaned over the keyboard and looked into the piano. He glared at the strings as if the force of his look would change what he'd discovered.

"This piano was tuned badly on purpose," he said. "And he did it in a very clever way such that any piano tuner would immediately realize that the result was intended."

"How can you tell?"

"Because he only mis-tuned the left string of each set of unisons, while he put precisely the correct pitch on each of the other two, the center and the right unisons. To do that requires using a wedge over and over as you remove the felt. It is twice as much work to do what he did as it is to tune all the strings correctly."

Wellsley looked at me to see if I was understanding him. "That clearly communicates to any tuner that he adjusted every string with great precision. It was deliberate. No one else would ever figure it out. But to a piano tuner, it's like he was leaving a message or something."

"You lost me back on the unisons."

"Oh, sorry. Come and look into the piano. I'll show you."

I walked over next to him. He pointed inside the piano to the strings at the far left of the piano. They were thick and copper colored and were made of coiled wire.

"The lower bass notes of a piano have a single string each." He pointed a bit to the right. "The higher bass notes have two strings per note." He moved his finger to the middle of the piano where the strings were not coiled, but single, and shiny silvery steel. "But up here in the temperament octave, there are three strings per note. We need more strings for each note because the thinner, higher-pitched strings don't make much volume, so more strings give the piano more sound.

"This temperament octave is where we start tuning. Not only do we want the notes to be in a proper relationship with each other, we want to make all three strings of each note - what we call the unisons - be exactly the same pitch as each other. If not, the sound has beats, a sort of a wah-wah-wah waver." He played a single note. "Hear it?"

It made a strong vibrating wah-wah waver, several times per second, and was unpleasant to listen to.

"If I tuned this note beatless, it would sound pure." He inserted the felt strip in between each group of three strings. "The felt silences the outer strings, leaving only the center string in each group to vibrate." He played some keys, running up the scale and back down. Each note sounded pure and beautiful.

"Sounds pretty good to me," I said.

"Yes. The center strings in each group of three are perfectly in tune. This is how Herman is saying to us that he tuned the piano, that he knew what he was doing. Now, I will pull out the felt and I'll dampen only the left string of each set of three unisons and let the other two sound."

He inserted his rubber wedge and played a note. Again, it was smooth and beatless. He moved the wedge to another left string and played that note. It also sounded great.

"You see, out of each group of three, the center and right strings are correct. Together, they are beatless. This is another way that Herman is saying that he has tuned them this way on purpose. They don't match the left string, but they match each other."

"And because it was clearly done on purpose, you think it might be a code."

"Well," Wellsley said, "I stress the word might. Obviously, the notion seems ridiculous. I've never heard of a tuner doing such a thing. What on earth would be the motivation? I'm just looking for some kind of explanation for a bizarre tuning."

"Okay, let's proceed with the ridiculous notion. Pretend that

Herman put a code into the piano. How do we determine what it is?"

Wellsley shook his head. "I know nothing about codes. What's that called? Cryptography? You would need a cryptographer."

"Yes, but the cryptographer would come to you, the piano tuner. They would ask you to measure this phenomenon, this out-of-tune piano, to quantify it."

"But how? All we have is a piano that has been precisely mis-tuned." Wellsley shook his head in frustration.

"What can you quantify about the mis-tuning?" I asked.

"I don't know. The frequencies, maybe."

"How do you do that?"

"It's easy with my electronic tuner. It has several functions including a simple frequency readout. When I set that function, I play the note, and it shows the frequency."

"If the center and right unisons are correctly tuned, then we would measure the incorrect ones, right? The left unisons?"

"Yes, I suppose," Wellsley said. "I can put the mute between the right two strings of each group, play the key, and see the readout for the left string."

"How long will that take?"

"Just a few minutes."

I stepped out onto the front deck. Lily and Spot were down on the small front lawn. He was lying on a patch of grass, and she was riding her bicycle in wobbly circles around him, giggling as if it were the funniest thing she'd ever experienced.

Ten minutes later, Wellsley came out of the cabin, looking much more fatigued than when he first arrived. His eyes were shadowed with dark eye bags. His previously combed and gooed hair was now messed up, strands coming down into his face. It wasn't that he'd done much work. It must have been the stress of contemplating what would drive a fellow tuner to commit such a crime to such a beautiful instrument.

"Any luck?" I said.

"I suppose I should say, yes, I was able to get the frequencies, but I've had no luck in imagining how all those numbers can mean anything." He handed me a sheet of paper with the letters of the notes followed by numbers.

"I'm a bit of a natural at math," Wellsley said. "But if the left unison of C-sharp vibrates two hundred eighty-one point six times a second or whatever it says on that paper, instead of two seventy-seven point two, which is what C-sharp is supposed to vibrate at, how is that going to reveal anything? You'd certainly need a cryptographer to decipher it. And besides, no matter how intelligent Herman was, I doubt he'd have learned some complicated math formula."

Wellsley sat down on the chairlift seat and rubbed the back of his neck while I looked over the paper with its inscrutable numbers.

"And anyway," Wellsley said, "why would Herman go to such trouble?"

"I'm an investigator, trying to solve a murder. It may be that Herman knew something about the case, something he was afraid to tell anybody."

Wellsley stared at me. "You didn't say anything about a murder. What am I getting mixed up in?"

"Nothing. I asked you to analyze this tuning, nothing more. You don't need to worry. You're not at risk merely helping me understand what Herman did to his piano."

My words didn't ease the worry on his face. I went back to studying the paper with the frequencies. Wellsley had written the frequency of each note and then, in parentheses, written the correct frequency. The actual numbers varied from the correct numbers by small amounts. And the amount they varied was inconsistent from one note to the next.

I knew nothing of cryptography, either, but my instincts told me that I was looking for a pattern, for something neat and clean and regular. It seemed that a message would stand out by looking like order in the chaos.

Unfortunately, I saw no pattern in either the actual frequency or in the variation from the correct frequency. Every aspect of it seemed messy, and a message, by its very nature, had to be unmessy, unequivocal, clear to the observer.

Wellsley continued to rub his neck and rotate his head for another ten minutes while I added and subtracted and transposed numbers. Nothing I did revealed any order or pattern.

"Tell me again about the wah-wah waver that you mentioned."

"The beats?"

"Yeah. What is that about?" I said.

"When notes are close in pitch, or when they have harmonics or what we call partials that are close to one another, the frequency interference produces beats. What happens is that the sound waves add to each other at some points and subtract from each other at other points. That produces the wah-wah sound.

"As I mentioned, we tune the unisons of a single note to be exactly the same, which makes them beatless. The intervals between the notes produce beats as well, but that's a little different. Does that make sense? If I play a C note, I want no beats. But if I play a C and a G together, I want a slow beat."

"Why do you want a slow beat when you play two different notes?"

"Tuners put slow beats on all of the main intervals. That is what we call a tempered scale. Before the seventeenth century, we tuned some basic intervals, like fourths and fifths, beatless. But that made other intervals like thirds and minor thirds have really fast beats. The really fast beats made certain music played in certain keys sound bad. Thus a piece by Bach could only be played in the key in which he wrote it. You couldn't transcribe it to a different key, or it would sound terrible.

"So tuners realized that if they put slow beats into the fourths and fifths, then the other intervals didn't have to have such fast irritating beats. As the evenly-tempered scale took hold, you could play any piece in any key, and it still sounded pretty good. Of course, many purists resisted the change well into the nineteenth century, but now the tempered scale is quite universal in the Western world."

"Could Herman have done this tuning with a focus on beats?"

Wellsley thought about it. "I don't think he could have used the beats of intervals as a way to communicate something. If so, how would we know what he wanted us to consider? There would be too many choices. But the beats of each single note stand out as a more obvious message device."

"You're saying that he may have wanted you to play one note at a time and consider the beats because the obvious mis-tuning is a red flag."

"Yes."

"But how do you quantify it?" I asked. "What are the qualities that tuners pay attention to when they hear beats?"

"There isn't any way to qualify or quantify beats other than counting them." He led me back inside the cabin, and struck a note. The beating was pronounced and uncomfortable.

"How do you count them?" I asked.

"By how many times it beats per second. What I'm playing now beats about three and a half times a second."

"How do you know that?"

"It seems like a good trick, but anyone can do it with a little practice." Wellsley turned sideways on the piano bench. He smacked his leg with his palm. "I can watch a clock and slap my leg once a second. Or, if I'm pretty good, I can count one-one thousand, two-one thousand, like that. Now watch. I keep hitting my right leg once per second. One, two, three, four. That's my down beat. Then I hit my left leg with my left hand on the up beat. One, and, two, and, three, and, four, and. I've just paced out two beats per second."

He pointed at my hands. "Try it. First, you go once per second with your right hand. One, two, three, four. Perfect. Now add in your left hand. One, and, two, and, three, and, four, and. See, even you can figure out what two beats per second sounds like."

I continued to pat my hands on my legs, ignoring his remark.

"Now, I double the pace," he said. "One, and-and-and, two, and-and-and, three, and-and-and, four, and-and-and.

"That's an easy way to count off four beats per second. You can do it with your hands, or you can just count silently.

"Now that you know how fast four beats per second is, you compare it to the beats you hear when you play a note." He hit middle C again.

Immediately, I could tell that the wah-wah-wah-wah waver was close to the four-beats-per-second rate. With a little focus, perhaps I could do as Wellsley did, and realize that it was a touch slower, hence about 3 1/2 beats per second.

"You can see how easy it is to establish the pace of four or three or two beats per second," he said. "It's not hard to count. Of course, there is a more accurate way. I can use my little magic machine to count for me."

"Can you do that? Write down the count of the beats for each of the out-of-tune notes?"

"Sure. Give me another few minutes."

Again, I went outside to wait. Spot had flipped onto his back so that his bent legs were in the air. His head was turned toward Lily, who lay next to him, also on her back. She had the piece of paper with the outline of Matisse's paper cutout painting. It was colored with bright crayons. She showed it to Spot, pointing.

"Heat is the horse, and I'm the rider. But you can't be the clown unless you look funny. Do you look funny, Spot?"

Spot straightened his head. It was now perfectly upside down. His jowls flipped open, exposing his fangs. Lily turned and stared. She exclaimed in a much louder voice. "My what big teeth you have, grandma! You certainly look funny now. Maybe you are the clown."

Wellsley came out and handed me another piece of paper. Like the previous piece, this one had the notes, followed by the beats per second.

C - 3.6
C#- 2.6
D - 11.6
D#- 6.9
E - 9
F - 2.5
F#- .4
G - 9.1
G#- 2.2
A - 2.3
A#- 1.5
B - .6
C - 7.7

The notes were labeled by letter. But I couldn't see how the letters of the notes could be part of the code. It seemed that they were irrelevant. The likeliest code was a simple number/letter conversion. 1 = A, 2 = B, and so on.

Without any reason other than that we read from left to right, I thought it would be most logical that Herman would put his message from left to right. So I wrote what the letters would be that corresponded to the numbers, rounding where appropriate. That gave me the following string of letters:

DCLGICAICBBAH

It made no sense. As an alternative, I substituted the logical alternative where the numbers were in the middle, rounding down, instead of up. So 2.5 became B instead of C. 1.5 became A instead of B. 7.5 became G instead of H.

That gave me a new set of letters:

DCLGIBAICBAAG

It still made no sense. Wellsley was gathering his tools, sensing that his work for me was done.

"Another question, if I may," I said. "I've transcribed letters for numbers, but I can't make any sense of it. Is there any other way that beats are used?"

"No. We just count them and set the strings accordingly."

"Always beats per second," I said.

"Yes. Although with slow beats, we count how many there are in five seconds. It's hard to hear that a beat wavers zero-point-four times per second. But multiply by five, and you get two beats every five seconds, which is much easier to quantify."

"Right." I looked at my sheet. "Unfortunately, multiplying these numbers by five would eliminate many corresponding letters. There's only twenty-six letters, yet five times these numbers produces several results that are more than twenty-six. I couldn't assign them letters."

"You've got yourself a real puzzle," Wellsley said.

"What is the slowest beat that you can count?"

"We can count one beat in five seconds, which would be the equivalent of point two beats per second. At the other end, we can go up to about ten or twelve beats per second. Beyond that, it gets too hard to hear them."

"Got it. Thanks."

He finished collecting his gear, I thanked him and paid him, and he left.

Lily had arranged pine cones in lines to designate a series of squares, perhaps the different rooms of a house. Spot was sitting in the middle of one square.

"You are the magenta horse, Spot," Lily said. "You are in your horse stall. But the clown wants a ride."

Spot looked at her, then lay down and rolled over onto his side. I could hear his sigh from a distance.

I looked again at the numbers, tried to think like Herman, tried to imagine what happened.

Herman is in his cabin tuning the piano when someone walks in the kitchen door. In order to keep the neighbors from being alarmed, the burglar tells Herman to keep tuning. Herman fears for his life and wants to leave a message about the burglar. He composes a simple sentence or phrase. He can't write it down, or the burglar might see it. So he wonders if he can put it into his tuning. He realizes he can put beats into his scale. What did Wellsley call it? The temperament. But if the beats are too fast or too slow, they can't be easily counted or accurately produced.

So Herman thinks about the letters of his message and the numbers those letters correspond to. He needs a system that goes from 1 to 26. But according to Wellsley, his beats should only range from less than 1 per second, up to about 12 per second. How can he adjust for letters ranging from 1 to 26?

Multiply by 2.

So I multiplied the beats by 2, and wrote them down.

7.2, 5.2, 23.2, 13.8, 18, 5, .8, 18.2, 4.4, 4.6, 3, 1.2, 15.4

Then I wrote down the corresponding letters.

GEWNREARDECAO

It still made no sense. I couldn't find order in the chaos. It did have the word REAR in it. So I separated the components out.

GEWN REAR DECAO

Easier to remember, but still no meaning.

I folded the paper, put it in my pocket and gathered Lily and Spot from the pine cone stable.

TWENTY-THREE

An hour later, I was working on the code when Ryan appeared and, sounding very nervous, asked if Street might like to come over again, and he could make us dinner.

Early that evening, I left to go pick up Street. Although I was living at Ryan's, and Street was bringing clothes for another sleep-over, we rang Ryan's doorbell just like dinner guests. We heard Spot's deep, ragged woof, woof, and I allowed myself the brief pleasure of thinking that even if Smithy weren't on duty out front, no person would dare break into this house.

I carried wine, and Street brought a small bouquet of flowers. Ryan opened the door. His face was blotchy-nervous, and he looked scared. He stared at the flowers.

"Hi. Oh, I can't believe... nobody has ever brought me... you are so kind." He took the flowers from Street, sniffed them and then hugged her. When he pushed away, the flowers were bent, and he was even more nervous and embarrassed for his effusive emotion. Street showed no reaction except to smile.

He stood in the doorway, not yet inviting us in. "I, um, I made an eggplant manicotti with marinated white beans. I hope that is okay. You are probably real epicures, aren't you? I've never made it before, but this is the first time I've ever had two people over for dinner who weren't, you know, like gamer friends, where you eat in front of the screen while you're blowing up the world, and I thought... Now I'm talking too much."

"Not at all," Street said.

Spot came up with Lily at his side, her arms wrapped around his neck. Her feet were in baby-blue socks, and she had them out in front of her, sliding on the wooden floor as Spot pulled.

She said, "I can water ski next to Spot. He's my boat. Isn't that a good idea?"

"That's a great idea," Street said.

Spot seemed to ignore Lily, and her feet slid along as he walked toward us, tail wagging.

Ryan looked at me, his forehead creased. "Is that okay, the manicotti? I flavored it with roasted garlic cloves, and crushed oregano and basil. There's no meat. Is vegetarian okay?"

"It sounds great," I said.

I must not have said it right, as Ryan looked more worried.

"You have to understand," Street said, "that Owen is kind of a meat-and-potatoes guy who thinks he's trapped in a vegetarian world. But he actually likes all kinds of food, including vegetarian." Without pausing, Street swung her elbow out into my side and said, "Here's where you nod and say, 'Right, I totally love veggies.'"

I nodded and said, "Right, I totally love veggies."

Ryan cracked a little smile.

We were still standing on the doorstep.

"Okay," he said. "I'll take that at face value. Now, what about a drink or something. Oh, I should invite you in. Please." He moved aside. "I'm thinking that a meat-and-potatoes guy would drink beer. But then you brought wine."

I handed him the bottle.

"Calera Central Coast pinot. This will be perfect with dinner," he said. "Or do you think I should open it now? If it makes a difference, I also got a Kenwood Jack London cab from Sonoma. Is that okay? I don't know which would be best."

"Either would be great," Street said. "Besides which, Owen has a thing about rules. If someone states that there is an order to something, he will subvert that whenever possible."

Ryan looked at me for direction.

"Tell you what," I said. "We're celebrating. Let's open both and we'll have a tasting."

Ryan's eyes grew wide.

"Tasting doesn't mean we have to drink it all," I said.

"Yeah. Of course," he said. "That's a great idea. Both wines. I'll keep the corks." He turned and went into the kitchen.

We went into the family room where the drapes were closed. Spot followed, dragging his water skier at his side.

Ryan came back out with the opened wines, then made another trip and returned with three wine glasses. He set them down on the table and then looked at us.

"I'm not sure how you do a tasting," he said. It was difficult to match up this shaky, nervous, insecure kid with the rich bio-tech genius who was the subject of business magazine features.

"I'll show you," I said. I poured a splash of pinot into each of the glasses. I took one and raised it high. "To dinner at Ryan's."

Street raised her glass. Ryan followed suit. We clinked.

I swirled mine, sniffed it, sipped it, chewed it, swallowed it. Then I poured a bit of the cab into my glass and did the same.

"Very good," I said.

"You don't need to rinse the glass?" Ryan said.

"One flavor informs another," I said.

"Really?" Ryan's earnestness was a little bit heartbreaking.

"Like I said," Street said.

Spot lay down and sighed. Lily was still attached to his side, and she flopped down next to him.

"The boat went too slow," she said, "and my skis couldn't stay up. So now that I'm in the water, I'll just hang onto the boat." Lily kept her arms wrapped around Spot's neck. He put his head down on the rug and appeared to fall asleep.

Lily looked at our glasses. "Don't I get to do a tasting? A kiddie cocktail?"

"Sure," Ryan said. He went into the kitchen, returned with a glass of yellow soda, and handed it to her.

Lily sniffed it, took a sip, swished it around her mouth, then swallowed. "Very good," she said, mimicking my voice.

We all chatted a bit and then, too soon, we ate dinner, the result of Ryan fussing that he wasn't being a good host if he didn't get lots of food into us right away.

Although Street and I avoided talking about the case, Ryan couldn't stay away from it. He asked me many questions to which the answers were largely 'I don't know,' and 'I'll have a better idea in a few days,' and 'Let's enjoy dinner,' and 'You and I will go over this tomorrow.'

Dinner was tasty despite being meatless. Street made interesting conversation. Ryan was too nervous to say much. Because I was the only one with an obvious appetite, I decided it was my job to eat.

After we'd cleared our plates, Ryan seemed relieved. He worked in the kitchen for a while. Sometime later, he came out of the kitchen carrying a cookie sheet. On it were fresh cookies, some kind of chocolate extravaganza. I looked to see how Lily reacted, but she was asleep next to Spot.

"It might be a mistake to bring out an entire batch and set it within Owen's grasp," Street warned.

Spot lifted his head off the floor, his nostrils flexing, eyes sleepy but intense.

I reached for one.

"Wait, don't eat it yet," Ryan said.

I already had a cookie at the gates.

"Wait, wait, wait!" He stood in front of us, his arms out, palms up, pleading. "It's like that line in the Yeats poem about stepping softly because you're stepping on my dreams."

I put the cookie back.

"It's okay for each of you to pick up a cookie," he said, "but don't eat it. Just hold it."

We did as he asked.

"Now close your eyes. Pretend it's nine hundred years ago. You are stone carvers in Paris, creating the gargoyle monsters for the Notre Dame Cathedral. Like many artisans, you've spent your entire life on this project in service to the Church. Food has never been anything but calories. The best treat you've ever tasted is a chunk of tough, singed deer meat. And heavy bread. Coarse enough to break your teeth, flavor like old leather, as hard to chew and swallow as tree bark. You need the water jug nearby just so you can wash it down."

With my eyes shut, Ryan sounded rapt and focused, maybe even unflinching for a moment.

"Are you there?" he asked. "Is your taste and smell completely deadened? Is your tongue still dry with the dust of chiseled stone from a long day's work?"

I opened my eyes and looked at him. His eyes were shut, but his face was wild and intense. He held his own cookie out in front of him. Street still had her eyes shut, always the good student, waiting patiently.

"Okay," Ryan said. "You can eat your cookies."

Street took a tiny bite, her eyes still closed.

I chomped mine, chewed it up and swallowed. It was chocolaty and warm and chocolaty and chewy and very, very chocolaty. I shut my eyes to consider again what it would be like to be a stone carver in Paris a millennium before, yet tasting a chocolate astonishment such as I'd just eaten. Just to make certain it wasn't a culinary aberration, I ate another, and then another. Washed it down with the Jack London cab. Perfect.

"Well?" Ryan said, the essence of the kid who cannot suffer delay. He looked both excited and worried.

I gave him the thumbs up.

Ryan's relaxation at my approval was palpable. This from a kid who'd made tens of millions in a high-tech business at an age when most of us were still trying to figure out what we wanted to do when we grew up. But then, maybe that was exactly where Ryan was, trying to figure out his future. His riches were just a collateral benefit from his hobby, like snowboard trophies or scout merit badges or spelling bee ribbons or publication credits for poems or travel articles.

Street was still chewing her tiny piece of chocolate dream, slowly, carefully, with what appeared to be great deliberation. She opened her eyes. "Is that Calera pinot all gone – I hope not?"

Ryan jumped up, nearly ran to the dining table, and lifted the bottle to the light. "There's still a taste," he said, excited. He brought it and, with flare, poured the last few drops.

Street lifted her glass up, swirled the wine several times around, then put it to her nose and inhaled, shutting her eyes once again. She tipped the glass up, and drank it, taking time to chew the wine with the lingering flavor of cookie, then swallowed. After a long moment, she spoke in a low voice.

"Amazing," she said.

Ryan grinned like a kid witnessing a revelation. He picked up another cookie, then noticed Spot.

"Spot is staring at me like I hold the key to the universe." he said.

"You do," I said.

"Are you supposed to feed dogs human cookies?"

"No. But that hasn't stopped fifty million dog owners before. If you want to give it a try, just set it on top of his nose," I said.

"You're not serious," Ryan said.

"Owen calls it delayed gratification training," Street said. "Spot will just stare at it until you say okay. Then watch out."

Ryan looked at us some more, decided we were serious. He walked over toward where Spot lay. He moved slowly, tentatively.

Spot looked like he might launch a cookie death-leap at any moment.

Ryan reached out with the cookie.

I thought a steadying word might be in order. "Spot, stay," I said in a stern voice.

Spot made the tiniest of movements as if he might look at me, but couldn't bare to pull his attention away from the approaching cookie.

"Stay," I said again.

Spot ignored me, every one of his visual, auditory and olfactory receptors focused on Ryan's gift.

"He's safe, right?" Ryan's voice vibrated. "He won't accidentally bite me?"

"He won't bite you," I said as streams of drool dropped from Spot's jowls. "But you have flood insurance, don't you?"

Now Ryan ignored me. He held the cookie by its edges, a delicate grip with thumb and forefinger, his other three fingers arched up to minimize finger loss should the carnivore miss the cookie. Ryan's other hand was tucked behind his back, the most effective hand and arm insurance.

With great trepidation, Ryan reached his shaky hand out and gently set the vibrating cookie on the top of Spot's nose. Had the cookie and nose been made of porcelain, the staccato tinkling would have been notable. When the cookie was half-balanced, Ryan jerked his hand back.

Spot went cross-eyed looking at the cookie. The cookie leaned sideways. Teetered on the edge of the nose. Drool-flow increased to flash-flood level.

Ryan squirmed with excitement. "Okay, Spot!" he shouted.

And the cookie was gone. Just like that. Whatever dramatic flair of motion happened, it was too fast to see without slow-motion photography. No sound effects beyond a clink of fang on fang and a quick guttural gulping sound. Just a simple blurred movement, and the cookie went from existing to not existing. If we hadn't been looking toward Spot, there would be no indication of what had happened except for the largish ball of saliva on a high pop-up toward third base.

Spot licked his jowls. A thorough tongue swipe down the left side and then up the right. A secondary swallow. He stared at Ryan, then turned his head toward the cookie tray where more helpless treats were lined up awaiting execution.

"Oh, God," Ryan beamed. "That was fantastic! Spot could be in the movies."

"Let's keep this as our secret," I said. "If word got out that we were feeding him chocolate cookies, the rule makers would charge me with cruelty to animals."

Street, nodding, pointed at Spot. "Look how he's suffering." We all looked at him.

Spot looked at us, wondering who would step up and fill the cookie void if Ryan was not going to put more on his nose.

"This calls for some classical music," Ryan announced. He walked toward a set of shelves that were his media center. "I'm thinking that a great romantic composer would suit chocolate and Paris. How about Mahler? I have much of his work. Maybe you have a preference?"

"Over my head," I said. "Famous composer is all I know about him. Grand and important symphonies, right?"

"Do you have the Symphony Number Five?" Street asked.

So we sat and listened to Mahler, and Ryan poured himself another half-inch of the cab, his eyes glimmering, and he talked about how exciting it was to devote an entire evening to an extravagant dinner sans video games, and he raved about celebrating the elixir of fermented grapes and the culinary delights of chocolate, all while we imagined life as stone carvers in medieval Paris. And when it was time to turn in, he said with great sincerity that it was the best evening he'd ever had in his entire life, and my heart broke a little bit once again.

TWENTY-FOUR

In the middle of the night, I awoke to an explosion. I rushed out of the bedroom and down the stairs. Spot was already at the entry to the great room. He stood in the dark, growling ferociously.

I found the light switch. The floor of the great room sparkled with a million small pieces of glass. One of the huge, double-pane windows had blown apart as if from a bomb. Cold air was rushing in.

In the middle of the pool of broken glass lay a fireplace poker, a sharp point on one end, and a looped handle on the other. Tied to the loop, like streamers on the back of a throwing spear, was a tail of long, red hair.

"Should I call nine-one-one?!" Ryan yelled. He was peeking into the room from around a corner. Street stood behind him.

"No. The person who did this has already gone. There won't be anything for the cops to do in the night. I'll call Diamond in the morning."

Ryan came into the room, saw the poker and gasped. "It's her hair! God, no, that's Jeanie's hair!"

"Why do you think that?" I said, even though I'd already had the same thought.

"Long and shiny, and the exact same red-orange color!" Ryan melted down onto the couch, his eyes tearing. Street walked up behind the couch and kneaded his shoulders.

I didn't know what to say. "Maybe you should go check on Lily. Hopefully, she slept through the noise."

I ran outside. Praeger was alert and in his car, but he hadn't heard the noise.

I told him about the poker. "The guy must have approached

from the back side of the house."

"You think I should cruise the road in case the guy is getting into a vehicle?"

"I'm sure the guy knows you're here. So his plan would have taken that into account. I don't think you'd find him. The guy probably saw the motion lights being installed, so he threw the poker from far enough away that he wouldn't trigger the lights and cameras. Then he would sneak off through the woods. I'd send Spot on a search, but I'm sure the guy has already left in a vehicle like the last time. I think it's best if you stay nearby."

An hour later we had the glass swept up and the dust vacuumed. Ryan was shaky. Street eventually thought to suggest that he look up window repair companies, and that gave him a focus.

I found a staple gun and step ladder in the garage and put up a large bedspread over the window opening to slow the flow of cold air.

I put on coffee. It was 4:30 a.m.

At seven o'clock, Lily appeared, holding a small stuffed giraffe. She was unaware of what had happened. She noticed the bedspread up on the window wall and asked why it was there.

"The window broke. Made a real mess, but Ryan's getting a company to replace it."

"Why did it break?" she asked.

I hesitated. "Sometimes, if glass is really stressed, it will break. But don't worry. It's very unusual for this to happen. It probably won't happen again."

She seemed to accept that answer.

Street cooked up a nice breakfast, doing a good job of keeping things relatively normal for Lily's benefit.

The window repair van came in the morning. Street had to leave. Ryan, Lily, Spot and I went outside. Praeger had been replaced by Vistamon. We said hi to him, then wandered up to Herman's cabin. Ryan sat on the chairlift seat. Lily joined him.

I asked her to hang onto Spot's collar while I took a look around. I made a circuit of the house, looking for footprints or some other sign of the suspect, but found nothing. Perhaps finding clues would have to wait until the party.

I looked into an old lean-to shed on the north side of the cabin. Its door was open, the bottom edge jammed into the dirt. Inside were some yard tools, a coiled hose hanging on a large hook, an open bundle of roofing shingles, a small workbench with miscellaneous hardware on it, an old, rusted barbecue and next to it, a half-bag of charcoal. In the middle of the shed was parked a late-model motor scooter.

"Herman had a scooter?" I called out to Ryan.

"Yeah," Ryan said.

"Who does his stuff go to?"

"Us. He had no family." Ryan came over.

"You ever ride it? It looks fun."

Ryan shook his head. "I'll probably sell it."

"You won't get much. Might be fun to keep it. Great for nice summer days. Looks like one of the tough ones, too. Good clearance. Decent-sized wheels. Be a fun toy. You should give it a try. You'll probably feel like a kid again."

Ryan shook his head again. He frowned. Looked somber.

"Ryan, I don't want to pry, but do you ever play?"

"What do you mean?"

"I mean, do you ever have fun? Goof off? Do something sporting?"

"I play video games."

"I meant, do you do anything outdoors? Skiing. Water skiing. Snowboarding. Tennis. Golf. Riding a bike."

Ryan's face darkened. He shook his head. "Nothing like that," he said.

"You and I should go for a bike ride together. Better yet, let's fire up this scooter and see how she goes."

He shook his head again. "I don't know how to ride a motorcycle."

"It's just a scooter. Variable speed transmission. You don't have to shift or anything. You just turn the key, hit the starter, and go."

"Motorcycles are dangerous."

"Ryan, this doesn't go any faster than a bicycle. You should try it. You need to learn how to have some fun."

"No, I don't!" he yelled at me. His face was red. He walked

over and sat on the steps to Herman's front porch. He bent at the waist, lowered his head between his knees, took deep breaths.

Lily was still sitting on the chairlift seat, petting Spot, hanging onto him. She looked at Ryan, concerned.

I followed Ryan. "I didn't mean to offend. I just thought the scooter looked like fun."

Ryan looked out at the construction site.

"I don't try it because it frightens me," he said. "I have no courage. I'm the ultimate coward. I'm afraid of everything. Someone honks their horn too close to me, I lose it. I start shaking. I have to pull over to the side of the road and breathe deep for ten minutes. I drop a glass in the kitchen and break it, I fall apart. I start crying. Not about the glass. I could care less about a glass. But about the upset. The inner turmoil. My inability to be normal. If I'm at the grocery store and a car backfires in the parking lot, I nearly collapse. I have to watch the clothes drier and turn it off before it's done, because if I let it go until the buzzer sounds, I nearly have a heart attack. It's like I have Post-Traumatic-Stress-Disorder. But I've never been to war. I've never been through any real trauma, except the trauma of my delusions, the trauma of my fears, the trauma in my heart."

I sat next to him on the steps. We were quiet for a bit.

"I've heard that they've developed a simple and effective way to treat one's fears," I said. "What you do is approach the thing you're afraid of in a controlled way, slowly and calmly. Take people who can't get on an airplane. They bring them on a plane that isn't going to fly. You're just going to sit in the seat near the open door, have a cup of tea, read the paper. Then they shut the door. The plane still isn't going anywhere. They spend more time in the stationary plane. Eventually, they progress to flying."

"You're saying I should do that with the motor scooter. Just sit on it. Get used to the idea."

"Yeah. With anything that frightens you."

That night, I left Spot with Ryan and Lily in their house with the new motion lights and outdoor webcams and off-duty cop on guard. I picked up Street, and we drove around the lake to have dinner at Wolfdale's in Tahoe City. We had the King Crab and watched the lake as the sunset put on a spectacular show.

She asked how my day went.

I recapped how Ryan reacted to the idea of riding a scooter, of having fun outdoors.

Street brought her wine glass to her nose and took one of her long sniffs without actually drinking it.

"He's lived most of his life in a computer world," she said, "where he has the skills to find his way through it, to conquer it. For him, that is as real as this world is for us. Maybe more real."

"Can't ride a motor scooter in a computer world," I said.

"I agree. But our generation is trapped by our myopia. The stagecoach drivers scoffed at cars, but it was the horse-drawn world that disappeared."

"When I was a kid," I said, "if my mother had told me to go play outside, it would have been redundant."

"Because almost all play was outside," Street said.

"Now most play is in cyberspace. I can't help thinking that something important has been lost."

"Just like when people climbed off horses and got into cars," Street said. "At least Lily still has a bicycle."

"Yeah. I'm glad for that."

TWENTY-FIVE

B ecause Spot becomes the main attraction most places he goes, I thought it would be best if he weren't at Ryan's party. So I put him in the Jeep and parked it in the trees off Herman's drive. He would likely spend the evening snoozing.

The caterers took care of hosting obligations, so my help wasn't needed. Ryan and Lily and I had already agreed that we wouldn't advertise that I was staying at the house. I would be just another party guest keeping a low profile. We got both Smithy and Praeger to join the party in plainclothes. Praeger volunteered to spend the evening bird-dogging Lily and never let her out of his sight. I sat on Herman's front porch, waiting until there was a good crowd before I joined in.

People started showing by 7:00. While the acoustic music wasn't loud, by 8:00 the party was already getting boisterous. The caterers had two buffet tables of food and a third set up as a bar, so the party guests had their hands full of food and drink within seconds after they got in the door.

The drive quickly filled with cars, and it was a lesson in the socioeconomic status of the friends and colleagues of people who live on Tahoe lakeshore. Of all the vehicles, only my Jeep was old. The rest were the pearlescent, all-wheel-drive, leather-interiored, luxury wheel toys of the wealthy. Vehicles spilled like candy corn out onto the street, parked with a casual rakishness, some wedged between trees on the Forest Service lots across the street, some left partway up the slope on the side of the street, some infringing on neighbors' landscaping.

Like most of the cars, the people looked like the models one sees in the glossy magazines that cater to the nouveau-riche. They were a study in how the wealthy, educated, business class differs from the rest of the population. With a few notable exceptions, their teeth were whiter and straighter than natural, they were thin, their clothes were tailored, their hair was tended with brushes, not combs, their belts and shoes were soft, supple leather, and they didn't slouch.

I milled and mixed and mingled and thought that if I didn't talk very much, maybe they'd mistake me for an outsider venture capitalist who didn't have the social grace to dress appropriately to his class.

I was looking for Ryan when I felt a punch to my upper arm.

"Hey, tall boy." Female voice. I turned. It was Glenda Gorman, dressed in a dramatic, billowy blouse/pant combination, satin-smooth fabric, purple over purple, the color accentuating her tight little blonde curls. The look brought to mind silent film stars from a century before. She held a drink that was bright yellow green.

"Ace reporter Glennie, Sherlock for the Tahoe Herald," I said.

"Why's a guy like you hanging with the young rich? You got a case that brings you here?"

"I was hoping that some of their financial acumen would rub off. What's your excuse?"

"A girl haunts the moors long enough, she turns up the damnedest stories."

"There some hound here you're chasing?"

"Probably," she said. "I heard a rumor about a secret research facility in Incline Village."

"Thought you were in the facts business."

"I figured that research equated to intelligence, and the host of this party, whom I've interviewed on the phone but haven't yet met in person, seems to be the epicenter of a good chunk of Northern California's intelligence."

"Good way to mix cocktails and journalism," I said. I decided to play along with her subject even though I already knew about it. "You think that Ryan's company is doing secret research? Or some other company?"

"Don't know. What's interesting to me is, why in Incline?"

"If the rumor is true," I said.

Glennie grinned. "Speaking of chasing hounds," she said, "you should know that I just spent five minutes at an old Jeep parked in the trees, kissing and scratching the ears of a big, spotted dog." She held out her drink and pointed to a dusting of short white hairs on the sleeve of her outstretched arm. "He learn any new tricks?"

"No. He just practices the old standards. How to lie down and fall asleep in two seconds. How to sleep sixteen hours a day. And eating. He keeps perfecting that trick."

"But unlike Sherlock's hound, Spot's teeth don't glow in the dark." She looked around. "Probably can't say that about most of these people. I've been watching Ryan Lear's career. I sold a story on him to Esquire. Anyway, I learned that he's quite the young tech star. Look at this crowd. There's enough bank here to float an Initial Public Offering without having to go to Wall Street." She gestured with her glass. I followed her gaze to a man who was maybe ten years older than Ryan chronologically, but a full generation older in terms of suave polish. He looked like a smiley, rugged movie star, his strawberry blond hair artfully swept back like a sailor who just stepped out of the wind. The contrast between his tan and his teeth made me want to put on sunglasses.

"Recognize him?" Glennie said. "Preston Laurence."

"I've heard of him," I said, remembering that he was Ryan's 40% investor.

"He started a software company, which he sold. Then he invested in a long series of startups that all went platinum. Now he's a playboy philanthropist. He just set up the Preston Laurence Foundation with a fifty million-dollar endowment. The foundation will fund children's groups. They say he's got another billion where that came from."

"He doesn't look like a geek."

"Got that right," Glennie said. "I read about him in the Chronicle. They portrayed him as the ultimate business shark, engaging in philanthropy only as a way to direct attention away from some of his activities."

"Like what?"

"Rumor has it that he pressures the young kids with startups into selling him disproportionately large percentages of ownership for disproportionately small investments. The paper quoted a source who said that Laurence is always cruising, always looking for a tip. Apparently, he is ruthless."

Preston Laurence stood at the focal point of a half circle of people. It was like watching rapt actors surrounding an A-list movie producer. One of them had his mouth open in a sort of permanent gasp of awe. Maybe Laurence *was* an A-list movie producer. Half of what he said must have been hilarious. The other half was profound. Every movement and gesture was studied and memorized. His admirers would be adopting his mannerisms at a later date, say, five minutes from now.

His charisma was undeniable, all captivating charm and smile. He had a Heineken, and he held the bottle in an unusual way, his palm up, the bottle standing on his palm, his fingers rising up the sides of the green glass.

"Looks like Laurence is about to get some spectacular company," Glennie said. She aimed her drink toward a young woman wearing a clingy, blue, spaghetti-strap dress with a hem that stopped at upper-thigh. The woman pushed through the group surrounding Laurence, slipped her arm around his waist, then rubbed his butt.

Her spiky blonde hair, fire-hydrant lips, eye shadow, and cleavage scored high enough on the bimbo scale that even if she could prove she had a Ph.D., I'd still assume it was earned in the non-academic way.

Glennie sipped her drink and said, "Shame that someone so beautiful doesn't know that you can skip the excessive paint job, and people will admire the lines of the vehicle even more."

"If I had his money and genius, you think she'd rub my butt?" I said.

"Sure, but then Street wouldn't want to anymore, and it would be your loss. Look how they hang on him."

"I'm guessing Preston's magnetism is more than his financial statement."

"Cobblestone abs," she said.

"Explains the tight yellow sport shirt."

She nodded, then turned to me. "I bet you'd look good in that shirt instead of that loose sweater. But who would know besides Street? What is it with you? You drive a rusted, old Jeep. You wear worn-out jeans and old running shoes. You don't primp or wear cologne or even have any jewelry. I bet you never even look in the mirror. You don't have a shred of vanity, do you?"

"I can primp," I said, licking my thumb and carefully pressing down my right eyebrow. "But I learned long ago that his largeness upstages me so completely that no one notices me, anyway. So it doesn't matter how I show off my tail feathers."

Glennie said, "Well, at least Spot has an ear stud. You could take a style lesson from Spot. Strut your stuff a little."

I looked back at Preston Laurence. "He live around here?"

Glennie took my arm and pulled me over to the window. "Forbes Magazine showed a picture of some of his play toys." She pointed out to a large Hatteras yacht that was anchored off Ryan's beach. It probably had too much draft to pull up to Ryan's dock. "That's one of them. I can tell because the photo in the magazine showed those curved rows of twinkling lights. Gotta be the same boat."

The yacht had three strings of lights that sparkled in the approaching twilight, outlining the decks and the flying bridge. The bow was long and pointy.

"He live in Tahoe? Or is the boat just for vacations?" I asked.

"I've heard that he has a house near Carnelian Bay. Dollar Point, I think." She gestured toward the north, across the lake. "But Forbes also ran pics of his five-hundred acre spread in the foothill wine country. Down by Jackson in Amador County. I think he spends most of his time there tending to his grapes and his race horses and his Mustangs."

"Mustangs," I said.

"Yeah. I guess adopting wild horses is one of his hobbies."

Glennie looked at me looking at Preston and the people surrounding him.

"It's not polite to stare," she said.

"Any idea who the armpiece is?" I asked.

"None at all. I always knew that rich and powerful men can take their pick from the young and beautiful. But when I see it in person, I wonder how it is that so many women of each generation seem to care about nothing beyond a man's finances. Why don't they care about the deeper aspects to life?"

"Like his abs?" I said.

"Right, forgot that for a moment."

"Maybe she's a poet or an artist, and he's her patron," I said.

"Why didn't I think of that?" Glennie said. "Emily Dickinson, judging by the humble wrap and the plain presentation."

Ryan appeared at our side, looking tentative.

"Glennie, have you met our host?" I said. "This is Ryan Lear. Ryan, Glenda Gorman."

"We've spoken on the phone," Glennie said. "Such a pleasure to finally meet you in person." She gave him a big smile and then a gentle one-armed hug, holding her drink out so she wouldn't spill on him. Ryan blushed, awkwardness radiating from him like heat from a woodstove.

They made small talk, Glennie as polished a charmer as they come, Ryan as nervous as a shy teenager. A minute or two later, Glennie saw her graceful exit. Her eyes moved to a person across the room. "Excuse me," she said. "I just saw my rumor point man. Gotta go work."

She left, and I knew that her quick exit was the technique of a master reporter. By the end of the evening she would have met and spoken with every single person, and sized them up for potential as future sources. She would also know which ones were reliable and which tended toward exaggeration.

"Rumor point man?" Ryan repeated after she left.

"Someone who referred to a secret research facility."

"What? You were right! You try to keep something secret, and it makes the news spread even faster."

Another woman approached us, grinning at Ryan the way a proud aunt grins at a high-achieving nephew.

"Oh, hi, Mrs. Hughes," Ryan said. He swallowed, his Adam's apple bobbing. "This is Owen McKenna. He's my... He's a friend here at the lake. And this is Mrs. Hughes, my friend William's mother."

The smiling woman of maybe 45 was six feet tall, broad through the shoulders, and fit in a hard way that reminded me of Bruce Lee in his fighting prime. Her sleeveless tank top showed arms that could probably lift engine blocks out of cars, and her traps made distinctive triangles from her shoulders to her neck. She had on Capri pants that revealed taut, hard thighs and bicycle-racer calves.

She was one of the serious fitness buffs, and she chose her clothes to show it. Despite her fitness, she probably looked older than her age, because she'd had enough sun to turn her skin to spotted tan crepe paper. It was beginning to sag over her muscles.

"Good to meet you, Mrs. Hughes," I said, shaking her hand.

She rolled her eyes. "Please, Owen. I'm Holly to everyone but my children's friends."

"I didn't know that William..." Ryan stopped.

"Had brought his mother?" she filled in. "Well, you know my Willy. He still doesn't drive. I'd like him to get out a little more, but I guess I'm very fortunate that William is still living at home, helping me with all the chores when he isn't writing his games. You've probably heard about his latest launch? Tomb Warriors of Middle Earth."

"I, uh, knew he was doing the trilogy. But I didn't know he moved the venue to Middle Earth. That's bold."

She nodded, her eyes glimmering. "Twenty-five million copies in the first three months." She looked at me. "Needless to say, my son is my pride and joy." Her smile was dreamy.

"Is William here? I haven't seen him," Ryan said.

"He's down in your basement. You know how shy he is. And all of these people. You've got that new game console. He's doing some simulations on it. I guess that's what you expect of a true gamer. Always escaping the real world for the fantasy world."

Holly Hughes paused, and Ryan paused, and we three stood there in awkward silence.

Preston Laurence's girlfriend had left his side, walked near to us and began talking with another group, chatting with great animation, turning heads.

"So, how's the, um, meet and greet going?" Ryan said like it was a line he'd heard on TV and was embarrassed to repeat. "I see you've noticed Champagne," Ryan made a quarter turn away from Holly and stared at the girl. "She used to be Carol Pumpernickel back when we went to high school together in Reno, but she changed it to Champagne Forest. It's a stage name. She's trying to get into film. But from what I've heard, the competition is, like, way out there. Worse than trying to get into Stanford." He looked at her, his face sad as if he were contemplating a prize he could never have.

"She was a couple of years ahead of me. After she graduated, I never had any communication with her. Not like she would ever talk to a geek like me, anyway."

As Ryan spoke, I could see Holly Hughes's posture change, a rise of chest, a tensing of hands, a subtle shake of her head, the disbelief of a wise woman watching yet another young man fall under the spell of beauty, a spell that temporarily renders him stupid as a fence post.

Ryan continued, "After my company started doing well, I saw her here and there, parties and political fundraisers, stuff like that. Then she started hanging with Preston Laurence, and of course he's involved with all the tech hotspots. I've seen them together in Palo Alto and up here in Incline. Girls that hot pretty much just go with the jocks, and Preston is the ultimate rich jock. But it turns out she's real nice. We've had some nice talks. And she seems real interested in what I'm doing."

Holly Hughes couldn't contain herself any longer. "You don't see many girls that pretty who are also interested in DNA," she said. "Must be an irresistible subject for them."

The sarcasm went past Ryan like a line drive too fast to be seen against the ballpark lights.

"Yeah," Ryan said. Ryan looked at Holly Hughes and finally realized that her glare was ·not benign. "Oh, sorry, that was insensitive, wasn't it, talking about a girl like she's nothing more than a trophy."

"Honey, fish don't come any flashier. You want to rub some money scent on your fishing lure and go trolling, maybe you can pull in some beautiful, bottom-dweller, too."

Ryan looked at me, his face showing shock. Then he turned back to her, his eyes wide, his cheeks turning crimson. "I'm sorry. I didn't mean..."

"Hey, handsome, I'm just kidding." As Holly walked away, I thought that she wasn't just kidding, and I wondered why she would have such a volatile reaction.

Ryan looked like he was about to cry.

"I really screwed up now, didn't I," he said, his tone imploring, his look rapidly switching back and forth between my eyes. "I'm hopeless in social situations. The only way I don't say the wrong thing is if I don't talk at all. And when I don't talk, then that turns out to be the wrong thing, too."

"Best to talk a little when people expect it. But good to think about how something might sound before you say it. But even so, her reaction seems very strong. It's as if she were Champagne's age instead of the age of her mother. Unless there is something else about you that bothers her?"

Ryan shook his head. "Not that I know of. We've always gotten along well."

Ryan looked like he was going to implode under the pressure of self-critique. "The only reason I even focused on Champagne's beauty is that I'm trying to see it. It's so obvious to everyone else, but I don't respond to it the way other people do. Same when I've seen good-looking guys. I notice physical beauty, but it doesn't make my neurotransmitters fire. So I'm trying to train myself to think like other people. To be impressed with beauty."

"Don't try too hard," I said. "It mostly just gets people in trouble."

TWENTY-SIX

Ryan excused himself, and headed down the stairs, probably to find solace in talking to Holly's son William the gamer, who was so awkward that he wouldn't even join the party.

I hung out with the well-appointed crowd, sampling the catered buffet, looking out at Preston Laurence's yacht.

Street appeared at the entrance to the great room, demonstrating once again that they invented the word elegance to have a perfect description for her. She was wearing the black top with the rounded neckline and the snug three-quarter sleeves that showed off her arms. But instead of the black miniskirt, she wore the stretchy black pants with low pumps. Her hair was pulled up into a tight bun, with little wispies curling down near her ears. Below her hair were the small turquoise-in-silver earrings, which made an ensemble with the similarly small necklace and bracelet. She always had a knack for powerful understatement.

I waved and walked over to her.

"Good party?" she asked.

"Now that you're here. Find a place to park?"

"Barely. I squeezed in next to one of those classic seventies or sixties muscle cars. It looked like it was perfectly restored, everything shiny and polished. Probably worth a fortune. The cars are on a sideways slope, and when I opened my door it swung out fast. I envisioned having to pay for a paint job on the vintage vehicle, but I caught it at the last second."

"Can I get you some wine?" I said.

"Please."

I fetched two small glasses and some kind of Thai chicken on long decorative toothpicks, and brought them back to Street.

I saw Preston Laurence break away from the group he was

with and move toward the big, open kitchen.

"Will you excuse me? I've been waiting to talk to that man in the yellow sports shirt."

Street nodded and moved toward the open door that led to the deck.

I followed Preston, hoping to have a little chat. I was closing in on him as he ducked into a bathroom. Glennie appeared at just that moment.

"It looked like you were aiming for the great one," she said in a hushed voice.

"I told you I was hoping to acquire some financial wisdom."

She shook her head. "I'm not fooled. You have that competitive look. What is it with men, anyway? Just because he's so successful, you feel the need to lean on him or something?"

"I was only going to introduce myself. Express my gratitude that he is doing such an excellent job of keeping the capitalist system going."

"Right. You think he's involved with your case?"

"What case? I'm attending a party, same as you."

"You're working, same as me. I've learned quite a lot about Ryan's problems. And I know that he's retained you to help with those problems."

Preston came out of the bathroom.

"Here he comes," she said. "Good luck." She left.

I didn't have to make an effort to meet him, as Preston approached me, pausing at an ice and beer-filled tub in the kitchen. He picked up another Heineken, popped the bottle top and, as I'd previously seen, held the bottle from the bottom with the palm of his left hand.

"Evening," he said. "I'm Preston Laurence. I thought I knew most of Ryan's friends and business associates, but you are a new face." Smooth, friendly, charming even.

"Owen McKenna," I said.

He set down his beer so he could shake my hand with both of his. With a big smile he said, "Friend or customer or vendor or investor?"

"Friend," I said. "You?"

"All of the above," he said with the kind of laugh that was a little too warm to be believable. "I'm in lots of arenas, so Ryan and I intersect in many ways. He's really a promising businessman, and a promising scientist."

Laurence exuded polish. I'd only said a half-dozen words, and already he was acting like my best friend. I decided to play along for a bit.

"Were you able to get in on the ground floor of Ryan's company?" I said, already knowing that he was Ryan's 40% investor.

He gave me a knowing smile. "Pure luck," he said. "Got a good buddy who's a prof at Stanford. He periodically points out promising new ventures that his students start. As a help to them, and as their trusted advisor, he points them toward the most reliable resources for new tech businesses. Of course, when it comes to capital, the first resource to visit is me."

"I imagine that Stanford would frown on their professors getting financially involved with their students."

"You imagine correctly."

"Kind of a shame, isn't it?" I said. "Guy helps his students get rich, and all he gets is the joy of altruism."

Preston's smile reminded me of the eels in the Monterey Bay Aquarium.

"I buy him a nice bottle of Scotch now and then, if you get my drift," he said. "How about you? Do you have a stake in CalBioTechnica?"

I realized it was a test. As a major investor in a closely-held company, he would know exactly who the stockholders were, which numbered only four according to Ryan. Preston Laurence with 40%, and Eli's dad, Jeanie or her heirs, and Ryan with 20% each.

I shook my head. "I've stayed out of bio-tech."

His eyes briefly toured my clothes, sweater to jeans, paused at my shoes.

"Do you focus on high-tech, or do you believe in a balanced portfolio?" he asked.

I thought about all that I owned, from a large stock of dog food, a bunch of art books, a 500-square-foot log cabin, and my old Jeep. "I'm like Warren Buffett, eclectic in my investments," I said. "My primary holdings are agricultural, art, real estate, and automotive. Of course, I've taken a beating in a couple of those categories."

He nodded. "As have we all." He sipped beer. "I can tell that you are one of the thoughtful investors. Where do you see future growth?"

"Well, there are the obvious areas, like pharmaceuticals, but I'm working on a service sector endeavor. There's some risk in it. But if I'm lucky, I should make out okay."

Laurence's eyes seemed to harden. Maybe he suspected that I wasn't really an investor. He excused himself, and left.

Later, I saw Preston Laurence in Ryan's foyer, surrounded by another group of people, equally as focused on him as the earlier group. One of them held a beer the same way Preston did, standing up on his palm.

Preston's monologue was interrupted by a tall skinny guy. He had dirty brown hair that was plastered in a curve across his forehead. The hair had so little body to it that it looked like it was painted on. Despite his stick-like shape, the man moved with confidence, and he acted dangerous. His gaze at the partygoers made me think of the way a wolf looks at a herd of sheep.

The man whispered something in Preston's ear.

Preston waved his hand at the assembled group, said something, then turned and walked away with the thin man.

I'd met guys like the thin man in the past. What they lacked in muscle they made up in attitude. I had no doubt that under the loose clothes was at least one gun - probably two - an ankle knife, and other items that could be used as weapons. But the deadliest weapon of all would be his willingness to act in ways that no normal thug would act.

I went the other direction and found Street talking to Ryan. The contrast between the self-assured woman and the ill-at-ease young man could not have been greater. Street stood up straight, and her mannerisms projected competence and confidence. Although I'd always thought she was wonderful, it wasn't her angular face or her too-thin body that made her beautiful. It was her posture, her presence, and her attitude.

As if in opposition to Street, Ryan looked like a mess in spite of his handsome face. He slouched against a wall, his shoulders slumped, his back rounded.

Ryan's worried frown, flinching eyes, and obsessive hand-washing projected nothing so much as fear.

Street saw me, separated herself from Ryan, and told me she had to go. We walked out to my Jeep so that she could say goodbye to Spot.

"You think Ryan will get through this?" she asked as she rubbed Spot's head.

"He's a nervous wreck," I said. "But if I can catch this psychopath, I think there's a chance that Ryan will come out of this with some coping skills."

I kissed her forehead. I didn't want her to go, but I understood that just because I'd moved into a client's house didn't mean that she should or could or would.

"You talked to a several people tonight," I said. "Any thoughts on who I should follow up with?"

"I'd look up the beauty queen."

"Champagne?"

Street nodded. "I heard her say something disturbing."

"What?"

"I was near her and some other women out on the deck. They were all talking about the Mustang Heat. One of them mentioned Preston Laurence's Mustangs, then told Champagne that Preston was an amazing catch. And Champagne said that he scared her. She also said that Preston had made some frightening remarks about Ryan."

"She didn't elaborate?" I said.

"No. But the fear in her voice was significant."

"I'll look her up," I said.

As Street rubbed Spot, he had his head out the window as far as possible, sniffing us all over, deducing what we'd eaten, what the people we'd talked to had eaten, along with all of the other culinary treats that had been present but were not eaten.

I walked Street to her VW bug.

"How about a nightcap out on your deck?" I said.

"What about his largeness?"

"Spot is happy here with Lily and Ryan. I could help them

clean up a bit and then come over in an hour or so."

Street smiled, and I felt the familiar warmth.

"I'll be waiting," she said.

I watched as she drove away.

Back at the Jeep, I let Spot out. As he wandered around, I moseyed over to a group of people who'd come down the driveway. One of them had his back to me. But I recognized the red knit cap, and the voice of Travis Rundell, even as his words were directed away from me. It sounded like he was saying something about how a thrush can really hurt a frog. As before, he had his camera around his neck. He was wearing warmer clothes than the other partygoers. Losing his hair in chemo probably made him cold all the time.

He turned and saw me.

"Hey, Owen, good to see you again."

We shook. The group he was talking to moved toward some other people.

"Friend of Ryan's?" I asked.

"I don't know any Ryan," he said. "I was just out for my evening walk and saw these people pointing into the woods. I wondered if they had seen Heat."

"You live around here?"

He nodded. "I'm the caretaker for the Maxwells."

I shook my head. "Don't know them."

"About a mile down."

"So are you a bird expert, too?" I asked.

"Birds?" he said.

"You mentioned a thrush."

"Oh, well, I never go anywhere without my camera. So I've learned a few things. But as little as I know about birds, it's still more than what I know of horses. But horses are so beautiful, and I got so taken with Heat, that I wanted to see him and get pictures. The website grew from that. Have you seen him, yet?"

"Yeah. The evening of that day we last saw you in the woods across the highway. Not far from there. He saw us and then ran. But it was exciting."

Travis beamed. "That's great. Well, I best be going. It's getting dark."

"See you around," I said.

I called Spot, and he trotted out of the nearby trees. We were heading toward Herman's cabin, when I saw movement up on Ryan's side deck.

The woman in the blue dress was out there. She had her hands on her hips, knees locked, feet apart. She was bent slightly forward at the waist, an indignant stance. She was talking to someone who was just around the corner, out of sight. From my distance, I couldn't hear her voice over the din of the party. But the angry head motions, the hand suddenly raised, index finger stabbing toward the unseen person made her meaning clear. Then she turned and walked away, fluid of movement despite the emotion and the sky-scraper heels.

A half-minute later, the woman came out the front door. She apparently didn't see Preston off to the side, as she moved into a large mass of people who mingled on the front patio. She threaded her way through them, as unsuccessful at blending into a crowd as a Lamborghini is at blending into a traffic jam of Fords.

TWENTY-SEVEN

Most of an hour later, the band had quit, and the party wound down to a few small groups. I'd been waiting to catch the woman named Champagne as she left, but I hadn't seen her. I looked in each room. I found Praeger with Lily and William and Spot, playing a video game in the basement. But the rest of the house was mostly empty. I went back outside and saw her walking down the road with Preston, heading for one of the cars. If I approached her, Preston would be alerted to my interest, so I let them go. I could talk to her later.

I wandered out to the back side of Ryan's house. A sidewalk made of flat stones and lit by multiple lights on short posts made a long S-curve from Ryan's house to the lake. The backyard was the environmentally sensitive type. Unlike the front of the house, the back had no water-demanding lawn or other lush greens. Instead, the pathway meandered through artful plantings of native species that evolved to thrive in Tahoe's wet winter/dry summer climate. Manzanita, chinquapin, and other bushes graced the bases of large Jeffrey pines. Scattered wildflowers added color. Simple but comprehensive stonework defined the plantings. The landscape architect had made a careful study of the lot and put in strolling and sitting areas to take advantage of sight lines and sun angles and prevailing wind.

The pier also had low lights on the posts. I walked out the pier and picked up some beer bottles and a wine glass that were left by revelers. Under the boathouse roof, in the U of the dock, sat the Riva woodie on its hoist. Even in the darkness, it looked fast and sleek, a work of mahogany art that doubled as a boat.

There was a small bit of sand beach near the pier, and many natural stones and boulders. The stone campfire area had curved benches surrounded by stone walls about four feet high. A good distance away was a little stone arch with an indentation under it. Inside the cavity were some small split logs and a few bits of kindling. At the center of the circle was the fire pit. I sat on the curved stone bench.

It was a dream place to have a lakeside campfire, protected from the cool evening breezes and featuring a view of the mountains around the lake.

Ryan appeared, coming down the sidewalk. He sat near me.

"Good party," I said. "I met several people I may want to talk to some more."

"You think any of them could be my tormentor?"

"Probably not. But somebody could know somebody else. I'll see what I can learn."

"I worry that I didn't do it right," Ryan said. "All that socializing, hours of talk, a thousand opportunities to get it wrong. What if somebody figured out that the whole point of the party was for you to meet and vet people as possible bad guys?"

"The good people will never think that. And if a bad guy thinks it, that's good. It will pressure him, encourage him to make a mistake."

I gestured at the fire pit. "Great place for an evening fire before you go to bed," I said.

Ryan scowled. "I've never used it."

"I bet Lily would love a hotdog roast."

"Too cold in the winter, and too dangerous in the summer."

"Nothing dangerous about this location," I said. "There isn't anything combustible for fifty feet in any direction. You're surrounded by rock and stone and sand and water." I pointed toward the closest Jeffrey pine. "The lowest branches on that tree are sixty feet above the ground. You couldn't get it to burn if you tried."

"But that bush under it," Ryan mumbled.

I realized he was looking for an excuse not to use the fire pit.

"Even if you purposely lit it on fire, it couldn't light the tree on fire. Mature pines have evolved to be fire resistant. They lose all their lower branches. Without large amounts of what we call ladder fuels, a fire can't get up into the crown. You couldn't find a safer place to have a campfire unless you went out to a barren desert. But don't let me pressure you into using the fire pit. I just thought it looked fun."

Ryan frowned as if it were a concern of huge importance.

"I've been near fires, but I've never actually made one," he said.

I tried to act casual as I again considered the implications of his admission. This master of the scientific universe had never experienced the most basic of life's joys.

"No big deal," I said, pointing over at the firewood. "A bit of crumpled newspaper under a little kindling and a log or two, and you'll have a great time winding down from your party. Any chance you've got marshmallows in the house?"

"I think so. Lily loves them."

"Then you could roast some with Lily. Anyway, I'm thinking of taking a night off. I'll leave Spot with you. Officer Vistamon will be outside. Are you okay with that?"

"If you think it's safe."

"As long as you keep Spot nearby, I can't imagine anyone giving you much trouble."

"Okay. William's mom already left without him, so he's staying over. That will give our little army one more recruit. For that matter, maybe he knows about campfires. He could make sure I don't screw it up."

"You'll have fun," I said.

I picked a small bouquet of wildflowers from around Herman's cabin, and showed up at Street's a few minutes later. The flowers seemed to have contracted into little crispy bits of colored paper. By the time Street opened the door, they looked like weeds from the side of the road.

Street was gracious as always, reacting as if I'd handed her a dozen red roses.

Because we'd only eaten a few hors d'oeuvres, she broiled some Halibut fillets, steamed some broccoli and red potatoes.

My cell phone chimed out a burst of Brubeck and Desmond playing one of their duets.

"That's a first," Street said. "You actually remembered to turn that thing on."

"Slow, but trainable," I said. I answered the phone.

"You were right," Ryan exclaimed. "William and I made a fire, and it worked just like you said. We kept it small, and it was perfect. Lil', say hi to Owen."

I heard the phone being shuffled.

"Owen, guess wha'?" came Lily's voice. It sounded like someone had stuffed her mouth with glue.

"What, Miss Lily?"

"We roasted marshmawohs!"

"Mmmm, mmmm" I said.

"Do you like marshmawohs?!"

"Yes, I do," I said.

"Me, too. And Spot too. Here's Ryan."

"Don't worry," Ryan said. "She only gave him one. Anyway, thanks. It worked great. And I have the hose nearby, so when we go to bed I can put it dead out."

"Good idea. Thanks for the call."

I told Street about Ryan's first experience building a campfire. "He's led a very sheltered life."

"Sounds more like a very impoverished life," she said. "All his riches don't change that. It takes someone from outside of his world to prod him into new experiences. You could change your business card. Owen McKenna, investigation and motivation. Personal coaching is big business," Street said.

"But I don't want to be a coach. I want to be your valet, your houseman, your caretaker, your gardener. I want to attend to your every need."

"My every need?"

"Indeed." I reached up and touched her earring, traced a line down her neck.

Street set down her wine glass.

TWENTY-EIGHT

L ate that night, the phone woke us up.
 At first I thought I was home. I turned the wrong way, covers catching on elbows and knees as I tried to figure out who I was and where I was.

Street picked up the phone.

"Hello?" A short pause. "Just a second." She handed the phone to me.

"Yeah?" I said into the phone.

"Terry Drier calling. Called your cabin. Thought you might be at Street's. Sorry to wake you so early, but I thought I should give you time to come and form your own opinion before the media gets to the scene and complicates matters."

I was trying to think of why the Fire Department Battalion Chief would be calling me.

"Good morning, Terry," I finally said, blinking my eyes at the clock, which said 4:15 a.m.

"Sorry, that was kind of a brusque how are you, wasn't it?"

"What do I need to form an opinion about?"

"You are working for Ryan Lear?" Terry said.

"Correct," I said, an instant knot twisting my stomach.

"His neighbor's house burned down a few hours ago. We're just repacking our hoses."

Like a punch to the gut. "Anybody hurt?"

"Not that we know of. Apparently, the place is empty most of the time. We contacted the owner in LA. He said he's only up here during the holidays."

"Is this the big mansion to the north of Ryan's?"

"Yeah."

"Sorry to hear about it. What does it have to do with me or

Ryan?"

"Looks like the fire started from an ember that popped out of Mr. Lear's campfire."

Adrenaline made my heart thump. "Ryan said he had a hose to put the fire out," I said. "And I've seen the setting. There is nothing combustible within many yards of Ryan's fire pit."

"You better come look again. It looks like Ryan Lear will be facing some serious charges."

I hung up feeling devastated. I explained to Street what had happened, how I'd pushed Ryan to enjoy a campfire against his fears that the fire could spread.

She was speechless. Her face, white-pale, made me feel worse.

While Street's coffee maker gurgled out its brew, I dressed. Before I went to sleep, I'd turned off my cell because my charger was in the Jeep, and the battery was nearly dead. I turned it on and found two messages from Ryan, calling in a panic because the neighbor's house was on fire.

When there was enough coffee in the pot, I poured a mug, nuked it for 20 seconds to give it reserve heat, kissed Street's terrified face goodbye, and ran out to the Jeep. I pulled into Ryan's drive ten minutes later. His house and yard were lit by his new motion lights.

The fire trucks were still in the driveway next door, and out on the street, and down the road next to an additional hydrant. Red strobes flashed through the trees. Floods shined in all directions from the trucks, lighting up the yard, illuminating burned wreckage that was as wet as if we'd just had a hurricane. On the street were two patrol cars, their lights making up in flash what they lacked in noise. A couple of spotlights shined on the hulking skeleton of the neighbor's mansion. The place looked like it had been fire-bombed. Blackened portions of exterior walls stood tall, but the windows looked in on roofless rooms. The roof on the west side of the structure still had its main gable, but it sagged toward the east side. Halfway across the house, the roof had collapsed and fallen into the rubble.

I parked and found Terry Drier near the burned-out house.

"Place was sprinklered," Terry said.

"Hard to tell."

"The owner had turned off the main shutoff because he was going to be out of town, and he'd once had a pipe burst."

"Saved the pipe, lost the house," I said.

"Come over here," Terry pointed. "I'll show you what we found."

We walked toward the lake.

"Owen. Owen!" came a shout.

I turned to see Ryan standing with two cops. They were in the wash of light from Ryan's back deck. One of the cops was writing on a clipboard.

"Hold on one second?" I said to Terry.

I walked over.

"They say it was my campfire!" Ryan said, his voice frantic. "But I put it dead out. Just like you and I talked about. I flooded it with the hose. Lily said I was making a charcoal lake."

Ryan was wearing jeans and sweatshirt and flip-flops. His lips were blue, and his teeth chattered as he spoke.

"It couldn't have been my fire!"

"Easy, Ryan." I stepped to his side, put my arm around his shoulders, gave him a reassuring squeeze. He was shivering violently. "We'll get this sorted out. I'm sure there's an explanation."

"They can't blame it on me!" Ryan was shaking as if to self-destruct. "Tell them that I'm telling the truth!"

"Ryan, stop. Take a deep breath."

"But I..."

"Do it!"

He appeared to breathe.

"Now do that again. Ten times. Nothing is going to happen immediately. But you're freezing. You need to get some clothes on."

I turned to the cops. "Officers, I'm Owen McKenna. Diamond will vouch for me."

"We know you," one of them said. "Sergeant was just here. He's talking to Vistamon from the SLTPD. He'll be back any minute."

"Perhaps you can take Ryan inside and let him warm up. Hard to think when you're freezing."

One of them nodded. They turned toward the house.

I spoke to Ryan. "I'll talk to you before I leave."

I walked back to Terry, and he took me down to the fire pit. They'd turned on Ryan's beach lights, and the area was lit like a stage set.

"Ryan Lear explained about the campfire, the s'mores and whatever." Terry pointed to the fire pit. "And like he said, the fire in the pit is totally out. Charcoal soup. Now walk over here. We didn't see this until we'd drained our hoses."

Terry walked toward the neighbor's property. "This is due north. I called the National Weather Service. According to their data, the wind at this part of the lake was likely blowing this direction for most of the last six or eight hours. Due north, five to ten, is what they estimated."

"They surmise direction and speed, but they don't have actual measurements," I said.

"Right." About fifteen yards from the fire pit, he stopped and pointed his flashlight at the ground. "A classic marker. A burned cone shape, as if from an ember. Pine needles smoldered, then eventually caught fire. From there the fire progressed north, not expanding much, not moving fast, but moving nonetheless. The duff on the ground probably burned like a cigarette, not with flame." He shined his light around. The blackened area stretched from the small starting point toward the neighbor's house. About ten feet from the ignition point, the blackened duff appeared to shrink and then re-expand farther along, gradually widening until it was a ten-foot-wide ground fire when it reached the house. I knelt down nearby and shined my penlight on the area where the fire appeared to have died down.

"What do you make of this?" I said to Terry.

He came over to look.

"It almost looks as though the fire went out at this point," I said, "and then rekindled an inch or so over. There's a small bridge of unburned duff."

"Don't touch it. We'll get lights over here. I'm guessing that just the top is unburned. The combustion probably went underneath for a bit, then came back up to the surface."

"Or the firestarter realized his first attempt fizzled out, so he restarted it here."

In the harsh glow of the distant floods, Terry scowled so hard that I could sense his venomous feelings for the subject. Like all firefighters, he'd dealt with arsonists over the years, and his disgust with them was obvious. His lips compressed, his jaw muscles bulged.

"Your reasoning?" he said, his teeth clenched.

"This evidence, the fact that Ryan took great care to put his fire out, and the distance from the campfire to the first point of ignition. How often have you seen an ember from a campfire explode itself into a forty-foot long jump? And the ember would have had to be good size. Hard to light pine needles or anything else on fire with hot ash drifting down from above."

"I've seen embers go a good distance. The updraft from the fire can loft them farther. It can happen."

"Sure. But think about this kid. He's scared of fire. I'm the one who suggested a campfire. He protested that it would be dangerous. I had to persuade him that a campfire in that fire pit was safe."

"Wait, wait. You're telling me the kid thought it would be dangerous, and you convinced him otherwise?" Terry narrowed his eyes at me.

I ignored what he said. "Ryan kept the fire small. Barely used any logs by the look of the woodpile. If an ember had popped that far, it would have made a serious crack. Certainly Ryan or his sister would have heard it. Ryan would have searched it down and put it out. If he hadn't easily found it, I bet he would have searched with a flashlight. If he still hadn't found it, he would have sprayed all of the surrounding grounds with a hose, or set up an all-night sprinkler."

"You've got a lot of confidence in this kid's character. Known him well for years, have you?"

"I just met him a few days ago. I don't know much about his character, but I have confidence in his dysfunction. I think his neuroses would cause him to worry so much about a potential fire that he would not have gone to bed had a significant ember escaped the fire before he put it out with the hose."

Terry shook his head, disbelieving. "Could be an act. A psychological setup. He's obviously brilliant. Diamond told me about him starting the tech company and all. Maybe all that just hides his sickness."

"Maybe, but I doubt it. I've got a feeling about this."

"You being in the hunch business." Terry's verbal edge was strong. "But this doesn't fit with what I know of arson. Most fire starters do it because it gives their sick, twisted minds a thrill. An arsonist would have set fire directly to the house, not played some game seeing if he could get it to burn the hard way from a distance. And, if Ryan Lear is truly a sicko, he probably wouldn't start a fire near his house."

Terry continued, "If arson is, as you're suggesting, the cause of the fire, the most likely explanation is that the fire was set by the owner of the burned house so he could collect on his insurance. But you and I both know that lakeshore houses are so pricey, his insurance wouldn't come close to making up for the market-value loss. Now if we find out that the guy was thinking about tearing down the house to build something fancier on the same lot, then we'd have a financial motive. But that seems very weak."

"Do you have a time estimate of when the fire started?"

"Our best guess is two a.m. or two-thirty." Terry said.

"And did you ask Ryan what he was doing at that time?"

"Yes. I assumed he would be asleep. But it turns out he was up playing computer games with a friend who was staying over. Someone name William."

"So he has an alibi for that time," I said.

"Hey, McKenna, no one's accusing Ryan Lear of arson. The question is only whether or not it was an ember from his fire that started this conflagration."

"If so," I said, "he'd be responsible. But I have another motive, which will seem weak to you. Ryan hired me because someone is trying to destroy him. He's been kidnapped and tortured. This fire may have been set just to make it look like Ryan was responsible for it. Just to try to unhinge him. From the standpoint of lighting a fire and making it appear that it came from Ryan's fire, this is a good place. It's even out of range from the motion lights. As long as the firestarter had his back toward Officer Vistamon, he wouldn't be seen even if he used a lighter."

"You're saying Ryan Lear could have been framed."

"Right."

Terry shook his head. "Sounds like some kind of a conspiracy theory, like he's a paranoid nutcase."

"He may be paranoid. But this is my idea, not his."

"I'm sure he's got plenty of his own insurance." Terry turned to look at Ryan's house. "Big bank account, too. Being accused of negligence isn't going to destroy him."

"With Ryan, it might. He's wired pretty tight."

"This kid ever been in trouble before?"

"Not that I know of," I said.

"Why would someone want to unglue the kid?"

"To get control of his company, maybe."

"Have you considered that this idea you have that this fire was arson kind of takes you off the hook for telling Lear how much fun a campfire is?"

I looked at Terry. "If expert analysis demonstrates that the fire started from a campfire ember, then my responsibility is greater than Ryan's. They can charge me, not him."

Terry stood back and swept his light from the fire pit to the point of the cone where the ground fire started, and on across the grounds to the steaming, smoking wreckage of the house.

Terry looked at me. "When that guy was torching Tahoe's forests two years ago, I hated it. I woke up every night, two, three in the morning, hating it. It was like some kind of evil had gotten into my life and I couldn't shake it. I couldn't imagine why someone would burn the forest, burn trees, burn animals, burn houses, burn people. I suspected everyone, even my firemen. I don't want to go through that again, McKenna."

Terry was as hard a man as they make, but there was emotion in his eyes as he thought about what he might be facing. This was an intrusion into the sacred part of his world.

"If I'm right," I said, "if this was an attack designed to destroy Ryan Lear, then this fire will be a one-time event. The next will be something different."

Terry called out to one of the firemen.

"Nugent! Get Mack over here. Tell him to bring his camera and gear. And find Sergeant Martinez. This is now an arson investigation."

TWENTY-NINE

Ryan was in full stress when I went back into the house. Diamond hadn't charged him with anything. But the cops' questions had scared him about as much as a person could be scared. If the fire was caused by arson in an attempt to unravel Ryan's tenuous grip on sanity, it was working. He paced and air-washed and talked to himself. And when I got him to stop and talk to me, his right eye was twitching, and his face was blotchy red. I told him that I had a plan to figure out the cause of the fire.

He didn't respond other than continuously shaking his head.

I called Ellie Ibsen at her dog-training ranch down in the foothills. It was only 7:00 a.m., but I knew she'd be up.

She answered with cheer as warm as sunshine in her voice.

"Ellie, darling, Owen McKenna calling."

"Nobody calls me darling anymore," she said.

"I'm sure you've heard that word a lot over the years."

"Yes, but the ones who used to call me that are all dead."

"Not me."

"No. Not you. How are you? How is Street? How is his largeness? Is summer at the lake as glorious as always?"

"Fine, fine, fine, and yes. I'm calling for sage advice from a wise woman."

She laughed. "Oh, Owen, I'm afraid you've reached a wrong number! When I was about fifteen years old, I knew everything. You should have called me then! When I got to twenty-five I was certain that I still knew quite a lot. At fifty, I was starting to doubt some of the basic assumptions that I'd always lived by. And when I got to eighty-five, I came to believe that I really knew only a very few things. Maybe if I live to one hundred, the progression will be complete, and I won't know anything at all."

"Isn't that what Socrates said? That true wisdom comes from realizing that one doesn't really know anything?"

"I think I read that about six decades ago. But that's too philosophical for me now."

"Tell you what," I said. "Here's something that I know. You are the best dog trainer in the world, and I have a conundrum that I would only trust to one of your dogs."

I told her about the fire that burned down Ryan's neighbor's house.

"You think someone lit the fire to make it look as if it had accidentally started from your client's campfire?"

"That's what I suspect. If so, the fire has succeeded in putting a really dark cloud over my client. Is Natasha still your best accelerant dog?"

"Yes, I believe so. But her hips don't work very well anymore. We couldn't take her on steep slopes. She's like me, still alert, but not so spry anymore."

"You were amazing on the mountain above Emerald Bay just last winter. And your Golden, Honey G, was amazing. You could bring him. But this is actually on a flat yard by the lake. No ascending or descending."

"Okay," she said. "Natasha is still more tuned to accelerant searches. So let's use her. When do we go?!" Ellie sounded as excited as a child 80 years her junior.

"How about today? I can be there about nine this morning."

"We'll be ready!"

When I pulled into Ellie's ranch in the foothills town of Coloma near the river where gold was first discovered, Ellie and the small German Shepherd named Natasha were out in the yard. Natasha looked up and trotted out to meet me.

"Where's his largeness?" Ellie sounded concerned.

"He's on duty, staying with Ryan and his sister Lily."

I took Ellie's day pack from her, she got in the Jeep, and I let Natasha into the back seat. We drove back up the American River canyon, came over Echo Summit, and dropped down the cliff-edge road into the basin.

We pulled up to Ryan's house on the East Shore twenty-five

minutes later. Smithy waved from over by the side yard.

Lily and Spot came running out of the house. I introduced Lily to Natasha. The German Shepherd wasn't so sure she wanted to be held by a little girl, and she kept her distance.

Ryan didn't appear. Perhaps he was too upset to come out.

Spot was excited, and he and Natasha ran in circles like the good friends they were. Natasha didn't run as fast as she used to before she broke her hip in the forest fire, but she still moved at a good pace.

Lily was jumping with the excitement of the romping dogs, but she held still long enough to be introduced to Ellie. She asked Ellie a dozen questions in a row, and Ellie patiently explained why she was here and what her dog was going to do.

Then Ellie and I compared notes on our project. I showed her the burned mansion and walked her over to where the burn had started in the pine needles some distance from Ryan's fire pit. Ellie shook her head at the magnitude of the loss, but she didn't dwell on it. She'd spent her career searching for lost hikers and earthquake victims and crime suspects and arsonists. She wasn't immune to tragedy, but she wasn't overly emotional. She was here first and last to do a job.

The dogs ran around, sniffing this and that, including areas that were burned, but paying no particular attention to the burn.

"Let's move downwind from the dogs," Ellie said.

We walked away. She reached into her daypack and pulled out a little vial and a handkerchief.

"I washed the outside of the vial with detergent, so there should be no smell on it. Just one tiny drop into the handkerchief will be enough," she said. "This is lighter fluid, which isn't as aromatic as gasoline. But it will still serve as a trigger for any smell associated with VOCs."

"Volatile Organic Compounds that a firestarter would use."

"Correct," Ellie said.

I told Lily to hold onto Spot, and Ellie called Natasha and held her while I went fifty yards down the road heading downwind.

I unscrewed the eye-dropper, and squeezed out the tiniest bit of fluid onto the handkerchief. I replaced the dropper, taking care not to get any lighter fluid on me or the bottle. Then I folded the handkerchief up so that the moist part with lighter fluid didn't touch my skin. I walked back to Ellie.

"Ready?" she said.

I nodded.

"Okay, Natasha," she said. "Are you ready to do an accelerant search? Find the scent?" Ellie bent down and put her hands on Natasha's body, gave her a shake to get her excited. Then she reached for the handkerchief.

I handed it to her. She put it on Natasha's nose.

"Do you smell the scent, Natasha?"

Natasha pulled her nose away.

Ellie put it back on her nose. "Do you have the scent, Natasha? Okay, find the scent!" She gave Natasha a little pat.

Natasha ran toward the burn area, moving in expanding S-curves and, here and there, in circles. She slowed to a trot, put her nose near the ground, then lifted it high in the air, trying to get a whiff of any scent that might be similar to what Ellie had scented her on with the handkerchief.

It was fascinating to watch this small shepherd who possessed a fierce intelligence. It didn't appear that Natasha picked up any scent, but there was a breeze that would carry away any smells. She'd have to get downwind from the spot where an accelerant had been used. Without slowing, she crossed directly over the small area where the burn had started. This was an immediate disappointment, but I didn't say anything.

Ellie and Lily and I watched the dog work. Back and forth, and up and down. Natasha stayed near the burned area, presumably because her past experience taught her that the odor she was looking for would be found there.

For a while, Spot trotted behind her, curious about her mission. Then he got distracted and stopped. I thought about scenting him on the handkerchief, as well. He'd done a range of searches for accelerants, and suspects and bodies, too. But he wasn't a pro at it, and I didn't want him to distract Natasha.

It was difficult to imagine how a dog can pick up a few unburned molecules of accelerant hours or days after a burn. The fire would have consumed nearly all of whatever chemical was used. And it would seem that any remaining accelerant would have evaporated.

Yet, as Ellie had pointed out in the past, dogs have noses that are ten thousand times as sensitive as our own, and they can outperform the most sophisticated electronic detectors.

I pointed to the narrow area where I believed that a person had purposely started the fire. "Do you think we should direct her to this place?"

Ellie shook her head without looking at me. She was as serious and focused as Natasha.

After several more minutes of searching, Natasha widened her search pattern, and she came back to where she started, directly downwind of the fire's beginning point. Still, she showed no sign of picking up an accelerant.

"Nothing," Ellie said. "I believe there are no VOCs anywhere near."

"So it wasn't arson," I said.

"I didn't say that. Just that if a person did light this fire, they didn't use lighter fluid or gasoline or any similar VOCs. But a person could have picked up an ember from the fire pit and set it down where the fire started."

"Ryan put it out with a hose before he went to bed. I believe he was very thorough."

"The ember or embers could have come from a different fire and were brought to this location," she said.

"Which would make it very difficult to tell unless the ember was from a kind of wood that we don't have here. Like oak."

"Or a charcoal briquette," Ellie said. "We could scent Natasha on embers of ash from woods that wouldn't be here naturally. But I think it would be very difficult for Natasha to tell the difference with any accuracy. It would be like distinguishing between regular gasoline and gas that was mixed with ethanol."

"What you said once about signal-to-noise ratio."

Ellie gave me a huge grin. "You remembered that?"

"Any other ideas before we take you and Natasha back home."

She nodded. "There is still the simplest thing we can look for."

I raised my eyebrows.

"If I want to start a fire with some tinder, it can be done

without an accelerant."

"Of course," I said. "I can bunch up a bit of pine needles and a few twigs and light it directly. A cigarette lighter would probably leave a trace of accelerant that Natasha could smell. So that is unlikely. But I could also strike a match. Natasha would be able to find that, right?"

Ellie nodded. "I didn't bring any, did you?" she said.

I shook my head. "Ryan will have something." I walked over to his house and rang the bell. Lily let me in and yelled for Ryan.

He came, still looking nearly as blotchy as he had that morning, but he was holding a bunch of stapled sheets of paper, and he was talking on his hands-free phone, something about theoretical models. He gave me a questioning look.

"Matches?" I said.

He frowned, thinking, talking as he walked into the kitchen and found a book of matches in a drawer. It was obvious as he talked shop that he was very self-confident in the world of science, the opposite of his frightened, nervous persona the rest of the time. He handed me the matchbook.

"Thanks."

Back outside, I held them up for Ellie to see.

She nodded. "Take them a good distance downwind, then strike a few of them and let them burn out."

I did as she said, and brought them back.

Ellie held out a tissue, and I dropped the charred pieces onto it. She called Natasha, who immediately stopped what she was doing, ran to Ellie and sat in front of her.

Her movement caught Spot's attention.

"You see how Natasha comes when called?" I said to him.

He ignored me.

Ellie went through the same routine with Natasha again, this time scenting her on the burned matches.

"Find the scent!" she said.

Natasha ran directly to one of the small spots where the fire had started, and pounced on it with her front paws. Her tail was up and wagging, a classic alert. She pawed at the dirt, stuck her nose in it, huffed and puffed, and pawed some more.

Ellie walked over and praised her effusively, then stepped over the area where Natasha was alerting, displacing the dog. "Natasha," Ellie said. "Find more scent! Find the scent!"

Natasha looked up at her, wagging, staring at Ellie's eyes.

"Go on, girl. Find the scent!"

Natasha turned, trotted a few paces over to the other place where it looked like the fire had dwindled and then been rekindled, and pounced on it, digging with her paws.

"Good girl, Natasha!" Ellie said. She looked at me, beaming.

"Helluva dog, Ellie. You just saved Ryan about ten million dollars."

"What?!"

"You've demonstrated that the fire was arson. And Ryan has an alibi for the time of the fire. He was playing video games with his friend. So you've absolved Ryan of negligence. The fire wasn't his fault, so he won't have to pay."

"Oh, my goodness! I'm so glad. No one could possibly have that kind of money in the bank, never mind a man as young as Ryan."

I smiled at her. I went to the house. This time Ryan hadn't locked the door. I opened it without knocking and hollered for Ryan. He came down the stairs, still talking on the phone. I made the quit sign by drawing my hand in front of my throat.

"Call you back," he said, then touched a button on the phone that was clipped to his belt. He stopped halfway down the stairs and put his hand on the railing as if to support himself, assuming I was about to report bad news.

"Ellie Ibsen scented her dog Natasha on burned matches. Natasha made a strong alert on the two places where the fire was started. That means the fire was started by an arsonist in an effort to frame you for negligence. You have an alibi. You are clear."

Ryan's permanent frown disappeared as his face relaxed. He shut his eyes, tipped his head back and breathed long and deep.

"That is so great! I mean, it's a terrible tragedy that my neighbor's house burned. But it didn't come from our campfire."

Ryan ran down the rest of the stairs, and bolted out the door. I looked out the door just in time to see him hug Ellie, and lift her off the ground. He set her down and began bouncing in front of her the same way Lily liked to bounce.

I went out and watched Ellie closely to look for signs of broken ribs or any other internal damage. But she just grinned.

"What do we do now?" Ryan said. "Is there some affidavit or something to sign? How do we make the authorities believe it?"

"We don't have to," I said. "Ellie's rep is more pure than George Washington's. She says what happened, the fire investigator Terry Drier says okay, and he no longer considers you as he begins his arson investigation. Diamond tells the DA, and the DA also accepts it as fact."

"Oh, I'm not that golden," Ellie said.

"Yes, she is," I said to Ryan.

Ryan went to hug her again, but Ellie got her palm up and in between them.

"Please, I'm still trying to breathe after the last hug."

"Oh, I'm so sorry. Did I hurt you?" Ryan looked sick.

"Don't worry, I'm okay."

"I didn't mean to..."

"Ryan," I said. "It's okay. Go tell Lily the good news."

He realized he was going overboard in his reaction, stopped himself, thanked Ellie again and left. I made quick phone calls to Diamond and Terry Drier. Then Ellie and I put Natasha in the Jeep, and I delivered them back down to the foothills.

THIRTY

It was the middle of the afternoon when I got back to Tahoe. There is a lot of dead space coming up the American River Canyon. When I got back into signal range, two messages popped up on my cell, one from Ryan, one from Diamond. I called Ryan first.

"I need to take Lily over to the school for a meeting. They're trying to decide whether to skip her a grade. Should we go alone? Or take Praeger with us?"

"Ask Praeger what he thinks. My guess is that it's okay to go alone in broad daylight as long as you keep your doors locked, and don't get out except in public places where other people are around. It's good for Praeger to watch the house."

"What about Spot? Should I just leave him in the house?"

"When do you leave?"

"An hour."

"I'll be there by then."

Next I returned Diamond's call.

"Douglas County spends all this money on patrol units," he said when he found out it was me, "but they don't check the batteries," Diamond said. "It's dead."

"McKenna transit company at your service, sergeant."

"I called both deputies that are up here at the lake. Both are busy. Then I called our road service provider, and they said it's an hour and a half wait."

"Where're you at?" I asked.

"We've had some vehicle break-ins at the trailhead at Spooner Summit. So I stopped to check. I heard a noise I couldn't place, so I hiked up the trail a bit. Didn't see anything, so I came back. Now my patrol unit won't start. I'm down to two options. One, you come get me. Two, I hitchhike."

"Looks bad for passersby to see Douglas County's finest hitching a ride. I'll be there in twenty-five minutes."

Diamond's SUV was easy to spot. I pulled up.

"Solenoid not kicking in?" I said.

"You gringos are so into cars. What's that gearhead thing about? You read art books, yet you know about solenoids."

"I don't know anything about solenoids. Just a word I heard. But I also heard that when the battery gets low, the solenoid won't pop out and engage the starter. It just clicks."

"So?"

"So, did it click?"

"I turned the key. No click."

"Then it's more than just a low battery." I looked at the hood latch. The sheet metal was bent. The release cable had been cut.

I popped the hood and showed Diamond. "Check it out. Battery cable was cut. These are big cables. He must have had a bolt cutter. Or a hammer and chisel."

I dropped the lid.

"For every bandito in Mexico," Diamond said, "we've got a norteamericano vandal making our life miserable up here."

"Is this the same patrol unit you brought to Ryan's house?"

"Let me think. Yeah. Twice. You think this is the guy screwing with Ryan?"

"Could be."

Diamond got into my Jeep, and I drove down the long and winding road from Spooner Summit.

After we went through Cave Rock, I said, "I need to pick up Spot at Ryan's house."

Diamond shrugged.

I turned off toward the lake, and drove to Ryan's drive.

In the lot next door, a small articulated crane was lifting a Glulam beam up onto a framework of posts. Two men on each end were fitting it into heavy metal brackets. Eventually, the Glulams would hold up the roof of the Washoe Spirit Center.

Lily, Spot, and Ryan came out of the front door as Diamond and I got out.

"Any news?" Ryan asked.

I shook my head. "I want to talk to the woman at your party named Champagne."

"Why?"

"She knows you."

"Not really."

"Sort of, then. And she knows other people who know you. She's close to Preston Laurence."

"Do you suspect him of something?"

"Everybody who knows you or knows of you is a suspect until we catch this guy."

Ryan widened his eyes. "That's not what... I didn't think you would pursue my friends."

"The killer is probably a friend or an acquaintance."

Ryan frowned. He looked at Diamond. "Is that really true?"

Diamond nodded.

"I don't like thinking that," Ryan said.

"No one does," I said. "Do you know how to reach Champagne?"

"I don't have her phone number. But she lives with her parents in Reno. Or at least she did last I knew. The number is probably in the book. I think her father's name is Paul. Paul Pumpernickel."

"Thanks. I'll let you know if I learn anything."

"What will you ask her? Will you be sensitive?"

"Asking questions is the nature of my job. I poke around. I look under rocks and see what slimy creatures crawl out. Sometimes I ask uncomfortable questions. I try to trip people up, catch them in inconsistencies, get them to say things they later wish they hadn't said. Champagne may not like talking to me. But she won't hold you responsible for that. If she gets upset, she'll just think that I'm a jerk."

After a moment, Ryan said, "Okay."

Diamond and I got in the Jeep. We waited until Ryan and Lily pulled out, then we followed them to the highway.

The tourist traffic was heavy enough to reduce us to slow-and-go before we even got to Kingsbury Grade. In front of us were a bunch of motorcycles. I got into the left lane just as the light turned red. Everybody eased from crawl to stop. We were the last in line. Should have stayed in the right lane.

"Two, four, six, eight, ten, twelve bikers," Diamond said. "All riding two-up, all wearing black leather. Like a uniform."

To the side of the road was a constant line of bicyclers. Part of some Tahoe circumnavigation ride.

"Even more bicyclists," I said, "all wearing brightly colored Spandex and special shoes."

"Bicyclists are mostly skinnier people than motorcyclists," Diamond said. "Need narrower uniforms."

"You Mexicans are observant."

"The cop in me."

I pointed at Edgewood golf course. "Numerous foursomes on the links, all wearing the same cut of pants and shirts."

"Just like the bikers," Diamond said. "You rode some over the years."

"Nothing more fun. Still got my jacket and helmet," I said.

"They black?"

"Yeah."

Diamond nodded approval. "Just making sure you fit in."

"But my helmet is a full-face model. Makes it a lot harder to spill your brains."

"Always a nonconformist in some way," Diamond said.

Spot pulled his head in from the right rear window. He shook his jowls. Nothing hit me, but Diamond made a show of wiping his cheek.

A silver Mustang convertible with the top down pulled up next to us on Diamond's side. There were four young women in it. They all wore bikinis in different colors.

"Mustang uniform," Diamond said under his breath.

They all talked and laughed with great animation. Maybe they were practicing for a Mustang commercial. Maybe there was a helicopter and cameraman above at that moment.

Spot put his head back out the window.

"Oooweee!" one of them shouted, pointing. "Look at that dog! Mister, what kind of dog is that?"

Before Diamond could answer, another one shouted, "It's a Dalmatian."

"No it's not," said another. "It's, like, waaaay bigger."

"No kidding," said a third.

"What is it?" repeated the first.

"Harlequin Great Dane," Diamond said.

Spot was wagging at the attention. He looked like he might jump into the Mustang.

"I'm calling Bo," the driver said.

"No way your sugar daddy gonna buy you a Great Dane," another woman said.

"He bought me this car. He'd buy me a Great Dane to sit in it. Right where you're sitting." She pointed at the other woman.

The light turned green and the motorcycles all roared so loud that two of the women put their fingers in their ears. Everybody moved ahead. I rolled my window up against the noise.

"Too loud for you?" Diamond said when the bikers finally got far enough ahead that we could hear something else. "You could put your fingers in your ears like those girls."

"I would have if I weren't driving. Protect my hearing. You coulda put your fingers in your ears."

"I don't put my fingers in my ears," Diamond said.

"That the cop in you, too?"

"That's the Mexican in me."

I turned left on Kingsbury Grade, drove up and turned into my office parking lot.

Two guys in muscle shirts and cowboy hats came walking down Kingsbury Grade carrying beers in tall glasses. By their walk, they'd had more than a few.

"Check out the cowboys," I said to Diamond. "Street and I saw them up on the mountain. Jerks on horseback. Making cracks about the color of Lana's houseguests."

I got out of the Jeep, let Spot out the back door. Diamond didn't immediately get out. Maybe on purpose. Maybe calling for backup.

"Lookie here," one of the cowboys said. "We got the big doggie and McKenna the private detective."

"Hey guys," I said. "You know my name, but I don't know yours."

One of them gestured with his beer. "Up at the bar, two different people had a quick answer to the question about the tall guy and the big, spotted dog."

"Still didn't get your name," I said.

"Didn't offer it," the other said.

They walked up to a white Ford pickup with a full-width silver tool box at the front of the bed. It reminded me of the pickup that belonged to Lana and her nephew Tory. The cowboys paused at the pickup's doors.

I willed them to get in and start it up so that Diamond could use the powers of the state to shake them down for drinking and driving. If they didn't, he could still probably get them on public alcohol consumption, but it would be much easier if they got in and turned the key. They didn't move. They each drank beer.

"On your way, boys. Hope you enjoyed your stay in Tahoe." I took Spot's collar and walked toward my office.

"Not very welcoming to tourists, is he," one said.

"Mountain cretins everywhere," the other said.

I turned and walked toward them. "It's been a long day. Please leave."

"Polite," one of them said.

"Standard attitude for *those* kind of guys," the other said. "That's how they try to avoid confrontation. Let's go."

They got in their truck, started it up, revved the engine, and drove out of the lot only to jerk to a stop as one, and then two, Douglas County patrol units pulled up, light bars flashing.

Diamond got out of my Jeep, and the men saw him, and their eyes were aflame as the Douglas County deputies put them through the routine.

Spot and I sat down on the curb and watched. When they took the men away in the back of one of the SUVs, the one on my side of the back seat looked out at me with rage.

"Names?" I said to Diamond as he walked up afterward.

"Mark Marwell and Evan Paguette. Oakland address for the former, Hayward on the latter. Both went silent as if they've been through this before. I'll let you know when we learn more."

Diamond got into the other patrol vehicle, and left.

THIRTY-ONE

I went into my office to check the machine and scan my calendar. I pulled the Reno book off the shelf and found Paul Pumpernickel's phone number. I dialed. Spot lay down while it rang. A woman answered.

"Hello, Mrs. Pumpernickel. My name is Owen McKenna. I'm calling for Carol. Is she in, please?"

"Who are you, again?"

"Owen McKenna. I met Carol at a get-together up at the lake."

"Chrissakes, that girl attracts more boy pals than a show horse attracts flies."

"I'm not interested in her in that way," I said.

Long pause. "Are you one of Mr. Laurence's men?"

I thought about her tone. Suspicion and worry.

"I'm not connected to Preston Laurence. I'm a private investigator, and I'm working on a case that involves Laurence."

"Don't tell me that Carol has done something wrong." She sounded like she was pleading.

"Did she give you a reason to think that?"

"No. But Mr. Laurence did. I've only met him once, but he scares me. I'm worried for my girl."

"Have you seen her recently?"

"That's just it. We haven't heard from her for a week, no, eight days now. That's not like her. If she was back living in LA, I wouldn't expect her to check in much. But when you're staying with your ma and pa, it's just common decency to call if you're not going to come home at night."

"You're saying she's been missing for eight days?"

"Yes."

"Have you heard from any of her friends?"

"Five, six days ago, I got a call from her friend Darin, and he said he saw her a few days before, but he couldn't find her. He wondered if she was at home. I don't know what to think. Mr. Laurence worries me. He seemed like his interest in my girl wasn't... healthy. Please tell me that your investigation doesn't mean she's been involved in a crime. She has hung around some bad men in the past."

"I can't say that for sure, but our primary interest is Preston Laurence. Do you think Darin has found her?"

"I don't know. You could call him."

"Do you know his number?"

"No. But his last name is Smirnoff. Like the vodka. You could look in the book. Or you could try his work. He works at that big condo development in Incline Village. I forget the name. He's the concierge or something like that."

"Which development is that?"

"On the main highway there in Incline. It's on the corner of... There I go. Talk about senior moments. Lake side. Brown with dark brown trim. Maybe six or eight different buildings. Good looking place."

"Got it," I said. "Thanks, Mrs. Pumpernickel."

"Will you ask her to call me when you find her?"

"Will do."

I dialed information for Incline Village, but they didn't have a Darin Smirnoff. So I got in the Jeep and went back to Ryan's.

He and Lily weren't back from the school appointment, yet. I let Spot run around while I waited. I got out my wallet and pulled out the note with Herman's code.

I took it from another direction. Instead of multiplying the beats by two and figuring what the letters would be, I multiplied by three. Unfortunately, there were several notes with beat rates of more than eight per second. Multiplying by three gave results higher than twenty-six, so there were no letters that corresponded. I stared at the letters, willing them to make sense. A few minutes later, Ryan and Lily pulled up.

"I start second grade instead of first," Lily said as she ran up to Spot.

"Because you're smart?"

"Because I have good ideas."

"Actually," Ryan said, "it mostly gets down to her reading level."

I congratulated them. Then I explained to Ryan that I needed to borrow Spot for the evening. I asked Ryan if he could take Lily out on the town, go to the movies, dinner, stay in public, maybe hang out in one of the hotel lobbies for a duration to be determined. When I got back to his house, I'd call and tell him that the coast was clear.

He agreed.

So I waited while he checked movie schedules, and found warmer clothes for Lily.

When he and Lily left, Spot and I left, too.

I drove up to the north shore.

I cruised the main drag in Incline, saw a possible condo project, continued on. When I got to the Mt. Rose Highway, I turned around. On my way back through town I saw no other good possibilities. So I parked, and went into the office.

A pleasant woman greeted me and asked if I had a reservation.

I smiled. "No, I just stopped by to see Darin, tell him I found his sunglasses."

"Oh, he's on break. Said he was going to grab a chocolate shake. I swear I don't know how that guy stays so skinny with all the shakes he drinks."

"Me neither," I said. "Any idea when he'll be back?"

She looked at the clock. "Ten minutes or less. He can't be late, 'cause that laundry's got to be all folded and stored before he clocks out."

I thanked her, and waited out in the lot, thought about what it meant that Carol's mother thought that Carol's good bud in Incline was a concierge. Five minutes later, an old rusted Subaru drove up and parked. The guy who got out was in his early thirties and was skinny like the picture on a famine-relief brochure. His white shirt was untucked on the left side. He shambled his way toward the office, walking so slow that it was obvious that work wasn't at the top of his list of hot activities.

"Hey, Darin," I called out as I walked toward him.

He turned and stopped.

"I'm Owen, a friend of Carol Pumpernickel."

He shook my hand, looked me over, looked at my old Jeep. I was glad I wasn't driving a new BMW.

"Wassup?" he said.

"I was trying to reach Carol. But she hasn't been home for awhile. Her mother thought you might know where she is."

He regarded me. "I never heard nothin' 'bout you. You even know what her new name is?"

I chuckled. "Oh sure, Champagne Forest. I'm totally onboard with the showbiz thing. You want to get on the big screen, Pumpernickel probably ain't the ticket. But I haven't made the switch to calling her Champagne myself. How 'bout you? Champagne or Carol?"

He made a little grin. "She'll always be Carol to me. But Champagne's kind of a babe handle. Makes sense when you think about it."

"You heard from her lately?"

He shook his head. "But she doesn't keep me up to date. Ever since that party got busted over on the California side. They made like my medical marijuana card wasn't valid. She was smoking, too, and she didn't have a card. They let her go and hauled me in. What's that about? But I guess when you look like her, life is easier, huh?"

"Yeah. Any idea where I'd catch up with her?"

He shook his head. "I'd probably talk to Grady at O'Leary's. You know how she's always been into that Irish beer. Me, I'm a Coors guy myself."

"Really? Me too. Guinness makes your mouth pucker," I said.

"Right on," he said, high-fiving me. I did the palm-smack. We were practically blood brothers. "Thanks, man, I'll check out O'Leary's."

I drove to the nearest gas station and asked where O'Leary's was, and was directed to a pub one block off the main drag.

It was dark inside, the major light source being two TVs, one at either end of the bar. There was a program on that showed a bifurcated screen with a news logo at the bottom. Two guys were screaming at each other, blaming each other's politics for the state of the world. No wonder I listen to NPR. Behind the counter was a guy who wielded a dishrag like it was the star of a ballet, all swirly moves and pirouettes as he wiped down the thickly-varnished mahogany. He wore a dress T-shirt. Above the pocket was the word Grady, stitched in swirling, green thread.

"Hey, Grady. I'm a friend of Carol Champagne Pumpernickel Forest. Darin said maybe you would know where to find her."

"I'm with you on the name change," he said. "But she looks like champagne, I'll give her that. I don't know where she is, but your timing is good." He jerked his head toward the window. "You catch that guy who's getting into his pickup, maybe he can help. He was just getting his afternoon bump and telling me a story. Sounded like her."

"Thanks." I trotted out the door. The pickup had backed out of a parking place, was starting to move forward. I got in front of the truck and waved. The driver's window rolled down.

Inside was a cowboy wannabe, a big guy with the bad-guy hat, black, with a curved brim that looked like it was snarling.

"Afternoon," he said with post-beer cheer.

"Hi. Wondered if I could ask you a question. Bartender Grady said you just told him a story about a woman, and he thought it might be our friend Champagne. Several of us have been looking for her. Any idea where she is?"

"Hold on while I park." He pulled back into the parking place. He got out and made a show of getting into position, his back to his truck, his feet out from the truck just enough that he could comfortably lean back. The man eased his butt back against the driver's door, holding the ring of keys on his belt so that they didn't bang against the truck's paint. It was a Silverado pickup of one of the earlier vintages, but freshly polished and shiny black as if it had been recently repainted. His hitched his thumbs into his belt loops, cocked one knee and hooked the under-cut heel of his glistening cowboy boot onto the running board of the truck. His curved hat brim swooped down over his eyebrows and cast dark shadows over his face.

"Tell you what," he said. "I'll relate to you the story I told Grady, and you can decide if it might be the girl you want. See, me and my lady were coming through town last night, and we saw this girl get out of the car in front of us. I remembered it because it had been raining and it didn't seem like a good time to take a hike. I also remembered it because she was one sweet package, and she got out of one sweet ride."

"Any chance you saw the make of the vehicle?" I asked.

"Make? Mister, I'm in the oil business. Knowing my wheels is how I put cheese on my burgers. It was a nineteen-seventy Hemi 'Cuda hardtop, painted Wheaties-box orange with the deep-gloss finish, tricked out with TQ wheels and Pro-Trac tires. And by the sound of the pipes, I'm guessing he's got the four twenty-six big-block in it. Very rare. I saw in Auto News how one like it went for seven-hundred thousand at the Strasbenner Auction in Palm Springs. Only car I ever saw sold for more money was the sixty-six Shelby Cobra Supersnake. That 'Cuda's the sweetest ride I ever saw in Incline. You cruise the land of Lexus in that baby, not much chance of going unnoticed by an oil man."

"What area of the oil business are you in?"

"I'm an R double L. Retail Lubrication Liaison. Which means I work at a Jiffy Lube in Reno."

I nodded.

He made a quick, short-lived grin. "So this 'Cuda stops in front of me at a red light, and she gets out, slams the door, and walks down the highway past me and the missus. She goes right by our truck, teetering in these heels that are so high she had to do the wobble walk to keep her balance. I've seen circus acts weren't that impressive. We'd had a little pretend thunderstorm, and the streets were still wet so they reflected the headlights and taillights. It was like she was walking on glass. She had on a long black coat that kept flipping open in the breeze so we could see the little blue dress. It was clear as day what with my new xenon headlights. I said to my lady, 'Musta been a real hot argument for the model to walk away from that 'Cuda ride.'"

It sounded like the same dress as the one Champagne wore to Ryan's party. I'd seen her arguing with someone, but I couldn't see who it was. Perhaps the driver of the 'Cuda.

"You knew that she was a model?"

"No. But if she ain't, she should be."

"Where'd she go?"

"Don't know for certain. Kept walking on down past the cars behind me. Then 'Cuda half-turns, half-spins a U-eey in the intersection, those big Pro-Tracs steaming as they spun the rain into burning rubber. He raced away in my rearview mirror. Then I heard him screech to a stop. So I assume he picked her back up. Unless she climbed into one of those local Lexuses. Now how would you say that in the plural? Lex-eye? Lex-ees?" The R double L laughed and then hacked and spit.

"All I know is, I love my lady. But if I had a piece of work like that model, I sure as hell wouldn't let her walk away and climb into any Lex-eye behind me. I know that like I know the oil business."

I thanked him, got into my Jeep and dialed Ryan. I was thinking about how Street described parking next to a muscle car at Ryan's party.

When he answered, I said, "Do you know anyone who has an orange, nineteen-seventy, Hemi 'Cuda hardtop?"

"What's that?" He said. The noise in the background was loud like a movie theater lobby.

"Plymouth Barracuda with a special engine that featured cupped, hemispherical combustion chambers. One of the hottest rides of the muscle car era."

"Never heard of it. By muscle car, do you mean lots of horsepower?"

I didn't think Ryan could keep sounding even younger and more naive, but he kept surprising me.

"Yes," I said. "Big displacement engines, lots of horsepower."

"Well, I wouldn't know about makes and such, but Preston Laurence is into cars with lots of horsepower. That might be like him to buy old cars with muscle, as you call it. Why do you ask?"

"Because Carol Champagne was seen getting out of such a vehicle on the highway last night after your party. Would she do that? Is she tempestuous?"

"Yes, she's sometimes moody. I've seen her temper flare. It wouldn't surprise me."

"Is there anyone you can call to see if Preston has a Hemi 'Cuda?"

"Let me think. Yeah, maybe. Call you back?"

"I'll be waiting," I said.

I headed for a local fast food and was waiting for my serving of salt and fat when my phone rang.

"Yes," Ryan said when I answered. "Preston does in fact have a Hemi 'Cuda."

"Thanks. Where is Preston's place in Tahoe?"

"It's over on Dollar Point. Hold on, I might have the number in my contact list."

I waited.

Ryan read me the address. "There's a couple of streets in that neighborhood that are on the lake. There's a cul-de-sac on one street that looks like a turnaround, but at the end is the entrance to a private road. You'd never notice if you didn't know it was there. After you go in, you won't miss the house. Preston bought three adjacent houses and tore them down to put up his."

"Got it. Thanks."

I hung up. Spot had his head out the open Jeep window as I approached. He knew what I was up to, and he leaned as far toward me as he could, his nose flexing. He struggled to stick a front paw out next to his head, hanging down over the window sill. He looked ready to jump out, except I knew he couldn't fit his chest through the window with the glass partway up.

"Stop, Spot," I said, holding my hand up like I was a rookie back on traffic detail in The City.

He stared at me.

I reached into my bag. "You know this stuff is bad for you."

He licked his chops.

I Frisbeed a french fry toward him. He snapped it out of the air. Then his tongue carefully rimmed the edges of his cavernous mouth. He stared at the bag. Then at my eyes. Then at the bag. We ended up splitting the fries and the burger, and I rationalized it by deciding that we each prevented the other from having a full onslaught of health-degrading decadence.

We got back in the Jeep.

Time to pay a visit to Preston Laurence.

THIRTY-TWO

I went west around the top of the lake on one of those late afternoons when the sun has turned everything so golden that tourists decide to quit their jobs in New York, cash out the retirement account, put on the mother of all garage sales, sell the house in New Jersey, the beachfront condo in South Carolina, dump the Suburban for half of Blue Book, and point the Mini Cooper west, with no cargo to speak of except the snowboards in the roof rack and the swimming suits in the daypacks.

There was a light chop on the water, which fractured the low sunlight into a billion pieces of glowing amber. Each time I came around a curve, it seemed that I spied another ribbon of perfect sand beach. Here and there were glam-tan teens who were maybe doing a volleyball or sailing shoot for the next Abercrombie & Fitch catalog. Their lithe sculpted forms belied the national obesity epidemic and reminded vacationers that there were still places on the planet where outdoor recreation pulled rank on video entertainment and left as its result a level of fitness and sports skill so high that despite Tahoe/Truckee's tiny population, 14 of our young adults competed in the last Winter Olympics, a percentage perhaps unmatched anywhere else in the world.

Behind the athlete-beach dwellers was a backdrop of water that served as the color model for artists who are always on the lookout for the purest, deepest, bestest blue. And beyond the far shore were the mountains, still dappled with patches of snow, small at a distance, but large enough up close to provide a corn-snow-dream descent for the hikers who carry their boards and skis strapped to their backpacks.

Past Crystal Bay and Agate Bay and Carnelian Bay, I turned off on Dollar Point, and made my way through the street maze that was designed by its planners to reduce the amount of riffraff traffic on the streets by the lake. I found the cul-de-sac and turned down the nearly hidden road.

Preston Laurence's lakeside cabin was probably a dreary step down from the castle on his 500-acre horse and vineyard ranch in the foothill wine country. But a glimpse at the outside still suggested a living room that could hold a Polo match, a fireplace that could roast a small elk on a spit, the kind of kitchen that made the chef at the Cape Cod Room in Chicago envious, and bathrooms in each of eight or ten bedroom suites that would please Louis the XVI even when he was drunk and ornery.

Preston's palace was surrounded by a stone wall at least two feet higher than was allowed by county code. The gate to his estate was wrought iron with a shiny golden coat of arms mounted in the center. It had a logo design incorporating a P and an L, and underneath it was an illustration of a horse and a vineyard. It looked impressive on the gate, and was probably monogrammed onto Preston's underwear, too. The gate was big and heavy enough that it didn't swing, but instead slid on roller tracks, retracting into a stone housing. The gatehouse was stone and timberframe with a pointy copper roof.

From out of the gatehouse sauntered a big guy. He was not sculpted, bodybuilder big, but NFL-linebacker-gone-flabby big. Under the beer-and-cheeseburger roundness would be heavy slabs of well-marbled beef. I couldn't see it under the Hawaiian shirt, but I assumed he had a belt-clip holster with a semi-automatic pistol. Despite the approaching twilight, his eyes were hidden behind Ray-Ban Wayfarers. On his left forearm was an Aztec tattoo that meant he'd once been part of the Norteños, a Northern California Hispanic gang that required murder on your resumé before you were admitted.

He radiated brusque toughness, every move a veiled challenge to any other alpha wannabes. I knew the type well, big guys in their thirties and early forties, past their athletic prime, with no attributes other than their bigness. Some were ex-military, some were ex-construction workers, some were ex-bar bouncers, some were ex-cons. But all had difficulty maintaining continuous gainful employment. Their more focused and disciplined contemporaries were making the transition from physical labor into mental labor, gaining a new level of responsibility in the job world. But the guys like the one in front of me weren't up to the mental exercise. They could only hope to parlay a stint as an occasional bodyguard into an ongoing gig as muscle for a rogue rich guy whose activities weren't clean enough to employ professional security firms.

"Help you," he said. Airy voice that indicated past damage to the vocal cords.

"I'm here to see Preston," I said.

"You have an appointment?"

"Buddies don't make appointments. Actually, it was Champagne who I just talked to on the phone. I'll check in with her and catch up with Pres some other time."

He waited a beat too long before he said, "I don't know any Champagne."

"Maybe you don't know her, but you've probably seen her around. Homely girl with blonde hair. But she's real nice after you get to know her. Pres seems to like her enough."

He looked at me with dead eyes. "I'll have to ask you to leave." He came closer. There was stitched lettering on his shirt. Above the P and L logo was the word Joe in fancy script.

"Look, Joe. I'm sure we can work this out. Champagne wants to see me. If I go in and talk to her, we'll all be happy. Pres won't know the difference. But if she finds out that you obstructed my visit, she'll complain to Pres. I'll complain to Pres. What will happen to you, crossing the wishes of his dream girl?"

Joe snorted. "If she was his dream girl, he wouldn't have given her the..." The guard caught himself and stopped.

"Given her what, Joe? The shiner? The bruise? The broken nose?" I was ready to jump out of the Jeep.

He pointed toward the turn-around loop. As he raised his arm and the shirt lifted a little over the belly, I saw the holster clipped to his belt, and next to it, a radio. Which meant that he wasn't alone in his duties.

"You realize you are an accessory, Joe? Do you want to go back inside?"

He lifted his shirt to show me his gun.

I nodded, drove around the loop, and left.

THIRTY-THREE

I parked on a side street on the opposite side of Dollar Point. The twilight was fast turning to a black, moonless night. I went over my evidence.

At Ryan's party, Street overheard Champagne talking with other ladies about Heat, and then saying that she was frightened for herself and for Ryan. After the party, Champagne was angry enough, or frightened enough, that she'd gotten out of Preston's muscle car on the highway at night. Champagne's mother said that Champagne had disappeared, and that she was worried about Champagne and scared of Preston Laurence. Preston's guard denied Champagne's existence, then more or less admitted that Preston had hurt her.

There was a big risk in breaking into Preston's house. Eli and Jeanie had already died. From everything I'd seen, Ryan's life was at stake. If Champagne was in fact being abused, then her life was at stake. I didn't have any other leads. And I'd learned over the years that pulling on the errant thread often unravels the fabric.

I let Spot out of the Jeep. I took his collar. Spot is tall enough that I don't need a leash. He matched his pace to mine. We walked under the stars down a dark street that led to large houses on the lake. Some were nestled behind serious fences. The rest had the size and style that suggested the presence of comprehensive alarm systems. I wasn't planning to break into a house, but I still didn't want cameras covering the grounds.

A vehicle approached from a side street, its headlights washing over us as we walked through an intersection. It came to a stop, then turned away from us, but not before they got a good look at the neighborhood interlopers. After its headlights moved on, I looked to see the vehicle make. There was only a dark shape and taillights to see.

Spot was alert, focusing eyes and ears at things that were invisible to me. As we moved along the lakeshore houses, my idea of borrowing a boat to get around the fence at Preston Laurence's castle seemed ridiculous. I could see boats down at the docks, but they were all powerboats. I needed something silent, like a kayak, or a rowboat, or a canoe.

Spot and I walked down another street, then another. A pickup came up from behind me, went on past, and pulled into a short driveway. The driver got out, shut the door, and pushed a button on his key fob. The pickup's lights flashed and the horn beeped as the alarm was set. The driver went into the closest house.

The pickup's bed was covered by a topper. Attached to the topper was a custom rack. Strapped to the rack, and extending out over the pickup's cab and even its hood, was a two-seat rowing shell. The shell was about 18 inches wide. I'd seen narrower, longer shells in the past. But this looked to be as precarious a boat design as one could imagine on Tahoe, which is so big it rarely has calm water. With a length of maybe 24 feet from one pointed end to the other, it looked more like a double-ended missile than a boat. The hull was round from side to side, and it would no doubt be very tippy to sit on. The shell had two sets of triangular frames that projected out from the sides of the boat and served as the oarlocks. Two seats were perched up above the deck and mounted on tracks that allowed them to travel forward and backward as the occupants rowed. While the design was perfect for practiced rowers, it was a capsize-waiting-to-happen for a landlubber like me.

By any reasonable measure, a precariously-balanced rowing shell was not an appropriate vehicle with which to rescue a maiden from the castle tower.

But there were two considerations that were as attractive to me as a fire truck is to a person in a burning house. The first was that it was the only boat I could find. The second was that, if I could row it without dumping myself into the drink - a big if - I could probably propel the sleek craft at near water-ski speed. To silently race through the darkness at high speed would make me hard to see, an ideal attribute for escaping the gendarmes guarding Preston's estate.

I stood in the dark, staring at the boat, visualizing how it could work. The seats faced backward. If I sat and rowed from the front seat, I could possibly get Spot to hunch down over the rear seat, with his feet on the floor of the boat, and I'd be able to keep an eye on him.

But that didn't answer the question of how to fit two people and a dog into such a tiny escape vehicle. I could eliminate the question by leaving Spot in the Jeep. But I'd learned many times that Spot's presence almost always has a bigger upside than downside. In a standoff, Spot can be more intimidating than I would be with a gun.

I thought about it. But I couldn't see how to turn the tiny rowing shell into a three-passenger craft.

Of course, first I had to actually find Champagne. And she had to be persuaded to come away with me. But getting beat up by Preston would motivate her.

I could call the Placer County Sheriff's Office and give them my hunch. I have a good hunch record. But cops can't get a search warrant on a hunch, and cops are required to play by the rules. I play by rules, too. But my rules say that a woman's life is more important than waiting on proper paperwork, even if my idea is based on supposition and hunch.

I quietly unstrapped the rowing shell from the carrier rack. I had no idea what kind of alarm the truck had, so I was very careful to prevent rocking the vehicle.

Four oars lay in cradles on the roof rack. I only needed two. I took them out one at a time and set them into the front set of oarlocks. There were clips positioned on the sides of the boat to hold the blades. Once I had two oars attached, the question was how to carry the boat. It had two handles, perfect for two people to carry it.

I lifted gently on each end of the shell to gauge the weight and balance. It looked sleek and light, but the seats and rigging hardware made it heavier. After several deep breaths, I took hold of the middle of the boat, and hefted it up onto my right shoulder, palming the bottom of the hull in my hand like a waiter carrying a giant, long tray that weighed 50 or 60 pounds.

The shell teetered, the front end dropping fast toward the

pavement. I shifted it on my shoulder, altering the balance point just before the bow would have hit the asphalt in a loud, damaging bounce.

Once I had it balanced, I rotated until I was facing down the street that led to the lake. Spot turned circles below the boat, lifting his head, no doubt wondering what craziness I was up to.

I walked down the street, grateful that the shell's owner didn't come running out to cleave my brain with a spare oar. If I didn't capsize and lose his boat, I had every intention of bringing it back. If I did lose it, I intended to figure out a way to get Preston to pay for it along with usage fees and interest.

At the end of the block, I set the shell down on the ground, careful not to dent the fragile hull. I scouted up and down the street looking for an unfenced path to the lake.

A block down was a possibility. A wooden fence with a utility gate. I ran my hands over the dark wood near the edges of the gate, feeling for a catch. My hand caught on a short, stiff wire protruding through a hole. I gave it a pull. A latch clicked on the other side, and the gate swung inward. I stepped in through the opening, listening for alarm bells.

No sound broke the silence. I peered down a dark, terraced yard that stepped down to the lake below. I doubted there'd be a watchdog reception because Spot normally senses an approaching dog and alerts by puffing an airy woof through his jowls. I stood in the dark for a long minute, watching the big dark house, looking for the faint light that always turns on when a home owner reacts to a silent alarm. No telltale glow appeared from behind the edges of the drapes, no slits of light coming through blinds. It was probably a vacation home, empty most of the year. Even if an alarm dispatch was dialing my law enforcement colleagues as I stood there, I'd be out on the water before they got there. They'd puzzle over what seemed like a false alarm.

I lifted the shell up onto my shoulder and headed down the slope under the black canopy of the trees. Now that I was away from the house lights out on the street, it was so dark that I could barely see the white background fur that showed Spot's spots.

There was a dock that was just visible below as a vague gray stripe stretching out over the black water. I moved slowly, feeling with my feet for the steps that led down to the dock.

Once I was on the dock and out from under the trees, the dock had a faint, starlit glow. I walked out to the end, lowered the shell off my shoulder and, careful not to bump the hull on the dock posts, gently set it into the water.

It was like floating a large cigar. The boat exhibited little resistance to rolling. I sat on the dock and held the shell with my feet as I took each oar blade out of its clip holder and set it in the water. Then I slowly transferred my weight onto the tippy craft, leaning on the dock with my hands.

It was like balancing on a floating log. One faces backward while rowing, so the bow was behind me. I experimented with the sliding seat, which allowed a rower to move with each stroke, increasing power. By straightening my legs, I pushed the seat back as far as it went. I reached out and pushed on the dock. The shell coasted away, the oars dragging in the water. When I was several yards from the dock, I reached for the oars, pushing their handles down to lift the blades out of the water.

The right oar came out first. The shell immediately rolled that direction. The motion was so fast, I almost fell off the seat. My uncoordinated reaction was to let go of the right oar and reach for the boat. The oar flopped back into the water, fortunately stopping my roll. I learned the first important lesson: Make sure both oars leave and enter the water simultaneously.

Moving slowly, I pushed down on both oar handles, lifting them out of the water at the same time. The shell rolled, but it didn't tip over. I pushed my hands forward, the handles coming close together, then lifted my hands up, dropping the blades into the water. I gave a gentle pull back on the oars. The shell shot forward, the direction my back was facing. I carefully repeated the cycle, and the shell moved away from the shore at a surprising speed. Spot stood on the dock and whined as I disappeared onto the dark lake.

"Quiet, boy" I whispered to him. "Coming right back."

I lowered the oars back into the water, using them to brake to a stop. Then I reversed the motion, pushing forward to drive the oars the other way and send the shell the way I was facing, backward, toward the dock. It was too dark to see Spot's tail, but I could tell by his motion that he was wagging at my approach.

"Ready for a ride?" I whispered.

He wagged harder.

I eased the shell alongside the dock. Spot lowered his head to look. I pointed to the rear seat. "C'mon, your largeness."

Spot took a step back.

Regardless of my tone of voice, he could tell that I was suggesting a ridiculous proposition.

I pointed to the empty seat and snapped my fingers.

Spot spread his front legs wide and lowered his head so he could sniff the shell. He no doubt remembered the explosion from the year before. He had clung to the over-turned boat hull for a very long time, almost succumbing to hypothermia. He wasn't going to be easily convinced that this was a good idea.

I patted the shell's hull. "Easier than riding a unicycle."

Spot backed up. I saw a way to improve the situation.

I took off my windbreaker, wrapped it over and around the seat, creating a very thin pad with a familiar smell. I pointed to my jacket. "Okay, let's try again." I patted my hand on the seat.

If he were a Shepherd or a Lab, I could have picked him up and set him on the boat. But you can't force a 170-pound Great Dane to do what he doesn't want to do.

He reached a tentative paw down and put it on the seat.

"Good boy, atta boy, you can do it."

He reached his other leg down. The shell wobbled. With much cajoling, I got him into the boat. His chest lay on the seat. His elbows gripped the hull to either side of the seat, and his front paws straddled the rounded hull.

With Spot semi-stabilized, I made a slow stroke with the oars, then another. The shell moved away from the dock at a good pace. I paid close attention to the feel and motion. I knew that once I was well away from the shore, a misstep with the oars, or any other action that tipped the boat, could be disastrous. Tahoe's water is much too cold to survive long enough to swim any distance to shore. If Spot slipped off, I wouldn't be able to get him back on the shell. Same for myself. But we'd already accomplished the hardest part.

THIRTY-FOUR

After 30 seconds of rowing through the dark, I found a steady rhythm. I kept my legs extended, preventing my seat from sliding. The extra movement seemed too risky.

Still, I had the shell moving much faster than any other kind of human-powered boat. The fact that I faced backward and couldn't easily see where I was going added to the sense of speed.

The bow hit the waves hard enough to throw spray up and onto my back. Soon, I was soaked. The spray was icy cold.

After several minutes, I glanced over my shoulder. The Laurence estate was maybe a quarter mile away. The faint sound of a big band swinging Billy Strayhorn's "A Train" floated across the water. The Hatteras Motor Yacht was docked at Laurence's pier. The light strings were off, but a single light came from the stern, silhouetting two jet skis that were suspended from a boom just off the rear deck. As I rowed farther, there appeared another light from up on the flying bridge, but I saw no movement up there or from anywhere else on the yacht.

Beyond the boat, up near Preston's palace, was a well-lit backyard patio, and above it several windows in the house that spilled light out onto the lawn. I couldn't tell if the music came from the boat or the palace.

I turned back to the oars and rowed until I was once again moving fast. The shell knifed through the oncoming waves. Spray continued to soak my back and occasionally went over me to land on Spot, making him shake his ears.

The Laurence pier was only 100 yards away. The yacht looked as sleek as a great white shark. The big band was loud, blasting, I thought, from speakers up by the patio. It sounded like a big party. But I saw no people as I approached.

Nevertheless, I knew that people were around. I'd met one guard at the gated entrance, and he had a radio. A mansion like Preston's required people to run it. Even if Preston were at his horse-and-vineyard estate in the foothills, or an apartment in New York, or just traveling the world, he was the kind of guy to keep staff around, if only to keep his ego buffed and polished.

I sensed movement in my peripheral vision.

I turned and saw a man up on the flying bridge of the yacht. He was a big guy, possibly the man I'd seen at the gate.

He reached out with his arm, and the light went off. The man disappeared into darkness.

I gently rowed toward the yacht, trying to get into a position where if he climbed down to the dock, I'd see him silhouetted against the lights up by the house patio.

When the dock was lined up in front of me, I stopped and waited. Nothing.

Maybe he was sleeping on the boat. Or was down in the onboard theater watching movies and pounding Budweisers. Or maybe he'd gotten a glimpse of me and was sitting up on the bridge in the dark, looking at me through binoculars, calling reinforcements on his radio.

After fifteen minutes, I decided he was below decks.

I rowed to the farthest point from the yacht, where the east fence came down the property line to the beach. I coasted until the bow just touched sand, then took off my shoes. I stuffed my socks into them and tossed them up onto the lawn. I rolled up my pants and stepped out into the frigid water.

I helped Spot into the water with minimal noise, never letting go of his collar. With my other hand, I dragged the shell up onto the beach, then walked Spot onto the lawn and had him lie down next to my shoes.

He stayed still while I put my socks and shoes on.

After watching the lawn and house and yacht for any movement, I took Spot and walked up the fence line, hoping that there were no motion lights or trip lasers. The tree shadows gave me good cover from the lights at the house.

Spot and I crossed an open area of lawn and stopped when we were next to the house corner. The house was lit by a perimeter of ground floods that showed the world just how grand the house was. Spot and I were in one of the not-quite-so-bright areas between the floods, and probably couldn't be seen from more than fifteen or twenty miles. The music was loud and appeared to come from the ground. It took a puzzling moment and some bending and squatting to figure out that the tunes came from faux boulders that contained hidden speakers. Down the east side of the house were more boulders. At the far southwest corner, another large boulder. Although Ellington's band had taken a recess, a big symphony orchestra began Gershwin's Rhapsody In Blue, and I was standing, courtesy of Preston's faux-boulder speaker system, center stage. Preston's taste in music was the classiest thing about him.

The house was set into a gentle slope. The lowest level was a walkout basement tucked under the center of the main structure. The house was built like his gatehouse, timberframe and stone. Even the windows looked strong and imposing. The doors would be difficult to jimmy. A forced entry would bring the beefcake up from the yacht, or bring his twin down from the gatehouse, or bring more employees from within the mansion itself.

However I got in, it would have to be silent.

But first I could try the patio door. Preston and/or his minions might think there was little harm in leaving the backdoors unlocked. Especially when the gatehouse is manned, the shore is patrolled, and the property is well-fenced.

The only problem was getting across the brightly-lit patio.

I turned Spot toward our destination, and we ran out into the lights. The doorknob of the walkout basement wasn't a knob, but one of those big brass handles with a thumb lever. I pressed the lever down as softly as possible, but still it made a loud snap as it clicked open.

The door swung inward with a swish as the weather stripping separated from its home position. Spot and I walked in, grateful to the gods of breaking and entering.

I was in an indoor grotto, with rock walls and rock floor, and a strong odor of chlorine. Hidden in the masonry were blue and green and red uplights that shined at the ceiling. The pool curved away from me in several directions, arcing into other caverns. The water glowed turquoise, lit by more unseen lights. It reminded me of pictures I'd seen of Hugh Hefner's grotto, although I imagined that Preston, with his software billions, had probably ordered up a larger, fancier version.

The pool water had a gentle swell rocking its surface. Someone had used it recently, or someone was currently lounging in one of the hidden bays. There was standing water here and there, but no clear sense of tracks leading anywhere.

Spot's nose was flexing, though I couldn't tell if from chlorine or the scents of men with guns and radios. I considered getting into the pool and exploring the watery part of Preston's world, but Spot turned his head away from the pool and looked toward a large arched opening. I went that way.

We stopped at the opening. I peered around the corner. It was another stone room with three regular doors and one large glass door in a curved glass wall that wrapped around a large circular staircase, which in turn wrapped around a Dale Chihuly-style glass chandelier. The chandelier hung down from the floors above. It emanated thousands of blue and amber lights.

I opened the regular doors. Two changing rooms, and one sauna. I walked through the glass door into air much cooler and drier than in the tropical grotto, and headed up the staircase.

One full revolution around the chandelier brought me to a large grand entrance hall. To one side was the grand entrance. To the other sides were grand openings leading, probably, to grand rooms. If I wanted more choices, the staircase no doubt provided grand options on the upper floors.

Although the music seemed to emanate from everywhere at once, there were no faux boulders. The most likely sources looked to be a series of abstract expressionist paintings that may have been serious art or may have been serious speakers. With abstract expressionism, one can never be certain.

I glanced into the huge rooms, each done in an elegant-but-rustic décor, with lots of leather and dark wood and everything big enough to fit athletes who've gone to seed. I didn't pay much attention to Laurence's size when I met him, but I was pretty sure that if he sat all the way back in most of his furniture, his legs would have to stick out straight like a little kid's. Maybe the big furniture made him feel like a king.

As with the grotto, all of the rooms had lights on. But there were still no people.

I took another trip around the Chihuly glass extravaganza. The next level up was quieter and not so grand. The carpet lost its elaborate red pattern and was now a single muted green, although a very lush nap. There was a large central room around the staircase with two distinct sitting areas. Hallways stretched to the east and west.

I went west. Four open doors led to four separate suites. I stepped inside the first two. Each had a bedroom, sitting room, media wall, and bathroom with double sinks, double-sized Jacuzzi tub and double-sized glass-and-marble shower.

Still no people. No personal stuff lying around. No magazines or half-eaten bags of tortilla chips or cell phone chargers or clothing or crumpled grocery lists. The place was sterile, like a new luxury hotel that had been decorated but hadn't yet hosted its first guest. I couldn't even see any foot tracks on the carpet. The only sign of people was the wavy water in the pool, two floors down. Maybe I'd have to go swimming.

But I still had a floor and a half of suites to check out.

I went east.

Except for a laundry room that replaced one of the bedroom suites, it was similar to the west wing. The last door was open. Spot and I walked in. It appeared to be Preston's room. But still, it looked like a hotel. His clothes were in the closet. His newspapers were neatly stacked in a magazine rack. He had some personal toiletries in the bathroom cabinet, but more were in one of those zip-up carrier bags that hung from the door hook.

He may have been staying at his lake house, but he wasn't living there.

Another trip around the central chandelier resulted in a plainer, simpler top floor, narrower from front to back because of the roofline. The music floating up the stairway was much softer. To the west was a large game room with a pool table, ping-pong table, pinball machine, an elaborate gaming console with a wall-sized screen, and deep leather armchairs.

To the east were the odds and ends of what people with too much money focus on. One room was Ode-To-Horses, with framed pictures of jockeys sitting astride race horses, or jockeys standing below the horses' big, beautiful heads. There was an aerial shot of a big, hilly, horse ranch - probably Preston's foothill estate - with white fences and multiple barns and vineyards stretching into the distance. There were horse books and a big map showing racecourses across the country, and a small wet bar with two barstools made from English saddles. There was a TV screen on the wall and a stack of DVDs nearby and two big easy chairs. It was certainly the most comfortable room I'd seen yet, and it would be a nice place to lose an afternoon drinking Kentucky bourbon and watching reruns of all the Triple Crown winners. Spot eyed the leather chairs.

The last room on the top floor was also locked, but this time with a simple brass slide bolt on the outside of the door. I looked closely and saw that the brass screws had bright, untarnished marks where the screwdriver had slipped. It was recently installed. The only possible explanation was that Preston wanted to keep someone in the room but didn't want the trouble or the attention of hiring a locksmith.

I put my ear to the door, and heard muffled voices.

I wondered if the door lock was also turned on the inside, making it so the door couldn't be opened without agreement from the people on both sides. One way to find out.

I slid the bolt back, turned the knob and opened the door.

Champagne was lounging on a chair in the sitting room, watching the big-screen TV up on the wall. She wore blue sweats, and her hair was no longer spiky. She didn't appear to be wearing any jewelry or makeup. But for her beauty, she looked almost ordinary.

She turned and saw Spot and me and gasped.

I put my finger to my lips and shut the door behind me.

THIRTY-FIVE

"Who are you?" Her whisper indicated a hope that I might be on her side regarding her situation. She stared at Spot.

"Owen McKenna. This is Spot. Friends of Ryan Lear. I was at his party, but we didn't meet. We've come to take you out of here. If you want to go. Judging by the bruise on your cheek and jaw, I assume you'd like out."

She reached up and touched her jaw. "I'm not... I mean, he didn't intend to hit me like that. He tried to pull his punch, but he misjudged."

"That's not true," I said. "He meant to hit you. They always mean to hit you. He will do it again. Next time it will be worse."

She shook her head. "No. He loves me. He really does."

"The bolted door?" I said. "You're being held against your will. That's called kidnapping."

"No, seriously, it's just a game. He's actually very sweet. He buys me anything I want. And he's only locked me in the room this last day because he's gone. He..."

I heard thumping noises from down the hall. I held my finger up to my lips, stepped to the side of the door. Spot turned to look at me.

The footsteps got loud. The door burst open. The man I'd met at the gate came in, saw Spot, frowned in confusion.

"Joe, look out!" she screamed.

He turned, saw me to his side, reached to pull his gun out of the holster.

I grabbed the arm with the Norteños tattoo as he raised his gun toward me. I jerked it down as I raised my leg, and cracked his forearm over my knee.

He yelled as his arm made a popping snap. The gun flew out of the man's hand, firing as it left his finger. It made a huge boom in the enclosed space. The round punched a black hole in the flat screen TV.

He grabbed my shoulder with his other arm. His grip cut like a pliers into my muscles and tendons. He jerked me toward him. I didn't want him to get his good arm around me.

I tightened my grip on his damaged arm, and dropped to the floor. He grunted in pain, let me pull him down. I landed on my butt, and got my feet into his gut. I rolled onto my back, and lofted him on a fast trajectory into the wall.

He hit head-first and dropped to the floor.

Champagne had jerked herself up into a ball at the explosion of gunfire. Her knees were up, hands over her ears. In a moment, she lifted her head, looked at the gun on the floor.

"Don't even think about it." I kicked the gun into the corner behind the door, then opened the door all the way.

"Don't worry," she said. "I'm not crazy." She looked crazy.

I looked out the door and down the hall, listened for footsteps, pulled my head back inside the room. I reached down to the prostrate guard and turned off the radio on his belt.

"Does Joe have a pal, here?" I asked.

She looked at me, hesitating.

"Does he?!"

"Willy."

"Is he in the house?"

"I don't know. A while back I saw him out the window. Down on the boat."

"Spot, come here." He walked over. I pointed to the floor about six feet in front of the door. "Sit."

He sat down facing the door. He would draw all of the attention of anyone who came to the door.

I looked around for a blunt weapon. A heavy candlestick. A baseball bat. A fireplace poker. There was nothing but the other man's gun, and I'd given up guns a long time ago. Near Champagne was a floor lamp that shined at the ceiling. The lamp was delicate. It would snap in two if you swung it at someone.

I realized that I didn't need to swing it.

I brought the lamp over to the door, plugged it in and turned it on to make certain that electricity was flowing to the bulb. Then I unplugged it, leaving the switch on, and used my pocketknife to take off the glass and wire shield. I popped out the halogen bulb, then plugged the lamp back in. The two protruding metal parts of the bulb socket were now exposed and electrified. Unless I could ground my target on plumbing, the lamp would just give him a bad burn. But it would startle.

"This time you won't warn Willy." I glared at Champagne. It had no observable effect. "You warn him, and Willy gets the jump on me, my dog will use his teeth on you."

She looked at Spot.

I put my finger across Spot's nose. "Silence," I said.

I stood next to the door and waited.

Spot sat in front of the door, looking at me.

Even if Willy had been sleeping on the yacht, the gunshot would probably have awakened him. He'd radio Joe. Getting no response, he'd be suspicious. Eventually, he'd come up to the third floor. From down the hall, he'd see light coming out of Champagne's open door, the door he knew was supposed to be bolted.

When he saw the light, he'd either run to check it out, or he'd be crafty and tiptoe down the hall to peek inside.

I'd be ready.

I looked at Champagne, gave her a stern look, held my finger to my lips.

Spot watched me.

We waited.

Spot kept watching me, trying to figure me out.

Then he looked at the doorway, his ears twitching, hyper focused on sounds I couldn't hear.

I got ready.

Spot growled.

"What?!" came Willy's voice as he appeared in the doorway, his gun out, his hand shaking with fear as he stared at Spot. I poked my electric prod into the side of his neck. There was a singeing, crackling sound when the electrified metal hit soft, moist neck skin.

Willy's arm went out and windmilled, the gun tracing circles. His body jerked. My electric poker came off of his neck.

I swung my foot up and kicked the gun out of his hand. It flew to the far wall and fell to the floor without discharging.

Willy lunged toward me. Like Joe, he was shorter than me, but he packed a lot more muscle. I didn't want him to get his hands on me.

I got the lamp pole replanted against his forehead. His head jerked back. I put a hard sidekick onto his knee. He screamed, fell to the floor, writhing as he grabbed at his leg.

I walked over and kicked his gun behind the door next to Joe's gun. He grabbed my leg. I bent down, and used my other knee under his jaw.

He went limp.

"Is there anyone else here?" I hissed, panting hard.

"No," came Champagne's whisper.

"What about Preston?"

"He had to go out of town for a meeting. He's supposed to get back tonight. I think he said one-thirty."

I looked at Champagne. "You said this is just a game Preston plays, locking you in a room. The guards with guns make it more fun, right?" I was angry, and I knew that her emotions were overwhelmed by fear, but I get impatient when people act stupid.

"I didn't mean that... The truth is that I have no place else to go." Her eyes were wet. "I'm broke. He offered me a life. Yes, he's a jerk. But I don't think he would really hurt me."

"Look, Champagne. I'm an ex-cop. Twenty years SFPD. I know how this works. Answer one question for me. Has he ever hit you before?"

"You already know that he hit me. But I told you that he tried to pull his punch."

"Before that. Has he hit you more than once?"

She looked down at the floor. Then over at the TV with its new dark orifice. Up at me. Teary eyes. Real tears.

She nodded. She looked afraid of what was to come. Afraid of what had already happened.

"If you'd said that he only hit you once, I'd say that he was a serious risk, and that there was a high chance he'd cross the line again. I'd say that there was a small possibility that it was a one-time aberration."

I sat down on the nearest chair. "But you know what I'm going to say, now that you've said he's hit you again."

She looked at me in fear, bit her lip.

"Men who beat up women are like men who beat up children. They are sick. They can be successful in the outside world. They can be charming. They can be very kind at times. They can bring you flowers and tell you how much they love you. They can compose love sonnets. But inside, they are rotten in a way that is hard to cure. We put them in prison and give them the best psychological treatment because we think that unlike child molesters, the wife beaters can get better. Then they go right back to it.

"Bottom line is, if you stay with him, you will end up seriously injured, maybe dead. Preston will always have this disease. When he feels a loss of power, when things don't go his way and his insecurity about his masculinity erupts, he will act like the emotional two-year-old that he is. He will lash out at the weaker people in his life. That ain't Willy, and it ain't Joe. You are going to take the brunt of his sickness."

She stared at me, horrified at the picture I painted, the picture that she, like so many victims, had already suspected.

"What should I do?" she said in a meek voice.

"Come with me. I'll take you to Ryan's house. You'll be safe there for awhile. We'll help you find a new place to live."

"What will he do when he finds me gone?"

"When a woman leaves a beater, it's common for him to become enraged and try to track her down. The safest thing is to get off his radar for a long time. You've heard of women's shelters?"

"Yes, of course. But they're for women who are in really bad situations. Not for people like me. I'm living with one of the richest men in the country."

"Then you will end up dead or maimed for life." I stood up. "C'mon, Spot." He jumped to his feet.

We were walking out the door when she called out.

"No, wait! I'll come with you. I don't want to get hit again. He locks me up and hits me. I can't live like an animal."

I walked back into the room. Willy was stirring.

"Do you have any packing tape? Or cord or rope?"

"No. I have masking tape."

"A T-shirt I can tear up?"

She found two and handed them to me. I tore them into strips and tied the wrists of both men behind their backs. I tied their ankles, pulled them up and back and tied them to their wrists. I put a wads of cloth into their mouths and tied gags around their heads. I asked Champagne for the masking tape, and used it to tape their eyes shut.

"Is there anyone else here?" I said.

"No. Miguel and Stefan come on at midnight."

I looked at the readout on her TV. 11:37 p.m.

"Let's go," I said. "Put on a jacket or something. Shoes. It's cold outside."

"They're downstairs by the garage."

We went out the door, and ran down the hall, and went down the stairs and around the fancy chandelier once, twice. Champagne headed for the kitchen.

At the far end was a closet. She slipped into a pair of hiking shoes without tying them, and pulled on a black fur coat.

"Where's your car?" she said, breathless, scared. She looked across the kitchen to the giant brick pizza oven where the readout said 11:51 p.m.

"We came by boat. Doesn't Preston have a car here?"

"Then we should go by boat," she said. "If we take one of Preston's precious cars, he'll kill me."

"He'll want to kill you anyway. And you don't want to ride on our boat. Where's his car?"

She turned, opened a door, ran down a broad stairway to an underground garage. Now I understood why the grotto level was small compared to the rest of the house. The garage was big enough for ten or twelve vehicles. In one corner was the 1970 Barracuda, Preston's pride and joy. Nearby were a Chevy Camaro and a Mazda pickup. Probably Joe and Willy's vehicles. In another corner were two black Audis.

"Where are the keys?" I said.

"They keep them in the cars."

We ran to the first Audi. It chimed as I opened the door, key in the ignition. I opened the back door. Spot jumped in. Champagne ran around the other side. I got in front, turned the key. The Audi quietly came to life.

"Does the garage door open automatically when you approach it?"

"No," she said. She pointed to the opener on the visor in front of my forehead.

"What do the workers drive?"

"Miguel drives a Ford Fiesta. Stefan drives one of those muscle cars from the nineteen seventies. A Challenger or some name like that. Preston helped him find it."

"They carry guns like Joe and Willy?"

"Yeah. But you don't need to worry about Miguel. It's Stefan who is dangerous. You need to worry about Stefan." Her voice was tense when she said it.

The garage door began rising.

"That means one of them is reporting for work?" I said.

"Yes. Shit. I'm dead."

"No." I talked fast. "Get in the other Audi. Start it up, and stay down low. As soon as the incoming car gets in far enough that you can get by, drive out fast, then stop when you get outside. I'll use this car to block the entrance and run to your car. Hurry!"

She jumped out, got in the other Audi. I heard it start just as the garage door stopped rising.

I saw nothing out the open garage door except the paving stones of the driveway. The incoming car was around a curve to the right.

I heard its engine rev just a touch, a throaty rumble as deep as Spot's growl. The low nose of a car appeared, hideaway headlights off, low yellow parking lights on. It looked like a 1969 Dodge Charger. It could chew up any Audi in a chase. It rolled down into the garage.

The Charger was painted deep purple, and it had smoked windows. The garage lights reflected off the windshield. I couldn't see anything of the driver.

I slid down in my seat. No time to try to get Spot to do the same in the back seat. The Charger drove in front of us, made a turn, stopped, then backed into a parking spot.

The Audi next to me shot forward with a squeal of rubber, up out of the garage. I followed even faster. Just as I got to the garage door opening, I stomped on the brakes and cranked the wheel hard to the right, hoping to set up a skid.

But the anti-lock brakes pulsed, and the car wouldn't slide. Nevertheless, I got it turned across the drive, shut it off, took the key, and jumped out. I let Spot out of the back, and we ran up the drive.

Champagne had stopped well away from the house. As I jerked open the back door of her car, I turned and saw Stefan leap over the hood of the Audi I'd left in front of the garage. It was the man I'd seen at Ryan's party. He was thin like a sword, and he ran like a sprinter. Even from a distance, I could see that the gun in his hand was bigger than what Joe or Willy had carried.

Spot jumped in first, and I followed him into the back seat.

"Go!" I yelled.

She hit the pedal like a getaway driver, and we shot down the drive.

THIRTY-SIX

The gatehouse had an automatic gate for exiting vehicles. I worried that Stefan would have a way of over-riding it. But it opened after an agonizing wait, and Champagne raced out, making the tires squeak again.

"Which way do I go?" she shouted to me in the back seat.

"Out to the highway, then make a left."

She drove fast and well, if nervously. At the highway, she turned toward Tahoe City.

"A half-mile or so up, you're going to take a left," I said.

"Back onto Dollar Point? You're crazy."

"We'll be obvious in this car. Mine is close by. I think it's the next street. Yes, up here. Turn."

She did as told.

"Slow down," I said. "No one is following us. We don't want to call any attention to ourselves."

She slowed, and we crawled down the street.

"Up here," I said, "take a right. Then the next left."

We approached my Jeep. I had her drive past it and park.

"Leave the key under the floor mat. Don't lock it."

We got out, went back to the Jeep, and got in.

"Why are you rescuing me?" she asked as I drove away. Spot had his head over the seat back, sniffing her. She put her hand up to fend him off.

"At Ryan's party, you told someone that Preston had said frightening things about Ryan."

"How do you know that?"

"You weren't discreet. You were overheard. Preston's guard wouldn't let me in to talk to you, but then let it slip that Preston had hit you. Even your mother said she was frightened for you."

"You called my mother?!"

I ignored her outburst. "She said that Preston scared her. It started to look like you were being held at his house rather than staying there voluntarily."

"I can't believe you found my mother and called her."

"She cares about you. Worries about you."

Champagne stared out the window, shaking her head.

"You said that Preston was coming back tonight?"

"Yes. He went to San Jose. He was coming in late. I think he said that Raul was to pick him up at one-thirty."

"Raul is his driver?"

"Yeah," she said.

"Do you know the airline?"

"Preston has his own jet."

"How does that work when he arrives? Does he come out in the baggage area like everyone else?"

"I don't know. I've never flown on his jet. You're not thinking of going there."

I got to the highway, turned east toward Incline Village.

"I need to talk to him. I'll leave you with Spot, far away. He won't know where you are."

She didn't speak for a minute.

"Raul will be there in the Escalade. It's black like the Audis. Maybe you could find him that way."

"Good idea," I said.

"You should know that he's dangerous. If he wants to, he could have you seriously hurt. Or killed."

"You think he would do that? Have someone killed?"

She paused. "I don't know if he would have you killed. Taking me isn't that huge of a deal. But yes, if someone crossed him in the worst way, I believe that he'd order a murder. And Stefan would kill for money."

"Do you think Preston's personally capable of killing?"

"No," she said. "I think that's why he hits me, because he doesn't have the guts to hit someone else."

We drove for awhile in silence. I came to the Mt. Rose Highway, turned left and headed up the mountain above Crystal Bay. As we came around the big turn by the overlook, lights were visible around the entire shore of the lake. They twinkled like a necklace that was 12 by 22 miles big.

"I understand that he has a place in the foothills," I said as I accelerated up a long straight stretch.

"Yes, a horse ranch. He's taken me there a few times since we started dating. Raul drives us. It's wonderful. I don't know how much he goes there without me. He doesn't tell me much about where he goes. I don't really know Preston well. I've dated him for a year or so, but I've only lived with him for a week."

We kept climbing up past the meadows and crested the Mt. Rose Summit pass, which, at 9000 feet, is the highest year-round pass in the Sierra. I realized that we had driven by the turnoff to the CalBioTechnica research lab, but I hadn't seen it in the dark. A short distance later the huge splash of Reno's lights appeared on the desert floor, 4600 feet below us. I slowed for the long network of hair-pin curves as we wound our way down the mountain.

"You could just drop me at my parents' house. They live here in Reno."

"Too dangerous. Preston will look there."

I saw her nod in my peripheral vision.

I hit the brakes as I came to a sharp switchback. I turned the Jeep through 180 degrees on a steep pitch, the lights on the desert floor distracting me from the dark highway. A hundred yards down were two more switchbacks.

"I could try going back to LA. But the competition is brutal trying to get acting or modeling work."

"You ever study acting?"

"No," she said.

"Modeling?"

"What's to study?" she said.

"How is it that you think you could get any kind of acting or modeling job if you don't know how to do it?"

"I've watched it. I've seen thousands of movies."

"I've eaten tens of thousands of meals. Doesn't mean I can be a professional chef."

"Let's face it," she said. "The main thing they want is looks, right? They're looking for people that other people want to look at. I grew up being looked at. It's not the fun thing that everybody thinks. But I should at least be able to get some employment in that looking world, or whatever you want to call it."

"The acting business cares about much more than looks," I said. "But even if they did focus on looks, you said yourself that the competition is brutal. So how do you make yourself stand out among an ocean of beautiful people?"

She didn't respond, but I saw her make a single nod.

"You could try a normal job," I said. "Save some money, study acting on the side."

"I would, but I don't have any job skills. Besides, I don't think I could stand a regular job. Too boring."

"That's what school is for. Skills will get you a job that isn't boring."

"School is too expensive," she said.

"Not community college."

"I wouldn't go to a community college."

For awhile, I drove without speaking. But I couldn't stay quiet. "Should everything be handed to you? When everyone else puts in uncountable hours at school and boring jobs, should you be able to go to the head of the line and take your pick of opportunities?"

"You don't know how hard it is these days." I heard the waver in her voice, saw her hand wiping tears.

"Ryan Lear never did anything but work," I said.

"Yeah, but he's brilliant." Now she was crying at a steady pace.

"An advantage that he used while he went to school, and studied hard, and went to more school. And when he wasn't doing any of those things, he made a business plan. Have you ever thought about how much work goes into writing a Master's Thesis? He's done all this while he suffers from every social dysfunction known to man." I stopped talking as I steered around another switchback. "You could use your advantages while you did all the same things."

"My only advantage is my looks. You're saying that there's no substitute for work?"

I could barely understand her as she sniffled and sobbed.

"Here's an idea," I said. "Go to the library and check out three or four biographies of the people you most admire in the field of acting or modeling. Read them and see what they went through to get where they got."

She thought about it, turned away from me to look out the side window, found a tissue, blew her nose, and turned back.

"You think I'm gonna find out that they had to work and study and claw their way to the top. That no one handed them anything no matter how gifted or talented or good-looking they were."

"Just like sports stars or singers or artists," I said. "You can be born with advantages, but for everyone who makes something of themselves through torturous hard work, there are ten thousand people just as talented who sit back and think that the difference between them and the successful person is luck."

Champagne was quiet all the way to the bottom of the mountain. As we turned north on the freeway into Reno, she spoke in a low, hushed voice, thick with fear and pain and self-critique.

"That's what I've always said. I look at a pretty girl who's in a good movie, and I say, 'I wish I was as lucky as her.'"

I got off the freeway at Plumb Lane, and headed into the airport.

THIRTY-SEVEN

It was 1:30 a.m. as I cruised up the passenger drop-off lane, looking for Raul. Champagne spotted the black Escalade.

I drove on past without slowing, went around the entire traffic loop a second time, then pulled into the ramp. I went up a level just to be safe, and parked.

"Keep the doors locked, and don't open them for anyone," I said. "Someone comes and tells you a story about me, don't believe it. Stay in the Jeep with Spot, and you'll be safe."

Champagne looked worried. "How long do you think you'll be?"

"I'll just talk to him briefly. If his plane comes in now, as you thought, I'll be back soon."

I got out of the Jeep, went down the stairs, and crossed over to the terminal.

I walked down the sidewalk until I could see the Escalade. It hadn't moved. Reno's not a large city, and passengers were sparse so late at night. I loitered outside near one of the doors. The dry desert air was cool. When people periodically came out of the terminal, the warmer air that came with them was welcome.

Preston walked out fifteen minutes later. He wore an expensive suit and carried a brushed aluminum briefcase.

Raul jumped out of the Escalade. I met Preston just as Raul opened the back door for him.

"Have a good flight, Preston?"

"I remember you. Owen McKenna. I looked you up, asked a few questions. I don't think you're an investor, as you allowed me to believe. I discovered that your main business is investigation. Does this visit mean I'm being investigated?"

I held out the car key. "This is for one of your Audis." I dropped it into his hand. "I came to tell you that a guy from your neighborhood will show up at your gatehouse some time soon. He will be returning your other Audi. You're going to provide him access to your backyard, where his rowing shell is sitting on your beach near your east fence line. In exchange for your payment of one thousand dollars cash, he is going to take the shell off your property."

Preston squinted at me. "And if I don't pay him?"

"Then he will file charges with the Placer County Sheriff's office regarding your theft of his boat. And Champagne will file assault and kidnapping charges."

"That's absurd."

"You had a slide bolt on the outside of her door. She was locked in your house. But she's free now. She's found her strength."

Preston's jaw muscles bulged in the terminal lights.

"She wants to stay with me. She loves me. She will be home as soon as she's away from your influence," he said.

"Not this time. If you try to contact her, I'll send photos of the bruises on her face to the media along with photos of her with you at Ryan's party. The news websites will think they've been given a sweet gift."

Preston reached for the car door that Raul was holding. "People who interfere in my life always regret it. Do I make myself clear?"

"Yes. One more thing. I don't think you will ever see her again. But if by some chance you do and you touch her again, I will find you, and I will break your arms."

Preston's jaw moved left, then right. He smiled. "Let me be sure I'm understanding you correctly. Are you threatening me? Are you actually threatening Preston Laurence?"

I nodded. I pointed at his arms and walked away.

From a distance, I watched to be certain that Laurence got into the Escalade and that it drove away.

When they were gone, I went back to the Jeep.

Spot was excited. Champagne was glum.

As we drove away she said, "I don't think I'm going to be Champagne anymore. I think I'm Carol again."

THIRTY-EIGHT

It was very late, but I didn't want Street to worry. I called hoping that she'd turned off the phone to let the machine get it, but I woke her up. I briefly told her that I was taking Champagne, now Carol, to Ryan's house, and she could find me there in the morning.

Next, I called Ryan.

"You're okay?!" he nearly shouted at me. "I've been so worried!"

"Where are you?" I asked.

"I did like you said and took Lily out so we wouldn't be at the house. We did everything we could think of, but now we're in a twenty-four hour café at Stateline, just waiting for your call. I was about to check in to one of the hotels."

"Sorry. I didn't know it would go so late. But I'm driving from Reno, headed toward your house. We'll be there in a bit over an hour. Don't go there before we get there. Even with the off-duty cop there. If for some reason my Jeep isn't in the drive when you get there, leave and come back later."

"You said we. Who is we?"

"I've got Spot and Carol Pumpernickel with me. She will be joining us at your house for a day or three, if that's okay."

"Of course. Whatever you think is best."

I said goodbye.

We drove in silence for a time. The highway left the bright lights of south Reno and arced into the low mountains that separate Reno from the flat, beautiful Washoe Valley. Spot seemed asleep in back. Carol had her head back against the headrest and sideways against the window. She didn't appear to be sleeping. But she was fatigued, no doubt trying to figure out what she'd gotten into, and where she was headed next.

"I'm sorry I got upset earlier," she said. "But the things you said, they were too close to the things that Preston said to me."

"How is that?"

It was a minute or more before she spoke. I waited.

"Preston first met me at an audition call in LA a year ago. He'd bought an interest in a movie production studio. A casting director was holding the audition, and Preston was there acting like the big man on campus. What he really was doing was checking out the women.

"When he asked me out after the end of the second day, I already thought he was more hot air than anything else. But I also believed that I was a hungry young actor, and going out with him seemed a smart move. It was only later that I realized that I may have been hungry, but I didn't know anything about being an actor.

"However, Preston knew. And from early on he told me that I didn't know anything about acting. He once asked me if I'd ever done stage work. And I said, 'What do you mean?' I'd honestly never thought about acting on stage. He's been joking about that ever since. His jokes are mean. It's not like good-natured teasing. So that's why you struck a nerve back there. What I have to offer and what I don't have to offer is clear to everyone else. I'm the only one stupid enough to be blind to my ignorance."

"Why did you keep going out with him?"

"I've asked myself that a hundred times. Of course, there's the obvious. He's got massive amounts of money, and I grew up poor, and... Well, I'm not proud of that. And he can be nice, believe it or not. When he wants to make you feel good, he knows what to say and how to act. Also, when you're on the arm of someone so important, it makes you feel a little important. I'm not proud of that either. Where I should be focused on character, instead I've always been focused on money and access and those things I've never had.

"But I'm not totally naive. The first time he brought me onto his yacht, I wondered how many other girls came before me, their mouths open as they stared at this toy that is fancier than anything they've ever imagined.

"Even so, I think the main thing that attracted me to him was his connection to that production studio. I had stars in my eyes from day one, thinking that if I made him happy, he'd arrange to put me in a movie. Of course, he never did, and he was totally clear about why not. I didn't have a clue about acting. So when you said the same thing, it brought that all up again."

I was cresting the rise at the south end of Washoe Valley, and began the descent down into Carson City.

"I have some questions if you feel up to it," I said.

"Now is as lousy as any other time," she said.

"I saw you arguing out on Ryan's deck the night of the party. I couldn't see who the other person was."

"Stefan. The bodyguard who drives the purple muscle car."

"Tell me again why you think he's dangerous," I said.

"Because he's not normal. He's got guns and knives and this chain with a weird metal thing with spikes on it."

"What were you and Stefan arguing about?"

It was a moment before she responded. "It's embarrassing."

I waited.

"He made a comment about the way I looked in my dress. I told him that he was rude, and that Preston liked me to look nice. He said that all Preston cared about was that I look like a good piece of meat in front of his friends. So I yelled at him. It's stupid to yell at someone dangerous, but I was very upset."

"Later in Preston's car, what was that about?"

"How do you know about that?"

"I talked to someone who saw you get out and walk down the highway."

"It was about the same thing. I asked him if what Stefan said was true. He said no, but I could tell he was lying. We argued, and I got out at a stoplight in Incline Village and walked down the highway. But he drove back and pulled me into the car. When we got to his house, I told him that I was done being his piece of meat. I said that he could never get a woman if he didn't have a giant bank account to dangle in front of her. I knew that wasn't really true, but I was so angry... Of course, he was outraged. He hit me and shoved me down onto the slate floor in the kitchen. My knee is a giant scab. After that, he had that bolt put on my door and locked me inside. He said I would have to earn my freedom by learning respect."

I took the new freeway south through Carson City, and headed up Highway 50 toward Spooner Summit.

"What do you know about how Preston got started?" I asked.

"In business? I don't know much. He's good at writing software. Started a company and then sold it. Made a bunch of money. Whatever his talents as a software engineer, I think he's much more of a businessman. I've never heard him talk about programming. He's got a lot of pans on the stovetop."

We crested Spooner summit and dropped down the mountain, getting a V-shaped glimpse of the big dark lake with the lights on the far shore. In the far distance across the water were the lights of the High Camp complex at the top of the Squaw Valley cable car.

At the bottom of the slope, we curved past the gated community of Glenbrook and went through the Cave Rock tunnel a short time later. The turnoff to the neighborhood where Ryan lived was only a mile later.

His drive was empty, the house dark. Spot ran around, triggering the new motion lights. I introduced Carol to Smithy, then used the key Ryan had given me to let her into the house. I told her to help herself to food or anything else. She got a glass of water. I fetched a beer.

Ryan showed up fifteen minutes later. He carried Lily, who was asleep. It was 3:30 a.m. While Carol used the bathroom, I quickly explained what had happened, and why Carol had the bruise on her face.

"Preston hit Champagne? I'm... I'm astonished!"

"I think she's left him for good. I think she's also decided to put that part of her life behind her. She said she doesn't want to go by Champagne anymore. She's back to Carol."

"I can understand why," Ryan said. He was still holding Lily. "Let me put Lil' to bed."

He took Lily to her room.

Despite the late hour, we went into the family room. Carol joined us. Even though there was no fire in the fireplace, Spot lay on the rug in front of it.

"Look," Carol pointed. "It's like he knows that fireplaces make heat, but there's no fire."

"Ever hopeful," I said.

"The night air is chilly," Ryan said. He walked over to the wall and touched a thermostat. With an audible puff, large, blue-yellow flames curled up around faux logs.

Spot lifted his head and looked. Then he lay his head back down and sighed.

Carol sat cross-legged on the adjacent couch. Ryan fidgeted and flinched and air-washed. He perched on the fireplace hearth, then moved to a chair, then stood and asked if he could get us anything. Carol and I declined. Ryan got himself a beer and set it on the fireplace mantle. He paced back and forth, now and then peeked out the drapes, but mostly stared at Carol. If she felt like she was under a spotlight of attention, she didn't show it. She'd been used to it for a good part of her life.

Carol and I tried to make light chat, staying away from the subject that brought us together. She attempted to bring Ryan into the conversation, mentioning the high school that she and Ryan had attended, telling him about her ten-year reunion the previous spring, and asking him if he intended to go to his.

Ryan didn't even speak his answer. He just shook his head fast, and looked alarmed at the thought.

"Hey," Carol said, looking at Ryan. "Remember when I saw you about a year ago in LA? Right after I met Preston and he took me to that dinner for the governor?"

"Yeah," Ryan mumbled. "I hate doing that stuff."

"If you hate it, why did you go?"

"Bob Mendoza, our CEO said I needed to go. He said that I put a human face on bio-tech. Which basically means that they parade me as the weirdo geek poster boy so that the legislators don't see us as just another big-business trying to buy influence. Bob uses me for the pity factor. When the legislators meet me, they feel sorry for our company. The issue they were discussing then didn't even have anything to do with bio-tech. It was all about some legislation that would favor infrastructure investments."

Carol nodded. "That's when you told me about the whole construction thing in Venice."

I gave Ryan a questioning look.

"One of those things my accountant told us we should invest in," Ryan said. "A real estate investment trust. An REIT."

"Venice, California," I said.

Ryan nodded. "Preston put us onto it. The REIT bought a block of rundown housing on one of the Venice canals just south of Santa Monica and put up a new, green, cottage townhouse project. I don't know what's happened with it."

"I do," Carol said. "After you told me about it at that governor's dinner, I asked Preston about it. He said that the new development couldn't break ground for eight months, and that they were renting the old units out real cheap. The only catch was that the renters had to be out in eight months. So I sort of became your best rental agent outside of Southern California. I'd moved back to my parents house in Reno. Whenever I was talking to my friends about landlord hassles and such, I'd tell them about this super cheap rental deal. I'd kind of make a joke out of it. I know a deal where you can rent a house for a fraction of market value. Of course, the catch is that it only lasts for eight months, and you had to move to Southern California, ha, ha. But, hey, I've been to Venice, and it's a pretty hip place. Anyway, maybe you got some business out of my recommendations."

Ryan looked at Carol, his eyes flinching. "Um, I don't know. But thanks."

"So then," Carol continued, "I asked Preston about it a few weeks ago, and he said that the manager had problems getting all the renters to move out in time."

"I don't know about that," Ryan said. "But I appreciate your recommendation."

"No problem," Carol said.

We talked a while longer, then I said that I was turning in. Ryan hadn't touched his beer. He showed Carol the guest bedrooms and told her to take her pick.

We were all in the kitchen a few hours later, drinking coffee for breakfast, trying to wake up.

I Googled the address where I'd borrowed the rowing shell. The name and phone number were listed. I dialed.

"May I speak to George, please," I said.

"Speaking."

"I'm Detective Owen McKenna calling about your missing rowing shell. We have located it."

"You found it already! That's fantastic. I only just discovered it missing. I was about to call it in."

"We're working on an ongoing case, and we'd like to enlist your help. You'll receive a fee, of course."

"Sure. What do I do?"

I told him about the black Audi in front of his house with the key under the floor mat. I told him where to drive to retrieve his rowing shell and one thousand dollars.

"Thanks, man. You cops do a great job."

Lily had hot chocolate, and she was entertaining us with a story she'd made up about a wild Mustang when Spot made a short woof.

I listened and heard the soft sound of tires on the drive. I stood and looked out the window. A black Escalade came to a stop between my Jeep and Lily's bicycle.

"Stay here," I said to them. "Spot, let's go outside."

He jumped up, always excited for yet another run. I hung onto his collar.

We walked outside as Preston got out of the back door, and Stefan got out of the front passenger door. They stood side-by-side like two gunslingers in a western.

Smithy stood up from his chair in the shade. I held out my hand, palm out. He paused and watched from where he stood. Smithy wasn't in uniform, and his gun wasn't visible. If Preston and Stefan noticed him, they didn't show it.

Preston wore a black knit shirt that showed his muscles. He looked like a model. Stefan was skinny-hard and ugly, the opposite of a model. The Escalade was still running. I could see Raul through the windshield, his hands gripping the wheel.

Stefan held his left hand in front of him as if to make a fast-draw of the gun that was bulging his shirt on the front of his belt.

"I'm here for Champagne," Preston said.

I walked up to them, still holding Spot's collar. I gave him the touch on his neck that means to be on guard. Spot looked up at me, then turned his laser eyes on Preston and Stefan.

Preston looked at Spot. Stefan's eyes stayed on me.

"Carol doesn't want to see you," I said. "I told you not to come near her."

"Doesn't matter. Go get her," he said to Stefan.

"You are trespassing. Time to leave," I said.

Stefan looked at me with dead eyes.

"Go get her," Preston said again.

"Get in your car and drive away," I said, "I won't give you trouble. Take a step toward the house, my dog will stop you."

Except for a slight adjustment of his left hand, Stefan stood like he was carved of stone.

"Pull your gun, my dog will take your hand off your arm." I made the neck touch again. "Watch him," I said to Spot, and pointed at Stefan.

Spot made the deep rumble in his throat. He lifted his lips, exposing his out-sized fangs. The hair stood up on his back. His growl intensified, he held it for a long five-count, took a quick breath of air, resumed the growl, and took a half-step toward Stefan.

Preston's lip trembled with rage.

Spot probably out-weighed Stefan, but Stefan showed no reaction. A bullet doesn't care how big a dog is.

Spot made another quick inhalation, and began his third long growl.

"Get in the car," Preston said.

He and Stefan got in.

The Escalade backed up in a fast, sweeping curve, went off the driveway and rolled over Lily's bicycle. Then went forward. For a moment, the bicycle got caught under the vehicle. Raul gunned the engine, and the spinning tires shot the bent, broken bicycle out from underneath. The Escalade went out the drive fast, skidding a little as it turned onto the street, then raced up toward the highway.

THIRTY-NINE

"Good job, Spot," I said, petting him. He wagged. Smithy ran over. "You want me to chase them?"

"No. Best to stay here, please."

I walked over and picked up the bicycle. The frame was bent thirty degrees, one wheel was folded, spokes broken, tire flat, and the front brake cable was sprung out from the handlebars like an antenna. Ryan came running out, followed by Lily. Lily had her hands at the sides of her face. She stared at the bicycle carcass. Carol came out behind them, looking frightened.

"Don't worry, Lily," Ryan said. "We'll get you a new bike."

"I'm sorry, Lily," Carol said. "It was my fault. That man was looking for me."

Lily walked toward the crushed bicycle like she was approaching a dead pet. She reached out, touched the bicycle frame where it was bent, then turned her hand to look at the shiny red paint chips on her fingertips. She turned to Carol. "It's not your fault. You were inside the whole time."

Carol picked Lily up. "Thank you. You are kind to think that. Let's go inside and make those waffles you were talking about." She carried Lily back into the house.

"Last night," I said to Ryan. "Carol mentioned the real estate deal in Venice. Tell me about it."

Ryan looked startled. "Do you think that could have something to do with this situation?"

"Possibly."

"I know very little about it. Preston was in charge. His lawyer set up a real estate investment trust and bought the old townhouses and single-family houses down in Venice. He had an architect design a green, eco-sensitive, multi-unit housing complex. Four-unit cottages arranged around courtyards. It was going to take up an entire block on both sides of one of the canals. Bridges, walkways, common areas and such. The idea was to quadruple the density, but make it more livable. That's all I know about it."

"Carol mentioned renters not moving out when their leases were up?"

"That's the first I've heard of it," Ryan said. "I'm really on the periphery on this."

"Could a disgruntled renter learn your name? Were the investors made public?"

"Not really. I suppose that all of the ownership information is available in the county records, but you'd have to be good at research." He stopped and frowned. "Wait. Someone printed up a prospectus. It was like a glossy magazine that showed the design and computer renderings of what the development would look like when it was done, and how it would be energy neutral, consuming less energy than the rooftop solar panels would produce. They distributed it throughout the neighborhood and to the Venice officials as a way to soothe any concerns."

"And that sales magazine listed the investors names," I said.

"Yeah. It was part of the sell-job. Like, if the Chairman of CalBioTechnica was on board, it must be an upstanding project. I think it had my name on there along with Preston's and the other investors and their corporate connections."

"A disgruntled renter could see your name and decide you were to blame for his or her troubles."

"It sounds like a reach," Ryan said.

I ignored the comment. "Do you have a copy of that sales booklet?"

He shook his head. "I'm not sure where to get one. Preston must know. But he's not going to be forthcoming now that I'm sheltering Champagne. I mean, Carol."

"Do you know the property manager who was in charge of the project when the tenants were being evicted?"

"Again, Preston handled that. Or one of Preston's secretaries. I never knew any of the details."

"Any chance that Eli and Jeanie also invested in this trust?"

Ryan paled. "Yes, they did."

FORTY

I got on the computer and booked a flight and hotel. I looked up people in Venice who knew about, or were in, the property business. Real estate agents, and property managers. I even called the Chamber of Commerce.

I had an hour before I had to leave. I found Carol.

"It would be smart to document how Preston hit you. I would ask some questions, you give the answers, and I record it with my cell phone."

She thought about it. "Okay."

We kept it very brief, but it was heartfelt.

"Good job," I said when we were done.

"I'm finally in the movies," she said.

Before I left, I went over a few rules with Ryan, Lily and Carol. The doors were to be kept locked, the window drapes shut. Carol and Lily were to stay inside and out of sight of the big un-draped windows of the great room. No one would go into the great room at night.

Despite the deputies on guard, Ryan would only go outside to let Spot run, and Ryan wouldn't stray far from the door. Not even Ryan and Spot would go out after dark. The restrictions were only for one day as I would be back the next night.

I told Spot to be good, then drove out of Ryan's and went south on 50 to stop by Street's lab. She was at the utility sink, washing out some vials. She poured me some left-over coffee, nuked it until it boiled. We went outside to the little stone patio in back of her lab, and sat on her wobbly, spindly-legged metal chairs that were 98% delicate looks and 2% wimpy function.

I went over what had happened and told her my plan to go to

Venice and see if I could learn something of this real estate deal that was yet another connection between Preston Laurence and Ryan Lear.

"Will Ryan and Lily be okay with Carol there? Is she stable enough not to cause upset?"

"I think so," I said.

"But she poses like a starlet. That wouldn't be good for Lily."

"I think the starlet act is mostly an act. Carol seems aware that the attention she gets is for a shallow reason. During the ride to Ryan's, she was candid about what she lacks."

Street frowned. "Please don't tell me that she's thinking physical deficits. There are few things more irritating to us normal people than having a gorgeous person lament that something about their person isn't perfect."

"Not physical deficits. I meant she's aware of how much she lacks in skills. That gives me hope that there is a solid foundation under there."

"She and Ryan are opposites," Street said, "but maybe they could help each other a bit. If she takes a break from the makeup and fancy clothes, Ryan could see how one can project physical confidence by simply having good posture. And she could see the benefits of hard work and goals. Hanging around Ryan will emphasize that knowledge is power."

"No better example than him," I said. "I know you're busy, but if you were to pop in, that would help even more. It would help Lily, too."

"Maybe I will. Lily has gotten herself into my hourly consciousness. Do you know when she gets her next blood test?"

"I think Ryan said it was in a few days."

"I can't sleep," Street said, "I worry about her so much."

"Me, too."

Street made a sudden grin, a forced change of mood. "You think Ryan has any more of those chocolate cookies left?"

"Probably. If not, he could make some more."

I told Street I'd be in touch, and kissed her goodbye.

From Reno, I took the shuttle flight to LAX, and caught the 13th cab in the line outside of the terminal. The driver was an old

Chinese man who drove the 405 like he was Jeff Gordon in car number 24.

My hotel had the words Marina del Rey in its name, and the glass doors had a sand-blasted design of two sailboats. But I couldn't see the ocean or the water of the marina or even a sailboat mast poking up above any of the nearby buildings.

I went to the lobby and asked the well-dressed concierge where the marina was.

"Not far," he said in a Mexican accent, his black, pencil moustache stretching to accommodate his big grin. He pulled out a small map and made some marks with a felt-tip pen.

"How far is not far?" I asked.

"Very close. Just around the block." He pointed to the map, then pointed out the window. "Only five minutes."

"Five minutes by car, or five minutes by foot?" I asked.

"By foot, of course." He grinned some more. "You run fast, sí?"

"How far is the ocean?" I asked.

"Not far. Ten minutes."

"If I run fast," I said.

He grinned. "Maybe fifteen minutes for you."

"If I follow the main channel to the ocean, and then walk northwest up the beach, I'll come to Venice, right?"

"Venice, California." He shook his head like a father thinking about a child who has failed. "Nothing much good to say about Venice. Of course, there are many nice places in Southern California. Santa Monica. Malibu. Beverly Hills. And you will find that Marina del Rey has everything you need."

"I'm sure you're right." I thanked him for the map and went to my room.

The next morning, I called Ryan to make sure they were all okay. Then I started calling the names on my list. Most people were out, but according to their voice messages, my call was very important to them, and they'd get back to me pronto.

I managed to get through to four actual people, all of whom were realtors. All claimed to know nothing about any problems associated with the Village Green On The Water. But they did know all about the 168 condo units in the four-plex cottages, complete with customizable floor plans, energy-neutral designs, and the promise that my purchase included the planting of one seedling in the tropical rainforest for every twenty-five thousand dollars of my purchase price. Also, my name would be inscribed on a community plaque as a defender of the environment. And one of them said that if I came in today before noon, she was certain that I would still qualify for the free kitchen upgrade with granite counters and my choice of eco-design, soft-focus wallpaper in a limited edition, signed by the famous artist.

When I pressed about problems, just one of the realtors said that she supposed that I could call the Venice Connection Association president, a woman named Ingrid Johanssen, and maybe she could answer my questions.

She gave me the number. I dialed, and a woman answered. After a long explanation on my part, she agreed to meet me for a happy-hour drink later that day.

That afternoon, I walked several long blocks over to the main entrance channel to Marina del Rey, and then followed it past a line of mansions for another long block out to the ocean.

The channel led me to one of those Southern California beaches that is to a normal beach like a Hollywood blockbuster is to a home video. It was two hundred yards of fine sand from the sidewalk to the surf, and the beach stretched as far as I could see.

I headed northwest, and after a mile or so came to Venice, the hip, black-sheep sister of glamorous Santa Monica and sensible, everything-you-need Marina del Rey.

Runners, skate-boarders, and roller bladers careened past gaudy shops and street vendors that specialized in tie-dyed T-shirts with raunchy catchphrases, and whole-body tattoo services, and sunglasses that no one but a feather-boa-ed drag queen would ever purchase. I bought a fun pair for Lily.

A group sitting on the grass passed around a joint. Near the Muscle Beach sign, a group of young men focused their steroid-drenched bodies on pumping weights. Some nearby girls didn't seem to notice. Some nearby boys paid close attention. In the distance beyond them, surfers wearing wetsuits rode low waves. A beach vendor had stacks of rental kayaks.

Now and then I passed people who appeared to be auditioning

for unseen casting directors. A mezzo-soprano deeply lost in a Puccini aria, a pundit in a trench coat explaining to the world the great Federal Reserve conspiracy, a ceramic artist on a pedal-powered cart, complete with rotating potter's wheel, raising a glistening, graceful pot as she recited what sounded like gibberish. Or maybe it was Beat poetry. When a unicycler juggling bananas pedaled past me, I turned to watch.

Spotting a tail without being noticed by the tail takes practice. The trick is to not react. I didn't jerk or stare or even pause to look as the familiar face came into view in the crowd behind me. I just watched the juggler for a moment, then turned back and continued to amble along up the sidewalk.

Coming up on my left was a tent canopy with panels displaying framed photographs. I stopped to look at colorful, vertical towns on the cliffs of Italy. I concentrated on my peripheral vision, noticing the movement on the sidewalk. I moved from one photo to the next, looking at the seaside towns but seeing only the people to my side, getting one more glimpse of the thin, hard man with the dirty brown hair that looked painted across his forehead. Stefan, bodyguard for Preston Laurence.

I tried to put it together as I studied the photographs. Preston was probably so enraged by me that he had his man follow me to see what I was up to. Not an easy trick getting a last-minute ticket on the same plane as me, or watching me get on the plane and then flying Preston's jet to my destination.

Either way, it seemed likely that Stefan was sent to find a way to take me apart, physically, or financially, or both. The billionaire had made it clear that no one threatened Preston Laurence. And if Preston had murdered Eli Nathan and Jeanie Samples, he would want to prevent me discovering that, regardless of the cost.

I decided to make Stefan work for his pay.

The worst work in the world for a tracker trying to shadow a target is having to wait while the target sits still in a public place, enjoying a cool libation on a warm summer day.

The sidewalk café where I was to meet Ingrid Johanssen had several small bistro tables roped off from the passersby. One was vacant. I stepped over the rope and sat down. I was a half-hour early for my meeting, so I ordered a beer. They didn't have

Sierra Nevada Pale Ale, so I ordered a West Coast IPA by Green Flash Brewing. The beer was good, and the scenery, an endless parade of bizarre people in front of the vast blue-gray Pacific, was entertaining.

A 6 p.m., a tall woman in a navy pantsuit stepped through the tight formation of tables and stopped at mine.

"You're the only person alone, so I'm guessing you are Owen McKenna," she said.

"Then you must be Ingrid. Thanks for meeting me." I stood and reached across the table to shake her hand, then nudged the opposite chair out a bit.

She carried a large leather shoulder bag. She hung the strap over the back of the chair and sat down. She had silver hair cut short, and her dangling earrings looked to be miniature wooden chairs, painted a brilliant red that contrasted with her eyes, which were the color of turquoise swimming pools.

"Let me guess," I said. "Your day job involves furniture."

"Oh," she smiled, "you mean my earrings. No, these little chairs are what I call wish-prayers. For twenty-five years, I've been a tradeshow demonstrator for a library services company. When I'm not on planes, I'm on my feet all day long, setting up a ten-by-twenty booth, then chatting up librarians, then taking the booth down. I do my song and dance in forty-two states and twelve countries in the EU. What I pray and wish for is a future where I can just sit a bit. That's what the earrings are about." She touched one of them, gave it a little swing.

"How was I fortunate enough to find you in town?"

"I have an agreement with the company. When I'm stateside, and if I have two or more consecutive days where I'm not at a show, I always get a ticket to fly home."

"So you can work your other job as the Venice Connection Association president."

She smiled and nodded. "I know. It gets a little crazy sometimes. But when you travel for a living, you recognize more than most the importance of community."

"So I'm not taking up your valuable personal time?"

"Yes, you are. And Howard is almost certainly upset with me as we speak. He's probably sitting in the kitchen window waiting for me. I will get an earful when I walk in the door."

"Your cat," I said.

"All twenty-two pounds of him, yes."

The waiter came back. Ingrid ordered a vodka martini. I had another beer, and we decided to split a calamari appetizer.

"You told me on the phone that you are an investigator. What is it that I can help you with?"

"My client is an investor in the Village Green project. He has received threats at his home in Tahoe by an unknown person or persons. I understand that the property manager had trouble evicting some tenants. I wonder if one of them could be the person threatening my client."

"Where does your client live?"

"The Bay Area and Lake Tahoe."

"And you're wondering if a tenant from Venice has gone to Tahoe and threatened your client?" Ingrid's tone was dismissive. "If a tenant is under enough financial stress that they are unwilling to move out, how are they going to find a way to go up to Tahoe and harass the landlord? The whole idea seems melodramatic." Ingrid said it with a certain disdain. I was suddenly in the enemy's camp. Evil by proxy.

"Yes, but the threats are real."

"So you're turning over rocks," she said.

I nodded.

The waiter brought our calamari. We ordered dinner, grilled sea bass for Ingrid, salmon for me.

"Been a long time since I've visited Tahoe," Ingrid said. "It is one of my favorite places. Does your client work for a living? Or is he one of those portfolio princes?"

"He works out of both the Bay Area and Tahoe. But he's Washoe, so his roots are Tahoe."

"Washoe?"

"The Native Americans who lived at Tahoe for ten thousand years while our ancestors were hanging out in caves in Europe."

"He's an Indian who also happens to be rich?" She said. "Casino money?"

I was disappointed in Ingrid, but I needed info, so I didn't comment. "Yes to the first. But he made his money in bio-tech.

He's the founder and chairman of CalBioTechnica, a genetic engineering company. You may have heard of them."

"CBT? Oh, my God. They've donated money to some of my librarian customers. I've really put my foot in it, haven't I? I'm so sorry. You must think I'm a terrible bigot. Really, I'm not. Please don't think that. I have great respect for our native people. Indians. Or Native Americans. Whatever the proper term is these days. Really, I do."

"Right." I ate the last calamari. "Can you tell me about any problems you've heard of with tenants at the units that were torn down to put up the Village Green?"

The waiter brought our food on hot platters. Our fish sizzled.

"It's the same whenever developers try to build new projects." She stabbed a large chunk of her fish, chewed with vigor, and swallowed it fast. "The difference is that our situation here ended in tragedy. They had a tenant who wouldn't move out. A woman had started a new commercial cleaning company. I think it's pretty obvious that she understood the eight-month term of the lease. But there was some vague language in the lease. I gave it to a guy in our association who is a lawyer, and he agreed as well. Of course, the landlord filed an unlawful detainer. The tenant brought up the lease-language ambiguity, but the court held for the landlord.

"The eviction came at the worst time for the woman. She'd gotten several contracts, and she had three teams out working all night long. But two of her biggest accounts were companies whose headquarters were back east, Atlanta and DC, I think the paper said. And they were shuffling her invoices up the ladder for approval because she was a new vendor for them. They'd strung her out to a hundred twenty days. But of course, her cleaning teams wanted to be paid every week, just like she'd promised."

"And she didn't have enough capital," I said.

"Nor credit. So she resisted the eviction and was eventually moved out by the sheriff. She had to lay off her workers. Her contracts fell through, and the business fell apart. She couldn't rent another place because she couldn't show income.

"In the end, she ended up homeless. A week or two later, the woman was killed by a hit and run driver. An observer said it appeared as if the woman had deliberately stepped off the curb at the wrong moment. It made a big impression on our little community. The Times did a story on her. 'Entrepreneur Squeezed to Death by System,' or something like that."

"Do you know the woman's name?"

She shook her head. "No. The property manager was so shaken by it that she quit and moved back to Hawaii. But it was in the newspaper. You could look that up."

I nodded, and changed the subject to the local town.

As we ate, Ingrid explained to me how the original developer dredged out the canals in an attempt to create a West Coast Venice. They dug many canals back in the early 20th century, but later most of them were filled in to make streets for the burgeoning population of automobiles.

Ingrid finished her dinner and looked at her watch. I told her that it was fine if she needed to leave. She said that Howard the cat needed her, and after two more apologies for her insensitive remark about Native Americans, she left.

I took my time with the rest of my dinner, formulating a plan to talk to Stefan, my tailgater, on my terms.

I paid the bill and left, taking a leisurely stroll up the winding boardwalk on the beach side of the street. I didn't need to turn around to know that Stefan was out there, his gun on his belt, and his brain on his plan to exact a revenge for how Spot and I turned them away without Carol the day before.

Learning from Ingrid about the tenant tragedy at the Village Green suggested that not all the clues pointed to Preston. Which made Stefan's presence more interesting.

FORTY-ONE

My plan to trap Stefan was simple.

I walked northwest up the beach, staying on the boardwalk so I'd be near other people and Stefan would be less likely to put his gun in my back. My demeanor was calm, and my pace was slow enough that the sun set, and twilight gathered in close. I went a mile and then another, my sights set on the Santa Monica Pier, twinkling with lights like a fantasy spot for teenagers on first dates.

A quarter mile from the pier, I went past a second kayak rental operation, then turned down the sand and followed the water's edge toward the dark pier posts. I slipped into the shadows under the pier, picking up a piece of driftwood. The tide was out, and there was a long expanse of wet, mucky sand. I walked into the darkest area of posts, moving at a steady pace. There was a place where one post met another. I didn't know if I might end up tussling on the wet sand, so I wedged my cell into the V of the posts.

I knew that the darkness would temporarily hide me from Stefan's vision until his eyes adjusted. I stepped to the ocean side of one of the posts and stopped. I watched for Stefan from behind the post.

He came running, then slowed and walked under the pier. His movement made his position easy to track. Then he stopped, and he disappeared into the darkness.

I stared at the vague black shapes of posts, watching for movement. Crowd noises came from above. Mechanical rumbling from the rides throbbed through the structure of the pier. In the distance behind me, the surf worked its calming, rhythmic music.

Patience is everything in cat and mouse pursuits. I stood still for four or five minutes. Behind me came more water sounds, waves slapping against posts, the gurgling of little eddy currents in the wave backwash, the fizz of wave foam seeping into the sand, other water noises that sounded like a disoriented fish slapping its tail in shallow water.

The first movement I saw came from left of where Stefan had disappeared. He stepped out from behind one post and over to another. From his position, I could tell he was looking for me far to the right of where I stood. He probably had his gun out, but it was too dark to see.

I moved from one post to another. I focused on his position, never looking away. The sand was wet, and I had to lift my feet with careful deliberation to avoid a sucking sound as they came free. It was a slow circular navigation, coming around behind him, one soft step followed by another.

When I was twenty yards away from him, the sand became drier. I thought I could sprint to him, silent steps on soft sand, and get hold of him before he realized what was happening. I readied myself, one foot back like a sprinter, my hand on the barnacled post for support, the other hand holding my driftwood club.

Just as I burst forward there was a stunning crack on the back of my head. I collapsed onto the sand and was out.

FORTY-TWO

Play dead.
   I didn't know where I was. My head was on fire. I went with my instincts.

You want to buy time with a pair of killers, you need to convince them that you are not a threat.

So you play dead.

Perceptions came in bits.

I was on my back. Being dragged. Two men. One on each foot.

Stay limp.

My head dug in to the soft sand. Water soaked my hair. My arms trailed out behind me. They pulled me over a log. Something caught on my belt.

"Damnit, he's stuck."

"Roll him."

My feet twisted, legs twisted. I flopped over onto my front.

Stay limp.

"Wait, let me get his wallet." A hand dug into my pockets, found the wallet and my pocketknife. "Okay, pull."

My face gouged the sand, my nose filled with muck. I scraped over the log. It caught on my chin. I shut my eyes hard and turned my head just the tiniest amount as if twisting were natural to they way they dragged me.

The log ripped at my ear and temple.

I struggled to stay limp.

My head dropped back down to the sand. Harder now. Sand over rock. Or cement.

"You sure he's dead?"

"I cracked him hard. He wasn't breathing, far as I could tell.

But I've learned, it's hard to know if someone's really dead. That's why we drop 'em overboard. They get dead eventually."

"Stick him and make sure."

I knew I could never lie still for a knife stick.

"Here, roll him over on his back."

They twisted my legs again. I flopped over. I left my mouth open, tongue bulging the sand pile inside my mouth. Eyes half-open. It was very dark under the pier.

"Gimme that paddle."

I gritted my teeth and tensed my stomach muscles. If he aimed at my head or neck, I really would be dead. I pretended that I was outside of my body. It was a rusted, dented vehicle. Bang it up some more, it wouldn't make much difference.

I heard movement. An intake of breath, a tiny grunt of exertion.

The blow hit my stomach.

An explosive wallop unlike anything I'd ever experienced. Babe Ruth hitting one out of the park.

But I stayed limp. I'd never had such discipline before. My body jerked with the impact, my lungs exhausted their air, then I was still. My diaphragm was paralyzed.

"He's dead. Or next thing to it. Nobody coulda took that without squealing."

"Help me roll this carcass over the kayak. On his stomach. Like he's strapped over the back of a horse."

They dragged me out into the water, rolled me, lifted my limp form over the center of a kayak. The motion helped disguise my efforts to suck in a little air.

"Okay, you get in the forward seat, I got the rear. I'll push us out."

They got the kayak into the water and paddled.

On one side of the kayak, my legs were in the water. On the other, my arms and head were in the water. I spit sand and muck out of my mouth, and turned my head a little so that my mouth and nose were a bit closer to the surface and one ear was exposed to the air. The wave motion rocked the kayak, brought my face out of the water for a quarter second.

I sucked some air.

"How you gonna weight the body?"

"Two twenty-five pounders from muscle beach. I've done it before. They're just the right size to put in the front and back of a guy's pants. It's enough weight to keep the body down through decomposition. Eventually, the fish will chew through his pants. But by then, he'll mostly just be bones."

The paddle of the guy in the front seat hit the side of my head as it came out of the water at the back of his stroke. A sharp blow. Then again.

"Guy's head makes it so I can't paddle."

The boat rocked a bit. I sucked more air.

"This far enough?"

"Not even close. Boss always stresses the half-mile rule. Except for this place we use down the coast where there's an underwater drop-off. Here, you go out a half mile 'cause otherwise the surfers and snorklers and boaters might see the body on the bottom on the clear days. Don't want that."

"No. Wouldn't make my boss happy. Wouldn't make your boss happy, either."

"This is freelance for me. My boss doesn't know."

As the kayak rocked, my micro breaths barely sustained me. A swell lifted the boat. My head came clear of the water. I got a larger breath.

"I always thought you dumped bodies in the desert."

I heard the words, but I wasn't tracking well. The hot poker was still thrusting into my head. My lungs felt empty, unable to get a comfortable breath. But I knew I was running out of time. I needed to move while they were distracted.

"It's the Rodriguez family always uses the desert. But this is so much easier. It's right under everyone's noses, so they don't think to look. Takes less time. Easy for a cop bird to see headlights out on the desert. But not us out here in the black of night."

"Right."

I felt another swell lift the kayak, rolling it so my head popped out again. I took as large a breath as my spasmed diaphragm allowed, shifted my weight so that the boat rolled back fast, then snaked into the water. As I went under, I grabbed the edge of the boat with my fingertips, putting my weight into it.

The boat capsized. I heard the men yell as I dropped beneath the waves.

Long ago, when I was a kid at my uncle's cabin on the lake in New Hampshire, I learned the basics of survival under water. You relax. You don't thrash for the surface, gasping for air. No matter how much you need air, you recognize that it's there, just above, just a few relaxed seconds away. Staying relaxed allows your brain to go many more precious seconds without oxygen.

I took three breast strokes through the black water, staying several feet under. Then I rose to the surface slowly, head tipped back. I broke the surface with only my mouth and nose, forced myself not to gasp, just breathed four deep breaths in and out.

With my ears under water, I heard muffled yells and thrashing bodies. Maybe their frantic movement would bring the sharks.

I was on the ocean-side of the kayak, a bit to the north. I submerged and swam the length of an Olympic pool, northwest toward Malibu, then resurfaced, treading water, breathing more comfortably, watching the vague dark shapes, listening to the men swear as they tried to climb back onto the slippery kayak.

"Hold it still!"

"I am!"

"Damn thing's full of water!"

"Get in! It still floats. We can still paddle it."

"Christ, what was that! Hurry! Something bumped my leg!"

"Maybe it was the body."

"You think maybe he's still alive?"

"No way."

"Good thing I got his wallet. That'll slow the cops down when they find him."

"The current, sometimes it keeps bodies at sea long enough the fish chew on the face. Gotta use teeth and DNA for an ID."

"Let's hope."

With my lungs better fed, but my head and stomach still screaming, I submerged again, swam another swimming pool, breathed more, then another.

Soon, I was a hundred yards away from the men. I swam to the beach and walked out of the water northwest of the pier.

I seemed to be alone on the dark beach, well away from the

commotion on the pier. And with the tide out, I was a long way from the people up on the sidewalk and street.

I stripped and wrung out my clothes, then put them back on. My running shoes remained squishy.

I walked back to the pier, and retrieved my cell. I looked for another piece of driftwood, but there was nothing but smooth sand. I walked up to Appian Way, the road parallel to the beach, and flagged a passing cab, got in.

"I'm Detective Carver," I said. "I just tangled with two suspects out on the water in a kayak." I pointed. "You can see them out past the pier."

The driver looked, nodded.

"Pull over to that dark spot under those palm trees."

He drove forward and stopped.

"When they come out of the water, they may separate. If so, I need you to follow the taller one. He walked here from Venice. He may walk back. But he might boost a vehicle. Can you do that? Follow him so he doesn't know it?"

"No sweat, amigo," the driver said.

We sat there ten minutes before the men paddled their water-filled kayak up to the beach.

They walked up toward the parking lot closest to the pier, then split. Stefan, the tall guy, went across the street and stopped. He was just visible from where we sat. Even from our distance, I could see water dripping from him.

The shorter guy walked up to a Camaro that was parked with its parking lights on. He bent down to the driver's window. Stayed bent. Straightened up and began gesturing. Lots of arm movement. Then gave the driver the finger.

Both driver and passenger doors opened. Two burly young men got out. The guy stopped gesturing and ran. The young men ran after him.

Stefan calmly walked over to the Camaro, got in and drove away, past us in the cab, beeping the horn.

One of the young men turned at the sound of the horn, saw his car leaving, yelled. The other young man turned, and they both ran after the Camaro.

The Camaro went past us at medium speed. My driver followed

at an easy distance.

After a block, the Camaro turned off Appian Way, drove back streets the other way, came back to the boulevard and picked up his wet comrade who was leaning against a palm tree a couple of blocks southeast of the pier.

They drove back to Venice, stopped near the boardwalk and got out, leaving the Camaro's parking lights on, the engine running, windows down, like an advertisement for a free ride.

The two men split up again, Stefan walking down a side street, the other continuing down the boardwalk.

My driver was a pro. He stayed back, did a slow-and-stop pattern so that any time Stefan might look back, he would just see normal cab motion, not a vehicle on slow cruise.

Two blocks in, Stefan turned. We came around the corner, and I saw my opportunity.

"Drive past him, pull over at that yellow apartment building a block and a half ahead of him. I'll get out, make like I'm paying you through the window. Then you drive ahead another block, take the first left and wait for me out-of-sight. I need to question the suspect. I'll find you in about ten minutes."

"No hay problema, amigo."

The driver drove past Stefan at a good speed, like a typical cab in a hurry, then pulled over where I requested.

When I got out, I stayed bent, moved with difficulty, like an old man on his way home. I turned away from Stefan as he approached from a block back. I held my keys in my hand, out in front of me, and stepped over into the entry of the yellow building. I didn't think he'd recognize my wet clothes in the dark. After all, he thought I had drowned.

Without a weapon, I had only surprise. My head throbbed, and my abdominals were still seized up, but I ignored the pain. I stayed hidden against the entry wall.

Stefan appeared on the sidewalk. I waited until he was past me. I exploded out, hit him hard low on his back, my arms wrapped around his hips. Saw the bus at the last moment. Angled his body to give me maximum cushion.

We hit the side of the passing bus. Stefan bounced hard and dropped to the street. I fell on top of him.

The bus braked to a stop.

I felt Stefan's pants, wondering which man had my wallet. I found my pocketknife and wallet in his right front pocket. I pulled them out, opened the wallet up to my Virginia City 19th century Sheriff's badge, and held it up as the bus driver ran up.

"LAPD official business. I need you to leave the area. Now! GO, GO, GO!"

The driver turned and ran back to the bus. He drove away.

I dragged Stefan up to his feet. His eyes rolled. Blood coursed from his nose. I sleep-walked him over to the shadowed side of a red brick building. I patted him down, felt the gun. Using the fabric of his shirttail, I pulled it out, ejected the clip, put it in my left pocket, and the gun in my right pocket. I took his wallet, his phone, and his keys out and slid them into my pockets.

Stefan moaned and started to regain consciousness. I remembered from his and Preston Laurence's tough-guy visit to Ryan's house, that Stefan was a lefty. I stood behind him, took his left wrist in my right hand and bent his arm behind his back. I pushed it up hard, then put my left hand on the left side of his chin, put his face up against the rough brick, and held it there with serious, skin-break pressure as Stefan started to mumble.

"What is Preston trying to do to Ryan?"

"Dunno what you mean, man."

I grabbed the hair above his left ear, pulled his head back a couple of inches and slammed it to the brick, hard enough to maybe break the zygomatic bone under his right eye.

He grunted. Impressive self-control.

"What is Preston's game?"

Stefan relaxed. I knew what was coming. He wanted me off-guard. I pretended to relax. He tried to spin, pull his wrist out of my grip. But my hand was a vice. I jerked his arm up, twisting the wrist. I heard loud squeaks and pops from his elbow or shoulder. Maybe both.

Stefan screamed.

"You make one more loud sound, and I'll twist your arm out of its socket like a chicken bone."

"Okay!"

"Did you kill Eli Nathan?"

"Who?"

"What about Jeanie Samples?"

"Never heard of her."

"Did you set the fire?"

"I dunno know what you mean. You lost me, man."

He sounded sincere, but pathology takes a lot of forms, one of which is the ability to fool any listener, including shrinks and professional lie detectors.

"How many guys have you dropped in the ocean?"

"None, man. I swear." He sounded like he was crying. "You were gonna be the first."

"How many in Tahoe?"

"Never. I can't say for Pres before I was around. But you took his girl, man. No one takes Pres's girl. He, like, cracked."

"You work for the Mob?"

"No. I know some guys, that's all. I've done some things to a couple dudes who deserved it. But they didn't die or nothin'. You were the first to die. 'Cept, you didn't die, either."

"How much did Preston pay you to kill me?"

"I get regular pay."

"He would give you a bonus if you succeeded. How much?"

"Ten large. I promised Carlos I'd split it with him."

I swept my foot under Stefan's. I gave his arm another twist as he fell. He cried out, landed face first on the concrete. I bent down, positioned my knee between his shoulder blades, jamming the broken arm up toward the back of his neck. I put some weight on my knee. Stefan moaned.

"What is Preston's goal with Ryan?"

Stefan could barely utter the words through his pain. His lips were against the sidewalk as he spoke.

"Pres wants Ryan's company. Either Ryan caves and sells him controlling interest in CBT, or Pres steals the research and starts another company. That's my call, anyway."

"Why? What is it about Ryan's company that is so special?"

"He'll kill me if I say."

"I'll kill you if you don't."

"CBT has a research facility up by Mt. Rose. They've made some kind of discovery."

I thought about it.

"With only one good arm left, you can still continue your scumbag occupation," I said. "So I planned to solve that. But I just thought of a way that you can keep me from breaking your other elbow before I leave."

"What, man?" He was frantic.

I got out my cell phone. "Gonna do a quick little video interview. I ask your name, and how long you've worked for Preston, and the details of some of your nastier jobs like this last effort to drop me in the Pacific. And we'll talk about that discovery."

"Whatever you say."

He performed like a star on Oprah, sincere and earnest and heartfelt.

I clicked off my cell video.

"I'll leave you with one thought," I said.

"What?"

"I ever see you in Tahoe again, I'll tie a concrete block to your neck and drop you in the middle of the lake."

"I promise, man, I'm never going back to Tahoe again."

I stood up, walked away, found my cab down the next street.

I had the driver stop twice. Once so I could drop the gun down a storm drain, and once so I could drop the clip down another. I used my own shirttail both times. Then I had the driver leave me at a corner, five blocks from my hotel. I knew I had cash in my wallet that I'd retrieved from Stefan, but I paid him with cash from Stefan's wallet, still using my shirttail.

"I will remember you, but you won't remember me or this trip," I said as I gave the driver all of Stefan's cash, an amount that worked out to more than a 1000% tip.

The driver nodded once, his face blank. "Gracias, amigo. Never seen you before," he said, and drove off.

I dropped Stefan's wallet down a third storm drain.

My clothes were dry by the time I got back to my hotel.

FORTY-THREE

I made calls to Street and Ryan, explaining that I was delayed, leaving out the details of Stefan's efforts to drop me in the ocean. After I said goodbye, I ate a takeout sandwich and drank a quart of milk in my room, and I lay there in the dark thinking about Preston and his goal to unhinge Ryan so that he could persuade him to sell controlling interest in CBT. From what Stefan said, the scientists had made a high-altitude discovery that had enough potential to drive Preston to extreme measures. A discovery that Ryan hadn't told me about, an omission about which I was going to try to be calm when I talked to him in person.

But my bigger problem was that Stefan said that he had nothing to do with the murders and the other incidents involving Ryan. I'd put Stefan under considerable stress when he said it - and he revealed important information - so I believed him.

Which meant that I had two bad guys, and I didn't have a clue who the other one was. But Preston had a lot of employees. He wouldn't tell each worker what all the other workers were doing.

The next morning, I caught the shuttle back to Reno and was over Spooner Summit and back to Tahoe by noon. I drove up the mountain to my cabin to pick up some clothes and other personal effects, then drove to Kingsbury Grade.

I saw Street's VW bug at her lab, and pulled in.

Street was sitting on a stool by her microscope station. The ceiling lights were off. She turned as I came in the door.

What happened to your face and ear?" Street said, frowning, reaching up to touch the side of my face.

"Had a scuffle with Stefan, the guy who works for Preston."

Street's brow was furrowed with worry.

"I'm sorry that the bad part of my world is spilling over into yours," I said.

"I'm just afraid." The only close light was the one coming from within her scope. Yet even the dim light from the scope reflected in the wetness of her eyes.

"Of what?" I asked.

"Of losing you," she said, shaking her head. "Of coming up against darkness. Of revisiting the fears of my childhood. I see Ryan, who by all rights should have a perfect life. He's done nothing but work, nothing but pursue his genius, and look what happens. And I'm afraid for Lily."

I stepped close to hug her. She turned her face and put her cheek against my chest, and I held her head, caressing her hair.

Street continued. "It's impossible not to fall in love with her. But it's like her childhood is on an edge that no child should face. Of course, she doesn't go hungry, and she has clothes and shelter. But she has no parents, and her brother is overwhelmed, and her surrogate grandfather dies in a strange circumstance, and some twisted monster is pursuing them. She can't even have a bicycle that isn't crushed by a billionaire jerk who has no awareness of what it means to respect another person's life. A life that may be over soon."

Street pushed her head back and looked up at me.

"Do you know anything more?" she asked. "Are you any closer to finding out what is happening?"

"I've learned that Preston is trying to pressure Ryan into selling his company. But it appears that Preston's man Stefan isn't doing the sick stuff. Maybe one of his other men is."

Street searched my eyes, tears brimming her own. "They're just kids," she said. "People think money makes you invulnerable. But they're just kids."

I pulled Street to me and held her. "I know," I said.

Ten minutes later, I left and drove to my office, a block up and across Kingsbury Grade to check messages. There were two.

The first was from Diamond about the lab that Douglas County used for DNA testing. They'd analyzed the hair samples on the brush that belonged to Jeanie Samples, and found a match with the remains on the mountain.

The second message was from the lab to which I'd sent the tiny, bright red leather piece that I'd found on the cliff above the remains. The lab couldn't tell me anything about the color dye or the source. But they had determined that the leather was made from kangaroo hide.

I drove back to Ryan's house.

Carol said hi, Lily and Spot were excited to see me, and Ryan looked so weary that it seemed he'd lost his will to live.

Eventually, I got him alone. I told him about the DNA match on Jeanie. He swallowed and said that Diamond had already called him.

"What do you know about the renter at the Village Green who was evicted and then died?"

Ryan's eyes got very wide. "Nothing. Someone died?"

So I told him, and he looked like he was about to collapse. It was clear that he was just the kid that Street referred to. A kind of a business version of an ivory tower recluse who was so focused on his science that he didn't grasp what else was going on in his life.

"And you haven't told me the truth," I said, trying not to sound too stern, but not succeeding. "I can't help you if you don't give me all of the relevant information."

Ryan's perpetual look of worry turned to fear. "What do you mean? I've told you everything."

"What about the discovery at your research facility? The high-altitude breakthrough, or whatever it is?"

Ryan looked horrified.

"What discovery?" he said.

FORTY-FOUR

"In Venice I enjoyed a little incident with Preston's bodyguard," I said. "Under my encouragement, the man told me that Preston wanted controlling interest in your company. The reason why is that CBT has made a discovery at your facility on the mountain. He said if Preston couldn't buy sufficient stock to take control, then he would steal your research and start his own company. Apparently, something with a huge potential value is going on up on Mt. Rose."

Ryan stared at me as if I'd just announced mutiny in his company.

"I can't believe it. This can't happen. Our scientists are loyal to me. They know that I provide very well for them."

"Does Preston have access to the company facilities?"

"He's not invited, but he's not forbidden access, either."

"Do any of your people know that he owns forty percent?"

"I suppose so," Ryan said. "I haven't kept it secret."

"And your first big cash infusion came from his investment."

Another nod.

"Which probably allowed you to purchase some of the equipment that your employees use," I said. "Maybe even the building up on the mountain."

"Yeah, but..."

"So it could be that your employees feel that they owe their jobs and their sophisticated tools to Preston. And if they know that you only own twenty percent of the stock, they may feel as much, or even more, allegiance to Preston as they have toward you. Maybe he's been popping into your mountain lab, bringing people hot pizza for lunch, the occasional gift and such, after-work beers. It's easy to imagine that they would tell him of any discovery. After all, they would think of him almost as their boss."

"That's outrageous! He's an investor, nothing more." Ryan was purple with anger.

"Is there someone at the mountain lab who you could call and ask if Preston has been around?"

"I'm pretty close to Selena. I'll call her."

He looked at his phone, pressed some keys, found the number, dialed.

"Um, Selena? This is Ryan Lear. Hi. Is this an okay time? Oh. Could you call me back? Also, could you call from your car or something? It's private. Thanks." He hung up.

Ryan sat on one of his kitchen barstools. His skinny shoulders slumped. His back rounded so much that it looked like it would break. He put his elbows on the counter and leaned his chin into his hands.

We get an idea of the corporate executive, a person with a big ego and enormous self-confidence. A person who is in charge of hundreds of employees and is responsible for their livelihoods, yet can still go to sleep with ease, speak before large audiences, and go to dinners with powerful politicians.

The kid before me appeared overwhelmed, and he telegraphed imminent collapse.

His phone rang, and he answered it. He tried to sound upbeat at first, asking her questions about Preston Laurence, but soon sounded dejected. A minute later, devastated. He thanked her and hung up.

"All this time I was worried about corporate spying. That was part of the reason we built the facility on the mountain instead of building a hypobaric chamber in the Bay Area. And it turns out that the spy is our largest shareholder.

"She said that he's been by lots, and that he seems to have a special rapport with JJ. That's Jason Johnson, and that in the last week JJ has been cataloging some rapid hypoxic adaptations in paramecium, a ciliate protozoa that we are using for research."

Ryan slammed his palm down on the counter.

"And he never called me! I'm his mentor! I hired him even before we brought Bob on board! I gave him his big promotion!"

"I'm sorry, Ryan," I said.

"What do you think I should do?" He was pleading.

"I should see your high altitude shop."

"When do you want to go?"

"Now," I said.

"Do you want me to drive?"

"I'll drive. Is this a time when you would normally go there?"

Ryan shook his head. "No. I always get there early in the morning if I go there at all."

"Then I'll go in alone. Having the boss around always changes the tenor of things. I'll get a more accurate read if you're not there. If it makes sense for you to come in, I'll let you know.

"You can't just walk in," Ryan said. "It's a locked facility."

"I can knock, right?"

"Yeah."

"Before we go, I need you to write a letter of authorization for me. Put it on your letterhead, and make it out to Jerry Burns of ETR Analysis, Inc. That will allow me to poke around once I'm inside."

"Like, 'This authorizes Jerry Burns of ETR Analysis entry into CalBioTechnica's facility up above the Mt. Rose Meadows?'"

"Perfect."

Ryan went into his office and brought it out a minute later.

We headed up to Incline Village, turned up the Mt. Rose Highway and drove up to the meadows at 9000 feet. Ryan pointed out the turn-off, and we followed a winding dirt trail that was marked as a Jeep road on my US Topographical map. The road went across to a rise, then started up, steep in places, switchbacking several times. We came to a Forest Service gate.

Ryan got out and unlocked it. I drove through.

Ten minutes after we'd left the highway, we came over a rise. The closest topo line on the map showed us at 10,200 feet. Mt. Rose loomed above to the northeast. Ryan pointed to a small building in the trees about a quarter mile away. It was as plain as he described it, a concrete block box, painted green.

I parked some distance away, in some trees that gave us cover.

I reached into my box of useful items, pulled out the clipboard, my recycled electronic device, my ETR baseball cap.

"What is that stuff?" Ryan asked.

"Just junk that gets me into places I don't belong. The clipboard is standard stuff. I record dates and very important meaningless numbers and checkmarks. This other thing is pure wizardry. Got it from eBay."

"What does it do?"

"I have no idea. I think it's some kind of obsolete phone repairman computer. All I know is you turn on this button, here, then twist this dial, and a little graph comes up on the screen. Change the dial, the graph changes. If I take these wires and touch them together or to any metallic object, the thing beeps. And this yellow light blinks now and then in a random pattern, sometimes fast. It's probably supposed to be on all the time. Works like magic. You stay here."

I clipped the computer device onto my belt, walked through the trees, came out near four parked vehicles, and went up to the door that Ryan said was always locked. I turned the knob and stepped inside, shutting the door gently behind me.

The entry I was in was separated from the rest of the space by a wall of glass. Behind the glass was a large room. Everything was white on white, smooth hard surfaces, every corner bathed in bright light. There were techie-looking stainless steel appliances. Some counters were bare, others had pieces of equipment unlike anything I'd ever seen. In one corner was a washing station with a utility sink and what looked like an unusual dishwasher.

In the far corner of the large room was yet another, smaller glass room with a vestibule between double doors, some kind of air-lock. The entire building hummed with the loud whoosh of forced air, perhaps a system for filtering dust and other pollutants.

In the smaller air-lock room stood a woman at a counter. She wore a white coat and cap and a mask over her mouth and nose. She worked at a counter. Next to her was a cabinet with a glass front. The lights inside illuminated rows of glass containers that reminded me of Petri dishes from high school science.

In the main room, two men sat on stools in front of machines. They had touch-sensitive control panels, and computer screens with inscrutable numbers and letters on the display. I had no idea what they were.

To one side of the big room were two sets of low white counters with two built-in desk spaces each. Each space had a computer and telephone. The fourth scientist sat at one of the desks, his screen angled toward the wall so that the others couldn't see it. His video game was visible to me. He was hitting the keys fast. I guessed that he was JJ.

I took a step forward onto the welcome grate, and it immediately came alive. A vacuum roar turned on as rows of oscillating brushes rose up to scrub the soles of my shoes.

At that sound, all but the woman in the air-lock room turned to look at me. I smiled, angled my shoes so that the brushes could do a thorough job, then stepped forward off the grate. The vacuum roar dropped from class 4 hurricane down to basic forced-air heating and cooling, and the brushes stopped moving.

The man at the desk hit a button as he stood up, and his video game was replaced by a work screen with writing. He walked over to an aluminum circle in the glass wall, and spoke.

"Can I help you?" His voice sounded tinny.

I pressed my fake Jerry Burns driver's license and Ryan's letter of authorization up against the glass.

He took the time to carefully read Ryan's letter.

Then he pointed to a rack of white shop coats. I put on a coat, and he hit a button. The door buzzed and I walked in.

"What is the purpose of your visit?" he said, frowning.

"I'm the Sierra Corridor Field Officer for ETR. We've had reports of frequency interference from the Mt. Rose section. I'm here to check it out. Probably only take me about five minutes."

I looked around the lab.

"I don't understand," he said. "There are broadcast radio towers and cell towers and microwave towers on the nearby peaks. This area is like the Los Angeles of electromagnetic traffic jams. What could our lab have to do with this?"

"We don't know. That's why they sent me out to check." I looked around at the lab.

"What frequencies are you looking for?"

"Just the ones that this baby picks up." I switched my belt computer on. "See?" I pointed at the blinking yellow light. "You've definitely got some leaky equipment, here." I wrote down the date on my clipboard sheet, then fumbled my pencil into the air toward his desk. It bounced under his desk chair.

"Oops." I got down on my knees, fetched the pencil, leaned on the chair and desk as I stood up and looked at his computer screen. In the short moment of standing up, I saw the word Preston in the address bar.

I pulled the two wire probes out from my belt computer, reached around and touched them to the metal backing on the man's computer while I scanned the email on his computer screen. I saw nothing revealing except the word breakthrough. My belt computer beeped.

"Hmm," I said. "That figures." I twisted the dial, made the graph jump around.

I moved to another desk and repeated the process at another computer. "Uh, oh," I said louder.

"What's that mean?" the man said.

"Means we may have to require your boss to put on filters."

"Who is it that made the report about this so-called interference?" he said.

"Got me. My orders come out of the Vegas Division. For all I know, their clients could be the government. Or the military." I made some more marks, followed them with a checkmark.

I walked across the lab toward the other men. I nodded at them, held my little machine out, its yellow light blinking furiously. I touched my wire probes to one of their devices, and held it there. The beep sounded long and tortured.

Then I took a quick walk to each corner of the room, twisted my dial, made marks on my clipboard. At each stop and turn, I made a surreptitious study of the other three scientists, then thanked them and turned to go.

"Got what I need," I said.

"Do you have a card?" the video gamer/emailer asked.

"No, sorry, ran out last week. Keep that authorization letter."

I walked out, and went back to the Jeep. There was room to back out and turn around a couple of ways. I chose the one that would keep Ryan out of view from the lab windows.

"Did you find out anything?" Ryan asked.

"The woman in the air-lock room and the two men at the counters are probably good people who serve your best interests.

The guy at the desk with the little goatee probably isn't."

"That's JJ. Did you see something?"

"He's playing video games and writing an email to Preston."

"What? Preston?"

"Yeah. Even more, my gut instinct tells me that he's rotten. You know how you can walk into any business, and you can spot the bad fish? Sometimes it's workers who are lazy, and have an attitude that says, 'Why should I care?' Other times they are brusque and telegraph that they are too important to be working in a place like this. That was JJ."

Ryan rode in silence for a time, as if he were in shock.

"What do we do now?" he finally said.

"We need to know if Jason has sold you out," I said, knowing to my own satisfaction that he already had.

"How do we do that?"

"The slow inefficient way is for you to check with your lawyer and discuss the legality and repercussions of gaining access to Jason's emails, his computer, and his other papers. The fallout would be substantial. Other employees would find out. They would wonder if they were also under investigation. That would severely undermine their morale."

"You imply that there is a faster, more efficient way."

I nodded. "With your permission, I pay a private visit to JJ and encourage him to come clean about any activities that don't square with taking a paycheck from CalBioTechnica."

"Are you suggesting that you'd threaten him?"

"Words, first, is my motto. I'm often very persuasive. People like JJ usually see the logic of confessing their sins."

"If words don't work first, what comes second?"

"If that is a big concern to you, call your lawyer. For whatever it's worth, if I pay JJ a visit, I believe that he'll want to tell me the truth. I'll explain to him that we're looking to cut down much bigger trees than him. Unless of course he doesn't 'fess up. In that case, we'll charge him with stealing corporate secrets. He'll never get another job in corporate America."

Ryan thought about it most of the way back to his house.

"Okay," he said. "Do what you think you should do."

FORTY-FIVE

I waited on the side of the highway up on Mt. Rose Meadows, within sight of the dirt road that went to CBT's research facility. Other cars and pickups were nearby, tourists out for hikes. I was calm, but I was angry. If you have a problem with your employer, tell him or her, and work to fix it, or quit. But selling him out behind his back is way over in the wrong column on my ethics checklist.

JJ's shiny green Infinity all-wheel-drive came bouncing down the dirt road across the meadow, turned down the highway toward Incline Village, and raced by me. I followed.

The guy drove way too fast. I could drive fast, too. I saw him put a phone to his ear. His driving wavered, but didn't slow. He suddenly hit the brakes hard, turned off onto the overlook parking area above the lake, and stopped near the guardrail. There were no other cars.

I pulled up at an angle behind him, blocking his exit.

He got out, red-faced, shouting into his phone.

I walked up, grabbed his phone, and threw it over the edge into the woods.

"The hell you doin, man?! I knew you were an imposter."

I took a good grip on the front of his designer sweatshirt and pushed him back against his car.

He fumbled in his pocket.

"Go ahead, push your panic button. I'm happy to explain to the world about how you sold out corporate secrets. When you get out of prison, no company will ever hire you again. You can do volunteer work as a street sweeper."

"I...I didn't do anything wrong. Stockholders have a right to know what goes on." Jason stuttered his words.

"Your boss is Ryan Lear. You didn't bother to even mention your discovery to him." I twisted the fabric at his chest, lifted him up a bit.

"I was going to. Honest. The..."

I cut him off. "How much did Preston pay you?"

"I don't know what you mean, man."

"HOW MUCH!" With my other hand, I grabbed the fabric and belt at the front of his pants and lifted him a foot off the ground. "Tell me how much or I throw you over the edge."

He strained to look down at the precipice behind him, eyes wide with fear.

I brought him back as if to swing him out over the guardrail, took two quick steps forward.

"WAIT! I'LL TELL YOU!"

I stopped my swing and released my grip. He fell to the asphalt and curled up in a fetal position, whimpering.

"I'm waiting." I took out my phone and set it to video.

When Jason spoke, he whined like a little kid who got pushed over on the playground. His face was tucked into his hands making it hard to understand him.

"Sit up so I can hear you," I said.

He slowly pushed himself up and leaned against the guardrail. I pressed the button on my phone.

"Mr. Laurence was going to make me a vice president after he got control of the company."

"You sold out your boss for a title and raise in pay?"

He whimpered louder. "I'd have my own division. And I'd get to go on Mr. Laurence's yacht. He said I could even bring my girlfriend to his horse ranch. She loves horses."

It took control not to kick him over the edge.

"What was your discovery?"

"You wouldn't understand."

"I'm not asking you again."

"Telomeres. Telomeres are the tiny components in cells that determine how cells age and when cells die. We don't yet know what the driving mechanisms are for how telomeres behave. But we found something unusual in how they respond to high altitude. It suggests how the underlying mechanisms function. If we can use this to tease out how telomeres..." His breathing increased to shallow, rapid pants as panic set in.

"You might learn how to control aging," I said.

I turned off my phone and left JJ at the overlook.

My case was going in multiple directions. I decided to concentrate on a single component and see if I could make some progress.

I called Street at her lab as I drove back down the East Shore. We talked a bit, then I told her about the lab report on Jeanie's hair.

"Ryan has lost a good part of his world," she said.

"Yeah. I also found out that the little piece of leather was kangaroo hide. Does that ring any bells? Have you heard of any clothing line that uses kangaroo leather? Or any other product made of kangaroo?"

"No. I didn't even know that kangaroo hide was turned into leather. Of course, it's obvious once you say it. But it never occurred to me before. Maybe try Diamond."

I got Diamond on the phone and asked him the same question.

"No. Sounds exotic. You should ask Maria. She might know."

"They have kangaroos in Southern Mexico?"

"Not the last I checked. But Maria... muy inteligente. Never know what she comes up with."

"Cortez's horses," I said.

"As I said."

I called Maria.

We chatted about Mustangs for a bit. Then I said, "Diamond probably told you about the body below Genoa Peak."

"Sí."

"I found a little piece of leather up there, bright red, small, like a piece of confetti. I sent it to a lab and they said it was kangaroo leather."

"Kangaroo?" Maria said. "In this country. How strange. But

then you said it was red. It must have come from someone's clothes."

"Yeah. I was wondering if you knew anything about kangaroo leather."

"Me? Kangaroo? Owen, you are a funny man. I run a little horse boarding ranch on the other side of the planet from kangaroo country. What would I know about kangaroo leather?"

"I just thought it might be something you've heard of. Like maybe it was an equestrian thing, or perhaps backcountry people wear a certain something that is made of kangaroo leather."

"No, Owen. I'm sorry. I've never known of any clothing or riding tack that comes from kangaroo. In fact, the only time I ever even heard of kangaroo leather was from when I was a little girl in Chiapas."

"What was that?"

"It wasn't even about clothing. The ranchers used bullwhips. They used to say that the finest bullwhips were made of kangaroo hide. So I'm very sorry that I can't give you any more help."

I thanked Maria for her time and hung up.

Bullwhips. I'd never even seen a bullwhip except for when the actors in Virginia City, re-enacting 19th century customs, fired their six-shooters and cracked their whips up and down the main street to the delight of the tourists.

Outside of acting, I had only a vague sense that bullwhips were made for driving cattle into pens and such. There would be no need for a bullwhip up on Genoa Peak.

When I got back to Ryan's house, I went online and typed in bullwhips. On the second page of links I saw something called FMA. I clicked on it and went to a website about Filipino Martial Arts. They stressed the discipline of being able to use all kinds of different objects as weapons, from sticks to poles to bullwhips.

I looked around a little further and found that there was an FMA school in Reno.

I called and was told they had an evening class at 6:00 p.m. The man on the phone said I was welcome to stop by and discover my future of fitness, discipline, and self-defense.

FORTY-SIX

The FMA school was near the airport in Reno. I got off the freeway on Plumb, and turned east. Just before the airport entrance, I went north again and drove around the far end of the airport where the runway begins on the other side of the tall fence. A huge purple jet floated in out of the north, looking like a big boat that had slowed just to the point where it would drop out of planing mode and settle down into the water. It felt like the plane was 28 or 30 inches above the roof of the Jeep as it went by, and I resisted the urge to duck my head. The jet cleared the airport fence with several millimeters to spare, and its wheels puffed smoke as it kissed the tarmac a few seconds later.

As always, I marveled that such a big, ponderous, and complex machine could get off the ground. Yet even an ordinary guy like me could understand the bits and pieces of a flying machine, along with the principles that allowed it to get up into the atmosphere.

Although our ancestors would be astonished to see modern aircraft, creating and flying jet planes is relatively simple compared to manipulating DNA and the very essence of life's processes. The new frontier didn't look as flashy as big shiny jets, but it hinted at possibilities that would make flying machines seem mundane.

The address on my Post-it note belonged to one of six large commercial units in a long warehouse building. They each had oversized garage doors next to glass walk-in doors. A small sign said FMA OF RENO. The garage door was up.

The inside of the cavernous space was carpeted. A dozen people stood in three rows of four, facing a wall of mirrors. All but one wore a gi, the white robe that seemed to be universal to all of the martial arts.

Two of the students were women, and one was a boy of maybe

13 or 14. All had what looked like bamboo sticks, but colored dark brown, and they held them out in front of them at 45-degree angles.

The instructor stood with his back to the mirror. He too had a stick. As he called out commands, he demonstrated different positions with his body and with his stick.

I walked past the open garage door, opened the glass door, and entered a small office. The walls were unadorned concrete block painted cream, the floor was gray concrete with a large throw rug in garish colors that looked like a Walmart version of Persian.

A young man wearing a gi sat at a gray metal desk, eating a candy bar, talking on the phone. He nodded at me, and raised his index finger. Behind him was a window that looked out onto the dojo. The students all stepped into a new position, their left foot forward. They shifted their sticks to a new position. They moved mostly in unison.

"Yeah," he said into the phone, his mouth full. "Yeah," he said again. "Look, I got a customer. Gotta go. Right. Luv ya."

He hung up, looked up at me, taking in my height, maybe wondering if it would be an advantage or disadvantage in FMA.

He finished chewing and swallowed. "Hey, man," he said.

"I'm Owen McKenna," I said. I handed him a card. "I'm working on an investigation that may involve your brand of martial arts. I'd like to ask a few questions about it."

He studied my card. "McKenna Investigations. You're a private detective?"

I gave him a polite smile. Ever gracious.

"Owen McKenna, private eye. Cool," he said. "So what's the deal? Did someone get killed?" He jerked his head toward the window and the class beyond. "Jimbo stresses non-violence to all of his students, just so you know."

I nodded. "I'm sure he does. Is Jimbo the owner?"

"Yeah. I'm his assistant. I can tell you right up front, we're not allowed to give out info about our students. Privacy. Plus, some of our women students are probably keeping their martial arts secret from their men. Maybe they got boyfriends slap 'em around, and they want it to be, like, surprise kaboom, guess you shouldn'ta slapped me one more time, right?!"

He looked at me for reaction.

"Right," I said.

"Like to be there when that happens," he said. He peeled back the wrapper from the rest of his candy bar, and popped it in his mouth.

"I understand that some types of FMA involve bullwhips," I said.

"Kali," he mumbled, chewing.

"Kali?"

His cheeks bulged with candy, made him look like a hamster. "Yeah. Jimbo got introduced to it in Manila. But he didn't really pick it up until the school in LA."

"LA a good place to learn Filipino Martial Arts?"

"Yeah. It's actually in Long Beach. They got the best school for it in the country. Hands down. But they don't teach bullwhips much from what I heard. Not like someone's going to carry a bullwhip down the street. But Jimbo does a bullwhip segment in some of his classes. One of the principles of Filipino Martial Arts is using any object as a weapon. Impromptu weapons. You go up against a Kali expert, you're not gonna figure out how he's coming at you. A chair can be used in awesome ways. I spar with Jimbo often. And I'm pretty good. But Jimbo pretty much kicks my ass every time. You want to learn Kali, he's the best teacher. You got a gi?" He chewed and swallowed.

I shook my head. "No."

"Kali doesn't require a gi. Kind of unusual that way. Not like Karate and other disciplines. But Jimbo's personal rule says everybody's gotta have 'em. He says it puts students in the right mental state. Martial arts are mental as much as physical. We sell gis, but you're one long dude. You might have to go across town to the Korean Karate school to pick up a gi your size. But I can sign you up, now, anyway."

"I'd like to watch a class first, if that's okay."

"Sure." He pointed out the window. "Be my guest. Or, you might want to come back tonight and see a session on bullwhips..." he ran his thumb down the schedule, "Jimbo's got his all-weapons class at eight o'clock."

"Maybe I'll do that. Tell me, do they ever make bullwhips out of red leather?"

"Never seen one up close." He ran his tongue around his teeth, searching out hidden bits of candy. "But I've seen pictures of whips with red ends. Like they were dipped in blood. Makes them look like serpent tails."

I thanked him and left, got some dinner, was back at 8:00.

The warehouse garage door was still open, letting fresh air in and helping the dojo cool down in pace with the natural cooling of the desert in the evening.

In the center of the far wall stood Jimbo in his gi. He held a bullwhip in one hand, the long tail portion coiled up next to the stiff handle and held by his fingers. About twelve or fifteen feet in front of him was a pedestal with a candlestick on it. The candle burned with a small flame, nearly invisible in the bright light of the dojo space.

Four students were spaced out as far as the big space would allow. They faced him, their backs to me. They too held bullwhips the same way, in their right hands. Two of the students were small and had their hair tied up at the backs of their heads.

I hung back at a good distance.

Jimbo spoke to them. "You don't snap a bullwhip. You project it with a smooth throwing motion. With practice you will be able to project the whip exactly where you want it. The power of the bullwhip is in its speed. The intimidation of the whip is in its sound. The crack you hear is the tip of the whip breaking the sound barrier. In fact, the upper speeds of bullwhips have been estimated to approach one thousand miles per hour. This is bullet territory. So even though the end of the bullwhip has very little mass, you can imagine that it can inflict great injury. Small bullets have very little mass, too, and we all know what they can do.

"So take great care when practicing your whip thrusts. Until you are an expert, it is hard to predict where the whip will strike. And always remember that if you were to actually hit a person with your whip, you would create a serious wound. Without much effort you can take out a person's eye. With a little more effort, you can take off a person's ear or even their nose. If you were to strike a person, whether by accident or not, a prosecutor could treat it just as if you'd fired a gun at them. Using a bullwhip on a person is considered assault with a deadly weapon. There are situations where it may be justified. But like using a gun, you'd better make certain that you are in mortal danger, and you have no alternative. Do I make myself clear?"

None of the four students said a word.

"Okay. Here is a basic thrust." Jimbo opened his fingers. The long end of the bullwhip dropped to the ground. He brought the handle back, then arced it over his head, thrusting it forward and down almost like a fastball pitch. The leather whipped through the air, and snuffed out the candle flame with a crack that sounded like a .22 revolver.

Jimbo said, "Please step up to the candle."

The four students converged on the candle.

"You will notice that the wick is still in place, and the candle has no cuts in it. That indicates that my whip didn't touch the wick or the candle. It merely cracked the air a half inch away from the wick and blew out the flame. Now return to your places."

The students went back to the edges of the room.

Jimbo left the candle unlit, and returned to his earlier position. This time he thrust the bullwhip at a slight angle. The crack was less intense. The main portion of the candle and candle holder flipped off onto the floor. The pedestal wobbled. The top two inches of the candle rocketed through the air like a slap-shot hockey puck and smashed into the wall between two of the students. They both jumped back, flinching.

"That is what happens if you strike an object," Jimbo said. "Now watch again as I move my arm in slow motion."

He ran his hand and arm through the arc in slo-mo, the limp whip dragging on the floor.

"I want you to practice running your hand through the throwing arc. Do it real slow. Go ahead. Ten times each."

They each mimicked his motion, at slow speed. Jimbo walked over to the person on the right rear and helped him, holding his arm, demonstrating the position.

He returned to the front of the room.

"Now I want you to try to crack the whip. Same exact motion. But faster. Remember, you don't snap the whip. There is no jerking back with your arm. Just a forward throw. Don't worry about your aim, although be very careful to throw directly in front of you. You are each separated by enough distance that there will be no danger. Your goal is to use a smooth arm motion and to make the whip crack loud and clear. Okay? Give it a go."

The students all did the throwing motion, some fast, some jerky. Only the woman in the left front corner made the cracking sound on the first throw. Her motion was smooth as if she'd done it a thousand times. The others struggled, their whips hitting the floor. One accidentally let go of his whip, and it flew through the air and hit the end wall next to Jimbo. Jimbo picked it up, carried it back, and spoke in low tones, demonstrating how to grip the whip.

The woman at the left front cracked her whip over and over, each crack louder than the last. The other students watched her success, mimicked her motion, began to crack their whips, too.

Jimbo called timeouts a couple of times, went over adjustments in the ritual. The students gradually got more successful.

Through it all, the woman at the left front became more and more focused. Her intensity permeated the big room. It seemed as if she were having some kind of religious experience, exorcising her demons with each whip-crack. Or maybe she was doing what the man in the office spoke about, going through imagined revenge against someone who repeatedly abused her. Either way, she telegraphed anger.

I watched through the entire class. At the end, I left and got into the Jeep. I was pulling out when my headlights swept over the woman as she walked out, almost stomping as she headed to her car. The recognition came as a shock.

It was Holly Hughes, the big, super-fit woman that Ryan introduced me to at his party, the mother of Ryan's friend William, the video gamer. I remembered her lashing out at Ryan when he gushed over Carol/Champagne's beauty.

I slowed, pulled over and thought about turning back into the parking lot. But she was already in her car. She raced out of the lot, tires squealing. I had no desire to interrupt her anger, so I let her go.

When I got back to Ryan's house, I suggested we all go on a

night walk. Carol said she was too tired. I gave her a hard look.

"What, you think you can't trust me to leave me here alone?"

"Think, Carol," I said, irritated. "It's Preston who can't be trusted to not come after you if he sees you here by yourself."

She looked alarmed. "Let me get my jacket," she said.

We took a long walk. Lily rode on Spot's back, then Ryan's shoulders. After he tired, she asked to ride on my shoulders.

"Don't you think you should get some exercise?" I said.

"It's exercise just hanging on," she said.

So I boosted her up, and she rode the rest of the way on my shoulders.

"Your name is HeeHaw," she said. "You are both the horse and the clown."

"I'm Owen," I said.

"HeeHaw!" she giggled. Then she periodically shouted out, "Giddyup, HeeHaw, giddyup!" and, "Do a clown trick, HeeHaw," and, "Faster, HeeHaw." And once when her enthusiasm made her lose her balance, "Whoa, HeeHaw!" as she grabbed my head to keep from falling over.

When we got back to the house, I lifted her down and said, "You didn't have to walk a single step."

"I told you I have good ideas!" she said, laughing.

I reached to grab her, but she shrieked and ran from me, giggling uproariously.

Later, I sat up with Ryan.

"Got a question about your friend William," I said.

"William Hughes?"

"The gamer, yeah. Any problems there?"

"What do you mean?" Ryan looked and sounded nervous, worried. He seemed like a rabbit, unable to move as a gang of coyotes circled.

"Is everything in your friendship with him comfortable? Any animosities? Any past dustups? Arguments? Disagreements?"

"Not really. Why?"

"Just saw his mother at a martial arts class. Made me curious."

"Oh. Well, William and I have always been good friends. It's not like we're soul mates or anything. More like we share social dysfunction. Our common ground is that we don't fit in."

"Was he ever uncomfortable with your business success?"

"Hardly. He's made tens of millions with his games. He's one of the elite. Stanford B-School pressed him to come and run seminars. Of course, he's way too shy to do that. But he's at the top. Not like he would be jealous of me."

"What about his mother? Was she ever upset with how you and William got along?"

"Mrs. Hughes and I have always gotten along great."

"That's not what I asked," I said.

He paused. "The only time she got upset was when we formed CBT. I asked him to be a partner. After all, he did some really great computer modeling that helped us with our first genetic experiments. But he said no. He was a gamer. He didn't want to have anything to do with bio-tech. Even so, his input was important. So when Preston came in for his forty percent, and we got our big chunk of money, I sent William one hundred thousand dollars as a thank you. Eli and Jeanie agreed with me that he deserved it and more. William didn't even want to cash the check. But I insisted. Of course, William was already rich by that time. Even so, I think his mother thought that he should be part of the company even if he didn't want to be. I could see why she'd be a little upset. If he'd been part of the CBT team, his salary and stock proceeds would have been considerable. And if we go really big, there would be that much more that he could have split. I think his mother was blinded by that knowledge. She probably thought that William said no to us because of some subtle pressure from us, like a sense that our offer wasn't sincere."

"Was your offer sincere?" I asked.

"Of course. But his mother might not have thought so."

"Tell me about his business."

"His game designing? Basically, William was and always will be a classic programmer. He has a magical ability to take any part of the world, real or imagined, or any kind of experiential phenomenon, and render it in binary code. When he played video games as a young kid, he really got into the concept that you could create a world with ones and zeros. He inhaled programming like it was eating jelly sandwiches. He even went to the video game summer camp at Stanford when he was in middle school. By the time he got to high school he'd single-handedly written a good game. It was as if the game design, the script and the storyboards were fully formed in his mind, and all he had to do was write out the code.

"Of course, any game written and coded by an individual is necessarily very limited. A typical game can take fifty people over a year to produce. A game can involve some of the most complicated software there is, with millions of lines of code to create an entire three-D world.

"But William's game got him a full scholarship at Stanford, and he was a star there before he dropped out. That's where I met him. He and I talked about our ideas, and, frankly, he helped me more than I helped him. He figured out that parts of my premise of how to do recombinant gene splicing could be modeled with software. We could run scenarios on the computer and prejudge which approaches would be most likely to work. So he wrote a cool program for us. But that's where his involvement with us ended. And even if he wanted to be part of our company, there's no way he'd have the time. I even asked him if he would just serve on our board, but he said no to that, too. His game studio has been buried. All of his employees work seventy, eighty hours a week."

"Another question about Holly," I said.

"Sure."

"What's her background?"

"I don't know. To me she was just William's mom. Very supportive of him. Very protective. If you were one of William's school teachers, you wouldn't want to see her show up after school. She's so big and strong. It makes sense that she would be taking martial arts. I used to be a little envious of William. My dad was nice but distant, more interested in the world of education than in the world of his son or his daughter. William didn't have a dad, but he had a mom who would do anything for him, protect him from the world. Although, I have to admit that when I was younger, she scared me a little."

"How?"

"Just her intensity. It was like she had an on/off switch, and it was always on all the way. There was no part-way, softer setting. And she did things that left me with a frightening image that I'd think about in the night."

"Any you remember?"

"Yeah. Out in their backyard, she used to chop wood for exercise. But she was so intense about it, it was like she was attacking the wood. She had an axe, and she spent a lot of time sharpening it by hand. The axe was shiny from her polishing. That bothered me as a kid."

"I can see why," I said.

We sat in silence a moment.

"I called Sergeant Martinez," Ryan said.

"You can call him Diamond."

"I asked him if Jeanie's parents knew about the DNA test. He said that the Colusa County Sheriff's department had already informed them. So I called them to express my sympathy."

"Good move," I said.

"I talked to her father. He seemed pretty cold, but also resigned to the news as if he expected it after all the time since she disappeared. Then I told him that Jeanie and Eli and I had an agreement about each other's stock, and that if they didn't want to hang onto the CBT stock, I'd be happy to buy it from him."

"Where do they live?"

"The Central Valley."

"I'll see if I can visit them tomorrow. Maybe I can learn something."

FORTY-SEVEN

Ryan had an address for Ron and Silvia Samples, but he'd never been there. He thought the closest town was Colusa. I printed out a map, and asked Ryan to give me a letter of introduction on his CBT stationary.

Then next morning, I left Spot with Ryan, Lily and Carol, drove down the mountain to Sacramento, and headed up I-5. An hour north, I turned off on a county road, drove seven miles, during which I passed six tractors hauling large pieces of farm equipment, and came to a lonely intersection in the middle of a landscape that was flatter than your average basketball court. If you took away the mountain ranges on the west and east sides of the valley, you might think you were driving through eastern North Dakota. Five turns later, I found the long drive to the Samples farm. The farm buildings were big, the house small. I parked, walked up to the door and knocked.

The man who answered had red hair and a face of red-brown leather. Despite the Central Valley heat, he wore overalls of such heavy fabric that they could stand up without a person inside of them.

But his overalls were clean, his shoes had no mud on them, and there was no dirt in the cracks of his hands. It didn't appear that he'd been doing much farming lately.

The reason was in his eyes.

They showed a deep sadness, a broken sadness, the kind that makes you think he will never regain his spirit.

I introduced myself, and he nodded and turned without saying a word. He walked into a small living room and pointed at a chair near the door.

I sat.

He went around a corner into the kitchen, said something in a low voice, then came back with his wife.

I stood, made a little hand-out greeting motion, and introduced myself again.

She also nodded, but didn't speak. They sat down together on one end of a long couch, their knees touching, her hand on his thigh. They waited for me to speak first.

"I'm very sorry about your daughter Jeanie."

The man nodded. The woman just looked at me.

"I know Ryan Lear called you, but he asked me to bring you his deepest regrets. He was very close to her."

Neither of them spoke.

"Ryan lost one of his closest friends," I said. "He said Jeanie was a math wizard. He told me that she was critical to the formation of CalBioTechnica." Their faces were wooden.

"She'd be alive today if it weren't for him," the woman finally said, her voice monotone.

The man nodded.

"She never even cared about Tahoe until she met him," the woman said. "Next thing we knew, she was going up there on vacations, and taking stock in that boy's company in exchange for pay. We lost her to that boy's world."

"The company paid her very well," I said. "I understand that her pay was the same as what Eli Nathan and Ryan Lear were paid.

"They could have paid her even better if they hadn't made part of her compensation stock."

"Everything was done by mutual agreement," I said. "Ryan and Jeanie and Eli. Friends all the way."

"And now our baby's dead, and that other boy's dead, and the Indian boy is sitting pretty."

"I know you're devastated by what happened," I said. "But others are too. Ryan can barely function."

They stared at me.

"Anyway, I don't mean to take up too much of your time. I understand that Jeanie left her CalBioTechnica stock to you. Her wish may be for you to keep the stock as an investment. However, if you'd like to sell your stock in CBT, I want to reiterate that

Ryan's offer to buy it is genuine."

They looked at me for a long time. The man glanced at the woman, then looked back at me.

"Too late," he said.

"What do you mean?"

"We're selling the stock to Preston Laurence."

"You can't," I said, amazed.

"Yes, we can. We checked with our lawyer. He drew up the papers."

"But Jeanie and Eli and Ryan had an agreement never to let an outside party acquire majority interest in the company. You are Jeanie's proxy in this. It isn't right that you go against her wishes."

"Mister, we don't care what you say. We had three daughters. Two are no good. One was perfect. Because of her involvement in Ryan Lear's life, the perfect one is gone. So nothing matters anymore. We've got nothing except this farm, which we mortgaged to the limit to put the perfect daughter through Stanford. Now we have nothing in our future except back-breaking farm work until we drop. So when Mr. Laurence came and offered us two million dollars for our stock in the boy's company, we said yes."

"Is the stock sale finalized?" I asked.

The man looked at a miniature grandfather clock on the fireplace mantle. "If not now, in the next little bit."

I got out my phone and dialed Ryan. "It's Owen," I said when he answered. "I'm in the living room of Mr. and Mrs. Samples. They are selling their CBT stock to Preston."

"What?! They can't do that! I told them that I'd buy it if they wanted to sell!"

"He offered them two million."

"It's worth much more than that!"

"You talk to them." I reached out with the phone.

Mr. Samples took it. "Hello?" he said. After a moment, he said, "I know, but I didn't think you would have that kind of money." Another silence, this time longer. "Okay," he said. "We'll let you know." He shut my phone and handed it back to me. He looked at his wife, then back at me.

"The boy says the stock is worth much more, but if we want

cash, he'll pay us ten million for it. Does he have that much money?"

"As far as I can tell," I said.

"Is his word good?"

"I believe so," I said.

"Then I'll call my lawyer and see if he hasn't finished our deal with Mr. Preston."

"Thank you," I said, and left.

FORTY-EIGHT

When I got back from visiting Jeanie Sample's parents, I said hello to Smithy who was sitting on the folding chair in the shade of the entryway dormer. Inside, I found Spot lying on the rug near the entrance to the family room. He glanced at me, thumped his tail on the floor, then turned back to Lily, who sat in front of him. Between Spot and Lily was a little china tea set. She'd tied a red scarf around Spot's neck. He was propped on his elbows, holding his head forward with great attention to her, a posture that I knew meant food.

Lily saw me. "Spot and I are having coffee and coffee cake." She lifted up an empty cup and took a pretend sip. Then she lifted a little piece of bread out of her lap, and tossed it.

Spot snatched it out of the air.

Ryan was pacing, and talking on a portable phone. Carol was sitting at the dining table with a mug of tea, the little paper square at the end of the string hanging over the rim. She looked up from her magazine, made a little wave with her hand.

Ryan hung up, came over. "How did it go?"

"You got the gist of it when I called you. I left shortly after you made Mr. Samples an offer to buy their stock. Let's hope they got to their lawyer in time to call off the deal with Preston."

"I would have offered more - it's worth more - but I don't have more cash. They won't want to wait while I shuffle investments."

Ryan looked at Carol.

"Oh, sorry," Carol said. "I can leave."

"No, you can stay," Ryan said. "Maybe you will have some insight. I'm not getting anywhere by myself."

Carol looked at me. "Are you sure?"

"Unless you want to read uninterrupted," Ryan said.

She shook her head, shut her magazine.

Ryan and I pulled out chairs. I briefly explained that I had no evidence that Preston had anything to do with tormenting Ryan.

"You think Preston didn't kill Eli or Jeanie?" Ryan asked.

"I don't know. I've learned that he's capable of ordering a murder, but it's usually easier to buy someone off if you have endless funds. My guess is that the murderer is someone we haven't yet found. Maybe it's a person who works for Preston. Or a person with a deep hatred for you. I want you to revisit your past and try again to think of anyone you have crossed."

Ryan was already shaking his head. "I've been over this. We've discussed Preston and William and William's mother. JJ at the lab. I've thought of my employees, the ones I know, anyway. There are many I haven't even met, so how can I consider them? I've thought about the kids at Stanford, and no one seems like they would have a reason to come after me. I even went back through my old email records, looking for anyone who might have been mad at me. But I've found nothing."

"What about further back? High school? Was there anyone there who saw you as a problem, or an obstacle to their desires?"

Ryan did the sad grin with the snort and a shake of his head. "You mean like someone who thinks that I stole his girl or something? That's a joke, Owen. I told you about how I was the miserable little geek, picked on by everyone except the few students who were equally dysfunctional."

"Think about it anyway," I said.

I glanced at Carol, and saw her sadness at the subject.

Ryan shook his head again. "You don't understand. Nobody liked me. The jocks who purposely veered my way when I was coming down the hallway so that they could hit my shoulder with their arms and knock me down. The goths and the dirtballs shunned me because I played by the rules and went to class on time, and gave the teacher the answers when she asked, and, God forbid, did my homework. Even the preppies, who knew I was smart, called me Injun to my face. And in my senior year, somebody found out that my long-disappeared mother was white. So they changed their taunts and started calling me half-breed."

Ryan paused. "I think even the teachers didn't like posting the test scores because my name was usually at the top." Ryan looked at Carol. "Carol, maybe you can tell me if I'm wrong. But I always got the feeling that the only way the smart kid could really get accepted was if the smart kid was a joiner and could gain approval based on sports skills or social skills. Smarts by itself was always a detriment to acceptance. Am I right?"

Carol looked down into her tea mug. "Yeah, I think so." She blinked her eyes as if they stung. "And I've got to tell you something else." She pushed away her mug, then leaned her elbows on the table and mashed her mouth into her hands, bending her nose and making the beautiful face look ordinary.

"I'm one of them," she mumbled. "I was a joiner. Everything I did was about approval from my peers. I didn't see people as individuals with wants and needs and hopes and fears. I just saw them as part of this group or that group. Either you're with us, or you're the enemy. Like two football teams fighting it out, each one thinking that the other guys are somehow lesser stuff. It's like countries going to war. What's that called? Nationalism. Like we're better than you. Why? Because we're born in this country?

"That's the way I was, thinking that I was better because I was pretty and I've got blue eyes and blonde hair. Then we do bad things to the other group, the other country, the other race. We dehumanize them in our mind because that makes it easier for us to treat them so crappy.

"My group was about being popular and good looking. I used to think that was my achievement, being pretty. Like I deserved credit for it. Even worse, I thought that the not-so-good-looking kids were less valuable.

"So I'm sorry, Ryan. Please forgive me for being such a stupid kid. In fact, I think I'm only just starting to grow up now. I'd been trying to understand why my career never went anywhere, while yours skyrocketed. Then Owen said something in the car on the way out of Preston's place. It wasn't these exact words, but in essence he was asking, 'What do you know? What are your skills? Can you do anything? Have you worked and worked toward a goal? Or do you just stand around and try to look good and hope that someone will give you a morsel for it even though you never did anything to earn it.'"

Carol got up and walked over to the kitchen counter, pulled out a couple of tissues and blew her nose. She came back and sat down and wiped tears from her eyes.

"I never disliked you for any specific reason," she said. "But I disrespected you by acting as if you didn't exist. Like you were an outsider. I'm very sorry about that."

She and Ryan stared at each other. I expected Ryan to look away first, to bend as he always had in the past. But he held her look, and she swallowed and then mopped her eyes.

"You remember Monty Wales, right?" she said.

"I never knew him. But I always heard about him. The great football player," Ryan said. "The quarterback. He was in your class, right? A couple of years ahead of me?"

She nodded. "I dated him. He took me to the prom. It's probably a real long shot, but I'm just trying to do what Owen said about looking for anyone who might hold a grudge."

"What do you mean?" Ryan said.

"I wonder if Monty might still have a grudge against you."

Ryan shook his head. "That's a ridiculous notion. He was big and strong and handsome. He was the star jock. He dated you. And anyway, we never even knew each other."

"But you were his undoing."

"I don't understand."

"Do you remember when you worked at the coffee shop?"

"Of course," Ryan said, puzzled.

"Do you remember those guys you called the cops about?"

Ryan stared. "One of them was Monty Wales?!"

Carol nodded.

"But I... None of them looked like him. Was he... Oh, man. He had the long hair and the handlebar moustache?"

She nodded again.

"Nothing like the buzz cut he had in high school. I can't believe that guy was Monty."

"Fill me in?" I said.

Ryan paused, remembering.

"During my senior year in high school, I worked at a coffee shop, kind of like Starbucks but sitdown-style, with waiters. I had a group of three guys in my section. They were..." Ryan looked at

Carol, "Sorry to say this, but they were natural jerks."

She shut her eyes and made a little nod.

"They were loud and obnoxious, and they immediately started needling me. I had pretty bad acne back then, and I'd broken out really bad that day. So they started making cracks about my face, and how the girls must be all over me, and how my dating schedule must make it hard to find time to be a waiter. The guy with the moustache - Monty, I guess - he would say things like, 'It must be hard to find time to be a waitress, I mean waiter.' Anyway, after a bit I realized that he and one of the other guys were bragging to the third about a theft that they had put together and how they made thousands of dollars. They went on about it at some length, so I went in back and called nine-one-one on my cell and explained to the dispatcher that I was working in the coffee shop and that I was overhearing a crime being described. I told the dispatcher that if she was silent on her end, I could put my phone near the people talking.

"So I turned my cell phone on speaker mode and put it in one of those paper napkin holders behind a couple of napkins. Then I brought it out along with sugar and cream as if to freshen up.

"The guys kept talking. I came back a bit later and poured them more coffee to keep them going. Fifteen minutes later, a police car pulled up, and two officers came in. I nodded my head toward the guys, and the officers started asking them some questions. When they all went outside, I retrieved my phone. They didn't arrest them. I never heard what happened."

"I do," Carol said. "The news spread through my neighborhood pretty fast. Jamie Nye and Monty Wales. Jamie went to prison for two years. Monty was the leader, so he went three years and some months."

"Do you know if they found out that it was Ryan who put the police onto them?" I asked.

Carol said, "I saw in the paper that the nine-one-one recording was used in the trial, so they maybe figured it out."

"What did they steal?" I asked.

Ryan shook his head. "I never found out." He looked at Carol. "Did you?"

She nodded. "Yeah. Horses."

FORTY-NINE

"Did you ever hear how Monty got involved in stealing horses?" I asked.

"I never knew him to be a thief when he was in high school," Carol said. "But he was always involved with horses. He worked at a ranch. And he was a trick rider. He competed in rodeos."

"When was the last time you talked to him?"

"About a year ago," Carol said. She looked at Ryan. "Not long after I saw you at the governor's dinner. I was in the grocery store in Reno. He saw me and talked about his time in prison like it was summer camp. He wasn't ashamed of it at all. He showed me some tattoos he'd gotten there. I was put off by him. His tattoos, and his casual attitude toward being a criminal. And he'd switched from smoking to chewing tobacco. It was revolting."

"Have you seen him since?"

"No."

"Did he give you any indication of where he was living?"

"Yeah. He said he moved to the Bay Area after he finished probation, and was back visiting his parents. He also said that his girlfriend had a plan to start a business in LA. So I told him about the good temporary housing deal that I'd heard of." Carol looked guilty. "I didn't give him any personal names," she said. "Just the Village Green name I'd heard from Preston."

Ryan made an involuntary jerk that was so prominent it made Carol wince.

She said, "I didn't care about him, but I figured it would be nice if it could help his girlfriend."

"So Monty or his girlfriend could have ended up renting at a project that I invested in," Ryan said, his voice bleak. "I wonder if Monty would have made the connection to me."

"You're presuming that they rented, but you don't know it," I said. "Any idea what her business was going to be?" I asked.

"Some kind of cleaning company, I guess, because Monty made that old joke about sanitation engineering."

Ryan's sudden look of shock was acute. "The woman who died might have been Monty's girlfriend. And I got Monty sent to prison. If he knew that Eli and Jeanie and I were investors in the project, he could be thinking that we destroyed his life."

"We don't know if the woman who died was his girlfriend. And if it was, we don't know if he was still in contact with her. Carol, do you know where Monty went to prison?"

"The Carson City Prison."

I recalled what Maria had said when she was telling us about Mustangs. I said, "They have a program for wild Mustangs at the Carson City Prison. They train them so they can be adopted."

"Heat is somewhere in this, isn't he?" Ryan said.

"Maybe," I said. "I've learned over the years not to trust coincidences. Let me get on the phone and see what I can find."

Ryan got a phone call. Carol said she was going to lie down.

I went out by the lake and called Maria. The sun was setting.

"Have you learned anything more about that poor Mustang?" she said when I told her who was calling.

"That's why I'm calling. Have you heard of any horses that have been stolen recently in Carson Valley or nearby?"

"No. But I only have contact with a few horse people, so I am not a good source of information."

"Could you do a little investigation on that for me?"

"Of course. But how should I do it?"

"Just think of all the horse groups you know. I don't know what they would be. Riding clubs? Boarding stables?"

"Ah, sí, sí," she said. "I have an idea. Let me call you back."

We hung up.

I sat out at the fire pit and got out the piece of paper with the tuning code on it. Looked for order in the chaos. The fact that Herman left a message was obvious. I just couldn't see his meaning.

Twenty minutes later, my phone rang. It was Maria.

"Owen, I think I know where Heat came from. I just got

a callback from a woman who teaches riding lessons in Sparks. She'd heard that I was looking for info about a missing Mustang. She said that two of her horses were stolen a month ago."

"Should I call her?"

"Yes, but she's in lessons for the next three hours."

"Did you learn anything about it?" I asked.

"One of the horses was a Rocky Mountain gaited horse, very valuable. The other was a Mustang, cherry colored, triangular blaze. She said the Mustang had been gentled at the Carson City prison program. But like many Mustangs, while his bond with her was strong, he remained suspicious of other people, and he always ran from everyone but her. So it makes sense that the thief brought the horses to his stable in Tahoe. Or maybe he had a Tahoe buyer. Maybe the thief didn't even realize that he'd stolen a Mustang. So it could be that when he unloaded them, he wasn't careful to hang onto them at all times, and the Mustang ran away, and he's been running from people ever since."

"Did she witness the theft?"

"It was at night. A noise woke her up. She looked out to see a pickup and a horse trailer driving away."

"No identifying marks?"

"I thought to ask her. I could be a detective, no?"

"No doubt," I said. "What did she say?"

"The only thing she saw was that the trailer was silver, and the pickup was white. She thinks there might have been one of those big toolboxes in the pickup's cargo bed."

"Great, Maria. Thanks very much."

"One more thing I have to tell you. The woman said that he is trained to a wolf whistle. She said, if you blow it three times, he comes expecting grain. It might work. Except, I don't know what a wolf whistle is."

"You use your fingers," I said. "A wolf whistle is what boys used to do when they saw a pretty girl." We said goodbye.

I called Diamond.

"I just found out from Maria that a Mustang and another horse were stolen in Sparks, and the pickup hauling the trailer was white. The owner of the Mustang thought the truck might have had a big toolbox in the bed."

"Lot of white pickups out there," Diamond said.

"Yeah, including one that belongs to Lana Madrone that her nephew Tory uses to haul her silver horse trailer. Street found some bug evidence in it that indicates that the truck was recently at lower elevations. But I'm also thinking of the tourist cowboys in the muscle shirts that your guys busted in my office lot."

"Right. Carrying the beers. They spent one night in the cell, then bailed themselves out the next day."

"Do you remember their pickup? It was white, but did it have a toolbox?"

"I don't recall," Diamond said. "But it's a possibility."

"If Ryan was kidnapped into a pickup instead of a van, it must have been a four-door version based on his description."

"A six-pack," Diamond said.

"Lana and Tory's truck is a six-pack," I said. "Do you remember if the cowboy's truck was a six-pack?"

"Not sure. I think so. I do remember that the guys were from the Bay Area."

"Carol could look at their mugshots. Tory, too. She said there was a guy named Monty Wales from her high school. He liked to steal horses, and he took a vacation at Carson City Prison as a result of Ryan's tip. She said that he moved to the Bay Area when he got out. I'm wondering if he could be Tory or one of those cowboys."

"I'll look it up soon as I get out of this meeting."

"Sorry, I didn't realize you were working late," I said.

"No problem. We're taking a quick break."

I thought of the other thing Carol had said about Monty.

"Any chance you noticed if either of them had tattoos?"

"Hard to miss it on the one guy," Diamond said. "Sappy stuff like, 'Love my mama forever,' and stupid stuff like, 'Born to be bad.' Why don't people ever tattoo something intelligent?"

"Like Shakespeare?"

"Yeah. 'A horse, a horse! My kingdom for a horse!' That would be something, high on a woman's thigh."

"Diamond, you were born in the wrong century."

"Don't I know it. Meeting's reconvening."

FIFTY

In the morning, I left Spot with Lily and Ryan, and took a long walk through the forest. I puzzled over the tuning code, looking at my notes, trying to figure another way to convert beats to a message. Nothing made sense. After a couple of miles of trail, I saw Lana and Tory's Mondrian barn through the trees. The white pickup was parked nearby. I walked over. No one was around. The horse stalls in the barn were empty. I looked at the pickup, which had recently been to lower elevations according to Street's glowworm-lunch evidence.

The truck was a six-pack. The toolbox in the bed wasn't silver as described by the woman whose Mustang had been stolen, but a dull gray. Maybe it could look silver at night. But as Diamond had pointed out, there are a lot of white pickups with toolboxes.

An hour later, I was back at the lake, no wiser for my thinking.

In the afternoon, Ryan took Lily to the doctor for her next blood test. Carol went along. They were going to stop at the Lake Tahoe Community College, pick up a class schedule, and look in on the drama department. Ryan had told her that he'd be happy to pay for acting classes.

Ryan asked me if I might take Spot again. I realized that he was uncomfortable leaving Spot alone in the house. I understood. Never know when a Great Dane gets up on his hind legs and noses open the freezer to check on the steak supply.

"Maybe you all should grab a bite out on the town when you're done." I said. "Be good to do something once in awhile without me around."

So we made a plan to meet back at Ryan's house by 9:00 p.m. After they left, Spot and I headed into town on errands, then to

Street's lab for a visit, then eventually left her lab to head back up toward Ryan's as it got dark.

There was a thin line of sunset glow over the mountains across the lake. Silhouetted by the glow were several thunderstorms growing their cloud columns toward the sky. Heat lightning flashed orange in one of the gray clouds.

I was just past Lakeside Inn when a white, six-pack pickup with a toolbox passed me. It had a trailer hitch on it that looked heavy enough to haul a horse trailer. Maybe it was cowboys. Maybe it was Tory or Lana.

I couldn't see in the dark if there was one or two people in it. It turned off on a side street and stopped. I pulled off on the shoulder some distance back. No one got out, and the pickup didn't move for a minute. I envisioned its occupants realizing that they'd passed me, and that I was now following them. Perhaps they were just lighting up a cigarette. But maybe they were pulling out the bullwhip from under the seat.

The pickup pulled back onto the highway and accelerated.

I stayed hard on the its tail as it raced north past the Roundhill shopping center, around the big curves at Zephyr Cove and on toward Skyland.

The pickup driver tried to tempt me into passing him by suddenly slowing. But his truck was much bigger than my Jeep, and I knew that if I drew alongside of him, he could jerk the wheel to hit me and bounce me off the road. I stayed behind him as he dropped to 30 mph.

He clearly knew that I was following him. But I couldn't tell if he was fleeing from me or enticing me to chase him.

The truck suddenly accelerated again. But my old, rusted Jeep has the big engine they offered the year it was made, and I easily kept up with him. At one point on a curve, oncoming headlights shined through the truck's glass. I saw the silhouette of the driver but no one else.

We were back up to 50 mph when he made a sudden turn to the right and skidded off onto some kind of trail that I never knew existed. I hit the brakes and followed.

The trail was rutted and rocky and wound through trees and sage. The pickup bounced along in front of me, his rear wheels spinning and kicking up stones and dirt. I tried to keep up, but the Jeep was bouncing so hard, it bottomed out on the suspension and then popped into the air. My head hit the ceiling. I knew that Spot was being thrown around so hard that he could suffer real injury. Maybe the suspension of the pickup was less vulnerable to this kind of trail. Whatever the reason, it kept up an incredible speed, gradually pulling away from me.

I dropped back ten, then twenty yards. The pickup's dust plume grew to obscure its taillights. I had a harder time seeing where the trail went. I kept the pedal down and pushed into the dirt cloud as fast as possible.

After a moment, I burst into clear air and realized he'd turned off his lights, pulled off and stopped. I looked left and right, trying to see where he'd gone. I raced forward until I saw a place where I could pull in to the left. I turned around and came back down toward him.

I slowed as the dust cloud thickened.

The truck was off to the side between some trees. I turned at an angle as I stopped so that my headlights were on the truck. Either he was lying down on the seat, or it was empty.

I turned more, so that my headlights shined into the forest.

Nothing.

I backed up, angled the other way.

My headlights fell on him, a lone figure in dark clothes, dodging through the trees into the darkness. Only one thing about him stood out, the tool he carried, its shiny surface catching and reflecting my headlights.

An axe.

In the tortured space of a second or two that I could not afford to waste, I considered my options.

I knew that I could send Spot after him. But the man might hear the footsteps of the attacking dog, and turn with his axe.

I couldn't do it.

I grabbed the tiny flashlight out of the glove box and shoved it into my pocket. Before I turned off the Jeep, I turned on the brights and honked the horn, hoping he'd turn and look toward the lights, thereby reducing his night vision for a minute. Then I shut it off and left the Jeep with Spot in it.

The forest was dark. The sliver of moon was now behind the thunderstorms across the lake, and of no benefit to me in the deep woods. I heard vehicles on the highway, but they were below us down the slope, and there were far too many trees between us and the highway for their lights to get through.

I held my arms out and up in front of my face as I ran. I could just make out the tree trunks as vague stripes of black against the dark background. But I couldn't see the branches. They hit my outstretched arms and gave me warning to duck and bend and shut my eyes to avoid losing them on sharp, dried branches.

Every few seconds I stopped and held my breath, trying to locate the noise of the other person over the pounding of my heart. The third time I stopped, it seemed as if he was turning more upslope. The fourth time I stopped, he was angling back toward the two-rut trail. Then his noise stopped.

I assumed he'd stopped like me, listening to the darkness, trying to hear if I was close to him or not.

But as I stared toward the last sound, I realized that there was a large, vague dark hump that rose up. I moved that direction, struggling to make out the lay of the land. As I got closer, the rise became more evident, a sharp slope that rose toward the not-quite-black sky. I slowed, stepping carefully, aware that he could be near, listening for my footsteps. Twigs snapped under my feet. The occasional larger branch broke with a loud pop.

The closer I got to the slope, the more it looked like a big bump of ground, a hill on the broader slope. As I reconsidered the shape of his earlier sounds, it began to make sense to me that he'd gone around the backside of the hump. That would explain why his footfalls went silent. He was circling around the hump of ground to double-back to his truck. I was thinking about whether I should follow or try to intercept him by going around the other direction, when I heard a noise.

I stopped in mid-stride, the heel of my forward foot just touching the ground.

It sounded like a snap of some kind, high in pitch. It came from somewhere behind me. But I'd been moving, so my sense of direction was vague.

I had walked Spot in the forest at night countless times. I

always noticed how many noises there are. Numerous animals sleep during the day and come out at night to avoid being seen by predators. As a result, numerous predators have adapted to hunting at night. Coyotes and Great Horned owls and raccoons and mountain lions and house cats. All of which occasionally make noise. But forest sounds take on a new feeling when you know that somewhere nearby, there is a man with an axe.

Very slowly, I reached into my pocket and pulled out the flashlight. I put my thumb over the switch, pointed it toward the sound, ready to flip it on if I heard another sound.

Even more slowly, I lifted my left foot, moved it at glacial speed toward a nearby tree, set it down as if I were growing my own roots rather than walking. I repeated the process with my right foot, moving toward the tree like a movie on quadruple slo-mo. Despite how dark it was, being behind a tree would give me more protection.

Again I made another slow, silent step toward the tree, and finally got next to it. I shifted a bit so that I was on the opposite side from where I thought the noise originated. I leaned my head out, and stared into the darkness. My flashlight was still out, my thumb ready to push the button. If the man was actually there, given enough time, he'd eventually make a move.

I waited a long minute. Then another. I heard tiny rustlings, like the movements of a mouse. Or the sounds of my imagination. The noises were so soft, I couldn't discern a direction. They came from nowhere and everywhere at once.

I began a slow silent count, deciding I would move if I got to five hundred without any sound from the axe man.

The sudden crack of a breaking branch was loud in my ears. Directly behind me.

I spun, turning on the flashlight. The beam caught a flash of movement, the silver glint of a sharpened axe blade, arcing toward my head.

FIFTY-ONE

I jerked to the side. Raised my forearm against the striking axe. The wooden handle smashed against my elbow. The axe deflected a fraction of a degree. The blade missed my head and slammed into the tree, scraping my right shoulder as it went by.

The flashlight was knocked to the ground.

The man ran away into the night.

I tried to push away from the tree trunk to chase after him, but I was pinned. The axe head had sliced through my jacket and shirt, its cold metal grazing my skin, and nailed me to the bark.

Pain seared my right shoulder. I twisted my body so that I could reach over with my left hand and grab the handle. But the axe was sunk deep into the tree, and my grip was ineffective.

I raised my right leg and used my knee to apply sideways pressure to the axe handle. With my left hand and knee together, I forced the axe out of the tree. My right arm felt shaky, so I grabbed the axe in my left hand and the flashlight in my right and ran toward where I thought the man had gone. I shined the feeble light beam into the woods, trying to find my way, aware that it made me a target, but hoping that he had no more weapons.

I'd soon come a good distance, but when I stopped to listen, I heard nothing. After ten seconds, I decided he was too far away to hear, so I headed in the general direction that I thought would bring me near my Jeep. If I could send Spot after him soon enough, I still had a chance. The man might have a gun that he could use on Spot, but I doubted it, as he would have probably used it instead of the axe to try to kill me. Or used it after the axe failed to kill me.

I ran ahead, looking for my Jeep or his truck or the rutted trail. When it was clear that I didn't know where my Jeep was, I paused, pulled my phone out of my pocket and opened it to look at the display. No reception.

I wandered through the black woods. Five minutes later, I heard a truck down on the highway. The sound came 90 degrees from where I thought the highway was. Based on that new information, I adjusted my search for the Jeep. As I stumbled through the forest, I tried to imagine who would carry an axe around in his pickup, and what kind of a person could use it to kill another person.

The only one I could think of with that kind of inner fire was the fitness buff, Holly Hughes, master of the bullwhip, mother of Ryan's gamer friend William. Ryan had frightening memories of her chopping wood with an axe.

I stumbled onto the rutted trail. I went down it for a bit, but realized that my Jeep must be up the trail instead of down. So I turned and came to the truck and my Jeep after a short run.

The truck had been backed up and smashed into the front of the Jeep, then left to block the trail. The impact didn't look like it had been severe. The airbags in the Jeep hadn't deployed. Spot looked fine as he stood in the back seat. I ran the dimming flashlight over the truck, wondering why the man hadn't driven it away. The answer was in the flat, left front tire.

Two of the truck's wheels sat in depressions. I tried the truck's door. It was locked. But even if it hadn't been, I could never budge it from the depressions that the wheels were in unless I could start it. Hot-wiring a strange truck would not be fast or easy.

I shined my light on the ground, noted multiple boulders. A distant squealing of tires came from the highway. Then another screech of rubber. I wasn't sure what it meant, but I guessed it involved the man, or woman, who'd wielded the axe.

I walked back behind the Jeep, up the path, checking for a place where I might get through the forest. There were fallen trees and boulders and ravines everywhere I looked.

I went back to the truck, took a good-sized rock and smashed the passenger window. I reached in, opened the door, swept the broken glass onto the floor and slid in. Once behind the driver's seat, I released the parking brake, and I pulled on the shifter, hoping the truck was old enough that the shift movement wasn't integrated with the key lock in the steering column.

It wasn't, and I pulled the shift down to neutral.

I transferred to the Jeep and started it. Spot jumped around, eager to have me back, tired of being left in a vehicle in the forest and being rammed by a truck. He stuck his nose over my burning shoulder. I gave him a quick pat on the nose.

"Okay, boy, hang on." I put the Jeep in 4-wheel-drive and eased it forward until it contacted the back bumper of the truck. I gave it gas. The Jeep's engine roared, wheels spun, and gradually I pushed the truck forward. The driver had left the wheels turned, so it curved to the right.

After a few feet, the truck's flat tire and the rutted path created too much resistance. I floored the accelerator, and the truck rolled another few feet and hit an obstruction.

I backed up. The truck rolled back with me. So I pushed it forward once again, wheels spinning, engine racing as if to blow up.

When the truck again hit the obstruction, I stopped, put the Jeep in park, put the parking brake on as far as it would go and let my foot off the brake. The Jeep and truck moved a bit, but held. I got out and ran to the truck to put on its brake and shifted it back into park.

When I again backed up the Jeep, the truck didn't roll back with me, and I was able to squeeze by, scraping a tree on the left and the truck's bumper on the right.

I bounced down the rutted path, the Jeep lurching as if to come off its wheels. I drove as fast as possible, my head hitting the ceiling. Spot was flung back and forth despite hunkering down to get some stability.

It felt like the distance was triple what it was on the drive in. When I got to the highway, I turned north, thinking that was the direction I'd heard the screeching tires. As I sped away, I had a thought. I looked at my phone again, and saw that it had reception. I jerked to the side of the road, stopped, and dialed Diamond's number.

"It's me," I interrupted before he finished answering. "I just tangled with the killer in the forest south of Hidden Woods. It was dark, so I don't know who he is. He nailed me to a tree with an axe, then got away. He had a flat tire on his pickup and left it in the woods. I heard screeching tires on the highway. I'm guessing he hijacked a car on the highway. You had any reports?"

"No. Nothing," he said.

"Call me if you hear anything?"

"Yes."

I hung up and drove to Ryan's. The house was dark. Smithy's Toyota was in the driveway, engine running. I beeped the horn and waved my hand out my window.

I had a sudden, nagging thought about something Lily had said.

When she saw Matisse's painting of The Horse, the Rider, and the Clown, she talked about how the curve that symbolized the rider was almost the same as the curve that symbolized the clown. She said that a little change makes a big difference.

I parked and got out Herman's piano tuning code. I'd always approached the code by trying to figure out what the numbers of beats indicated. This time, I ignored the beats and just looked at the letters. GEWN REAR DECAO. Could I make a little change in the letters to create a big change in meaning?

I saw it in a minute. Staring at me all of this time.

Just to verify what it meant, I called Maria one more time.

"Sí," she said into the phone.

"Owen McKenna calling. Sorry to be brusque, but I have one more quick question."

"Of course."

"Some time back I heard someone say something like, 'A thrush can hurt a frog.' A thrush is a bird. But is it also something to do with a horse?"

"Sí. Thrush is an infection in the soft tissue of a horse's hoof. That part of the hoof is called the frog. Thrush can really hurt the frog. That is one of the reasons Mustangs do so well in the desert. The dry footing keeps their hooves from getting thrush."

"Gracias, Maria." I hung up.

The statement about thrush and frog came from someone who professed to know nothing of horses, someone who let me believe my mistaken notion that the statement was about a bird.

If the axe-man had hijacked a vehicle, Diamond would have heard by now. Which meant the killer was probably traveling on foot to the nearest alternative transportation. Lana's horses.

I shifted the Jeep and headed back out to the highway, driving very fast, emergency flashers on. When I got to the drive to Lana's house and stable, I made a hard, skidding turn, and drove up the narrow road.

Lana's house appeared in my headlights. I careened around it, and followed the road back to the Mondrian barn.

Light spilled from the open barn door. I jumped out, let Spot out of the back. Streaks of blood went from the parking area to the barn door. I ran inside.

Prancer and Peppy neighed at me, their heads over their stall walls, their eyes wide, hooves pawing the floor as they stomped back and forth.

Paint was gone.

Lana's nephew Tory was nowhere to be seen.

Lana was lying on the floor, her head bent up against the front wall of Paint's horse stall. Her elbow was on one of the stall's boards, her hand wedged against a deep circular cut across her throat. Blood bubbled out from under her fingers. The red river ran down her chest and dripped off onto the concrete floor. She was alive, but she looked groggy.

I ran into the tack room, found a dirty rag, brought it out to Lana. I put it under her hand against the pulsing blood flow.

I held her hand and the rag against her neck while I dialed Diamond with my other hand. Blood ran over my hand, dripped off onto the floor. As I waited while it rang, I thought, compress the wound hard enough to close the leak, you shut off the blood to the brain.

"It's McKenna," I said when he answered. "I'm at Lana's barn. She is severely wounded, bleeding profusely from her neck. Send help fast."

"Go," Lana interrupted. "He's after Ryan Lear." Her words were so thick they were hard to understand. "He's crazy... bullwhip. Cave Rock."

"I can't leave you like this."

Her words were weaker. "I... die... you're here or not. Save Ryan." She passed out.

FIFTY-TWO

I put Spot in the Jeep, gunned the engine, and raced down Lana's drive. I hit the buttons for Ryan's cell. It rang several times, forwarded me to page and voice menu.

"If you get this message, do not go home!" I said at the prompt. "I'll call you later."

I raced down the highway, slid into the turnoff, sped up the driveway. Ryan's motion lights were on.

I hit the brakes, skidded to a stop next to Ryan's Lexus. The car was caved in on one side as if from multiple blows of a kicking horse. It looked undrivable.

Smithy was sitting on the ground, leaning against a tree. He held his hands at his face, blood coming through his fingers.

Ryan was on his knees in front of his house, hands clasped in front of his chest, his head tipped back. The roaring scream coming from his upturned mouth was agonizing.

Carol was nearby, doing a frantic kind of dance as if she were on hot coals. She jerked and bent and spun. A whimpering terror rose from her throat. I realized that I was looking at people coming apart.

I ran up and saw blood running down Ryan's face, blood coming out of a large tear in his pants. There was an ugly 4-inch laceration above his ear. Blood soaked his hair.

Ryan saw me.

"HE TOOK LILY!" He screamed. "She had to go inside to use the bathroom. We each took one of her hands. Smithy was here to guard. We ran inside, then back out to the car to leave. But he rode out of the dark on a horse. He bent down and yanked her up into the air! Jerked her out of our hands! LILY SCREAMED. BUT HE GALLOPED AWAY INTO THE FOREST!"

FIFTY-THREE

"Carol!" I shouted. She turned and looked at me, her head bent and shaking.

"Go inside and get some towels. Put them on Ryan's wounds to stop the bleeding!"

She tried to say something, but her speech was gibberish.

"CAROL! GO NOW!"

She turned and ran, stumbling, jerky, toward the house.

Again I got Diamond on the phone, and explained.

"Which way did he go?" Diamond asked.

"I don't know. Lana said the words Cave Rock. It would be the ultimate way to destroy Ryan."

I hung up and sprinted for the Jeep, backed out of Ryan's drive, my headlights shining on Ryan's wavering form.

I shot out of his driveway, up his road, blasted out onto the highway, accelerator floored, skidding and swerving.

A mile north, I turned off the highway and drove up the steep pitch of Cave Rock Road. I didn't follow the switchback that climbed to the houses on the cliff. Instead, I headed toward an open area off the road, thinking it was a potential trail to the back side of Cave Rock, the easy way to get to the top. I hit the brakes at the switchback, skidded to a stop, jumped out into the darkness, and let Spot out.

I sprinted toward the dark forest. Spot ran ahead.

A sudden glow came through the trees from a vehicle down on the highway. The glow grew brighter, then shut off as a vehicle clicked from high beams to low beams. But before the light disappeared I saw that there was a path.

I had my little flashlight and turned it on, but the beam was feeble, the batteries low.

Lightning flashed from out on the lake. The storms I'd seen earlier were tracking east. Again, the light flashed, silhouetting the black shape of Cave Rock up above us on the left. Thunder followed a few seconds later.

In the distance came a siren. It was joined by a second siren keening in the background. Farther off came the whine of a small engine, revving like a chainsaw. Over the cacophony of sirens and engine whine came the terrifying scream of a child.

Lily.

I ran on up the path. I sensed a split in the trail, and I went to the left. A sudden bright flash lit the sky, directly over our heads, followed in an instant by a deafening thunder crack. Spot veered over next to me.

One of the sirens down below on the highway turned off, then the other, leaving the chainsaw whine sounding lonely.

The flashing of the cop car lights pulsed up from the highway into the night, eerie blue and red strobes that lit the clouds. The small engine whine receded, and I heard the soft clippity-clop of horse hooves ahead on the trail. Then the clink of a rock bouncing on another rock. From the same direction came a tiny whimper.

Despite the storm above, no rain had fallen, and I choked on the horse's dust cloud. Spot showed no concern for the darkness or the steep rock. The trail pitched down, then began to climb again, steeper than before.

Lightning flashed, pulsing three, four times, highlighting the black hulking form of Cave Rock above me. The clouds and trees and the trail and rocks flashed a staccato blue gray. Then the blackness returned, and I could see nothing.

The rock was steep. I had no idea how to get up it in the dark. Lightning flashed again. I saw a small ravine in the rock face, like a miniature crevasse. I ran forward. Spot understood my intentions and ran ahead of me, his white fur just visible in the night as a light arc of movement. He jumped up into the narrow V in the rock and climbed in leaps. I followed.

I clawed at the rock, trying to keep my center of gravity forward. That the rider above me had gotten Paint to make the same climb was amazing.

Another siren arose over my labored breathing. The chainsaw whine was louder than before. The siren quit, and I had the sudden vision that there would be a crowd of cops to watch Lily fall from the sky above.

Into the silence came the pistol crack of a bullwhip.

Lily screamed.

I charged up the rocks, trying to suck air. An outcropping turned me to the left. A wall of bushes slapped me back to the right. Spot pushed on through. I followed. I saw no trail, just rock that stretched up another thirty feet above us. To the left was nothing. If we went the wrong direction, we'd plunge to the highway below.

The dark sky grew wide as we came out onto the summit.

The top was a broad, rounded hump about fifty feet in diameter. I couldn't see anything but shapes in the dark. I sensed the horse and rider near the edge of the drop-off. I couldn't tell where Lily was.

From below shined the headlights of cars lined up behind the road block the cops had set up. I felt disoriented. The chainsaw seemed behind me.

The horseman turned on a big flashlight. He held it with his left hand. Something else hung from his left hand, but I couldn't tell what it was. I still couldn't see Lily. The light beam shined on Spot, standing about ten feet in front of Paint. The rider made a throwing motion with his other hand, and the whip sounded like a gun. Spot jumped. Lily screamed from out of the darkness.

Lightning flashed and I saw the horseman's red cap.

The rider made Paint leap toward me.

I backed up, stumbled, fell to my hands and knees. My left knee ground into a sharp rock. The pain was excruciating. I pushed up, my hands on my knees, warm, sticky blood oozing through the rip in my jeans. I got to my feet. The powerful light beam turned toward me. Before I could look away, it shined into my eyes, then went out, leaving me blind.

"Let the girl go, Travis. Monty," I said. "She is innocent."

Travis's scornful laugh rose in the night.

"What matters if she's innocent? She's a tool, a pawn. My pawn. I don't need to hurt her. But I will. Tossing the little Washoe girl off the big sacred Washoe rock will teach Ryan the final lesson, won't it?" His voice got louder with each word. "He sent me to prison. My life as Monty Wales was destroyed."

Lightning pulsed. Travis and Paint were silhouetted against the sky, his red cap looking purple in the blue-white flash. They had moved to the edge of the precipice, facing south. A rope wrapped around his left shoulder and down his left arm. At the end of the rope was Lily, tied under her arms and around her chest. She looked tiny and fragile. Travis swung her back and forth. If he let go on the backswing, she would land hard on the rock behind. If he let go on the forward swing, she would fall over the same edge where Eli had fallen to the highway below.

The pulsing lightning quit, and rain began to pour down. Travis flashed the light in my eyes, blinding me again.

I wanted to run up and snatch Lily out of the air, but I knew it was unlikely I could pull it off in the dark. I'd miss. The rock was becoming slick with rain. Travis would sense me coming and let her fly through space. I needed to delay him.

"This is a sacred rock, Travis. The Washoe shamans are the only people who can come here without repercussions. If you let Lily go, you can leave. But if you don't, you're performing the ultimate evil. The spirits will come for you. You'll never survive."

"If you believe that bullshit, you're crazier than the Washoe. I won't survive, anyway. Me and this little girl were in the same chemo program. We're both dying. I'm just going to speed up the process."

"You can walk out of here," I said. "I'll call off my dog. Lower Lily to the ground and you can go."

He didn't respond. The only sound above the pouring rain and the vehicles down below was a moaning cry from Lily, swinging from the rope next to Travis's left leg.

"When I played football," Travis said, "I was king. King for a game, king for a season, king for a year. I was unstoppable. And Carol was my girl, smart and beautiful. Everyone talked about Carol Pumpernickel and Monty Wales. But she didn't go with me because I was captain of the team. She went with me because she thought I had a future." He shifted, and his grip on the rope jerked Lily back and forth. She cried louder.

"Shut up!" he shouted at her. He cracked the whip in the air. Paint reared up. Lily screamed.

He resumed talking, his voice thin and soft and unnaturally high. "Carol and I used to drive up to the Mt. Rose overlook above Incline. We'd sit in the car in the dark and look at the circle of lights around Tahoe. One of those lights on the shore would be ours someday. Carol was going to be an actress, and I was going to own a horse stable, run trail rides for the tourists, use my riding skills to build a business.

"But Ryan Lear ruined it all. I went to prison. He got the house on the lake. Carol left me and ended up with a billionaire who owned a horse ranch.

"So I found another woman who had the ambition to start a business in LA. Carol even helped us find a place to stay. But it all blew up when the landlords kicked us out. And guess who turned out to be the landlords? Ryan and his buddies. My girlfriend died. Because of him, my life wasn't worth living. It was that stress that gave me cancer. I'm dying because of Ryan."

"You stole horses again, Travis. This time, one got away. You screwed yourself."

I heard footsteps to the side. Sensed a movement. Travis heard it, too. He flipped on the flashlight, swung it around.

Ryan ran out of the dark, leaped up onto Paint's rump, grabbed at Travis, got his arms around Travis's waist.

Travis's flashlight fell and bounced behind a shrub, its beam shining at wet, dark rock. I didn't think the skinny kid could hold Travis for more than a moment before Travis flung him off into the night. I sprinted through the dark, my knee burning, aiming toward the front of Paint. I grabbed at where I thought Lily and the rope would be and felt air. Lily screamed again, and her arcing form hit me hard on my left shoulder. I grabbed her before she fell to the ground.

"Spot! Come!" I said. I held Lily in my arms. I ran with her ten steps away to the far side of the little Cave Rock summit. I set her down and jerked the rope hard. It pulled Travis off of the horse. I ran backward with the rope. Travis rolled on the ground, and the rope came free from his shoulder.

I tried to slip the rope off Lily's body, but it was wrapped well, and the knots were tight.

"Lily, stay here. Do you understand? Don't move. Spot! Guard her." I put my arm around Spot's neck and held his head to Lily. "Guard her."

I turned back to the edge of the cliff.

In the dim glow of the flashlight on the ground, I could see Travis and Ryan standing facing each other, fifteen feet apart.

"I'm not afraid of you!" Ryan shouted, his voice filled with terror. He hurled himself toward Travis. Travis cracked the bullwhip. It sounded like a gunshot. Ryan screamed, falling to the ground, holding his face.

I ran in an arc, coming up behind Travis. He rotated and shot the bullwhip toward me. It caught the side of my neck, lacerating the skin near my jugular vein. I reeled, but kept up my run. He shot the whip again. It wrapped my right ankle, and I went down. He stepped to the side, shot the bullwhip at my face. I saw his arm move, tucked my chin to my chest. The whip cut across the back of my head. I pushed up to my knees. Before I could stand, he shot the whip out and cut my shoulder.

Paint neighed his terror from across the little summit.

I tucked my shoulder, rolled across sharp rocks to get away. Travis ran after me. He raised the hard butt end of the whip to stab it down onto the side of my head. I rolled. His missed my head and hit the base of my left trapezius muscle. My left arm and upper chest went numb. I kept rolling into the dark.

I heard a high-pitched yell. Ryan leaped out of the dark and struck Travis in a flying tackle. They both went down, sliding toward the cliff.

Travis stood up, shaking Ryan off onto the ground like a bear shaking off a small dog.

But Ryan clamped onto Travis's leg.

Travis used his leg to drag Ryan down a short slope to the edge of the precipice, 80 feet above the exit of the southbound tunnel.

I pushed up, my left side still numb. I did a fast, sideways crab crawl toward them.

Before I could reach them, Ryan twisted and swung his fist up into Travis's groin. Travis bent forward, stumbled back, then kicked at Ryan's head. He missed, and Ryan grabbed Travis's foot.

Travis went down, pushed up onto his hands and knees. Ryan was up, took a quick step toward him, stomped on one of Travis's hands, then jumped back.

This time it was Travis who roared. In his anger, he stood up tall, a long dark shape in the dull glow of the flashlight, silhouetted by the blue and red strobes below. His foot rolled on the tiny pebbles that littered the rock slope like ball bearings. He stepped back with his other foot to regain his balance, but he stepped too far. His foot was on the edge, his body movement still going backward. His arms went out, wavered and circled as he teetered.

Before he would have toppled backward off the cliff, he stepped backward into the air, shifting his center of gravity so that he could catch the top of the cliff with his hands as he fell. His hands swept the rock, didn't find a hold, but got the rope that snaked over to Lily.

Travis fell out of sight. The rope jerked tight and Lily was yanked from where she sat. She screamed. I dove for the rope as she shot across the ground. My hand grabbed rock and air.

Spot grabbed the rope just below Lily. He stumbled, went down on his side. The two of them slid toward the edge. She was pointing head-first, down the slope. Spot hung on. His paws clawed at the slick rock.

I dove for the rope where it stretched below Spot. It was tight against the rock. I dug my fingers under it, got a good grip, lifted it up.

Spot scrambled, got himself righted, his feet out and braced, his front paws on the rock next to me. The rope went under my arm. I felt Spot's nose just behind my armpit, his teeth locked onto the rope, pulling like tug-of-war.

I braced myself, sitting on the ground, pulling back at the unyielding rope. I could hold Travis's weight as he hung from the rope below the cliff. But I couldn't stop sliding down the wet, grit-covered rock. The slope was too steep.

"I have a jackknife!" I yelled to Ryan. "Right front pocket."

He dropped to his knees at my side, felt the fabric with panicked hands. He found the pocket opening, got the knife out, pulled the blade open.

Spot and I stayed clamped onto the rope as Ryan sawed. His

motions made little oscillations. Travis jerked from below us. I slid, pulling Spot and Lily behind me.

The rain pounded harder.

Ryan shifted to keep the knife at the same place on the rope. But the rope kept moving over the edge as Travis's weight pulled from below. Soon, Ryan's cutting location reached the edge of the rock and snaked over and down. He dropped to his belly at the edge of the cliff. He tried to keep the knife in the same cut mark. We slid farther.

My heels got to the edge of the cliff. I tried to dig them into the wet rock, tried not to bump Ryan over the edge.

Ryan lay on the ground sideways on the edge of the cliff, reaching over the edge, sawing furiously. I leaned back. My knees bent more. My butt came closer to the edge. Directly below us were multiple patrol cars, bathed in blue and red staccato flashing. A blinding spotlight shined up toward us, no doubt illuminating Travis, hanging from the rope, just below my feet. The rain increased to a downpour.

A voice crackled over a loud speaker, but I couldn't hear the words over the roar of rain. I only heard the repeating words in my head, Lily's words when Herman died, her voice tiny.

Life is too short.

Ryan grunted, furious panting breaths. He reached farther down as the wet rope slid. His left hand clamped onto my pants. He sawed faster. His grunts rose to high-pitched cries with each sawing motion. He was about to fall over the edge.

The rope went slack.

Ryan collapsed, his head down on the rock, arm dangling over the edge of the cliff.

Voices yelled from below.

I picked up Lily. I scooted back up the rock, set Lily upright, told her not to move, and went back to the cliff edge to help Ryan.

EPILOGUE

Three days later, Spot and I drove up to Preston's gate at 10 a.m. I had bandages on my neck, my face, my head. My bruises from being dragged under the Santa Monica Pier had darkened to a purple gray.

The guard named Joe walked out. His broken right arm was in a cast. Nevertheless, he did the big-guy waddle like I was going to be intimidated by his bulk. My patience was at ebb-tide.

I got out of my Jeep and walked up to him.

"Here to see Preston," I said.

"You don't have an appointment, so get out of here." He made an awkward move with his left hand, reaching for his gun.

I kneed him in the groin. He stumbled back. I stepped up close, bending my right arm. I rotated from my feet, swung my arm hard, and gave him a crushing elbow blow to his nose. As he staggered, I stayed with him and pounded him a second time on the backswing.

He stumbled back and hit the gatehouse wall with a thump. His good hand went to his bloody face.

I pulled his gun out of his holster and tossed it into the woods. Then I turned him around, propelled him into the gatehouse, sat him down on the desk chair.

"Open the gate."

He hesitated. Maybe stubborn. Maybe unconscious.

I took hold of the hair on the back of his head, aimed at the green button with the word OPEN on it, and punched his forehead onto the button.

The gate opened.

I got back into the Jeep and drove into the estate.

Spot and I found Preston sitting on one of the saddle-barstools in the racehorse room on the third floor. He had a glass full of amber on the bar, a half-empty bottle of bourbon nearby.

He looked up. Showed no surprise.

"Got some videos for you to see," I said.

"Screw you," he said.

I sat down next to him. I got out my cell phone, wincing at my shoulder pain from the axe laceration. I pushed the buttons, held the phone in front of his face with my left hand, and put my right arm around his shoulders, squeezing him to make sure he paid close attention.

First came the video of Carol explaining how he had beat her up, and then kidnapped her. Next, Stefan in Venice explaining how Preston had hired him to sink me into the deep blue. Finally, JJ telling of his future vice presidency if he stole corporate research from CBT and gave it to Preston.

"What the hell do you think you're going to do?" Preston said.

"TV and radio news programs, business magazines, major newspapers, supermarket tabloids, youtube.com, all the social networking sites, a hundred bloggers. Maybe Michael Moore would like to do a documentary. You're finished. The DA will love focusing county resources on you. Your colleagues will shame you out of their world. The girls you try to bring onto your yacht will laugh in your face. Life as you know it is done."

Preston made a fast grab at the phone. I was quicker and pulled it away. He made a fist and tried to convert his grabbing motion into a sweeping hook at my head.

I took hold of his wrist, shifted my other arm up from his back, and locked it around his neck. As I jerked down on his wrist, I used my headlock to roll him off the barstool. He landed on the floor, back down. I landed on top of him. The air came out of his lungs with a big whump. It was three or four minutes before he could speak.

"How much to hit the erase button?" he wheezed.

I told him the price.

Two days later, my last morning at Ryan's, we were eating

breakfast. I gave him the used CD I'd gotten on eBay. Queen's We Are The Champions signed by Freddie Mercury. Ryan exclaimed and stared at me hard.

We heard a vehicle on the driveway, and looked out to see the black Escalade pull up. It stopped. Preston Laurence got out of the back, walked up to Ryan's front door and rang the bell.

I answered it. He was wearing a suit. He handed me a 9 x 12 manila envelope, which I knew contained documents for the sale of his CBT stock to Ryan.

"I'm here to see Miss Lily, please," he said.

"Miss Lily," I called out. "You have a gentleman caller."

Lily came running. "I'm Lily."

"Good morning. I have a delivery for you." He turned and walked back to the Escalade, opened the tailgate and pulled out the shiniest, fanciest kid's bicycle I'd ever seen. He set it on the ground, carefully leaning it onto its kickstand.

He glanced up at me, lifted up on the creases of his trousers, then squatted down in front of her.

"Miss Lily," he said, "I'm sorry to have damaged your bicycle. This is a replacement. Please accept my apologies."

She nodded at him. "The pleasure is all mine," she said.

"Thank you for your understanding," Preston said. He got back into the Escalade. Raul drove away slowly, carefully.

The next morning, Street and Spot and I drove south down the East Shore.

"Now that it's September, the morning is cold," Street said to me, her arms across her chest, hands rubbing opposite shoulders.

"Thirty-one on the thermometer when we got up," I said. "One of the reasons why I'm a fan of sleeping in."

"Maria said it would be best if we got there by 7:00 a.m. She said that Heat would be looking for breakfast."

The coating of upper-mountain snow and hail from the series of thunderstorms had all melted, and the views across the lake had gone back to looking like summer after several days of looking like fall. The air was crisp in my lungs.

We pulled into the entrance to the trail where I'd chased Travis off the highway four nights before. Ryan's car was already there.

Diamond and Maria and Lana pulled up as we got out.

We said our good mornings.

Maria and Street went up the rutted trail first, apples bulging their jacket pockets. Behind them walked Lana and Carol, their pockets stretched by carrots.

Ryan and Lily went behind them, holding hands. Lily kept turning around to face Diamond and me. Ryan kept her hand in his, so that she ended up walking sideways-backward, her hand stretched up and across in an uncomfortable position.

Stubble had begun to grow where they'd shaved Ryan's head before laying down multiple tracks of stitches.

Spot ran through the forest, then came back to tag us. He'd clawed the bandage off the top of his head, but the stitches seemed to be holding.

"Coming to find Heat was a good idea, wasn't it?" Lily said to Diamond and me.

"Absolutely," I said.

The night on Cave Rock seemed like it had taken place just a few hours before. I knew that Lily would likely have bad dreams for a long time to come, but she was bouncing back the way only kids can. Life can be harsh beyond measure, but a kid can still take pleasure in having good ideas.

"Do you think Heat will let me ride him?"

"I don't know. We'll have to ask Heat."

We walked a mile up the slope toward the watering hole where the creek pooled deep and provided a place where wildlife could find all the water they needed.

I'd brought blankets in my pack, and we arranged them within sight of the watering hole. The big cooler that Diamond and I carried went where the blankets came together.

Carol and Street sat on either side of Lily. No visible wounds on their group. Lily didn't even have bandages. The doctors had just said to keep her clothes loose so that they wouldn't irritate the burns from where Travis's rope had bit into her skin. Spot sprawled in front of Lily and put his head on her lap, but after two minutes she found it was too heavy. She pushed his head to the side. He sighed, then snoozed.

Lana wore a kerchief around her neck, but it didn't fully cover up the bandages.

"It'll be like a permanent necklace," she said about her stitches. She laughed. "The scar will just look like I'm wearing some kind of choker. Very chic, really."

"Oh, Lana, you're so brave," Maria said. "Like Ryan."

"Gonna have some macho scars, kid," Diamond said to Ryan. "Where I come from, the girls would appreciate what you did to get them. Boys, too, for that matter."

"I just tried not to be a coward for once in my life," Ryan said. "Monty-Travis scared me to death. But Owen said I should confront my worst fears. I knew I had to try to help. I couldn't open the door on my car, so got on Herman's scooter and used it to get up to the back side of Cave Rock."

"Saved Lily's life," I said. "Mine, too."

"Took a bad guy out of circulation," Diamond said. "Always a good thing. Saved the state a lot of money."

"Diamond!" Maria feigned astonishment. "What if your fellow officers heard you say that?"

"They'd raise a toast," he said.

We munched picnic food.

"Here's how we'll work it," Maria said. "Before you whistle, Owen, we'll all be sitting down on the blankets. Remember, the only person he trusts is the woman down in Sparks. We have to overcome his distrust by being completely non-threatening. If he comes, we will notice him, but seem uninterested."

"When he comes," Lily said.

"When he comes," Maria corrected herself.

"Can I feed him an apple?" Lily asked.

"The whistle means sweet grain to him. So you will have some in your hands. After he eats the grain you hold out to him, then you should get more grain for him. In time, he will learn that you have apples and carrots, too. That will build trust."

When Maria was satisfied that everything was in place, she looked at me. I nodded at Lily. She went to Spot and covered his sensitive ears. I stepped away from the group and did a loud wolf whistle three times. Spot squirmed under Lily's grip on his head.

"Why doesn't it work?" Lily asked after a minute.

"It will work," Maria said. "We just need to give him some

time. He could be far away."

We waited a half hour, ate some lunch.

"When Heat comes out of the forest," Lily said as she munched watermelon, "where will he live?"

"With his owner in Sparks," Maria said. "She told me that you can visit him any time you like."

Lily grinned.

The next time, Diamond covered Spot's ears as I stood up and whistled three more times.

"What if he doesn't come?" Lily said.

"Let's give him more time," Maria said. She stared out at the forest, her eyes intense. She wandered into the trees.

Street got up and followed her.

Lily looked at Ryan. "Can I go with them?"

Ryan nodded. "Just don't talk too much."

She ran off after them.

The rest of us lounged in silence, listening to the birds and squirrels. By their movements and energy it seemed it was never too early to get ready for winter.

"How long did you know it was Travis?" Diamond said.

I shook my head. "Not until the last moment. I called you and said that the killer had gotten a flat tire, and I thought he had hijacked a car on the highway. But you said there hadn't been any calls about it. So I was confused. I took another look at the code from Herman's tuning. My best guess at the letters had been GEWN REAR DECAO. Something Lily said made me think to look for a few letters that could be changed to give the message some sense. If it worked, then it would just mean that Herman's piano strings had adjusted a little before the other piano tuner measured them.

"Either way, I realized that by shifting five of the letters just one notch forward or backward in the alphabet, it would say HE WORE A RED CAP. That told me it was Travis."

"Whose real name was Monty," Carol said. "And he was still stealing horses even after getting out of prison."

"Right. I was so startled to think that it wasn't one of the cowboys or Tory or William's mother Holly, that it took me a minute to process. It was one of those times when I had to rethink everything, from chocolate to Paris. Once I knew it was Travis who had gotten a flat tire on his truck, I figured he would go to Lana's and steal a horse for transportation. So I went too, and everything exploded from that point."

"That was why my horse trailer was moved when I came back from Chicago," Lana said. "It was a clever way to steal that woman's horses. Borrow the trailer and then put it back. If anybody had recognized it, it wouldn't lead to Travis. I'm so glad it wasn't Tory. He can be difficult, but I've always thought that he was good at some core level. Did they ever find the other horse that was stolen?"

"Not yet," I said.

Ryan watched us without speaking, still telegraphing unease. It seemed that he didn't understand how people could just sit around and talk, hanging out, being friends.

His world was about constant productivity. Maybe that staved off his fear of engagement. But I thought I saw a set to his eyes and jaw that I hadn't seen before. And his frown seemed less about worry, and more about responsibility and determination.

"Any word yet on that last blood test?" I said in a low voice.

Ryan nodded. "It was bad. The indicators suggested a full metastasis was in progress. The doctor said we should start chemo immediately. But that same afternoon, we got the first report back on the clinical trial for our new drug. It looked very promising. So the doctor gave Lily her first biological treatment an hour later."

Ryan took a deep breath.

"When will you know how she responds?"

"They drew more blood yesterday afternoon. The doctor called me at nine o'clock last night. He was excited and said that the indicators have begun to retreat. At best, it will be a long haul. But if it continues like this, he believes she could eventually be cured."

Diamond stuck out his fist with his upraised thumb. Carol and Lana broke into huge smiles. I leaned forward and gave Ryan a hug.

"Congratulations," I said.

Maria, Street and Lily came back in a hurry and sat down on the blankets. Maria waved her hand at us. Street raised her finger to her lips. Spot lifted his head up, and stared into the forest. I reached over and put a firm hand on him.

In front of Street stood Lily, her eyes round and struck with wonder, her mouth so stretched by mirth that she looked about to burst into song. She, too, put her finger to her lips. It was, I thought, an important moment in an important day for her, the beginning of a new life where excitement replaced fear.

Lily slowly raised her arm and pointed.

We followed her gaze into the forest.

I saw nothing. We waited. A big Jeffrey pinecone fell from a hundred feet up, hitting multiple branches on the way down. A treetop squirrel screamed for a few seconds, then settled down to nervous chattering. A group of three crows swooped through the forest, cawing to each other about the state of the world. They disappeared, and the woods went silent.

I kept my hand on Spot while I watched Lily. She scooped grain out of the bag, held it in her upturned hands and took slow steps toward the trees.

We all stared into the forest.

There was no movement.

I focused on the mass of tree trunks and saw a white mark among the brown stripes. An inverted triangle. In time, it moved to the right. It grew ears and a dark brown thatch of mane above and two large dark eyes. Below came the body of a beautiful cherry-brown horse.

Lily walked forward, her arms out. She quivered with excitement.

And Heat walked out of the forest.

About the Author

Todd Borg and his wife live in Lake Tahoe, where they write and paint. To contact Todd or learn more about the Owen McKenna mysteries, please visit toddborg.com.